THE MOON ABOVE

BRETT DAVIS

TEMPUS

ISBN: 978-1-953100-06-1

Cover design by Rebecca Poole Dreams2Media

Editor: Kimberly Comeau

First Trade Paperback Printing by Broken Arm Publishing: April 2020

10 9 8 7 6 5 4 3 2

SP

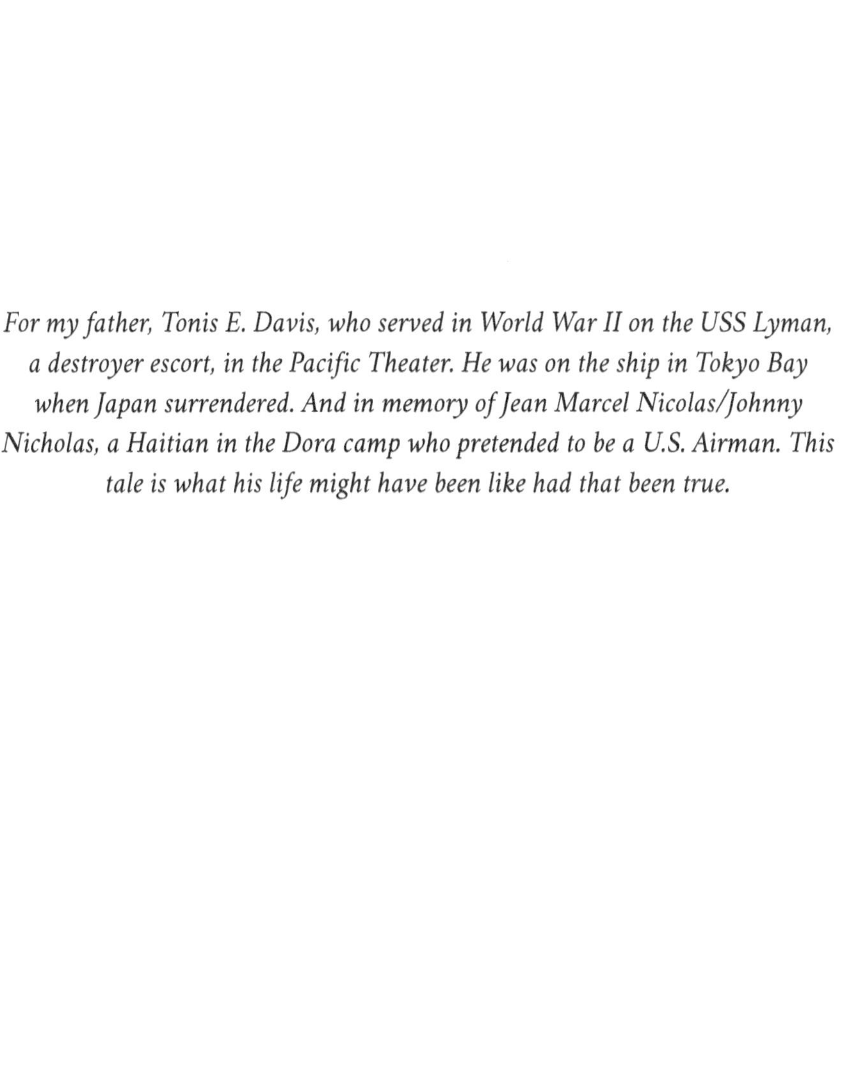

For my father, Tonis E. Davis, who served in World War II on the USS Lyman, a destroyer escort, in the Pacific Theater. He was on the ship in Tokyo Bay when Japan surrendered. And in memory of Jean Marcel Nicolas/Johnny Nicholas, a Haitian in the Dora camp who pretended to be a U.S. Airman. This tale is what his life might have been like had that been true.

Trademark Acknowledgements

Flash Gordon
>Ming the Merciless
>Buck Rogers
>*The Flash*
>Playboy Playmate
>Buick
>Ford
>Mercury
>Pontiac
>Cadillac
>Studebaker
>Walgreens
>Coke (Coca Cola)
>Shell Station
>First National Bank
>Redstone Arsenal
>Pan American Airlines
>*The Maltese Falcon*
>*Popular Mechanics*

A Note From The Author

You are the boy I used to babysit every once in a while. Your mother gave me some books to read to you, but you weren't very interested. They were stories about love and war and things like that, with talking animals and knights in shining armor. You told me your mother said I had better stories to tell, real stories about love and war, and you wanted to hear those. Particularly the ones about war. But those stories I wouldn't tell.

You thought you knew the answers to everything but were not so sure of yourself that you wouldn't ask a question now and then.

One warm spring day, I was sitting on my front steps wondering why I never put in a porch, when you came around, sort of sidling up to me like you always did. You were dressed for winter, with two or three baggy shirts hanging over your jeans and a ball cap on your head even though I have never seen you attempt anything athletic.

"Why don't you tell me some a' your stories?" you said to me, like you always did.

Then you cocked your head back and looked at me like I was going to tell you something this time. But I did what I always did when you came around and said that to me. I shooed you away and went back inside.

I got to thinking about your question that night, when the warm spring day had given way to a warm spring night. I went back outside and sat on my steps again, looked up, and watched a falling star flicker to its death behind the heavy limbs of my neighbor's oak tree. From where I sat, I could see the edge of your house. There was no light in your window, and I wondered if you were asleep.

If you wonder why I can remember all those things from that day so long ago, it is because that was the day I finally decided to give in to your request. I was not planning to do it, but I changed my mind. You got me remembering and I decided to tell you some a' my stories. You never know how things are going to go. Sometimes you need to tell people things while you can, while you can tell and they can hear. Because you never know.

I warn you in advance that some of my facts might be off a little. I'm not one of those people who can remember every single thing, in order. I remember lots of things, but sometimes I'm not sure when one came before another.

I may let some little things slide, but I remember the big things. I will tell you how a man can sit by and watch the very devils in Hell turn into the snowiest angels. I will tell you how a man can lose a son and gain a son, and I will tell you how a man can lose a woman and keep her forever. I will tell you how a man can build a pile of bones high enough to reach the moon.

ONE

I Learn a Trick

Father worked in the window of the small room, the only good natural light in the kitchenette. First, he put down a thin layer of silver, so smooth it appeared featureless until he tilted the big board and the sun caught the nooks and crannies of the wood. When it dried, he began laying in tiny specks of black, and thinning them out, sometimes licking his thumb and running it across them to water them down. Then he laid in tiny flecks of white, treating them the same way. After a while, his thumb became gray.

I watched him most of the time he worked. He sank into the job, occasionally surfacing to notice me and to smile. When he thought about it, he offered random pieces of advice.

"Just take your time. If you're going to do something, do it right."

He kept his brushes in an old green tool kit that made a sound like a mousetrap when he opened it. He found the smallest brush and began adding tiny spots of brown, then, squinting as if blind, he made their edges lighter, almost gold. It was something you could only see if you looked very closely.

"Fake rust," he told me with a smile, like it was a joke and we were the only ones in on it.

The words came next, big red ones that spelled out something. I was young and I couldn't read. The name of a grocery store, he said, over on 49th Street, down the way. He wasn't done when the words were dry. He put in small shadows under the letters, raising them up until they seemed to float. When he was done, it looked like a metal sign instead of a cheap board covered with paint.

"I hope they don't put it outside in the rain," he told Mother.

"Tell them not to."

"They don't listen to me."

He leaned the sign against the apartment wall, carefully, in case some parts weren't quite dry. It looked like a metal sign from any angle and in any light. He would never have settled for less.

"Looks good," Mother said.

Father stood up, balled his hands into fists at the small of his back and arched like a cat. Something popped deep inside and he gave a small groan of pleasure. "It's a good piece of wood. Derek did a nice job of trimming."

Father didn't care to alter the wood, he just liked to paint it. He always had someone else do the cutting.

"I think the paint has something to do with it," Mother said.

I felt maybe he needed some kind words from me, too.

"It's really good," I said.

He laughed and rested his gray-thumbed hand on my head.

"It's just a fake, Johnny. It's pretty but it's not what it seems to be. You just be careful with things like that. Some people want metal but they're only willing to pay for wood."

TWO

The Fall

I WAS BORN in Alabama but don't remember much about it. I was four years old when Mother and Father moved to Chicago, taking me and my sister Katherine. I'm sure I was startled at first. Chicago is all noise and bricks and dirt and stockyards and trains. The cows are there just to be killed, the trees are sparse and kept on reservations. Buildings rise up everywhere, square and squat, tall and slim. I was scared when I saw it through the train window. But it was in Chicago that I grew into myself. Katherine was older when we arrived. She was already into herself, or thought she was. She was not at all scared by Chicago, and she should have been. I think we started to lose her that day when we pulled into Union Station.

I don't remember any buildings in Alabama. I remember only Grandfather's house. We all lived there, too, Mother and Father and Katherine and me, but it was always Grandfather's house, never Father's.

Grandfather was a farmer. I believe now that he was a tenant farmer for another family. He had his small house made of gray boards that no longer fit well together, so that the gaps served as windows and ventilation. The yard was wild, full of tangled and scrubby bushes that made a great obstacle course for a careening child. I treated the yard as my personal jungle and Mother let me; she could always hear me fighting with imaginary lions and tigers as I pursued them through the trackless wilderness in front of our house. And, of course, she could usually see me through the gaps in the walls.

A lean, little-traveled road ran near the house, as thin and crooked as a stream. On the other side of the road, the fields began, the fields where Grandfather and Father worked. Those fields seemed to extend forever and were off limits to me because Father and Grandfather and other men worked there with animals and sharp implements. But the work was really Grandfather's pursuit. Father detested farming. He hated everything about it; hated the mules, hated the plow, hated the crops for growing and hated the scythe for cutting them down. He was content to let the Earth do what it wanted, which is why our front yard looked the way it did.

Father wanted to be an artist, but there was no opportunity for that in Alabama. He had taken to painting on unused two-by-fours with old mismatched house paint other people gave him, paint he would never have considered actually using on the house. He painted what he saw, hills and cows and blue skies and towering white columns of clouds, with tiny black people below them scratching out a living. Occasionally, he would use one of his boards to fill a gap in the rotting walls of his father's house, lending brightness here and there. I can see them in my mind, but I don't know if I actually remember them; he talked about them a lot and put them in my imagination. Most of his pictures he gave away to anyone who expressed an interest, and probably more than a few ended up filling gaps in other houses the way they did in ours. I like to think that a few are still out there, maybe tucked under a sagging window or holding up a porch rail, but I'm sure they're all gone. Either the houses themselves have been destroyed, or the cheap paint Father used has faded and the wood has gone back to gray.

Father moved to Chicago to get away from farming and because he hoped he might be able to put his artistic skills to some use. Mother moved to Chicago because Father was moving there and because she wanted some social justice. That was her phrase. She was tired of living in an area where everyone said the name of Jesus but then allowed white people to lynch black people and act like they were having a party. She was tired of living in a place where black people had to take it. She wanted social justice, she said, so much that I thought it was some kind of product she could not get in the South. I still don't really know what she thought she wanted. I think she just wanted the atmosphere, just wanted to breathe some free air.

She didn't find as much freedom as she expected, at least, not at first. She had no particular skills except the ability to cook dishes that convinced people to part with their money for church bake sales. In Chicago, she used that talent to get a job cooking for a wealthy white family who lived a few blocks east of Washington Park. Father got a job with a sign-painting company that was doing work all over town, for Negros and whites alike. It was a CIO union shop and, for the first time in his life, he worked alongside white men who would sometimes call him "Mr. Nicholas," which never happened down South. They both worked hard but made good money, maybe $80 a week. We lived in a pretty nice apartment and they thought they might be able to buy it someday. I don't remember all the physical parts of it, but Katherine never forgot them; she never lived anyplace better. She talked about it for years after, used to describe it like a palace, its smooth wood floors and the front door that was rounded on the top. We lived there for one year, and then the bottom fell out of the world.

"Mrs. Carson took me aside today," Mother said one day while she was folding laundry.

Father grunted. He was pawing through the *Chicago Defender* and the *Bee* looking for jobs, while Katherine and I gnawed on cold chicken still wet from the icebox.

"What did she say this time?" he asked after a moment, not taking his eyes from the words on the page. He was not a strong reader and did not like to lose his place.

Mrs. Carson taking Mother aside was not an uncommon thing. She took her aside to ask her to wash the sheets early because her son had a problem with his bladder, and again to ask her never to be alone with Mr. Carson because Mr. Carson sometimes drank and let his hands wander where they should not, and again to warn her never to store anything in the icebox without first asking permission, as it would need to be kept in a separate section.

"She said they want to cut my wages in half, and if I don't agree to it, they'll have to let me go."

Father looked up. "You're kidding."

She did not even answer that. She was obviously not kidding. Mother would never joke about money.

"She said the problems are hitting them, too. They're selling one of their cars and they're letting go of the cook altogether."

"That's just wonderful. Nobody wants signs painted anymore, they're happy with just cardboard and black paint, so I'm out of work, and now we're losing half your salary. Kids, maybe you should learn to pick cotton and we'll move back to Alabama."

"No!" Katherine and I said in ragged unison.

"I'm sure it's not any better there, Carl."

"I'm sure it's not. Not any worse, either."

"It's never any better or any worse, that's why we left."

He just sighed and looked back at the paper, but there was little there for him. He was physically large enough to work in the stockyards but did not want to. He wanted to make money doing something that interested him and challenged his talents, which meant he was born in the wrong place and time.

"She wants an answer by tomorrow. What should I tell her?"

"You know what to tell her," he said without looking up.

About two months later, we moved into a kitchenette apartment closer to the railroad tracks. The trains were not all that close, but you could feel them rumbling in your bones, all the time, so you could never forget they were there. The apartment was one of about thirty that had been carved out in a grand old house that once held just one family. The building had gotten old and feeble, but you could still catch glimpses of its former glory. Some of the doors had very elaborate archways, with glass transoms that had been painted shut; some of the ceilings were pressed tin, with tiny elaborate designs raised in them like veins under the skin; marble peeked out here and there from windowsills. Our kitchenette had none of these things. It had been slapped up in a corner of what used to be a much larger room. A false ceiling hid the tin, the door had been carved out of a thin dividing wall, and none too straight, and the windowsill was made up more of cracks than wood, leaking furiously when it rained.

The kitchen consisted of a stove and an icebox pushed up against the side wall like awkward guests at a party. The rest of the room was just a room and had to hold all four of us, as well as any guests who might come through. The bathroom was down the hall and was shared with half the building. That did not bother me all that much, but Mother despised it, and for Katherine, it probably proved to be her downfall.

It did not take us long to move. Everything we owned we had carried on a train—and we had added very little to it since—so the deed was done in the space of an afternoon, including travel time. The first thing Mother did was put up the small picture of Jesus that she carried everywhere. He was looking out at the viewer with a hint of a smile, and, with one hand, revealed a red, glowing heart.

"He looks over us, wherever we are," Mother said. "Even in the most degraded of circumstances."

"It's not *that* bad," Father said, irritated. It had taken him some work even to find this place.

THREE

The Promised Land

"Got one!" I said, but not too loud.

My friend Nelson Ray and I were playing World War I bomber pilots. Our bombs were acorns. Our targets, standing in for the Germans, were whoever walked under the largest oak on the western side of Washington Park.

In my memory, I spent nearly all my time in the park. I felt like I had the whole world open to me when I was there. It had everything: trees, horses, enough grass to make up two or three football fields, a lagoon as big as the ocean. That's how it seemed at the time, anyway.

In those days, our folks let us out to run all day in the park. I've seen how your mother keeps an eye on you from her kitchen window. You get out of her sight for three seconds and she's out the door after you. That's not bad, I know she means the best. But that's not the way things used to be. Kids were kids then, and they were supposed to be outside, and that was fine with me. If I dared stay inside too long, my mother would find me something to do.

Nelson was a tiny little boy, even smaller than me, but he was fast and could climb like a monkey. He lived to the east of the park somewhere—I never went to his house, and he never came to my kitchenette —but his father ran a dry-cleaning store in the neighborhood and was generally considered to be fair to Negroes. His father knew he played with me, because I sometimes met him at the store, but he obviously did not mind. That didn't mean anything to me at the time. It does now.

"I don't think you got her," Nelson said from above.

He was higher up the tree than I was, sprawled over a limb like a panther.

"I did, too."

"She didn't look up."

"I hit her, though. I saw it bounce off her foot."

It actually was a little hard to scope out our victories because as soon as the bombs were away, we pulled in our arms and legs as best we could to hide. But I did think I saw it bounce off her foot.

"Here comes somebody," Nelson hissed. "He's mine."

A large man passed underneath, wearing a natty suit and a fedora perched at a jaunty angle, complete with a small red feather. I waited to see the acorn go by, and to hear the simulated scream of a falling bomb, but nothing happened.

"What's going on?" I asked.

"Did you *see* that guy?" Nelson responded. "He was huge!"

"So? He's not going to climb up here after you, not dressed like that."

"I don't care. He's big. I just wanted him to go on by."

Just about then we heard a ragged, tearing sound. I looked up to see an old airplane towing a banner high in the sky above the city. The banner was touting a restaurant or something, but it was at an angle and I couldn't quite read it. The aircraft was a biplane, a two-winged contraption left over from the First World War. It either sustained serious damage in the war, or had gone without repair, or both. It sounded like a motorcycle as it sputtered across the blue. We watched it until it disappeared behind the apartment buildings on the other side of the park, and half expected to hear a resounding crash.

When it was gone, I flattened my stomach on the branch and held my arms out straight.

"When I grow up, I am going to be a pilot," I said.

"A pilot?" Nelson said. "What kind of pilot?"

"For the Army. A bomber pilot. Dropping *real* bombs, not acorns. I will bomb the Germans."

"But we're not fighting the Germans anymore. And anyway, you can't be no bomber pilot."

"Why not?"

"Johnny, take a look at your arms."

I did. They were black, same as they are now.

"That's why. You're a Negro. The government won't let you."

"So what? I can still grab a stick and bomb Germany."

"We're not fighting the Germans anymore."

"I know that. I can still bomb anyone who needs to be bombed."

"I know you could. I don't know if you'd be a good bomber, though, the way you drop them acorns. But anyway, it doesn't matter, they won't let you."

"Who? The Army? Or white people?"

"It's the same thing."

"Why not, though? It doesn't make sense." I knew he was right; I couldn't be born in Alabama and not know he was right. I couldn't grow up in America and not know he was right.

"They don't think you can handle it, I guess. You don't ever hear white people talking. Some of them don't even want you to drive, and so they sure don't want you up over their heads in a plane."

When Nelson was telling me things I already knew, it did not occur to me to hate him because he was one of the people wanting to hold me back. I knew he wasn't like that. I could separate him out from the people we were talking about. If a child can do that, I don't know why adults can't. Well, I do know now, but I didn't then.

That night, as I lay in my small bed in a corner of the kitchenette, I burned with the desire to be a pilot for the Army just because Nelson said I couldn't. The desire had stayed with me that entire afternoon. Nelson and I had wreaked holy hell on the Germans below us with our explosive acorns until some of the older boys who played in the park threatened to come up to where we were and make us eat those acorns, or something worse. We had suspended our bombing campaign then, but I still thought about it.

The desire to fly was born in me that day. Unlike so many childhood interests, it did not die for many years. Nelson is dead now, though. I saw less and less of him as life pulled us apart, to the point that I probably wouldn't have known him as an adult if I saw him on the street. I heard he took over his father's store, had a couple of kids and then got drafted. He made a mistake; he didn't fly. He was infantry. I heard he died in the Battle of the Bulge. So now he knows more about life and death than I do.

MY UNCLE ABE VISITED THE NEXT WEEK. I WAS STILL STEWING ABOUT MY lack of flying potential, so I took it up with him.

"Why so down, little man?"

"Leave him alone, Abe, let him be," Aunt Eveline said.

She was reading a stack of newspapers borrowed from the Jacksons down the hall. Eveline was perfectly content to be quiet for hours on end, but Abe was not a reader and was not himself if he was not talking.

"I'm just asking the young man a question," he said. "Read your papers, woman. Something's got him upset. Look at that serious face."

Abernathy, or Abe, was a big man with big appetites. He took up nearly an entire corner of the kitchenette whenever he visited, while Aunt Eveline would barely occupy a single chair. I do not know of any food he would not eat and eat a lot of. His chest was huge, almost as big around as one of the oaks in the park, and he draped it in the finest suits he could afford. He roamed all over the country in a gigantic yellow Cadillac with Aunt Eveline, moving fearlessly through the Deep South, even through the places where Negroes were not allowed to stop and go to the restroom, which was almost everywhere. Uncle Abe said he had the biggest bladder in the South and didn't need to stop.

"I was just thinking about something, that's all."

"Tell me. Tell your Uncle Abe. You and Uncle Abe and God can sort it out."

A few words about God and Uncle Abe: Mother's "little" brother was a preacher of sorts. He had held a variety of jobs—some of which made my parents argue—but the most recent was jack-leg preacher. He felt the calling of Jesus, he said, and he wanted a flock to lead.

"He feels the calling of George Washington," said Father when he heard the news. "And he wants some sheep to give him as many Washingtons as he can get his hands on."

The problem for Abe was that he roamed so much that he was not a known quantity in Chicago. He could not just show up and get a church going.

"You got to get in there with the people and get to know the church," he said. "You got to know what the people need. You got to find out why their current pastor is not giving it to them, then you got to provide."

Uncle Abe became an assistant pastor at the South Side Baptist Fellowship, which met in a building that used to house a Jewish deli. It was where Mother and I went to church regularly, sometimes accompanied by a reluctant Father, occasionally by an even more reluctant Katherine. There was another assistant pastor, too, another shark in the tank. The jobs were unpaid and were mostly filled in case Brother Johnston was sick. It also gave the assistant pastors the opportunity to undermine Brother Johnston whenever they could so they could get their own churches started. Brother Johnston was in good health, at the moment, so Uncle Abe did not have much to do but lounge around the kitchenette and talk to me.

"I'm not upset. It's just my friend said something the other day and I've been thinking about it."

"What friend?"

When Uncle Abe was paying attention to you, he paid attention to you. His face settled into what looked almost like a parody of concern, but he was serious. It was a good trait for an aspiring preacher.

"Nelson. Nelson Ray."

"That little redheaded white boy I've seen you with? His father has that dry cleaning place on 45th?"

"That's right."

"I hear good things about his father. I would rather see a Race man have that business, but if a white man must have it, I guess Nelson's father is good enough. So, what did this young man tell you?"

"He told me that I couldn't fly for the Army because I'm a Negro."

Aunt Eveline, who was supposed to be reading, snorted a little laugh at that.

"What are you making noise at, woman?" Abe asked. "The young man has a serious concern."

"Ain't nobody, white or Black, ought to be flying," Eveline said. "Birds and bats, because they have wings, and that's it."

She was quiet but consistent in her way and I don't think she ever did fly in her whole life.

"Shush," Abe said, turning back to me. "Well, Johnny, I have to tell you that your friend is right. You can't fly for the Army. But that don't mean you can't fly at all."

"But how?" I asked.

"You don't have to be a military flier. You can fly the mail, or just do barnstorming, if you want."

"Abe, why don't you just kill him now and be done with it?" Eveline said.

"I will not snuff out the dreams of the young," Abe replied. "Now, Johnny, there is one problem. You'll find it hard to get trained in this country. The white man will keep us down however he can, and that includes keeping us down on the ground. But there are places you can go where they are willing to look beyond the color of your skin. You need to get to France."

"France?" I said, in unison with Aunt Eveline.

"That's right, France. France has trained Race flyers. I read about it in the *Defender*. There was a Race man who went over to France in the Great War. The U.S. Army wouldn't let him fly but he flew for France and could shoot down German planes as well as anybody. He became an ace. And there was Bessie Coleman. You heard of Bessie Coleman?"

She sounded a little familiar, but I wasn't sure.

"She was from right here in Chicago. A woman, to boot. Used to do up hair right here in the neighborhood, but decided she wanted to fly aeroplanes. She went over to France and learned how, and then came back and showed everybody how a Race woman could fly."

"And she crashed her plane and died," Eveline said.

"Woman! I am trying to encourage this boy!"

"Encourage him to be safe, then."

Uncle Abe rolled his eyes.

"Come on, let's go out in the hallway."

He put his baseball mitt-sized hand on my shoulder and guided me out to the hallway, which was the opposite of our clean, well-organized kitchenette. It had three light sconces but only one bulb that held out against the darkness, and boasted several competing lengths of wallpaper, with old designs peeking out from under newer ones like the place was some half-finished archeological dig.

One of our neighbors, Mr. Roswell, was sitting in the hallway on a wooden chair, looking at the *Defender* under the dim yellow glow from the lone working bulb. He was about sixty-five years old, thin as a stick, but healthy. He never had two nickels in his pocket but always dressed like he was going to the opera. He kept the chair in the hallway because he could be sure to run across one of the many other residents of the kitchenette building, especially since his own tiny apartment was near the shared bathroom. The newspaper was an excuse to sit outside; he was barely literate. He sat on his chair and awaited his prey, like a spider.

"Abe! I didn't know you was in town."

Our neighbors always liked to see Uncle Abe, and he liked to see them. They tried to borrow money from him, and he tried to borrow money from them, and I think they ended up just passing the same old tattered dollars back and forth.

"Yes, George, I am. I see you're looking well, as usual."

"And hello, young Johnny."

"Hello, Mr. Roswell."

"You say hello to your mother and father for me, Johnny. And your sister, too."

Katherine was starting to catch the attention of a lot of men in the building, and not only the young ones.

"I will, sir."

"So polite. Abe, I hope you're not bringing this young man out in the hallway to punish him for something?"

"No, not at all, George. I'm just trying to get him away from the negative influence of that crazy wife of mine. I'm trying to tell him that he needs to go to France."

"France!" Mr. Roswell said. "Why would he want to do that? Do you speak French, Johnny?"

"No, sir."

"See there?" Mr. Roswell said.

"You're about as bad as Eveline. The boy can learn French, any fool can learn French if they want to. What he could get over there is freedom."

Mr. Roswell seemed to think about that.

"Well, the white folks there seem a little calmer about these things," he allowed.

"That's right," Abe said. "A Race man there can own property wherever he likes. He doesn't have to live just with his own."

"They have that Josephine Baker there, too, I heard," Mr. Roswell said. "She dances in front of white audiences."

"Who's out here talking about Josephine Baker?" another voice said.

It was Lance Wilson from upstairs. He was a lanky man, not much older than Katherine. He ran policy numbers from a shop down the street, a kind of constant ongoing lottery that didn't pay out much but didn't cost much to play, either. My mother said he did other things, as well, and told me to keep away from him. But I always thought he seemed nice. He was also very tall, and that impressed me at the time.

"We are telling this young man that he ought to go to France," Mr. Roswell said, delighted to have an additional source of conversation.

"France? He ain't going to France before I go," Wilson said. "I'd get a lot more out of a Josephine Baker show than he would."

"He wants to fly aeroplanes," Uncle Abe said. He always pronounced it that way. The first time I heard him say it I thought he said, "arrow planes."

"And he should fly aeroplanes if he wants to," Uncle Abe continued. "They'll let him do that in France."

"They'll let you do anything in France," Wilson said with an air of authority, as if he had not just announced that he had never been there.

"A Black man can go over there and have a white wife, if he wanted one. You can do whatever you want."

"They let a Race man fly in the Great War," Uncle Abe said. "You know, he shot down some planes, became an ace."

"Yeah, I heard of him, too," Wilson said. "Can't remember his name, though."

"I read about him," Mr. Roswell said. "I can't remember his name, either."

"I better be going," Wilson said. "Got a drawing soon. You all take care. You tell your sister hello, young man. And let me know before you head off to France."

"I will."

I started reading everything I could about France after that, looking at newspaper articles and books at the library. They spoke French. They had exquisite cooking and ate snails, which I found nasty but interesting. The population of the country was 40 million people. They used francs, whatever they were, for money instead of dollars. And they didn't seem to hate Black people. A woman named Josephine Baker was indeed getting famous for dancing there and didn't have to do it just in front of Black audiences. And Uncle Abe was right about the fighter pilot. He was Eugene Jacques Bullard. They let him fly for France in the Great War, and he shot down two German planes. He wasn't an ace, though. You had to shoot down at least five airplanes to become an ace.

I decided I wanted to become an ace, if there was ever a war again.

FOUR

Katherine Falls

MOTHER WAS LIVID. There was no sleeping in the kitchenette that night as she paced like a lioness. She was not a lioness protecting her cubs. She was going to eat one of her cubs, if that cub ever came home.

Katherine was entering her womanhood while she was barely a teenager. She was racing into womanhood, getting there as fast as she could, and she could go pretty fast. My sister was tall for her age, tall and slender but with curves budding in all the places guaranteed to attract men. There were plenty of men around with nothing but time on their hands. The economy was wrecked and there was nothing but time for them, and energy, with no work to sap it out of their young limbs.

She started staying out later and later. Times were tough and more and more people were following what our family had done and were pulling up stakes in the South and heading for Chicago, looking for the same thing we and everyone else were looking for. The schools were running in two shifts and Katherine had the late shift, and her arrival home kept getting later and later. She said she was studying but her grades did not reflect that.

"If those are the kinds of grades you get after all your studying, girl, you have a mental problem," Mother said.

"It's hard," Katherine said, her voice as tight and sharp as Mother's. "You wouldn't know about it."

They looked like bookends as they argued, because their bodies had adopted the same position: heads thrust forward, hips thrust out, right elbows crooked ninety degrees, hands on rumps. They looked somewhat alike, although Mother had gone round where Katherine was still angular.

"Girl, you know I am educated. There is nothing you are studying that I don't know. And I know that you're not studying. You don't seem to be looking around you. If you don't study, if you don't educate yourself, nobody is going to do it for you. If you don't educate yourself, you are going to go nowhere in this life."

"Like here? If I apply myself, I can end up in a shitty kitchenette, working for white folks for peanuts and married to a man who can't get a job? That's what I've got to look forward to?"

Mother wanted to keep her in the house but ended up chasing her out the door. I think that was the first night things really came to a head between them, and after that it was almost as if Katherine had died, because she became a ghost. People talked about her, particularly the men, but she was rarely around, although now and then I thought I saw her face just before she slid into the shadows. She still came home, although it was not like she actually lived there, and the first cross word from Mother or Father and she was gone again, like the dirt father blew off the wood before he painted his signs.

I don't think I ever really knew her well. She was four years older than me. That did not matter much in Alabama, but it was a lifetime in Chicago. She arrived in the land of temptation just at the moment she was looking for temptation. No road was closed to her. She was not a loud person, though. She was quiet, reserved, placid as the sea. She took after Father in that. She had his quiet ability to make friends, although, according to Mother, she used it only to make the wrong ones. She also inherited Mother's steely will, but I think she only used it to oppose her.

I will take this time to remember Katherine, who has been gone from me for so long. I don't know if she's alive right now, or long dead. I will remember her as I would like to remember her, when she was just a teenager headed for trouble. She was lean, with smooth skin that was light enough to worry Mother. Both my parents were dark, my father especially; my sister was fair, as I said, and I was somewhere in between. Light skin was something to be desired in those days, in that place. Virtually the entire social structure of the South Side was based on skin color, and the less of it you had the better off you were. Negro newspapers that assailed the doings of the white man stoked their coffers with ads for creams guaranteed to lighten skin. Mother complained about these ads every time she saw them, and she knew the danger that her daughter's hide placed her in, but she was powerless to stop it because it was something God had done and she always knew God was much, much bigger than her.

Late one afternoon, I was looking out the window watching a lot of people on the street. Then I saw Katherine, small down there, hugging her few books to her chest. There were other people around, but I hadn't noticed anyone walking with her. Mother peeked out the window and saw her instantly and smelled trouble. She could spot Katherine's wrongdoings a mile away, like a mother bat able to hear her babies' shrieks in the din of a darkened cave.

"Who was that who walked you home?" Mother asked Katherine when she came through the door.

"Just a boy," Katherine said.

I'll give her one thing, she never lied. She might not tell you what you wanted to hear, but she didn't lie.

"What have I told you about boys?"

"That I'm not supposed to pal around with them."

"That's right."

"But I wasn't palling around with him. He had talked to me at school and I told him where we lived, and he wanted to walk home with me to keep me safe. I thought it was very chivalrous."

She was very smart, too. I did not know what chivalrous meant, I had to look it up. It was a French word. It was a double-edged sword, what she said. It showed our mother that she was learning things and, at the same time, got in a dig about our reduced circumstances. Katherine knew full well that we were living no worse than we had been in

Alabama, but she rarely missed a chance to remind our parents that we could be doing better.

Mother leaned over the table and bared her teeth at her daughter like a wild dog.

"Chivalry is dead," she hissed.

The thing is, Katherine did not seem to care much about boys one way or the other. She could not help but attract them, just like a flower can't help but attract bees. She had only to open her petals and they would come. She was smart, when she felt like displaying it, and funny. She could draw wonderful pictures of anything. She once drew a picture of me looking out the window and I didn't even know she was doing it. My mind was a million miles away. I was Flash Gordon protecting Chicago from the evil hordes of Ming the Merciless, who were flying down between the rat-trap buildings, forcing people to flee so fast the men had to hold on to their hats. I didn't hear her scratching away. The picture looked like a photograph. I carried it with me for many years and wish I had it still.

She had more girlfriends than boyfriends, but they never seemed to last long because a boy always seemed to pop up and come between them. I remember her girlfriends coming over because Katherine would usually kick me out of the kitchenette, and I would have to do my homework in the park. My writing always looked bad because I never had anything proper to write on. I had to use the bark of the trees or the dirt or the cracked slats of the benches. But, like I said, then a boy would pop up and create some screaming hysteria between Katherine and some soon-to-be-former friend. I never understood it.

I made a few vows while watching Katherine grow up in Chicago. I vowed that I would never make my parents cry. She did that for sure, especially Mother. Katherine would make the rage rise in Mother like a volcano, but instead of lava she would erupt in tears, although only when Katherine left. She would never let her daughter see her cry. She would show only the rage, which was probably a mistake.

I also vowed that no one would tell me what to do. At first, I gloried in Katherine's independence, in her ability to come and go as she pleased. It took a while, and it took some listening to some of Mother's sermons before I realized, but it finally sunk in that she did not have real freedom. She was merely giving control to other people, namely the string of men that attached themselves to her. She was not free, any more than a picked flower in a vase is free. I know I keep mentioning her as a flower, but it is the only metaphor that seems to fit. She was a beautiful flower in a meadow, and everyone had to stand over it to see, and they cut off its sun and it died.

I also vowed, later, that I would be true to myself. I did not know exactly what this meant, not in a way that I could put into words, but I knew what I meant by it. Katherine had no goals for herself, no spine of purpose; she was happy to borrow the nearest spine around her. I would never be that way.

I broke all of these vows, one after the other. I made my parents cry. I most certainly did what I was told. And I lost myself, there for a while. But Katherine was always ahead of me. She made her mistakes rapidly, recklessly. It took me most of my lifetime to follow in her footsteps.

FIVE

The Competition

"Go and ask your father to pick up some lettuce, if he can find any," Mother asked.

She was busy baking bread for Uncle Abe's church fundraiser and didn't want to leave it because she had already heard the men in the hall, rustling like rats. She had once baked some cookies for a similar occasion but stepped out for a few minutes to get some laundry off the skeletal lines in the back of the building. She was gone only a few minutes, but her absence happened to coincide with one of Hurricane Katherine's appearances. One of her boys had swept in with her, followed by a few neighbors who suddenly decided to pop by, and mother returned to find her store of cookies severely depleted and Uncle Abe's dream of a church of his own that much farther away.

Katherine coming home was not much of a danger—she hardly ever did now—but Mother had never taken her keys away so the possibility could not be dismissed. Mother had told Father about the lettuce before he left, but he was prone to be forgetful. He did not drink to excess, chase women or blow the rent on playing policy numbers, three failings widely shared in our neighborhood, but he was not always reliable when it came to bringing things home.

He *was* reliable about the way he chose to come home. He worked all over the neighborhood and even outside it, in white parts of the city. But he always came back down 47th Street, like some pigeon following the sun home. It wasn't quite dark, so I went down to the bottom floor of the building. I halfway expected to meet him on the stairs on the way up, but he wasn't there. I waited outside the building, a little warily because mother didn't like for me to talk to many of our neighbors. Like me, she expected Father home almost any time.

He didn't come. I decided to take a little walk up the street to see if I could catch him so he wouldn't have to backtrack and go back to the Jewish store a couple blocks up. It was starting to get dark now, and people were headed for home, stockyard workers in overalls and shapeless hats and uptown types in ties and fedoras, all of them walking past me with dead eyes. I kept going up, past a couple of bars where the music tinkled onto the sidewalk and, looking inside, I caught glimpses of shadows tipping glasses. Still no Father.

I wandered back home and reported that I hadn't seen him. Mother was at first irritated and then upset. She paced the tiny kitchenette like she always did when nervous or bothered. She was frustrated because she could not imagine where he could be. Like I said, he did not drink, so he would not be among those shadows, and he did not play policy, so he wouldn't be coming home late bragging about the money he won or minimizing what he had lost.

It was dark and he was late. Mother was making me nervous with her pacing, so I slipped out again and walked up the street, even though she would not have let me if she knew what I was doing. I walked even farther up than before, past the bars, where the music had gone far beyond tinkling and now was crashing out to the sidewalk. I felt like an explorer, going beyond the known world to the edge of the abyss; I was at the edge of Bronzeville and near the invisible line that marked where the Irish and the Poles and the Italians lived. They worked at the stockyards. Their kids beat up Black boys.

It was an exhilarating place to stand. I felt like a one-man Lewis and Clark, standing at the edge of a broad river and viewing the rest of the New World, even though I was just looking across a well-worn street, one among many, and the houses and buildings on that side looked just like the houses and buildings on this side. And then I saw him. He was with other men, four other men, coming down the street from the direction of the train yards. The other men were white men, which immediately struck me as wrong. Father was not a hateful person. He bore only the usual justified resentments against the white man, but he was not one to have white friends. No white man had ever come home with him, or set foot in our kitchenette for any reason, as far as I knew. Stranger still, he seemed to be staggering. Maybe the siren song of the bars had gotten to him after all, become too attractive to resist. But then I saw he wasn't staggering. He was only walking upright because the other men were carrying him. And he was bleeding.

"Father?" I said, my voice faltering when I had intended it to be firm and manly. "Dad?"

"Here's a good reason for you to know your place," one of the white men said to Father. He was on Father's right, carrying him under the arm. In the dim illumination from the streetlights I saw that his skin was tough and leathery and nearly as dark as Father's. "Your little jungle boy here is waiting for you."

"Don't you talk about him," Father said, his voice even more faltering and soft than mine.

"You don't tell us what to do," the man on Father's left said. He was skinny but his muscles rippled against his bones like ropes. His fingers were long and lean. I still remember them against Father's white sleeve; it looked like an octopus clutched him. "You stay the fuck out of our territory."

They were almost upon me now. I stood before them in the street. They stood over me, Father a scarecrow in the middle. The white men looked down at me without malice, without much interest.

"You better tell your pop to come to his senses, little man," the man on the left said, and then, like it was some choreographed dance move, they threw my father to the street at my feet.

He let out a huff of air when he fell, sending up a tiny dust cloud that hovered around his head. He lay there a second and I stood before him, unable to help him, unable to move. I had hardly ever seen Father exchange so much as a cross word with anyone, white or Negro, let alone get beat up and thrown down like a sack of garbage.

"Wait...wait," he said, and began struggling to stand. I snapped out of it and grabbed his arm to help. He snatched it away so fast that the rough cloth of his sleeve burned my palm. He stood, tottering still, and turned his back to me. He ran after the men, who were sauntering back across the street, laughing as though one of them had just told a good joke.

"Wait!" Father shouted, and the men stopped and turned around, the laughter dying on their lips. "I need my things!" Father said. "Please!"

"You don't have any *things*," the skinny one said, drawing out the word as if he was talking about something especially disgusting. "You lost your *things* when you come over to our side to try to steal jobs from us. Anything you brought over with you is ours."

"Please," Father said again, more quietly now that they were listening. "Please, I won't come back. But I can't afford to buy any more. Please."

He didn't have anything with him, now that he had mentioned it. No brushes, no cap, no rags, no buckets. His "kit," as he called it, was heavier than I could lift.

"I say it again," the man said, his voice flat and cold like a snake's would be if it could speak. "Anything you brought over to us is ours."

"Please," Father said again, but softly, and the word fell away and the men did not hear it. I watched them walk away until they disappeared, small points of light that fell away like pebbles dropped in a well. Father turned and walked past me, then stopped.

"You go on ahead, Johnny. You go on ahead and tell your mother you haven't seen me."

"But I—"

"You go on ahead now."

"You haven't seen me tonight," he said as I began the walk home.

There was a note of pleading in his voice that I did not like, and never wanted to hear. I decided, as I headed home, that I would never let any man treat me the way those men treated Father.

I was very wrong about that.

SIX

A New Job

"LOOK AT THAT," Father said. "Have you ever seen anything like that?"

I had not. The thing was huge, taller than even Father, and festooned with levers and slots and buttons. It looked like a cash register that had swelled to several times its original size.

"It's a hot-type machine," Father said proudly. "A Linotype. This is what I work at now."

It had taken him a long time, after the beating, to really look me in the eye again. I never said anything about it and neither did he. I know he talked about it with my mother, because for weeks after it happened, I could hear their voices, low, quiet, like snakes talking, when they thought I wasn't around. But he never talked to me about it and I never asked. Once he warmed up to me again, I was just glad to have him back.

He had to get a new job, that much was obvious, even to me. I could pick up snatches of conversation—not hard to do in the kitchenette—and learned that the sign-painting business, never strong, was not recovering enough to continue bothering with it. Father could not make do in Bronzeville alone, where he complained that shopkeepers and other business owners were happy enough with badly scrawled cardboard signs. He had to work in the whiter parts of town, which is where what little money remained could be found. But he wasn't the only one working that territory, as I knew firsthand, and they didn't play fair.

He didn't do anything for about a month after that night. He looked for jobs but found nothing, and his smile, always so ready, became rare. Even Uncle Abe, often good for entertainment, at least, could not cheer him up during one trip into town. Father refused to try to find a job at the stockyard. There were union squabbles going on there, a dangerous situation, and he did not want to get involved. He also wanted to do something remotely creative, and I think he might have starved us to death waiting for that. Father was not a hard man but there was a hardness to him. Things were getting leaner than ever in the kitchenette, and it was secretly a blessing that Katherine had gone off to chase her own wildness, as it left more food and room for the rest of us.

And then he got what he wanted. The *Chicago Defender*, the newspaper that had brought him here in the first place, needed a man to set type and work on advertising art. One of the publisher's business friends remembered a sign Father had done for him and put in a word for him, and he got the job.

"That man has a lot of friends," Father said.

"It's not just that," Mother reminded him. "You do good work, and people remember."

"You hear that?" Father asked me. "You do good work, and people will remember."

He seemed to realize that I had learned a bad lesson from his humiliation, and he was desperate to replace it in my mind with a better one.

The *Defender* was more than just a newspaper. It was that, and it fought hard with its competition, and usually won. But it was also a cause. The *Defender* had brought more Negroes to Chicago than the Gulf Breeze train from Mississippi, one saying went. It drew us to Chicago, it defined us. It even affected how we talked. The newspaper did not like the words Negro or Black, preferring Race men and Race women, and that's the word my family started using, and I use to this day, although I may be the only one left who does. The word can have more than one meaning. Being a dark-skinned man in America is a race, a race to keep barely ahead, a race to keep from drowning.

Father had actually missed the earlier boat. Just after the First World War, the founder of the *Defender*, Robert Abbott, decided to push for Race men in the South to come north, where they were free from lynching and generally free from segregation, although there was only so much the law could do about that. It was time for Race men of the South to vote with their feet, and they did, by the thousands.

White people in the South did not care to associate with Race men, but they also didn't like the idea of having them go to Yankee country to better themselves, and many white cities banned the *Defender*. This is what Father told me, but I remember some of it myself; I remember copies surfacing from time to time in our house in Alabama, and I remember the way Father wrinkled his eyebrows when he struggled through them; a new world opening to his mind right then and there.

People were still drifting north to Chicago, but now that we were here this was making things harder on Mother and Father. They had more people to compete with, people driven by the same impulses they had followed. But, at least, Father now had a job that he liked, and this was a rarity for Race men in Chicago. Now that I have been alive for much longer than I was then, I realize it was a rarity for men of any sort in Chicago, or anywhere else. Father always wanted a job that would let him be creative, and he found it. He laid out the type for the newspaper, arranging metal letters in rows to print the words—I never did really understand how it worked—but he also got to do some artwork for the ads, including for the fair-skin creams Mother hated so.

I had not read the *Defender* much before he started working there, but my interest grew when I realized reading could connect me with my dream: To fly. I came across a story one day about two men named James Banning and Thomas Allen. They were smiling, good-looking men. They were Race men, and they had goggles pushed up jauntily on their foreheads. Because they were pilots. They were attempting to fly from Los Angeles to New York, and the *Defender* covered their stops as best it could. They apparently did not have a lot of money and their plane was not the best, so they had trouble every time they took off. That was mechanical trouble. They also had trouble of the usual kind for Race men trying to prove themselves. They might be proud aviators when they were in the air, but when they landed, they were just plain old Negroes, or worse. They had to sleep in barns, they were forbidden to land at some airports. The *Defender* reported that they were called the "flying hobos," but it would not call them that itself.

It took a long time, but they made it. I followed their stories so closely that I started to dream of them, and rolled out of bed one night onto the floor because I dreamt I was falling out of their rickety airplane.

Long before we arrived on the scene, the *Defender* had taken it upon itself to support flying Race men and women, including Bessie Coleman and Eugene Bullard. There was apparently a lot of interest in Chicago in having Race people up in the air. All the tall buildings just whetted their appetite to go higher. The paper had always been in the house but now Father brought me home early press runs every week, giving them to me from hands stained blacker than they already were. He even dug up old back issues for me. The papers were hard to read sometimes, full of smears and half-printed pages, but I could often find stories about courageous pilots. I was determined, more than ever, to be one of them, and I had never been farther off the ground than the third floor of my school. Father knew what I was reading the papers for and raised no objection. After I had seen him so humiliated, I think he would have let me do anything I wanted short of a life of crime, and I'm not sure he would have even ruled that out.

The paper's coverage of flying Race people made me so happy that I took a shine to the rest of the operation, too. I liked to visit Father at the newspaper offices. The place was some kind of beehive and it was almost always buzzing. Up front was a nice but worn entryway governed by some severe-looking women, hair usually tight in buns, but who smiled sweetly at visiting young men (like me) and anyone who might be coming, cash in hand, to buy an ad. Behind that was the news-room, where young men in crisp white shirts came and went, talking all the time, typing out stories on cheap paper or hunching over those sheets with editing pencils. The reporters and editors seemed to be in a state of constant warfare, and when I walked through there, I often heard language I would not hear again for many years, until I joined the Army.

Behind that was the back shop, where Father worked. He wore a filthy apron, as did all the men there. Their job was to take the paper that flowed from the white-shirted men and convert it into newspaper pages. To do this he arranged little metal letters into rows using that machine of his and then poured hot lead over them, or something like that. He never let me back there when he was actually doing it for fear that I would have some kind of metal-related injury and Mother would come and end his life. Plus, he said it would deafen me. For a long time, I thought he said it was a "Lion-type" machine because that's what it sounded like he said, and because he said the machine really roared. It made me want to roar, too. It helped me understand that what Nelson said was wrong, and what Uncle Abe said was right: I could fly. It wouldn't be easy, but if I believed I could fly, I could.

SEVEN

Coming Closer

I DID NOT EVER WANT to sleep in a barn or be forbidden to land at an airport, like James Banning and Thomas Allen. My time reading the *Defender* not only increased my interest in learning to fly, it increased my interest in going to France. I wanted to fly, not suffer.

There were some serious problems with this "plan." I was barely a teenager. I was a Race man in a country that did not value Race men. I had no money; my parents had no money. I was doing well in school, that was not a problem for me. I decided early on, after seeing Katherine give up on her brain, that I would not do the same. Also, I figured out that I needed math to do what I wanted to do. I did not want to be a pilot who didn't know anything about his airplane, didn't know what kept it in the air, couldn't fix it. After reading about Banning and Allen, I decided for damn sure that I wanted to know every inch of my airplane, I wanted to know what kept it aloft, I wanted to be able to calculate the best angle for landing if I was coming down hard at some out-of-the-way French airport.

In addition to knowing math, the universal language, I decided that I needed to know French, which was not the universal language. My school did not offer classes in French. I was reduced to buying an old, used textbook from a student who had transferred in from New York, where he had studied French but without enthusiasm. I paid him fifty cents for his battered, tattered, dog-eared reject. I loved it. It fit in my hand like the Bible when we went to church. I showed no aptitude for French on my own, and the book was hard going, but I loved it. It was the crack in the door.

Uncle Abe had the idea that he could speak French. He knew a few words and phrases that he liked to try out on me, especially after he saw my book. His attempts were meaningless—French, to me, was words on a page. As far as I knew, it was a dead language, like Latin. I was pretty certain that whatever Uncle Abe was saying wasn't quite right. Aunt Eveline agreed.

"Abe, that's not the way you say that," she would mutter after he unleashed a slick-sounding series of words.

"What do you know about it, woman? You don't speak French."

"I don't speak it, but I know it when I hear it, and I'm not hearing it. I used to work for that French lady in Charleston, remember? She talked an awful lot, and you have not said anything that sounds like anything she ever said."

"Well, men and women talk differently," Abe said, rolling his eyes at me where Aunt Eveline couldn't see. "Our throats are bigger and deeper, so the sound is different. That's all. I had forgotten about that French lady. I would have liked to have talked to her."

Aunt Eveline lowered her newspaper and looked at him.

"You would not be allowed within fifty feet of that woman. She was immoral. She had men coming and going out of that place like it was a train station. That French accent just drew them on in there like flies."

These comments brought some interesting thoughts to mind—I was getting to that age where I thought about girls a lot, and a French woman with apparently loose morals was an interesting variation on that—but I forgot about it soon after. Some months later, though, she came back to my attention. Uncle Abe was in town for an extended stay, during which he hoped to finally move a splinter group from church into a congregation of his own. He was around a lot, coming in late to the kitchenette, easing his bulk with a sigh onto a cot pushed next to Aunt Eveline's. He was out glad-handing during the day, all day, every day, talking to the flock and seeing who might be interested in a new shepherd. I actually didn't see him all that much during the visit, because I was busy with school, but one day he pulled me aside in the hallway.

"Listen, Johnny, I wanted to ask you. How serious are you about studying French?"

I looked up into his big sweaty face, which glowed yellow in the hall light.

"Very serious. You know that."

"Yeah, I thought so, I just wanted to make sure you hadn't moved on to something else."

"Well—no."

I didn't think he wanted me to go on about flying and math. He looked like he was in a hurry and I wanted to hear what he had to say. Maybe he would send me to France. Maybe he wanted to establish a branch of his church in Paris and he wanted me to be a missionary? I'd do it if I had to.

"All right. I got this deal cooked up with someone who's doing some work for the church. They're going to do a little extra work for me, but instead of me paying them, they got somebody who's going to tutor you."

"Tutor me?" I made good grades. I didn't need a tutor.

"Yes. In French. She speaks French, she's actually French."

"Who—"

"You remember that French lady Eveline told you about? That she worked for in Charleston?"

I did. I also remembered that Aunt Eveline disapproved of her highly, which certainly made her more interesting.

"She lives here now. She's going to tutor you. She's white. Did I mention that? She speaks good white French and she's going to teach it to you."

I didn't understand the deal, at all. I was getting good at math, like I said, and it didn't add up. Some people were doing extra work for my uncle, but I was going to be tutored in good white French.

"But why?"

Uncle Abe looked nervous.

"Look, it's hard to explain right now. Just—it's complicated to explain. Do you want to learn French or not?"

"Well, of course. Yes, I do."

"Good. You just go to her place next week to start. After school. You get out pretty early in the day, right?"

"Yes."

"That's perfect. You don't want to go too late. She has a, a bit of a drinking problem. You don't want to learn *that* kind of French. So, okay? You'll go talk with her?"

"Yes."

"And it would be better if you didn't tell your mother, or your dad. And especially your Aunt Eveline. You know why."

I just nodded.

"And," he said, leaning in close, "you keep your nose clean, you hear? Are you hearing what I'm saying?"

"Yes."

"Yes, what?"

"Yes, sir."

"You really do know what I'm talking about, don't you? I mean, you're old enough?"

He looked like he was willing to talk to me at some length about the facts of life. I knew something about it—I wasn't really clear on a lot of the details—but he looked so uncomfortable with the idea that I decided to put him out of his misery. I decided I did not want to talk about sex with a preacher.

"All right. You pay attention to your studies now. You go Tuesday to start. Can you go Tuesday?"

"Yes. Yes, sir."

"All right then."

I was still very confused by the whole thing, but it sounded like I was getting a good deal out of the situation, somehow.

"And thanks, Uncle Abe."

He put a meaty hand on my shoulder. "Young man, you are welcome. No offense to your folks, but I want to get you out of this dump. Even if that means you have to go to France."

He leaned in and looked me close in the eye. "You know I believe in moving around. But I think my traveling days are winding down. Yours are just beginning, and the world is starting to open up in a lot of ways. You could be right on the front of that. People see you can fly these aeroplanes, they will take you seriously. They will take *us* seriously, you know?"

"I just want to fly for me."

"I know, I know, I'm putting too much on you. You want to fly, that's what I want to help you do. You just work with this lady. But keep it quiet."

He gave me a wink.

I gave him an uncertain smile.

———

THE DOOR LOOKED LIKE ANY OTHER IN THE HALL. IT WAS UP SEVEN flights of stairs and I was breathing hard when I stood before it, so I waited about a minute before I knocked so my lungs and heart would settle down. The hallway was shabby, with wallpaper that was trying to quit its job in several places and a couple of weak bulbs barely clinging to light and life. The door itself boasted several coats of different-colored paint, green and tan and light blue, all of which were trying to show through at once. I was a little disappointed. I had always assumed white people lived better than Race people, but my French tutor hadn't climbed the ladder very far.

Finally, I knocked. After what seemed like half of forever, a woman opened the door a crack. I could see very little of her, just chalk-white skin and bright red hair. She looked like a secretive clown.

"You got my numbers?"

"What?"

"My numbers?"

Her words were not the smooth French I had been expecting. Her voice was raspy, like she had just put a cigarette out in it.

"I'm not a policy runner. I'm here for my French lesson. My Uncle Abernathy set it up."

She seemed to think about that for a few seconds, then opened the door wider.

"That's right. Don't worry about my numbers, I hardly ever win, anyway."

I stepped inside. Her apartment was everything the hallway was not: decorated well, lit well, orderly. I also saw that she did not, in any way, resemble a clown. She was beautiful. She was much older than me, but not really as old as I had expected. Maybe forty. She was slim and tall, with large breasts, which I noticed right away, even before I noticed her bright green eyes. Before I make her sound like some kind of Playboy Playmate, I'll say she wasn't perfect. Some of her skeleton seemed to be assembled from the wrong parts. Her jaw was firm, a little too firm and large, and her hands and feet were quite large. She could have wrapped her hands around my entire head. Her elbows and knees also seemed a bit sharp and extravagant, like the bones didn't know when to stop and take a turn.

The flaws didn't really detract from her looks. Like I said, she was beautiful, built out of big bones and luxurious curves, where needed, and bright colors. Her skin was the whitest I think I have ever seen. Katherine was about the fairest person I had ever seen on a regular basis, and this woman made Katherine seem like she was carved out of a lump of coal. Those "fair skin" cream companies could have just come to this apartment and scraped some of the white off this woman, she had plenty to spare.

She didn't have much furniture, though, which helped her apartment be neat and orderly. She had two small couches and a chair arranged around a small coffee table that was devoid of coffee table books. She sat on one of the couches, arranged her long legs in an interesting trapezoidal structure, and indicated that I should take the chair. I did, and crossed my legs, even though I didn't like to sit that way. I thought it would make me look more adult than if I sat there with my hands knotted between my knees.

"J'mappelle Dominique," she said after a moment of looking at me.

"What?"

"That was French. I said my name was Dominique. You should respond in kind. We are beginning our first lesson."

"Oh. Uh, jay mapelle Johnny."

"Zh. It's a zh sound, not 'jay.'"

"Zhhh."

"Better. French isn't just the words, Mr. Johnny. It's the sounds, the feelings."

I had brought a notepad and a pencil, but she frowned at me and shook her hand like she was shooing away a bird. She wanted me to absorb it, not just learn it.

"You speak French here," she said, tapping a spot above her left breast, "not here," tapping her red head.

We went on like that for about fifteen minutes, me memorizing the words because I just wasn't able to feel them yet, when there was a knock on the door. She had adopted a glazed expression during our lesson but perked up at the sound.

"Ah! That will be my numbers."

She walked past me like I was no longer there and opened the door the same crack she had shown me. I peered around the edge of the chair, which was not very well padded, so it was easy to do. The caller was another Race man, older than me by a few years but not yet in his twenties, I would guess. He had a sheaf of paper strips in his hand; he was her policy delivery. She was betting lots of numbers. Some of them came in, too; he had some money in the other hand, and she took it and made it disappear with the dexterity of a magician.

The older boy was smiling at her, a lazy smile, but she turned her face toward me, indicating she was not alone. His smile disappeared, replaced with a reptilian look.

"It is a language lesson," she said. "Nothing more."

She walked back to where I sat and extended a thin arm to help me up, like I was an old man.

"Mr. Johnny, that will be enough," she said. "I'm afraid you have to go."

Then, more quietly, so quietly that her new visitor couldn't hear her, and so quietly I almost didn't hear her myself, she said, "Come back next week, yes? But maybe a little earlier. A little earlier or a little later."

The policy man smirked at me as I left, but I didn't even look at him.

EIGHT

Lord of The New Church

"Look over here. This is where I will stand."

Uncle Abe stretched his arms like he was already preaching. He was looking at a blank wall. Next to it was an equally empty space where he had knocked out the wall and expanded.

"The pews can go here. I want some big aisles so if people get the spirit, they can express it and run and shout if they want to. And back there we can have the baptistry and a choir."

"I wish the pews were here *now*," Aunt Eveline said.

She stood holding her small purse, her tiny feet tucked close together. The floor was a mess of dust, crumbled brick and wood splinters, and Aunt Eveline was trying to minimize her exposure.

Uncle Abe had his own church now. A sizable number of the congregation had agreed to come with him. They would support him with "love offerings," which would include a considerable number of dinners. Aunt Eveline was a good cook whenever she got the chance and would prefer not to have to depend on the kindness of the congregation, particularly when she could do better, but she would go along and smile because she would be the preacher's wife.

Uncle Abe was wearing a dirty white shirt over an undershirt so stained with sweat you could see it through the cotton. He had been working all night to help knock down the wall. He had his church building and his flock ready to move in it, but, as Aunt Eveline could so obviously tell, the spirit was willing but the building was weak. Once he was able to rent it, he discovered the electrics were in bad shape and about half the wiring would have to be ripped out. The floor was also structurally unsound and would not stand up to the weight of a congregation, especially a congregation whose members might get the spirit and jump up and down. If they tried that right now, they would not get closer to heaven, but would go in the opposite direction and end up in the dusty basement.

Uncle Abe had rented the building from a man who once ran a shop there but ran out of money and closed it. He was happy to get it until he started working on it and saw what a pit it was. The man he rented it from was Jewish, and Uncle Abe had some unkind words to say about him, about how Jesus came down to change things for the formerly chosen people. I didn't understand much about what a Jewish person was, at that point, but it was something I would come to think about not too many years later.

Aunt Eveline called the church building a "rotten onion." It looked all right on the outside but once you got to the inner layers you saw the rot. Uncle Abe did not appreciate the metaphor.

It was Monday afternoon. Uncle Abe intended to hold the first worship service there the following Sunday. He had a lot of work to do, on top of all that he had already done.

"Oh," he said, shaking his head, sending drops of sweat to stain the floor further. "I wish I had a month. I've got to get those people in here, make sure they're safe, make sure they can express themselves if the Lord gets hold of them. All in a week."

My father walked in the door just then, still wearing the bluish-gray apron he wore to operate the Linotype. It was hot work and he was almost as sweaty as Abe. He nodded to his brother-in-law and walked around the building quietly, sizing it up.

"Looks like it's going to work, Abe."

"I don't know," Abe said, running a hand over his wet, bald head. "It's sure hard to tell it from here."

"I'll help you. I can make sure I just work my regular shifts this week so I can be here this time every night."

"And I can be here after school every day," I said, although I suddenly remembered my French lessons, the ones I was taking in secret. "Except tomorrow."

"Rosemary will help too, of course," my father said. My mother was at work now, but she had already been by earlier that day to survey her new channel to God.

"I'll help you too, Abe, you know that," Aunt Eveline said. "I can't do any of the heavy stuff but this place sure could use a cleaning and I can do that."

Uncle Abe hung his head and shook it like a horse. "I don't know what I've done to deserve such good people in my life."

Less than a week later, he stood in nearly the same spot where I first saw him in the church, his arms raised again, sweaty again, and this time he was preaching.

"Let me tell you all about the goodness of the Lord," he said in a voice that carried easily to the back and bounced off the freshly painted walls. "The Lord wants his word to get out. And so, he fills you good people with the spirit and tells you to form another church. And we have done that, Lord."

"Amen," said Mrs. Thompson, a rotund woman who was nearly as sweaty as my uncle. She had complained loudly about Brother Johnson's preaching, so it was no surprise to me to see her here. It *was* a surprise to see some of the other people. I had not really thought that much about who might come and who might not, since my father's disinterest in religion—at least the religion practiced in the churches that sprouted in Bronzeville like mushrooms—had only increased. But there they were, filling the church, showing that Uncle Abe's decision to knock down the wall was necessary.

There was Mr. Thornberry, so old and thin and dark you could hardly make out the features on his face until you got right up next to him. He expected more soothing preaching from Uncle Abe than he got from Brother Johnson. There was Jake King, his wife Anita and their three toddlers. Jake and Anita were always angry about something, mainly their station in life—Jake labored at the stockyard doing work he hated, working with people who hated him—and they wanted Uncle Abe to stoke their anger into something fiery and righteous. There was Alice Tonklin, whose husband, rumored to be a white man, had been killed in the Great War long ago. She had never remarried and seemed to have no further interest in males, except for Jesus. I'm not sure what she hoped to get out of the North Corner Church of God in Christ, but it could be that Uncle Abe's new congregation was just closer to her apartment.

It would be impossible for Uncle Abe to live up to the expectations of everyone who crowded into his church, but I realized then what a salesman he was. He wouldn't be able to do it, but they believed he could, enough to follow him to a new church in a building that looked sharp and shiny and new. I knew just how much of that was a front. A stack of two-by-fours was helping prop up the floor, and I knew that when Uncle Abe bowed his head and led us in prayer, asking the Father, Son and the Holy Ghost to protect our souls, he was also silently asking them to protect our bodies, at least for a couple of hours, so that he'd have time to get the floor fixed for good. I also knew that if things got too hot and sweaty in the church the fresh white paint was likely to come sliding back down the wall because it hadn't been up there long. The advantage of this was that Uncle Abe would be forced to keep the service comparatively short.

"Brothers and sisters, God has brought us here today," Uncle Abe said.

"Amen," someone said.

"He has brought us here to grow His church in this wicked city."

He was taking a little bit of a chance there, going after what little civic pride might be in the audience.

"Amen."

Not too much of a risk.

"He has brought us here to grow His church in this great country, a country that, sometimes, oh Lord, has been prone to wickedness."

I was reminded, again, of why Uncle Abe had his own church and the other jackleg preacher at the South Side Baptist Fellowship did not.

"We must work together now, putting all ego aside, to get the word out. We must keep our eyes on the goal, oh Lord, and not let ourselves get bogged down here in this vale of tears. This Earth is wicked, and we must not be part of that wickedness."

He could call Chicago wicked. He could not call the entire country wicked, but he could call the entire planet evil. It was a very fine tightrope to walk, but my uncle could dance across it.

"Amen."

When he got serious with the prayer and asked the congregation to lower their heads and close their eyes, I had a better chance to look around. I was near the back anyway to help keep an eye on the door. No one was afraid of crime—there was not really anything to steal except the church pews—but since it was a new church, Uncle Abe wanted me to keep an eye out for any curious passersby who might want to come in.

"The bigger the flock, the bigger the shepherd's salary," my father said, and my mother hit him lightly on the shoulder in rebuke, but it was true.

I sat on the far-left edge of the left row of pews so that I could see the edge of the foyer without turning my head like an owl. While Uncle Abe led the prayer, which piled phrases of praise and lamentation into a tower nearly tall enough to reach right into heaven, I looked around. That's when I noticed the two men. They must have just walked in or I would have seen them sooner. They were well dressed in dark suits and held their fedoras against their hearts. They were handsome men, tall but not threateningly tall, with close-cropped hair. But there was something disturbing about them, something hard in their faces. They looked fixedly at my uncle at first, although he was communing with Jesus and didn't see them, then surveyed the crowd. The one on the left saw me looking at him. He didn't turn away, but just gave an almost imperceptible nod and then continued to slowly swivel his head.

I was just about to rise and usher them to a seat when the one who had made eye contact with me turned quickly to the other one, said a couple of words, and then they both vanished. Not the churchgoing types, it seemed.

NINE

I Get Better

"Am I getting any better?"

Dominique looked at me with her curious manner, her eyes half open but strangely intense, as if she was looking into my soul but found it a little boring.

"You are about good enough to go to a tourist restaurant in Paris and order something to eat," she said, her voice its usual rasp. "That is about it. You try to talk to a regular Parisian, or Frenchman of any sort anywhere, and they would stare at you like you came from the moon and were speaking moon-speak."

I slumped back in the chair. We had been having my lessons now for nearly six months and I studied my French whenever I could. I had hoped to show more improvement. One problem was that I had no one to speak French with aside from Dominique. Uncle Abe had still not given me clearance to admit even to my mother and father that I was having the classes, so I couldn't practice it at home by myself, at least, not out loud. The French I spoke in my head was perfect but apparently was losing something in the translation. I had asked Uncle Abe if maybe there was somebody at the new congregation who could help, but he didn't seem to think so, and as far as I could tell, he had not followed up on the matter.

"Johnny, I keep telling you that French comes from the heart, not the head," Dominique said.

Her voice was syrupy and cooing—listening to her talk was like listening to a dove speak (a chain-smoking dove)—but her words frustrated me.

"But I still have to know the words and the grammar," I complained.

"That is true. But think with your heart, not with your head."

"You keep saying that, but it doesn't mean anything."

She reached over and slowly put her hand on my knee. From this angle, I had a view up her long white arm, a slender archipelago that led to the valley of her breasts.

"It means something, Johnny." She looked at me a long time then, with those half-lidded eyes, until I felt very comfortable. Finally, she seemed to reach a decision. "I can help show you a way to think with your heart."

Her fingers began to move on my knee. Before, the placing of her hand on my knee, her hand white and unmoving as marble, could be construed as the innocent act of a teacher reaching out to a student. Now, the fingers were writhing slowly like lazy snakes, and that could only mean one thing. I was not experienced with girls, not at all, and even I knew that. I would not say that I had tried to become experienced. There were some girls at school I knew and liked enough to become friendly with, and I had even kissed one of them several times, but I was not what you would call worldly. By today's standards, I would be hopelessly behind, but I was just normal then, normal and shy.

"Johnny, do you want to get better?"

I had not really thought about the time when I would lose my virginity. It seemed to be something off in the distance, like an airplane hovering over the horizon. I had vaguely thought it would occur after my marriage to a beautiful, smart woman, maybe even a fellow pilot like Bessie Smith. I had not pictured a lanky, slinky, raspy white French woman in a neat but nearly empty apartment in a dumpy building, but that was the choice that was presented to me. I looked into her bright, half-shut eyes and realized I had an opportunity before me that every boy—every man, probably—in the city would kill for. I am not saying that when opportunity arises you should always take advantage. But I did.

"I want to get better," I said, trying to make my voice deeper and scratchier than it was.

She laughed at that, but not in a way that made me feel bad, and slid a bit closer. She was not wearing any perfume that I could detect. In fact, she was nearly odorless. As her body moved before my eyes, I seemed to lose the ability to focus. I saw what looked like a wall of white coming across to take me over. So, I let it. I closed my eyes and she ran her fingers over my face, reached one inside my lips to touch my teeth. She ran one hand down my chest, peeling off to the right before she reached my belt buckle, making me want her more. I thought my pants were going to explode like a popped sausage. She took my hand and led me down the hall to her bedroom. I didn't notice anything about the hall or the bedroom. I only saw her shoulder blades moving under her thin dress.

Dominique was thin and angular, but she could move like melted butter. I had never seen a naked woman before—or, rather, not for any length of time, as I had occasionally spotted mother or Aunt Eveline or even Katherine in various states of undress—but Dominique answered all my questions about what they looked like, and then some. She used every part of her body and showed me what to do. I had masturbated before. I'm not ashamed to tell you that, it's a perfectly natural thing; so, I had some idea of what was to come, but it was so much better with her than I could have imagined. She looked me in the eyes as I shoved my young penis into her, after she helped me get there, and then she reached her warm hand down and pushed against my thigh and showed me the right rhythm. I began to move with her instead of just against her, or into her, and once I found that slow rhythm it felt like we were dancing.

After a short while, she started to lose that rhythm, became jerky and wild, and then gripped my back like a grizzly bear. She cried out and fell back against the pillow. I don't know whether she really had an orgasm, or whether she was trying to make me feel better about the whole thing, but it worked. I ejaculated into her after that and it felt like I was shooting away some vital organ. It burned deep in my core and left me sprawling atop her marble body, limp and exhausted.

"Say something," she said.

"Like what?"

"No, no. Say something in French."

I told her I did not want to say anything in French. But I said it in French. My voice was tired, husky, slurred.

"Very good," she cooed. "Very, very good."

She ran one hand up and down my chest. I was half dead but began to feel the stirring again in my groin.

"See, French is from the heart. And from here," she said, and began to stroke me back to strength.

We started having classes twice a week. I began to improve rapidly. C'est la vie.

TEN

Mr. Coffey and Mrs. Brown

THERE IT WAS, right in front of me. It was not much to look at; a flat stretch of ground, a strip of concrete with tufts of grass breaking through, a couple of tattered windsocks, some metal buildings that looked like one good storm would blow them away. On the far side of the strip of concrete, in one of those buildings, was my destiny. Because, as it turned out, I would not have to go to France to learn to fly. A place willing to educate Race men in the ways of airplanes was coming to me, right there in Chicago.

I heard about it, oddly enough, straight from the horse's mouth. I had been reading about Race aviation in the pages of the *Defender*, but I heard about the new school from the mouth of Robert Abbott himself, the paper's founder, the legend.

I had gone to the *Defender* office that day to carry some lunch to my father. He had forgotten his but was going to be eating so late that I had time to bring it after school. Today was not one of my French lesson days, or he might have had to do without. I was heading back to the press room when I nearly ran over Mr. Abbott. I apologized, but then he seemed to recognize me and started talking.

"Let me have a look at you, son."

He wore a shiny brown suit and sharp fedora. He looked me up and down in an exaggerated motion, like I was a horse he was interested in buying. His round face creased into a big smile. "You are the spitting image of your father. I believe that if you brought me an old photograph of your father, he would look exactly like you. I mean, exactly like you!"

"Th-thank you, sir," I stammered, wondering if he was paying me a compliment or not. He didn't say whether he considered my father and myself to look good, he was just saying we looked alike. Maybe we looked equally bad.

As I've said before, Robert Abbott's words, or the words his paper had published, were very strong among the forces that had brought my family to Chicago. His words calling for Race people to leave the South and get what they were entitled to had been read all over the country, carried from railroad porter to farmer to banker like some easily transported disease, although it was a disease that opened men's minds and made them move. In person, he was not that prepossessing, at least not physically. I was already taller than him and I wasn't out of high school yet. I was a lot thinner, too, because he was a man about town and he liked to eat and had plenty of chances to do it. His face was round and smooth as a baby's. He had a presence, though. You could not stand near him and not pick up on that energy that had driven him for decades, had driven him to uproot families like mine, to change, in fact, the racial layout of the entire country.

"Your father tells me you are very interested in airplanes and human flight," he said, having dispensed with the chitchat.

"Yes, sir, I am."

"You know about Bessie Coleman, about James Banning and Thomas Allen?" he asked.

"Yes, sir, I do."

"You probably know that the *Defender* has championed them all?" he asked, raising his chin in unrestrained pride.

"I do. I have read the stories."

"You're a well-informed young man," he said.

I started to laugh until I realized he wasn't making a joke. He was that proud of his newspaper, and I suppose he should have been.

"You know, son, that Race men can make a difference in every walk of life, don't you?"

"I think so, sir."

"I mean, your father makes a big difference by coming in here and helping me put out this newspaper, isn't that right? And Race men can make a difference as bankers and bakers and garbagemen and men that work at the slaughterhouses and put food on the table," he said in a big gust of words. "What I'm driving at is that sometimes people only pay attention to the flashy things, like Race people who fly airplanes. But there are other ways to make a difference."

The man whose newspaper had introduced me to flying Race men and women was trying to talk me out of flying? I didn't want to hear that.

"I know that, sir. But I want to *fly*. I'll go to France, if I have to."

He chuckled.

"You ever been to France, son?"

I had been to Alabama and Chicago and that was it, and not even much of either of those.

"It's just that you say that like it's a bad thing. That's not exactly paying a heavy price. You speak French?"

"Uh—no."

My lessons were still a secret, because Uncle Abe had not released me from my agreement with him, so I couldn't admit that I did, at least a little. I doubted that the issue would ever come up between Mr. Abbott and my father, but you never know.

"As it turns out, it's just as well. I have just been asking you all this because I want to make sure you're really interested. There are some things going on here, and we're going to have a story about it soon."

"About flying?"

"Yes, about flying. You ever hear of a man named Cornelius Coffey?"

"No, sir."

"No reason you should. But you will. He's going to establish a flight training school. He's a Race man, and he will teach other Race men to fly and maintain airplanes."

"This will be in the United States?"

He spread his stubby arms wide. "In the United States? Mr. Nicholas, it will be right here in Chicago! At Harlem Airport!"

I must have made a very funny face because he looked at me like I was about to float right out of the room.

"Right here on the South Side."

I couldn't believe it.

He left me after that.

Still stunned by the news, I took my father his lunch. And a few weeks later, there was the story, in black and white, complete with a picture of Cornelius Coffey. He was a hero to me, instantly, without my having met him, but he didn't really look particularly heroic in the picture. He stared off into the distance with a faint smile on his face. He did look determined, though, and the article backed up that determination with his story. He and another Race man had applied to the Curtiss Wright School of Aviation, also in Chicago, and were let in despite its whites-only policy. The school didn't know they were Race men and, when they found out, tried to turn them away, but their employer, a Chevrolet dealer, threatened to sue if they didn't get in. So, they got in, and graduated, but later Cornelius Coffey decided he wanted to create an aeronautics school where Race men could walk in through the front door with their heads high.

So, I went to see the place. Robert Abbott had exaggerated when he said the Coffey School of Aeronautics was going to be on the South Side. The South Side of the planet, maybe. It was a long stretch from Chicago, or at least my part of it. I had to take the L and two streetcars and then walk for a while. Then I took a bus. I took the wrong bus at first, adding about half an hour to my journey, but I finally made it.

A small plane buzzed overhead as I approached the airport, and I wondered if it was a white man flying it, or a Race man. It made me glad to think this was a possibility. I walked past the terminal building, where the ticket man had told me to go, and around the edge of the runway until I found the school. There was a young woman there, a Race woman, pretty but with a very serious face. I thought maybe she was some kind of secretary.

"The terminal is up that way, young man," her voice was stern but not unkind.

"Is this the Coffey School of Aeronautics?"

She looked at me funny and then stepped a couple feet to the right so that I could see the sign she had been blocking: Coffey School of Aeronautics. It was a plain metal sign. My father could have done better, and with wood.

"Can I help you with something?"

"I just wanted to find out more information about it. I want to study here."

"You're a little young, son."

"I know, but in a year or so I'd like to study here."

I was fourteen years old but the year before I had hit a growth spurt and was now as tall as my father; taller, if he stooped, which he was starting to do. If I remembered to keep my smile in check and my voice a little bit low, I could sometimes pass for an eighteen-year-old.

"More like five or six years," she said. "You need to get through school first."

"Is Mr. Coffey here?" I asked, purposely looking around her as if she were blocking my view of Cornelius Coffey, who might not be so hung up on age.

"He is not and would tell you the same thing if he was," she said. "But it is nice of you to show such interest."

I kept peeking around anyway.

"Ma'am, I would really like to speak with him, if I could. I came a long way."

She gave me a sharper look than before. A very faint smile had been hovering on her lips, but it faded away now and they drew back against her thin face.

"Young man, talking to me is the same as talking to him. I set up this school with him. I am not his assistant. Now, you just go on home and come back when you're older and have some money in your pocket."

"I'm very sorry, ma'am," I said, giving her my biggest smile. "My name is Johnny Nicholas and I very much want to go to this school next year. I guess I let my desire run away with me." I stuck out my hand.

She continued to give me that hard look for a few moments, but then the faint smile flickered back into view, barely. "Well, Mr. Nicholas, although I think perhaps next year may be too soon, despite what you say, I hope you get here if you want it bad enough." She gave me a firm handshake. "Willa Brown."

The name hit me like a brick. I had read about her. This same Willa Brown had marched into the newsroom of the *Defender* a couple of years before and demanded coverage of an air show out at this very airport, and had taken the reporter up in the plane, to boot. It was a terrific story and I remember laughing when I read it, but for some reason, her name had not stuck in my head until now. Her face hadn't, either. The paper with a photo of her had been an early print run and had a big smudge on it, which is what most of the *Defenders* I ever saw looked like. She looked much better in person, both prettier and more determined.

I started going back whenever I had a chance, which usually was no more than once a week. Sometimes, the trip would take me an hour, sometimes it would take two hours, depending on the buses, and there were a couple of times when I didn't make it at all and had to turn back. It was not an easy thing for me but, like Cornelius Coffey himself, I was determined. I talked to Willa Brown, or Cornelius Coffey, who I met on my second trip out. Coffey was almost always busy, talking to the students or up to his elbows in an engine showing them how to reach some half-buried part. Willa was always busy, too, but seemed to find me amusing and usually found a little time to talk. I spent most of my limited talking time with them trying to convince them I was nearly old enough to go to the school, and to see if I could wheedle some sort of scholarship.

"The young Mr. Nicholas," she would say.

"Next year, ma'am," I would say. "I'd like to see if we could arrange some kind of work-study."

"Next year, you will be planning to wear your first pair of knee pants," she might say. Or, "Next year, you'll still be wiping the milk off your lower lip."

This went on for a good six months or more, probably more like eight months. I'm sure my visits annoyed them, but they put a good face on it, and eventually my persistence actually worked. One day, after a particularly long journey out there, Cornelius Coffey offered me a job.

"It's not very much," he said. "Just sweeping up around the place and keeping things clean. I can only pay a few bucks a week." He gave me a little wink. "But if you want to come in and work during class hours, and keep your ears and eyes open, that won't bother me a bit."

I think I nearly flew all the way back to Bronzeville that day. I still wasn't able to come back and work every day, but I came as often as I could. I came as early as I could and stayed as late as I could, and just as he suggested, I kept my ears and eyes open while I cleaned up. I paid so much attention that sometimes he had to gently shoo me away and remind me to get back to work.

Willa Brown was often a little more direct. "There is a spot of grease over there as big as your head," she said one day when I was nearly peering over her shoulder to look inside the guts of an engine. "It would be really nice if you could find the time to clean it up."

The truth was that I was having a hard time following what they were saying. There was an awful lot of math involved, more than even I had expected or hoped for, and a lot of technical terms about engine and fuselage parts that most of the time I couldn't see, along with boring talk about regulations. I wrote down a lot of the terms whenever I could, carrying a pencil with me so much that it poked holes in all my pants pockets. Whatever I didn't understand, I looked up in library books from school.

Willa Brown was right—I did not attend the Coffey School of Aeronautics the next year. It took three years and a war before that happened. But it did happen.

ELEVEN

Beneath the House of God

I ARRIVED EARLY one day at Uncle Abe's church, which was still how I thought of it no matter what it was named. I came by once in a while, when I wasn't working my jobs or working on my French, to help out. I felt I owed him. On this day, I walked in and heard a thumping sound from below.

"Uncle Abe?"

Nobody answered but the thumping continued. I didn't think he was having some kind of real holy-roller service down there, not in the afternoon, so I walked to the back and out the service door. There was a set of stairs that led to the basement, which connected only from the alley through an old coal chute with heavy metal doors. The owners had used it to bring in food when the church had been a store, and it looked like that's what Uncle Abe was doing now. The metal doors were flattened back against the pavement like the petals on a dead flower, and he and my father were carrying boxes in from a ratty truck so old it looked like it should have a horse pulling it. My father was resting his arms on his knees and breathing a little heavily, and Uncle Abe, true to form, was bathed in sweat.

"Hey, little man," Uncle Abe said when he saw me. "Now that you're here, we can use your help."

I had come around to help however I could, which I had figured would include moving hymnals or straightening the pews, which were not yet bolted to the floor and had a tendency to move around when the service got a little boisterous. I had not expected to help load heavy boxes down a steep ramp.

"What is all this?"

Uncle Abe wiped his brow but did not look at me. I noticed my father wasn't looking at me, either, he was concentrating on the backs of his hands, which rested on his dirty knees.

"Just some stuff I agreed to store for some people. Since we have the basement of sorts down here, I thought I could help them out. Sort of the neighborly thing to do."

The basement was not so much a basement as a gaping void studded with two-by-fours to hold up the floor, and I did not like going down in it, much less dragging heavy boxes. I pictured myself knocking one of the two-by-fours loose and having the whole church cave in on me. I might go straight to Heaven by dying in a church, or I might go straight to Hell for knocking it down, and I did not want to find out which. But Uncle Abe looked like he was on the verge of a heart attack, and my father was not far behind him, so I decided I would help. Plus, Uncle Abe had helped set up my French lessons, and I owed him so much for that.

The truck was not all that big, but there were a lot of boxes and it took us a long time. They were heavy, too, and it wasn't long before I was sweating and panting along with my father and Uncle Abe. The boxes were all the same size and weight and seemed to be packed pretty much the same. After a while, once I thought about it, it seemed odd that they would be so uniform.

"What's in these?" I asked.

"Cans, I think," Uncle Abe said.

They seemed heavy enough, but they didn't slosh or rattle.

"Food? Books?"

"Not sure," he grunted as he carried another down the concrete slope into the basement. "Didn't ask. They said they needed some stuff stored, so I'm going to store it."

"Who is *they?*"

"Some people I know."

His tone indicated that perhaps I should stop asking questions, and I didn't really care that much, so I did. When we finally finished, we were all exhausted, sweaty and dirty. Some spiders had taken a liking to the basement, too, after the two-by-fours had been installed, and we were covered in gray webs. We had barely gotten finished when I noticed two men standing beside the truck. They looked familiar, but I couldn't place them.

"Just a minute," Uncle Abe said, and went up to talk to them.

When I saw them together, I realized where I had seen them before. They were the men who had come into the back of the church that first Sunday and looked around. Apparently, they liked what they saw, or at least liked the basement. Uncle Abe stood with his back to me, blocking my view of the men. They talked for a while and things looked like they were getting heated, but they kept their voices low, even Uncle Abe, and that was work for him. Finally, one of the men reached into his front pocket, pulled out a thick wallet and gave Uncle Abe some money. Then the men went away, giving my father and I nearly imperceptible nods of greeting.

"Sorry about that," Uncle Abe said as he walked back to us, counting out his new cash. "A little difference of opinion on whether I needed your help."

He gave some money to my father and some to me. The roll he handed to me seemed to be about half as thick as the one he gave my father. My father pocketed his without comment, but I was now more confused than ever about what was going on.

"Who were those men? What's in those boxes?"

Uncle Abe rested a meaty hand on my shoulder. Even his palms were sweating.

"Johnny, sometimes it's possible to ask too many questions. Those men are acquaintances of mine and they need some help and I'm helping them out, and I'm glad to do it. And they're glad I'm doing it so they're helping me out, too. I appreciate your help, and your pop's help, so I'm just sharing some of the appreciation with you. I don't know what's in those boxes, and I don't want to know. It doesn't matter to me. All I know is that they are in need and I'm helping them out. And it would be good if you would keep this under your hat. Your mother doesn't need to know about it. Nobody in your building needs to know about it. Nobody in the congregation needs to know about it. Let's just keep this between us, all right?"

I was learning how to keep secrets the more I hung around with Uncle Abe. But this time I spotted an opportunity.

"How often do those parishioners need help?"

My father looked mildly alarmed at my question, but Uncle Abe just gave me a long look, then the corners of his mouth started to tilt up.

"They are thinking that they will be in need about once a week, maybe once every two weeks."

"I was just figuring that you could use some help," I said. "The two of you looked like you were nearly worn out when I showed up."

In fact, I had noticed that once I arrived, Uncle Abe and my father seemed to take things a little easier than they had before, letting me bring down two boxes to their one. I was willing to work at whatever it was, and now I had a reason to get money beyond just the ordinary use for money: I needed to save up for my studies at the Coffey School of Aeronautics. I was already working some, but this seemed steady enough and, although I wasn't sure how much money my uncle had given me—thinking it would be rude to count it right there in front of him—I was pretty sure it paid better.

"I could possibly use some help," Uncle Abe said.

My father was getting angry. "Now, look here, Abe, don't get him involved in this. He's just a kid, he doesn't need to be here working with us."

"I don't need to be helping some parishioners?" I asked him. "That seems like something the nephew of the preacher ought to be doing."

My father fumed, but he was reluctant to tell me what was wrong with my assessment.

"Come on, Carleton," Uncle Abe said. "He is a kid. That's the beauty of it, I can see that now. God sent your son here to help me because he's a kid."

"That's ridiculous. Don't start in with this God told you to do stuff," my father said. "It seems that God is forever trying to find corners for you to cut."

"Maybe he is! The Lord works in mysterious ways, we all know that. He wanted me to have a church, now I have a church. He has seen fit to tell me to use the church building for other purposes when chance arises, and now chance has arisen. And he has sent a young man here to help me, a young man who is not likely to run afoul of the powers that be because of his age."

I was tired after all the work and didn't feel like continuing to argue about what God wanted. I knew what I wanted.

"Dad, just let me do this. Let me help unload these boxes of whatever they are. If you don't, I'll tell Mother."

He gave me a look that pained me. It pains me still; I never forgot it. I could summon it right now, if I wanted to, and it would make me feel as bad now as it did then, so strong was it. The years have not diluted it one bit. But at the time, I did not back down. I wanted some money, this was a way to get it, and he couldn't say much about it because he was taking it, too.

We never talked about it until it was too late. The "work" was steady, to the point where I eventually dropped one of my other jobs. I'm not sure what my father did with his money. I didn't notice any sudden increase in our standard of living. As for me, I squirreled mine away in a box that I kept under my bed. I kept some schoolbooks on top of it to weigh it down. After a while, the pile grew until it pushed the books right over the top. It was just getting me closer to the sky, I thought.

TWELVE

Establishing My Territory

I was leaving Dominique's one afternoon: Very fluent by this time, fluent enough that I believe if I had been dropped into France I could land in any restaurant and order anything on the menu. I couldn't read much French, and could write even less, but I could speak it, or so Dominique said, like a native. We had actually come to focus more and more on language lessons and a bit less on sex. We were almost like an old married couple, or at least what I imagined an old married couple to be like.

I was headed down the stairway, listening to my footsteps echoing off the cheaply painted walls. The carpet was thin as paper and did not absorb much sound. I heard footsteps ascending to meet mine and was halfway down when I saw a familiar face. Another Race man, a bit older than me. It was the guy who brought policy numbers to Dominique, and to probably half the other residents in the building. He looked at me and recognized me, too. I gave him a noncommittal nod and would have passed by if he hadn't opened his big mouth.

"You come around here too much," he said, his voice nearly a hiss.

"What?"

He was above me on the stairs now, looking down on me in more ways than one.

"You need to leave Dominique alone. She mine."

"She yours?"

He was so angry he didn't realize I was making fun of him.

"Yeah. She mine. So, you need to take a walk."

I had tried not to think about Dominique when I wasn't with her. I was busy with school, I was busy helping Uncle Abe and I was busy trying to worm my way into the Coffey school. She was a white woman, to boot, although one with physical skills I had never heard attributed to white women. I did not think of her as mine. I also did not like to think that she might be with other men, although I knew it was a possibility, and Uncle Abe had hinted as much. But I certainly did not think of her as belonging to this joker, and I did not appreciate him trying to stake a claim.

I should have thought about it a little more before I responded. He had a seedy look about him and wore a tight blue shirt that showed off his lean, muscled build. I was a skinny, tall kid who wore a loose white shirt that hid mine. He was tough and looking for trouble, and I was doing neither. And yet I seemed to have developed some sort of spine. I had filled my head with stories about Race men and women doing anything they set their mind to, and I guess that included not allowing themselves to be scared away from white women.

"She not yours. She can make her own choices."

It was difficult for me to talk like that. Mother would have come close to smacking me for saying something so grammatically incorrect.

He took a step or two back down. "What are you saying to me?" His mood was clear.

What I said next could determine whether I walked out of this building with all my teeth. "I'm saying you don't own her. If she wants to see me, she sees me."

He was on me like a panther. He hurled his whole body down the steps and slammed into me. I saw him coming and shifted to the left, so I was able to swing him around and keep most of his weight moving straight into the wall. A pile of dust fell from the landing below when he hit, and I heard his breath fly out of him with a whoosh. His eyes got wide. I didn't wait to see what he would do next. I tucked into a fighting stance and pounded away at his midsection. My shirt didn't show it, but my muscles had developed nicely from carrying all those boxes into the basement of Uncle Abe's church and from pushing a broom at the Coffey school.

He tossed me a quick punch and tried to push away from the wall, but I deflected it and kept punching at his stomach. I don't know exactly where I had learned about that. I must have read it somewhere. If I punched him in the face, I stood the risk of cutting my fist on one of his teeth or even breaking a knuckle on his jaw. He started spitting up blood and was getting it on my shirt sleeves, but I could not stop because I could still feel him trying to push off the wall, and if he ever got off the wall, I figured I was done for. My arms were getting tired, but I ignored the burning in my biceps and kept plugging away, hit after hit, none of them powerhouse blows but all of them steady enough to keep him busy just trying to breathe.

I finally stepped back when his knees buckled, and he fell to the carpet. My arms ached but the fight was knocked out of him.

"You don't tell me what's mine and what's yours," I said, trying to make my voice menacing, but it sounded like the wheezy threat of a scared kid.

"Hey!" someone shouted above, the sound echoing down the stairwell like the voice of God. "What are you niggers up to?"

A sizable white man in a too-small shirt, his belly jiggling like he was an out-of-work Santa Claus, came down the stairs with surprising speed. I did not care to talk about anything with him, and neither did my opponent, who staggered down the stairs before me, still spitting blood. I made sure to keep him in front of me.

"Ah!" the man shouted when he reached the landing where we had fought. "Nigger blood! On my carpet! I'm calling the police!"

I doubt he actually did, but I didn't stick around to find out. I saw which way the policy runner headed and I went the other way, mainly so he wouldn't try to jump me somewhere else. I ran toward an L station until I noticed that people were looking at me because I had bloodstains on my shirt. I quickly took it off and bundled it under my arm. I had on an undershirt, so nobody noticed or minded.

I ended up walking all the way back home, mainly so I had time to stop trembling before I got there. I was cool by the time I arrived, but I hid the shirt under my mattress so mother wouldn't find it. We didn't have enough money for me to go throwing away perfectly good shirts, but I couldn't very well let her clean it. I would have to scrub it myself, later. Or maybe I should ask Dominique to clean it. The whole thing was her fault, anyway.

I was no longer shaking but my nerves were still jangling long into the night. I lay there, awake, realizing that I could fight if I needed to.

"You caused me a lot of trouble last week," Dominique told me.

We were lying side by side, naked in bed, with the soapy afternoon light washing over us. It was no longer an erotic thing but just what we did after having sex. I liked the gentle slope of her hips rising above the tangled sheets like some surfacing fish.

"I'm sorry."

I wasn't, really.

"Are you jealous of me, Johnny?"

Her brilliant green eyes looked unblinkingly into mine. It wasn't any sort of accusation. She was just curious.

"Jealous?"

"I've been with that boy that brings me the policy numbers. And you got me in trouble with the landlord. He knew where you both have been. I had to give him a little taste, too."

She pulled the sheet back to expose dark hair, so it would be perfectly clear what she was talking about.

"And you saw what a fine specimen he is. But I gave it to him, same as you. What do you think of that?"

She was trying to shock me.

"I don't like talking about this."

The truth was that Dominique was very good about making me feel like I was the only person who mattered. I never went anywhere with her outside the apartment, I did not know any of her friends, I did not know very much about her family life. Looking back, I just remember her presence: her skin, her eyes, her hair, the way she moved underneath me and on top of me, the way she breathed in my ear. She could wrap around you like smoke and shut off your air until she was the only thing left. She could do this to the extent that I never thought about her with other men. I knew they were around, but when I was with her, she choked off those thoughts.

"It's who I am, Johnny. All my life, men have wanted things from me. Well, one thing, really. I have learned to give it to them."

"I never wanted anything from you."

"No? Or should I say, non?"

I lay back and the pillow fluffed around my head like water, covering me. I had not thought of it that way, at all. I had come here for language lessons and thought the more hands-on part of the training had just blossomed on its own. She thought it was part of the transaction. Then it hit me hard, as hard as that unlucky policy runner would have hit me if he had gotten the chance: I was in love with her and she was not in love with me, never had been and never would be. I actually cried, a little; a lone tear squeezed its way out and began moving down my cheek, only to be soaked up by the pillowcase that still hid my shame from her.

I had read about love, but only in an academic way, the same way I had read about engines and propellers and bearing grease. It was a means to an end, a way to move you to the kind of life you wanted. I had not expected to feel it in bed with a white woman who was much older than I was, whose world was close to mine but not part of it. I had not expected that the first time I would feel romantic love I wouldn't recognize it until it hurt, until it ached. It was gone the second I knew what it was.

I did not answer her until I had my voice under control.

"I never thought of it like that," I said finally, pulling my head up so she could see my face.

She still lay there, unblinking green eyes on me, a lioness waiting for its prey to emerge. She could probably have stayed that way all day, never moving.

"I know you didn't. I don't either. I wouldn't be with you if I didn't want to be, Johnny. I think you're the only man I have met who really didn't want this from me. Or at least, not only this."

"Do you want to be with the others? With that punk I beat up on the stairs?" I sounded so much tougher than I felt. I didn't beat up the punk, I just got the drop on him. I had resolved to keep a close watch out for him in the future, because if he ever got the drop on me, I would be finished.

"He's not a punk. He's actually a nice boy. But I don't want to be with him. That's just about money. Let's just say I get my bets at a discount, and I don't have to go over there and check on the numbers."

I didn't feel like my time with her was a transaction, and she didn't seem to feel like it was either, but there was definitely a transaction going on here. Uncle Abe had set it up, for one thing.

"Why did you agree to teach me French? I don't pay you."

"You don't pay me in *money*," she said playfully.

"But when I started, I didn't pay you in anything. You didn't get anything out of it. So why do it?"

It was her turn to lay back in the sheets. She lived in a cheap apartment, but her bed had the softest sheets I have ever felt, before or since.

"Johnny, Johnny. Sometimes people do things and they can't explain. I don't mean I can't explain it, I mean I'm not supposed to."

"Explain what?"

"Why I'm with you. I'm supposed to be with you, but it's my choice, too. I want to be."

She reached out to stroke my jaw, but I batted her hand away, a little harder than I needed to.

"What do you mean, you're supposed to be with me?"

"Are you going to beat me up? Like you did with that other boy?"

"No. I'm sorry. I didn't mean to hurt you. Did I hurt you?"

"No."

"But what did you mean?"

She sighed. "My brother. He does business with your uncle. He knew you were interested in learning French and he knew I was interested in —young men like you. So, he and your uncle worked out a deal."

"A deal?"

"That's all I'm going to say. I am not doing anything I don't want to do, if that makes you feel any better."

I got up and put my clothes on and left without saying goodbye. I was physically tired from the rollercoaster of feelings that our simple conversation had launched. I think I went home and went right to bed. I resolved that I did not love her, had never loved her, and would never see her again. My resolve lasted until the following Tuesday.

THIRTEEN

Happy Birthday to Me

I CAN ONLY REMEMBER one day when I regretted going out to the Coffey School. It was a Monday. I had a tough test at school, I moved just a couple of boxes for Uncle Abe, which was still enough to make me sweat. The end result was that I was tired, both physically and mentally, by the time I got out to Harlem Airport.

"Oh, we have a job for you today," Willa Brown said when I arrived. She smiled a big fake smile and seemed very happy about the news, which instantly made me suspicious. Usually she did not pay that much attention to me, except to point out dust bunnies I had missed or to yell for me to bring over a box of screws or ball bearings. I knew something was up.

"Concrete," Cornelius Coffey said. "We're going for a CPT permit. You know what that is?"

"Of course. Civilian Pilot Training."

War talk was in the air. Germany was showing its muscles; it was on all the newsreels. The federal government had started a program to make sure there were enough military pilots by approving schools to train them. The *Chicago Defender* had been running stories about how Race men and women could be part of it. Should be part of it. Apparently, Coffey believed so, too.

"We can't have a dirt floor in the hangar," Coffey explained to the class.

He had brought students out there that day just for the fun. I stood in the back. I was very tempted to sneak away and go home but I knew that Willa and Cornelius would know I had left, and leaving wouldn't help my case for getting in the school.

"The government wants concrete on the hangar floor, so the government is going to get concrete on the hangar floor. I've already got some of the wooden forms in place."

"Why couldn't they do this before I got here?" I groused to Willie Mason, one of the few class members who would talk to me some. He was not much older than me and liked to clown around some. Most of the other students were respectful but standoffish. They didn't have time to spend talking to a kid.

"Don't you wish," he said. "Cornelius wanted to, but Willa wouldn't let him. It was raining this morning and she said the humidity would hurt the concrete."

I had no idea if that was true or not, but Willa was not often contradicted.

"And here comes our concrete now," Willie said.

I shaded my eyes against the sun. There was hardly a cloud in the sky now, so the rain could not have been much. A massive truck was trundling down the edge of the runway, kicking up a cloud of dust. It couldn't have been all that humid in the morning, not with all that dust around now. Why didn't they just go ahead and pour the concrete before I got there? Then I could have the benefit of showing up without having to do any work, because they would all be tired and sitting around talking. I could have gotten a cold grape soda out of the icebox and had a nice afternoon. But I didn't.

The concrete truck driver did, though. He pulled up but Coffey wasn't ready, as the wooden forms weren't in place around the whole perimeter of the hangar. The concrete couldn't just be poured in without a form; the hangar's walls were always nearly spotless (not least of all due to me) but they had big holes here and there and the concrete would have just poured out on the ground forever. Adding to the problem was that the forms on the far end were taller than the ones close to the door, because the hangar stood on a slight hill. But concrete obeyed the laws of gravity and the forms had to be uneven.

So, we got inside and worked nailing the wood together. I got toward the far side with Willie. He was bigger than me in all ways, taller and rounder and softer, but he could work when he needed to. He was also smart, because he tried to ensure that he wouldn't labor *too* hard. We worked in the middle, which was pretty easy, and avoided the corners, which were more difficult, apparently, because I heard some of the students cursing as they tried to line up the forms straight enough that Willa would approve them. The concrete truck driver sat on the running board of his truck and watched us, sipping on a grape soda.

"Take your time," he said.

Once the forms were finally done, he backed the truck up to the hangar doors and we opened them as wide as they would go, which was pretty wide as the Piper Cubs had to go in and out. Then he poured in the cement and we raked it across and flattened it. It was hot work and even the grape colas could not put a dent in our thirst, and anyway, after a few hours they were all hot and sticky and unpleasant. My head was hurting, and the students were grousing that this was not the kind of work they signed up to do.

"Gentlemen, you need to know every single aspect of every airplane you fly," Cornelius said. "You may have to take them apart and put them back together in a field in the middle of the night, by yourself. Now, today, the act of knowing everything about airplanes includes the concrete they're going to roll in on."

"Just think of it as learning from the ground up," Willa said, and everybody groaned.

But they didn't just direct us. They pitched in and worked, getting as nasty and sweaty as everybody else. This concrete was literally the foundation of the school.

I decided I would not do this kind of manual labor for a living. The future for me was engines and wings: high technology, or at least higher technology. Race men and women had done such scutwork for too long, and it was time for me to break the cycle. And I did, for a while. But like most of my other vows and resolutions, I wasn't able to keep this one.

I was about to walk through the classroom door at the Coffey School of Aeronautics for the first time as a student, not a part-time janitor. They knew I was coming down the hall because I noticed a head peek out, then shoot back inside. Then the singing started. One voice that I could pick out was good—Willa's—but the rest were producing the kind of droning sound you might expect to hear from engineering students. Still, the singing was nice enough. I had a big smile on my face when I walked through the door and saw the wreckage of the Boeing P-12 that the secondary students studied like it was a corpse and they were in medical school.

On the stubby remains of the left wing sat a chocolate cupcake with a single white candle in the middle, already lit. Willa had been telling me forever that I was not old enough to get in the Coffey school.

"I'll bake you a cupcake and put a candle on it when you're old enough, and then you'll know," she said, but Cornelius told me later that she never baked anything.

I had been waiting for the day when I had enough money saved up and could walk through the door and get my store-bought cupcake, and now that day was here. I walked up to it and gave it a quick puff. Everyone clapped when the candle went out and the smoke made a break for the ceiling. Most of the faces were new, but it seemed that everyone had heard about the boy janitor who was determined to fly. They clapped me on the shoulder and wished me a happy birthday. Cornelius Coffey stood back, smiling for about a minute more, and then he put us to work.

I had my money saved and I jumped right in. Like Coffey had promised, I learned everything there was to know about airplanes at the school. I had soaked up as much information as I could while cleaning up around the place, but the pace of learning skyrocketed when I became a student. I learned how to pull an engine out of a plane, take it apart, put it back together and shove it back in (neatly). I learned how to disassemble all the controls of a 50-horsepower Piper Cub. I learned how to take the landing gear apart, how to disassemble the tail, how to repair rips and tears on the skin. Everything.

"You never know when you will need to know something," Cornelius said. "You may find yourself in a field in the middle of nowhere in the middle of the night after your engine gives out. There will be no one to help you. And depending on where you are—and who you are—you may be stalled out somewhere in broad daylight and there will be no one to help you."

Almost all of the students were Race men, and that's who Coffey addressed with this last line. He didn't stress the point, but we understood it. Race men still could not fly for the U.S. military, but white pilots were getting sucked into the war preparations and flying jobs were opening up. There was one white man in the class, a nice fellow named Jefferson who took the first level courses and then got called up. I heard later that he went off into the Pacific and got killed trying to sink a Japanese aircraft carrier. So, he knows more about life and death than I do.

Cornelius once told some of us a story about how he had been on a barnstorming trip in the South just a few years before and burned out a rod in the engine of his little Curtiss Robin. He had to land in Mississippi and fix it. None of the white men watching believed he could do it, but they also wouldn't let any Race men watch through the fence, figuring they didn't need to see a Race man do something so complicated as repair an airplane. It might give them ideas. The story made him wrinkle up his forehead in irritation when he came to that part, but he never did tell the story around a white student, as far as I know. He wanted everyone to feel welcome at the Coffey School.

This welcome extended to women. There was a female in my class, a Race woman named Sarah Carroll. She was small but wiry; pretty much the opposite of Willa Brown. Willa was proud and hard charging, both the gust of wind before the storm and the storm itself. Sarah was quiet. She moved through the school, both in the classroom and at the airfield, as quietly as an Indian sneaking through the woods. There were several times when she startled me by asking me a question or by asking for a tool, and I would jump because I had no idea she was there. But, like Willa, she knew her stuff. She could take an engine apart faster than anybody else in the class. She was also the most fastidious student. I would soak parts in gasoline as long as I felt was necessary, but most of the time she would double that time. When she put an engine back together, everyone knew it would run, and run better than new.

Of course, we all wanted to ask her out on a date. Willie actually tried it, and she told him no, thanks. She was too busy learning to waste time on boys. That's exactly the way she worded it, too, he told me later: boys.

"You could go out with flyboys, though, right?" he asked her, but she just smiled and kept her wall up.

It took me longer to get through the school than anybody. I kept running out of money. I should have paid the tuition all in advance, but Coffey and Willa went easy on me and let me pay in installments, but then other things kept eating up the money. Times were tough around the kitchenette. The *Defender* did not pay particularly well and Uncle Abe's church was not much of a moneymaking venture. Even the mysterious basement storage program wasn't bringing in enough money, so I contributed some of mine here and there, and it slowed me down. I should have been through the primary training in a little over a month, but it took me all of that summer and into the fall, while the war talk was heating up and life was passing me by.

But the flying; the flying was everything I had imagined. We had familiarized ourselves with every inch of our little Piper Cubs and WACO 9s and had learned to taxi them around as well as if they were cars we were driving. That was fun as far as it went, but it wasn't flying. I still remember my first flight; will always remember it. It's like your first time seeing the ocean, or making love, or looking at the face of your child. It burns into your brain, into your soul. I was flying with my instructor, a white man named Craig who had just gone through Coffey's secondary course and had become an instructor (and joined the Army Air Corps about a week later; Coffey could not keep instructors, the looming war kept eating them as fast as he could turn them out).

Craig was not physically large, and neither was I, at the time, but we were pretty cozy in the Piper's cramped cockpit. He watched carefully as I checked the instruments—which didn't take long because there weren't many, in those days—checked the flaps, blipped the throttle a little to listen to the engine, and got ready. I looked over at him and he gave me a little nod. I pulled back on the stick and we hustled down the short dirt runway, and then we were aloft.

It wasn't quite like I imagined a bird feels, not at first. I was concentrating too much on the equipment, on the rudders and flaps and stick, to really feel the magic. But after it became pretty clear that I wasn't going to plow us headfirst into the ground, Craig looked out the little plastic windows, which were rattling and shaking like a screen door in a tornado, and laughed. He wasn't laughing at me, he was just laughing because it was fun. We were flying, and he was looking out the window at the green fields below us and the little brown and black ribbons of roads that cut through them, and he laughed from the simple joy of it. At that moment, I ceased to worry about the controls and just felt them, felt my training start to sink into my bones a little, and I looked out the window. I didn't laugh. But I did smile.

FOURTEEN

A Door Opens

I BELIEVED that I became a man on December 7, 1941. You know what happened on that day or should be ashamed of yourself if you don't. Now, I had previously set this marker on different days. When I first walked to school by myself, I felt that I had become a man. When I had my first French lesson—my first *real* French lesson—with Dominique, I felt I had become a man. But these things didn't really change me. I'm not sure how I defined becoming a man, but I figured that one definition had to be that it was something that changed my life, that set me on the right course, the course of my destiny.

The country had been on a semi-war footing for most of the last couple of years, which is one reason Cornelius and Willa were able to finally get some government attention and start training pilots that might have to go and fight someday. But Hitler was doing his best to mash Europe under his heel and Japan was moving across the Pacific, and the United States didn't do anything. Even Canada declared war on Germany, and we didn't do anything. Dominique cried when France fell, and I didn't cry, but I felt sad. She watched newsreel footage of Hitler touring Paris and told me later that it was like watching a monkey desecrate a church. On one level, I couldn't understand it. It was white people treating other white people badly. I thought white people reserved their most bitter hatred for Race people, but apparently that was not so, or, at least, they were able to hate equally. Germans, who were indistinguishable to me from the French, hated and defeated the French. They hated the Jews even more, and I could not tell them apart. On the newsreels it was just a parade of pasty faces, with the ones in the black coats winning.

And then the Japanese bombed Pearl Harbor and we were in it. We were in it against Germany and Japan. Just like the stories I had heard about when I was a kid, the entire planet was at war again, and we were in the middle of it this time. I was eighteen years old. Congress had passed the draft the year before, and any man—even Race men—twenty-one years old and over had to register. That was three years away for me, maybe four before I could really get in it. The war would never go on for four years. I was going to miss my chance to be a military pilot, just when the biggest war in the history of the world was taking place.

I burned with the indignation of it. This made no sense to my parents, who were glad that I would be out of it. It made no sense to the old men in the building, and to some of the young men, who were old enough to sign up for Selective Service and were not at all happy about it. The only person around me who seemed to understand the need was Dominique, and she had an ulterior motive. She wanted me to go and liberate France. She was never going to live there again, had no real desire to live there again, but she wanted her homeland to be free. I could understand that.

Hardly a month later, the Army announced it would train Race men to be pilots and the draft age was dropped to twenty. My odds were looking up. To me, hearing the news about Race men flying from the assistant secretary of war was like trying desperately to understand another language. The announcement made no sense, not with everything that had gone before. Race men were going to fly U.S. Army Air Corps airplanes. The secretary was careful to couch it in language that would not offend any white people. It was to be an experiment, was the official word through the military ranks, at least according to Coffey. An experiment to see if Race men were smart enough to do what white people could do. Probably they could, or the Army wouldn't risk the airplanes, but the idea of actual combat was a long shot. Even if Race men got into combat, they would fly only fighters, never bombers, because if they flew bombers, they might be in a position to give orders to white crewmembers, and that would never do.

The Coffey School was not hurting for people to enroll. The concrete floor we had worked so hard to lay down was streaked with black from the constantly rolling tires of the planes. The school went full tilt, offering all levels of civilian pilot instruction for white and Race alike. The whites were being sucked into the burgeoning war machine. The Race men joined the Army's great experiment down in Tuskegee. Experiment or no experiment, for the first time in my life, I wanted to go back to Alabama.

"ALL RIGHT, GATHER ROUND," COFFEY SAID TO US ONE DAY. THE SUN WAS settling onto the horizon, flying was done, and people were starting to go home. "Got something for you."

He had some uniforms for us, jackets that made us look vaguely military, and matching pants.

"You need to look official," he said. "The military is watching us, watching what we do here. They're watching us while they're setting up down at Tuskegee Army Air Field. From now on, when you're training, you'll wear these outfits."

It took a while to hand them out. I shouldn't have gotten one, at all, because these were for the secondary students, and I was still treading water with my primary training. But I was becoming sort of the mascot of Harlem Airport, so they gave me one. Mine wasn't quite sized right—it was too big—but I didn't complain. If it got me one step closer to flying for the U.S. Army, I was happy.

"These aren't from the Army," Willie told me later. He complained that his was too tight, but really his stomach was a little too big. "They're leftovers from the Civilian Conservation Corps. Somebody was building a dam or a bridge or something and they had these left over so we get them. They don't have anything to do with Tuskegee."

"I don't care, I'll take mine."

"Yeah, you don't care, yours fits all right. Oh, wait, it doesn't, does it? You look like a little boy trying to wear dress-up clothes."

The thought struck us at the same time: his were too tight, mine were too loose. So, we traded.

"Going to have to go check these out," he said. "So long, sucker."

"Yeah, you enjoy those. I hid a razor blade in there somewhere, see if you can find it."

That's the way a lot of our conversations went those days, dumb joking around. We only got serious when we were talking about engines or transmissions or rudders. Willie laughed and walked off, stopping only to utter some witticism to Sarah, who was working with Willa to find something small enough for her to wear. Since Willa was there, he must have kept it clean, because Willa and Sarah just laughed at him and he went on his way, back to the barracks. The secondary students, or "cadets," as they were now called, lived in a barracks that had been hastily slapped up beside the terminal. It was some military requirement for the secondary students. Coffey had to start jumping through military hoops even when the military was only interested in any white students he could produce.

Since I lived relatively close by, I just went back and forth to home. I would have liked to live in the barracks, too, even though they were not at all luxurious, but I had things still to attend to at home. I kept a little locker in the hangar, stuffed behind a table that was usually piled with junk and random parts. I thought I would just keep my uniform there instead of having to lug it back and forth. I had just stashed it when I nearly bumped into Sarah, who had a pile of green in her hand, meaning she had found something close enough to her size to wear.

"Sorry. Hi, Johnny."

"Hi, Sarah. I heard you gave everyone a hard time up there today."

She couldn't literally do that, as we only had three planes and never flew them at the same time, but she was getting a reputation as a solid pilot. A little bit of a daredevil, too; the instructor, Craig, said she had gotten those little Piper Cubs to go faster than anyone else in the class, primary or secondary. This wasn't that big an achievement—the Cubs weren't fast, so it was maybe an additional five miles an hour—but it was something. Craig said one thing was clear: She was a better pilot than either Willie or me. He laughed when he said it, like he was joking, but I don't think he was.

She just shrugged. "It felt pretty good. But I think everybody is doing well."

I nodded at her uniform. "These will be neat, right? I mean, we'll look all official. Or, you'll look official," I added, remembering that I wasn't a secondary student, and didn't want to offend her by acting like I was.

She shrugged again. "I guess so. They kind of make me feel sad, though."

"Sad? Why?"

"Because they just remind me that no matter how good I fly, I probably can't get work anywhere doing it. I can't fly for the military."

"I can't either!"

"That's true, now. But when the white men are all used up or killed by the Japanese and the Germans, they'll let Black folks in. They'll get you all set up at Tuskegee and when they need you, they'll use you. But they won't let women. They won't ever let women."

I didn't know what to say to that. It was true, I had just never thought about it before.

"What is it you want to do, Sarah?"

"Fly fast. The fastest planes I can. Right now, that's fighter planes, but I won't ever be able to get in one."

"But they're dangerous—" I said before I could stop myself, and she gave me a look that would blister paint.

"They're all dangerous," she said, spun on her heel smartly, almost military style, and walked to the barracks.

She was right, they were all dangerous. The slow, tiny Piper Cub was probably more dangerous than a P-40 Warhawk or whatever else she wanted to fly. And she was right, I couldn't imagine the military ever letting her fly. I could imagine them letting *me* fly, but never her, and she knew that full well and it must have eaten at her every day. She couldn't even go to France for that kind of work.

I heard later, much later, that she ended up barnstorming around the country after the war, flying in air shows. She flew a battered old P-47 Thunderbolt, which was far from the fastest plane even during the war, but it could dive like a bomb because it was so fat and heavy. She crashed it into the ground at full speed and her body was halfway to China before they found her and dug her out. So, she got to fly a fighter plane, at least, although not the way she wanted. And now she knows more about life and death than I do.

As I watched her walk away that day at the Coffey School, anger rising off her like steam, the uniform in her hands representing a dream dead before it was born, I realized that no matter how rough I thought I had it, someone was always worse off. That's true for everyone. Somewhere on the Earth there must exist one person more wretched and miserable than anyone else, but that person would be difficult to pull out of a crowd.

FIFTEEN

I Fell in Alabama

I SAW her my very first day at Tuskegee. I was tired from the train ride, but I was hustled out along with the other guys from Chicago and points along the way and we were forced to attend a training seminar on how to behave around white people in the Deep South. We had hardly been able to put our duffels on our cots when a sharply creased young man earnestly explained to us that although the Tuskegee Institute loved us, the town of Tuskegee did not. Under no circumstances were we to enter into any dispute with the white residents of the city.

"All eyes are on us," he said, looking each one of us in the eyes as if to make the point. "We must succeed."

I admit that I did not pay attention. I was from Alabama and figured I did not need any explanation of its ways. I had heard it all from Father and Mother and Uncle Abe and Aunt Eveline. I knew well enough to leave white people to go their own way and to go mine. And anyway, my eyes were on something else. I was lucky enough to be sitting by the window. This was not lucky because it made the room cooler—the heat was worse than any I had ever felt in Chicago, and it made the wood sweat so that the cheap walls were already buckling—but because I could cut my eyes to the right now and then and catch a nice slice of blue sky. And, one time, a tantalizing glimpse of a female figure. She was walking away from me at a 45-degree angle. She must have already been closer to me, but I missed her because I was pretending to listen to how, if we got in trouble in town, which we should never do, we should make sure we got into the hands of base MPs and not the Tuskegee sheriff's office.

Some of the fellows were a little stunned when we got out and looked in dismay at the trees off in the distance, maybe calculating that these crackers had a lot of lynching spots at their disposal. Everybody knew the South was bad, but it's one thing to know it and another thing to be in it. They started talking about the racial situation, some of them bragging that if some white sheriff's deputy got in his way, he would regret taking on a Race man with military training; but they kept their voices low so the training session instructor would not hear.

I ignored them and walked around the building. I stepped off the wooden porch onto the dirt. I scanned the horizon for her, but she was gone, vanished somewhere in the Wild West town that was Tuskegee. The buildings were sturdy but not attractive. Most of them were banged together out of cheap wood and plopped right down on the reddish dirt. My angel had disappeared somewhere out in that Martian landscape.

I didn't have much time to chase after her. We started getting lectures on everything. How our uniforms should look, how our tiny metal beds should be made, what time we should roll out of our tiny metal beds, what time we should eat, how we should address everyone, and repeated warnings about avoiding the good white citizens of Tuskegee, Alabama.

"Makes you wonder how the Nazis and Japs will be any worse, huh?" a voice said over my shoulder during the bed-making session, where a lieutenant colonel showed us that he needed to be able to bounce a quarter off our tiny metal beds.

I turned my head ever so slightly to see the face of Willie Mason, the edges of his lips turned up in as big a smile as he could muster without getting yelled at.

"So, you're here, too," I said. "Is there anybody left in Chicago?"

"Who would want to stay up there? Too cold. Too much to do, too much freedom. I'd rather be down here in crackertown."

"I gotta wonder," I muttered back. "Do the white folks know they're letting us fly airplanes that have machine guns?"

And, somewhere in there, we learned about those airplanes with machine guns.

These were no Piper Cubs. These were P-40 Warhawks, the planes we had already heard about from the Flying Tigers in China, who had been shooting down Japanese planes before the war had barely gotten properly started. Piper Cubs were kites compared to them, and despite my flying time at the Coffey School, I could not let up for a second. Fighter aircraft were a whole new kind of language and I had to learn it.

The P-40 had a twelve-cylinder Allison engine kicking out more than a thousand horsepower. It could eat Piper Cubs and WACO 9s for breakfast. You could feel the power of that engine coming through everywhere: the vibrations in the seat, the shaking of the stick, the howl of the propeller, the creaking of the glass in the canopy. The P-40 wanted to get in the air, it didn't care how. The ground crew would pull the wheel chocks and you would crank on the stick and it would race for the other end of the runway, sometimes trying to pull hard to the left. Moving the pedals was like dancing with an untalented girl. The thing was a mess to fly, but it was fast. It took a lot of learning to figure the Warhawk out, and I was never going to be able to understand it the way I could a Piper. I would never be able to land it in a field some-where in the middle of nowhere and get it to work. If I ever crashed a P-40, I would most likely be dead.

This knowledge meant that I applied myself again, as hard as I ever had at the Coffey School. But there was a tiny bit of distraction present that I had never felt before, not even with Dominique. I saw the mystery woman a couple more times, but she was always far enough away that when I got to where she had been, she was gone like a ghost in the dust. It was Willie, of all people, who told me who she was.

"That cute girl? With the light skin?"

I had never been one to fixate on skin tone because my mother would have killed me.

"With the round little butt like this?"

Willie stuck out his own not-so-little round butt and I laughed and nodded. Not because I was necessarily looking only at her butt, but because she was always walking away from me when I saw her so that was what stuck in my mind the most.

"Her. Yes. That one."

"You don't want her, man, unless you like going to church. Her father is a minister in town. Something or other Baptist Church. She's a fine, upstanding churchgoing lady, from what I hear. Not your type, at all."

"You don't know my type, Willie."

"Don't I? Maybe I don't. But I heard rumors."

He laughed to show he was kidding and wandered off. For a moment I felt a pang of fear that he knew about Dominique, but I remembered that I had never spoken to anyone about her.

"Wait! Do you know her name?" I shouted after him, but he disappeared behind a clot of soldiers marching through.

Trying to find one particular Baptist preacher in Alabama, even in a small town like Tuskegee, could take a considerable amount of time, time I didn't have. I wasn't afraid of white people, but the constant warnings about the sheriff's office did not make me inclined to wander about the town. I decided I would keep my eyes open for her and whenever I saw her, I would drop what I was doing and talk to her. My chance came two weeks later during a class devoted to the P-40's .50 caliber machine guns. It carried two on each wing. Although we weren't going to learn how to field-strip them or do anything complicated, we did need to know what to do if they got clogged up while we were flying. The instructor was about halfway through when I glanced out the window and there she was, walking away from me, as usual. I remembered my pledge. I was listening to instruction that could very well save my life someday, but there she was, and I had made myself a promise. And I kept it.

I jumped to my feet, grabbed my stomach, blurted something about feeling sick and ran for the door. Once outside, I barreled around the building and ran to intercept her, making sure I would catch up to her just late enough that I couldn't be seen from the classroom window. I didn't think it was a very slick performance, but I thought I pulled it off until one of the guys later told me that the instructor smirked that I wasn't just sick, I was lovesick, and there was no cure for that.

But I wasn't thinking about that as I ran toward her. She turned when I got near, to see what kind of beast was clomping up on her, and I got my first good look at her face. To my faint surprise, she wasn't quite as pretty as I had expected. She *was* pretty, but on closer inspection there were a couple of oddities with her face that made her look more interesting rather than just plain beautiful. The bridge of her nose was a little wider at the top than usual, which set her eyes further apart. Her mouth wasn't quite symmetrical; her thin lips dipped down to the left as they crossed her face. And she had a tiny scar just at the tip of her chin's left cleft. All of that sounds bad in black and white but it just made her more attractive. I've seen lots of flawlessly beautiful women and I can't remember a thing about them. But I remember every aspect of her face. Her features burned themselves into my mind the very first instant I saw her.

So now she was looking at me and I realized I didn't know what to say.

"Hello?" she said, a slight smile playing across her uneven lips.

She was probably approached like this seventeen times a day.

"Uh, hi. My name is Johnny. I'm from Alabama, too, originally."

I ran my hand over my head. She just kept smiling. I realized that I sounded retarded.

"And where are you from not originally?" Her voice was honeyed. Definitely southern, with the vowels running all over the place, but not slow.

"Chicago. Illinois."

"I have heard of the place. I thought you must be from some big city. Your method of approach was a little—brusque."

I was very impressed. I had never heard anyone use the word brusque in a sentence before. She was smart and beautiful.

"I apologize for that. It's just that I've seen you around—you were practically the first person I saw here—and I've been trying to catch up to you, but you walk so fast."

"I have discovered that, as a woman, it pays to walk fast on a military base."

Hard to argue with that.

"I, I understand you're a minister's daughter." I had lost control of this conversation. I never had control of this conversation.

"That's right, Mr. Johnny from Chicago. Is that a problem?"

"Oh, no, no. No. In fact, my uncle is a minister back in Chicago."

"Are you a churchgoing man?"

"Yes, I am."

I had, in fact, gone to the church quite often, although most of the time I was loading boxes of possible contraband into the basement.

"A Baptist church. My uncle is a Baptist minister, like your father."

"Word has gotten around, has it? I guess if people are going to talk about me, that's not a bad thing for them to say."

"They don't talk about you. Uh ..."

"Virginia. Virginia Scott." She extended her hand in greeting, angled so I would know to shake it and not try to kiss it.

"Nice to meet you," I said. "Nicholas is my last name. And they don't talk about you. I *asked*."

"Did you now. Well, it was nice to meet you, too, Mr. Nicholas. But I need to be on my way."

"I—I would like to see you again." It had taken me so long to find her and cost me not a small amount of dignity among my classmates, I was not going to let her get away so easily.

"I'm very easy to find. If you were really a churchgoing man, you would have found me by now. I volunteer at the chapel on base. Goodbye now, Mr. Nicholas."

SIXTEEN

More Difficult Than Flying

"So, how long have you wanted to fly, Mr. Nicholas?"

The Reverend Scott was very formal. He presided over not only his church, located on the poorer side of Tuskegee, but over a modest house that was only three blocks away. It was Sunday. He had delivered a fire-and-brimstone sermon that very morning, which I had witnessed, but unlike Uncle Abe, he hadn't ended it in a pool of sweat. I actually don't think the man could sweat.

I was the one sweating. I had been dating his daughter for four months, but this was my first time to be invited to lunch at the Scott home. Flying a Piper Cub was easier; flying a P-40 Warhawk was easier; going on a ten-mile run was easier. Rev. Scott was a short, compact man who had no hair on his head. His head was almost perfectly round, and he didn't seem to have an ounce of fat on him. He looked like a bullet in a three-piece suit. Mrs. Scott was similar, although, of course, she had hair; a lot of it, dark and lustrous. She had married Mr. Scott when both were very young and had Virginia not long after. Although, judging by the air of quiet decency that seemed to surround them at all times, I'm sure it was at least nine months after the marriage.

I told him my story, leaving out many key details, including the existence of Dominique and that I financed my flight schooling with payments from my uncle for loading boxes of unknown origin.

"My, you couldn't get me up in one of those things," Mrs. Scott said, shaking her head. "Too dangerous."

"Not really," I said, but then realized I was talking about an airplane that carried machine guns in its wings.

"Son, do you really think the United States government will let Negro pilots fight in this war?" the reverend asked.

I figured the war would be over before I got near it, but said, "I'm counting on it."

Virginia gave me a funny look. I took it as a sign that she didn't want me to go. It was very little encouragement, but it was all I needed. I began to pursue her constantly, going so far as to attend chapel services.

There was really no reason to do this. I had a lot to learn at Tuskegee, material that could save my life. And I was preparing for the only role I had ever wanted in life: to be a U.S. Army Air Corps pilot in the service of his country. Getting involved with a woman could get in the way of that. If I gave my heart to Virginia, the rest of me might not want to go off to fight the Germans or the Japs, should I get the chance. And she was obviously not the sort of girl who could be won easily; there would be no casual encounters with her. All of this I knew, and it did not slow me down in the least. Fighting for my country, loving Virginia Scott; both of these seemed to be pure undertakings, almost holy.

I never had as much time to see her as I would have liked. I had things to do, and she had things to do, and I lived on a military base and she only worked there. But I almost didn't need to see her. I thought about her all the time. I mean, all the time. I was beginning to think I had some kind of mental illness. When I woke up, I thought of her and wondered what she was doing. During the day, while I needed to be concentrating on my flight lessons and learning about my aircraft, I thought of her. Her face floated before my instrument panel. Her touch, her gentle touch on my arm, which I had felt only a few times, made my skin burn when I thought about it. When I went to sleep, even though I was usually exhausted from a long day and a ton of information I needed to understand, I thought of her and lay there with my eyes wide open far into the night.

I spent a lot of time having conversations with her in my mind, talks in which she tearfully confessed her love for me and said she couldn't live without me. We planned out our future after the war, when I would return home an ace and start some kind of career involving flying—this part of the conversation changed a lot from day to day—and she would declare her loyalty. She would raise our children and follow me all over the country as I barnstormed, led military aviation programs, took aerial photographs, dusted crops; like I said, that part of the plan changed a lot.

In person, she did none of those things. She kept an icy reserve at all times and I often had the feeling that I amused her rather than aroused her. But she let me hang around. She smiled at me, very faintly, when I showed up at the chapel for a service. She let me take her to a movie one day. Just one time. *The Maltese Falcon*. It was an afternoon show and I had a small bit of leave. We had to sit in the balcony, of course, as we were in Alabama, and this infuriated me, but she didn't seem to care, and after a while I didn't either because it meant I could sit up in the balcony with her. I let my hand rest on the armrest very close to hers, and occasionally our fingers brushed against each other, but she never took the extra step and touched me in a way that signaled that our hands should join together. I would be willing to fly a warplane into enemy territory without much thought, but I could not summon the nerve to take that step myself. And so, we did not hold hands.

Everybody noticed that I was having trouble focusing on the task at hand.

"Man, when you solo you are going to fly that P-40 smack into the ground, because you know she's on the ground and you'll be looking for her," Willie said, although, from his tone, I couldn't quite tell if he thought this was a bad thing or an admirable thing.

"No, I won't. I know which way is up."

"Not the way you're walking around with the moon in your eye. Forget her, man. She's a preacher's daughter from small-town Alabama. You're a member of the United States Army Air Corps and you need to get your head on straight. We've got a war to win before you can get your willie waxed."

"Don't you talk about her like that."

"See?" he said, backing away with his hands raised in surrender but a big smile on his face. "When they ask me why you flew straight into the ground, I'll just have to say you did it for love."

There were times when I could shake her loose. When I was flying, I did concentrate, despite what Willie said. I had to make sure I was using the stick correctly and watching my gauges. When I soloed, I had to pay even more attention to what I was doing to avoid making Willie's prediction come true. But I could never get rid of her entirely. When I looked out the cockpit window while I was riding behind my instructor, I saw the green spread of Alabama stretching away to the horizon and wished I could show it to her. When I came flying above the airstrip on my first cross-country solo flight, I did imagine that she was down below, watching and waving.

So, at the time of my life when I was finally doing what I had been intending to do and training to do for so long, my mind and my heart were somewhere else. My preparation for my cross-country solo passed like a dream, in between her ghostly visits to my mind. My memory of the actual flight is more vivid, but she was there, too. I knew that Willie was right and my fixation on her was going to spell trouble for me. I missed her ferociously already and I was seeing her at least once or twice a week, sometimes just long enough to say hello, sometimes for a long time. What would happen to my addled mind if we got shipped off to war and I didn't see her at all? Mooning over her then could get me killed. Thinking about her the way I did, building my fantasy life around her, was probably going to end my real life.

SEVENTEEN

The Waiting is the Hardest Part

MOST OF THE people in my class at Tuskegee failed. Most of the people in every class failed. Flying an airplane is not easy. Being able to control an airplane like it's part of your body is not easy. Being able to flip an airplane over and stop it from rolling in a snap is not easy. Being able to fly at night using Morse Code signals as waypoints is not easy. They were not easy for me, and I was a man whose brain had suddenly gone AWOL on him and taken his heart with it. People who were giving the program their all, focusing on it with all their might, failed. Washed out. My brain had gone soft and sticky with the crazy electrical firings of love but still I made it through. Maybe that even helped.

I graduated in a class of six. We became Lieutenant Colonels in the U.S. Army Air Corps. I wrote my parents in advance to see if they could come. Mother wrote back to say how proud they were, but that they could not. Her letter seemed a little short and perfunctory to me, and I was a little irritated that they weren't going to make it. But Virginia came. The ceremony was in a tent on the main field. She came in late, probably hoping I wouldn't notice her, but, of course, I did, as did every other male in the place. I was the only one who caught her eye. I had been beginning to suspect that my love was unrequited, that all this madness in my brain was a waste of time. But I saw her sly smile from across the tent and hoped that was not true.

So, I graduated. I was ready to fly warplanes for my country against the Germans (the Navy pilots were tackling the Japanese). But nothing happened. Summer turned to fall and there I was, still in Alabama, which was still hot and humid even when September rolled around. I started helping train the next class coming through. The Army had reluctantly opened its arms to Race soldiers, had shown that they could fly an airplane as well as any white man, and there we sat on the ground. Some of the earlier classes had gone off to Michigan and other places to continue training, but I was stuck in Tuskegee. At least I had my wings. A lot of the washouts still hung around, unable to do anything else. If they had been white and washed out of a flying program, they could have gone somewhere else to train to be gunners or bombardiers or maintenance men, but the Army had not seen fit to offer those options to Race men, so they hung around like ghosts.

Willie was one of them. He was not a sad ghost, though. He had stuck in all the way through until the night flying test, when we had to find our way back from Montgomery. Willie ended up in Georgia, landing a rather expensive airplane in a farmer's field and causing some crop damage that the farmer wanted the U.S. Army to pay for. He was washed out the very next day, even before he got the plane back to Tuskegee. Getting washed out of the program did not seem to bother him, at all.

"I knew I was done for," he said. "I flew that old heap slow when I came back and just enjoyed the view. I figured that was going to be my last relaxation flight on the Army's nickel. And, you know, Johnny, I don't even care. All this bother and I still don't care. If I can't figure out how to fly at night, the Germans would get me for sure. I'll just wait out this war, take my commercial license and make some money. I'll get to fly all I want, and nobody will try to shoot me down. But they'll be after your dark ass. Especially with your head up in the clouds over that woman of yours."

I usually got mad when people said stuff like that, but I never seemed to get mad at Willie. And I could tell he wasn't kidding; he really didn't care that he had washed out. I'm not sure what I would have done if I had failed. I did have a commercial license now, thanks to the Coffey school, but I had gotten spoiled by military planes. I always wanted to go faster. Flying a mail plane or some biplane crop duster would never cut it for me. I sometimes wonder what would have happened to me if I had washed out. I would have had slightly more time to see Virginia, but I wonder if things would have worked out for us. Absence makes the heart grow fonder, and my heart was pretty damn fond.

The war went on without us. We watched it on the newsreels. Japan was on the run in the Pacific and it looked like the tide was beginning to turn for Germany now that it had made the mistake of kicking the Russian bear. We were ready. But our country was not ready for us.

Things got so relaxed for us, aside from our endless training, that I got leave and decided to visit Chicago. Aside from Virginia, I was tired of Alabama and there was nothing I wanted to see there. I actually thought about asking Virginia to go with me, but I hoped to clear my mind of her for a little bit, and maybe a week in Chicago would do that. As it turned out, I'm glad I didn't bring her.

I sent Mother a letter that I was coming. I walked down the hallway of our old building, getting nods of respect from the people I passed. They had never seen a Race man in uniform, and they moved against the wall to let me pass.

"Stand in the light and let me get a better look at you, son!" Mr. Roswell said. He was sitting in the hall with his unread newspaper in his lap, just like always. "You look impressive!"

"Thank you, Mr. Roswell. I'm just here on leave to see my parents."

"Well...good luck with that," he said, and turned his face to his newspaper.

I didn't know what he meant until I knocked on the door of the kitchenette. Mother opened it and gasped. She had not gotten the letter, or if she had, it was lost somewhere in the mess behind her. The kitchenette was piled with junk. Old hand washing machines, old sewing machines, meat cutters, who knows what else. It looked like a trash pile.

"Mother—what's happened?"

She drew me into the room and shut the door behind me. She gave me a fierce hug and then looked up at me through wet eyes.

"You look so good. It's so good to see you. I'm sorry we weren't there for your graduation, Johnny, but—your father and your uncle are in jail."

"Jail?"

"They were doing something in the church, of all places. Your uncle Abe was smuggling something through town. I don't even know what it was. Your father won't tell me. But whatever it was, the police caught them. They've been in jail for three months."

I was stunned. I dropped my hat and sat down, nearly on the floor until I righted myself and managed to fall into a chair. I knew whatever Uncle Abe was into wasn't exactly on the up and up, but it never occurred to me that it would be illegal enough for him to be in jail.

"Where's Aunt Eveline?"

"She left him. She said this is the last time he's going to pull something like this. I don't know what all he's been involved in, but she thought he was going straight when he built the church. But he just renovated it to smuggle things."

"Have they—have they said anything about me?"

"About you? Just that they're proud of you and ashamed of the way they've let you down."

So, they had let me down? I had gotten involved with something I knew was shady because I wanted some money out of it.

"I want to go see them. Maybe I can help get them out."

"Oh, Johnny, I don't think so."

She was right. There was some novelty for the white men at the prison to see a Race man in uniform—and I was not about to go in there in anything but my uniform—but my father and my uncle were awaiting trial and there was nothing I could do. The guards let me visit with each of them in their cells; another Race man behind bars didn't bother them, even if it was only temporary.

I had never seen my father look like he did. He looked gray, almost matching the jumpsuit they had him wearing. His eyes were rimmed in red. His hair looked like it was thinning. And he had only been in here three months.

"I'm sorry, son," he said, clutching me near in a weak embrace. "I let you down. And with everything you're doing for the country."

I broke down and wept on his shoulder, making his jumpsuit even more gray. I couldn't help it. A white guard walked by and looked in, shaking his head. I hated him, just for that second that our eyes made contact. He didn't see a father and son having an emotional moment; he saw two Race men who couldn't control themselves. I stayed in there for a little while longer, but we really didn't have too much more to say. He was ashamed, and I was ashamed that he was ashamed.

I had a lot more to say to my Uncle Abe.

"How could you do this? Why are you smuggling shit and getting my father involved?"

He looked just the same as always, rotund and full of energy. He probably had something going on the side with the guards already.

"Your father knew what he was getting into," Uncle Abe said.

My eyes were hard and red, and he was avoiding them.

"And what about me? I knew you were up to something. I took the money, too. I should turn myself in."

He met my eyes then.

"Don't you even say anything like that. No one knows you were involved. Boy, what you've done with the money you got is the only good thing to come out of this. Eveline left me, this time for the last time. Your father is a wreck. Your mother is so mad at me I doubt she'll ever talk to me again. My ass is in jail, and I've lost my church. But you've gone on and you've made history, for the Race and for the country. You do not want to mess that up. You hear me?"

He was right, sort of, and anyway, I had no intention of getting myself entangled in this mess again. I figured that he never told me what we were doing so I didn't know, and that's actually the truth. I don't know to this day what was in those boxes we put in the basement of the church.

I had only been in Chicago two days at this point and I was already ready to leave again. I felt the tug of Tuskegee and the sky. I had been ready to get away from there just hours before but now I couldn't wait to get back. And Virginia was there, squeaky clean Virginia. No more of the tall, dull buildings and my uncle's slimy doings and my father's weakness. It was time to get back to the land of the blue sky. And the waiting.

EIGHTEEN

A Free Trip to Europe

WE DID NOT TRAVEL MUCH in those days, at least, not my family. I had been to Alabama, Chicago, back to Alabama, back to Chicago and then back to Alabama. When I got back from my trip to see my incarcerated uncle and father, I learned that I was going to go overseas on Uncle Sam's nickel. Race airmen had already been shipped over from Tuskegee and other advanced training locations and were flying out of Italy. The Race press said they were doing great; the white press said they weren't. I believed the Race press because I intended to do great myself. We were due on a troop ship two days after I got back.

"All y'all will get over there and I'll lose all my card partners," Willie complained.

Willie's great contribution to the war effort was to set up a roving card game designed to suck the money out of the pockets of most of the soldiers at Tuskegee, to keep them from spending it in town. Airmen were a specialty. Since he had washed out of flight training himself, he seemed to take great delight in taking the money of the men who could fly.

"I'm doing y'all a favor," he said in the fake Southern accent he had adopted during his extended stay well South of the Mason-Dixon line.

"All that money won't be weighing you down while you're trying to fly. I'm helping save your lives."

Willie was genuinely not bothered by the fact that he was not going to fly. I couldn't understand that, at all. I was ready to go. In my mind, I was already there, pinwheeling over a Europe I had never seen, shooting Nazi aircraft out of the sky. There was just one thing I wanted to do first.

"Oh, son," the Reverend Scott said when I showed up at the door. "She's gone to see her sick aunt in Birmingham. She won't be back for a week."

He knew why I was there, and he looked genuinely sorry that I would not get to see his daughter before I left, which I appreciated. He invited me in for lunch. I ate lunch with him and his wife like a zombie. I could not believe that I was not going to get to see Virginia before I left. It felt like somebody had punched me in the gut. I had no appetite and could hardly choke down the wonderful ham Mrs. Scott made. I left them with the address the Army had given me, which they said would allow me to get mail. But mail would take an eternity and I wanted to see her now. I was not going to get my way. The Army was not exactly going to let me miss my ship so I could see the woman I loved one last time. So, I left, and I didn't get to see her or talk to her because her aunt did not have a telephone.

And I still did not know for sure if she loved me. She had never said so, or even anything of the sort. I thought she did, but I wasn't sure. I was headed into the jaws of Hell and I wanted to know if the woman I loved also loved me, but there was nothing I could do.

The trip over was my first time on the ocean. I remember the steely blue of the open sea, which sometimes matched the pale blue of the sky but was more often topped with a gray expanse of clouds. Dolphins swam alongside the ship, leaping like happy children. The card game continued in Willie's absence, with the airmen getting a chance to win a little money for a change. The trip passed like a dream for me. My mind was with Virginia. She was in my thoughts from the minute I woke up until the minute I collapsed back on my bunk. I lost more money than I ever had to

Willie, and none of these guys could play particularly well. I desperately wanted to shut Virginia out of my mind but I could not. I could occasionally nudge her aside for a little bit with worry about Father and Mother, not to mention anger against my uncle, but she never stayed away for long. I thought I was going insane. I was going up against an awesome war machine and all I could think about was love. And the worst part about it, always, was that I didn't know if she loved me. I felt rejected by her faint response. Was her smile ever big enough? Was her touch ever long enough?

In my fantasies, she wrote me a letter and confessed that she would do anything for me, that she could not live without me. We arrived in Italy and there was no such letter. I was getting ready to take on the Nazis and all I really wanted to do was die, because that would be the only thing that would silence my raging brain.

Actually, my raging brain was silenced pretty quickly after we got to Italy. The weather was terrible. It seemed to rain nearly all the time. I had pictured Italy being nothing but swarthy men wandering around playing mournful songs on squeezeboxes, but we didn't see any actual Italians. We spent most of our time inside studying mission plans.

"Jerry is trying to move supplies. We have him on the run," said our instructor, Lt. Gen. Peter "Cappy" Capps. He smacked a stick against a paper map stuck against a wall. It made a faint pop that was drowned out by the rain striking the roof. He had to hit the paper hard to make even that much noise; the map was peppered with little holes and indentations.

"Our job is to escort bombers as they eliminate these supply routes. We've had some good success so far. We have not lost a single bomber that we have escorted. I do not intend for you to start."

We had lost some Race fliers, but we had also shot down some German planes. The brass was starting to take notice. High-level visits to the base were common but I missed most of them. I was busy getting ready. I was determined to be the first Race airman to become an ace. That meant I needed to shoot down five German planes. I wanted to see that row of swastikas along the side of my plane, underneath the cockpit. Every day I worked the mission maps, getting ready for the day when one of the other pilots would rotate out and I would finally get to fly for my country. This determination had one great side effect, one that I had been seeking for weeks: It kept me from obsessing about Virginia. It didn't keep me from dreaming about her—nothing could do that—but now my conscious mind was busy with the war, and that made me very happy.

We, the proud Race flyers of the 99th Squadron, were still flying Curtiss P-40 Warhawks. This was in 1943, and these planes dated to before the war. Virtually anything the Germans had would be better than the P-40. I heard the ME-109s had almost twice as much horsepower. There were probably worse things flying, but not many. I had been very excited to fly a P-40 in Tuskegee but had hoped to have something fancier in the actual war. A P-47, maybe, the Flying Milk Jug, or the best thing in the sky, the P-51 Mustang. But I took the P-40 I got and named it. You know what I named it. Virginia. Some of the planes had curvaceous women painted on the nacelles but I couldn't imagine representing her that way. I just had the name painted on it. The letters weren't even that big. It was probably the least flashy P-40 that ever had ripped across the sky. That suited me just fine.

My first mission in the war was to fly over coastal Italy, making sure the Jerries weren't bothering allied ships. I barely slept the night before as I replayed the mission prep over and over in my mind. I didn't want to miss anything. As it turned out, I might as well not have bothered. My patrol saw exactly one German plane, way off at nine o'clock, and he hightailed it out of there as soon as he got wind of us. I don't know what he was flying, but whatever it was, the P-40 could not begin to keep up with it. Our slowness probably saved us from a fight. By the time we landed back at base, I realized that the mission was no more eventful than one of our training flights over Alabama, maybe even safer.

The mechanics hustled out to the runway as soon as we landed and taxiied in. They dragged huge hoses over to the P-40s and blasted the engines, which were nearly overheated even though we had barely done anything. No high-speed pursuits, no dogfights, nothing, and the P-40s were gasping and hissing like exhausted birds. The mechanics hosed down the nacelles, and they didn't always wait until the pilots got out of the cockpit. I made my getaway, but Lt. Col. Gary "Hardcore" Keck, hopping out of the P-40 next to mine, wasn't so lucky. He got a big snort of the nasty water right in his face. He hadn't taken off his goggles, but he also hadn't shut his mouth. Once he spit out the water, he had a few choice words for the mechanics.

"You want your plane to explode?" the mechanic shouted back. "Get out of that heap and let us fix your mistakes!"

I hauled Hardcore away before he could get in a fight. The steam coming off the engines was blinding us anyway; he wouldn't know which mechanic to punch, and we needed them all.

I finally got him far enough away to where he wouldn't start something and made my way to my bunk. I sat on the edge and realized that the whole mission had been a letdown. I had crawled into the plane, took off, flew around, landed, and that was it. It really was just like a training mission in Alabama. The damn war was probably nearly over before the Army had let Race men get into it, and now we could never show that we could be heroes. Willie had the right idea: stay in Alabama and play cards.

That's how our days went for quite a while. We were busy, flying all the time, but it seemed like the Germans had left the continent. Occasionally, we shot up some planes that were sitting on the ground, but otherwise the war seemed as bland as one of our training missions. We flew; the Warhawks sputtered along, threatening to overheat at every turn; we got no closer to any Germans than we did to any Italians; and we came back to eat bad food and sleep badly on uncomfortable cots. The routine started to get to me. Virginia began to creep back into my thoughts. She did not write to me, which made things worse. I began to read her imaginary letters in my mind, letters in which she poured out her love for me, told me that she could not live without me, urged me to return home soon in one piece.

"Listen at this!" a pilot named Doughboy said one night, leaning over the back of his chair, pages of a letter shaking in his hand. "My dearest Daniel. I cannot wait to see you again. Be sure to let me know when you are coming home so I can wear something special just for you!"

The letter brought hoots and catcalls throughout the barracks.

"She just wants to know when you're showing up so she can run her boyfriend off!" Hardcore shouted, but nothing could wipe the wall-to-wall grin off Doughboy's face.

I got no letters at all. Virginia did not love me, never had, was not thinking about me. Even my mother was distracted, her life ruined, Father in jail, Uncle Abe in jail, so she did not write. I had been sent to the edge of the Earth for no reason except to fly outdated piece-of-shit airplanes so the Army could say it had tried to help Race men. My war was not going so well.

And then I found a new woman to be in love with.

NINETEEN

The North American P-51 Mustang

"Gentlemen, we have got a little surprise for you today," Col. Benjamin O. Davis told us one morning at our mission briefing.

I was still down in the dumps—figuring something was wrong with me if I went to war and got bored—but even I perked up at that because the Colonel usually didn't joke much. It was falling to him to make sure this "experiment" with Race flyers worked, and you could tell by looking into his eyes that he felt the pressure. But he looked happy this morning, and he almost never looked happy.

We walked outside and down the hill to where the metal chain-link runway snaked across a large flat field. Our antique P-40 Warhawks were gone. In their places stood the most advanced flying fighting machines on the face of the Earth: The North American P-51 Mustang. The Mustang did not look all that different from the Warhawk, or from any fighter plane, for that matter, but there was something special about it. Its sharp nose stuck up in the air like the P-40, and its flanks were lean, but it was beautiful and curvy where the Warhawk was stringy and tough. It's like saying that two women each have one nose and two eyes and two lips, but if one of them is beautiful and the other is just striking, or maybe not even that, you notice the difference.

The Nazi Messerschmitts were lean like the P-40s. Very functional, but no real style to them; or maybe it was because I had only seen their tails as they were leaving my P-40 in the dust. They wouldn't be leaving the P-51. This was the fastest plane in the sky. The wind would pour down over its thin nose, gently slide around the bubble cockpit and caress the curved underbelly, which could hold a drop tank for more range. They weren't going to get away next time.

"This is yours," a mechanic named Derek told me. He walked me to the airplane and sat on the lower part of the wing. "You don't have to worry about it overheating like that old rattletrap you've been flying. You got more envelope with this thing in any given direction."

"Great."

"And don't mess it up, because I just checked it out and everything's working. I don't want to see you come dragging in here with this thing, smoke trailing out of it, nothing like that. You bring this sucker back in one clean piece or don't bother coming back."

The mechanics could be touchy about the aircraft. They didn't seem to understand that the fighters belonged to us, the pilots, not them. They wrenched on the things and made sure the flaps worked and the valves were clear and the fluids were moving, but they could never touch the soul of an airplane. You could only do that in the sky. But I wanted Derek to keep my plane in top shape, so I just nodded. He was my regular mechanic, but I never got to know him well. Derek was a nice enough guy from Ohio. I wasn't even sure Ohio had Race men, but he came from there anyway. He always seemed lost in thought, frowning at the airplane as if trying to divine its secrets through the force of mind alone.

Our first mission in the P-51 was uneventful; we saw nothing to chase. I was beginning to doubt that Germany had any airplanes left, given my experience with them. But the plane was great. Over the course of my lifetime, I have come to hate the weapons of war, and I will tell you why later. I hate anything used for war. I almost hate the human hand, the first weapon of war. But I cannot hate the North American P-51 Mustang. It was built as a warplane through and through and it was the best of its kind at the time, but even though it was good for nothing else but war, I cannot hate it. That plane stole my heart. The first ones we got had canopies that had little windows in them, which later were replaced with clear bubble canopies. In other words, the airplane only got better looking with time. It could climb faster than anything I had ever been near and it could dive faster than anything but a P-47 Thunderbolt, which I have never flown. I heard the P-47 could dive so well only because it was a tub of lard, and it climbed like a fat man taking the stairs. The Mustang just danced in the sky.

I killed my first human being while flying in the P-51 Mustang. It was my third mission with Virginia II. The real Virginia had still never written me a line and still had never left my thoughts, so I named my second combat aircraft after her. It was more like her than the flame-spitting, smoke-belching P-40, anyway. Sleek and mysterious. I sometimes wondered if she could tell, way back there in Alabama, that a warplane with her name on it was scaring the hell out of the Germans. Well, I probably wasn't scaring the hell out of them. Annoying them, maybe, if they knew I was there, at all.

That is, until my third mission with Virginia II. It was my first day doing bomber escort duty. Our previous missions had not done much to bring out the Jerries, but bombers attracted them like Chicago attracts wind. Our job was to give the bombers a chance to do their work, deep in enemy territory. The P-51s had the range needed to go along with those big droning monsters and make sure they got there and back. On this particular day, we were going to accompany some B-17s as they blew up a railway that Germany was using for supplies. Germany needed supplies desperately, according to our briefing, and they were pretty keen to keep their trains on the tracks. Germany was stretched thin but was still a nasty enemy, and they were going to show us all the nasty they could muster.

I was on the left side of the B-17 fleet when I heard excited chatter from the other side, from the P-51s I couldn't even see beyond the olive-green bulk of the bombers. I recognized Hardcore's excited voice, "Bogeys! Two o'clock!" He was even more impressed with the Mustang than I was, if that's possible. I think Hardcore would have slept in the cockpit if his crew chief let him.

I dropped down underneath the big plane and then I could see them; tiny malevolent specks on the horizon, headed our way. I checked to my left to make sure there weren't any others coming the other way, then I went after them.

"You boys let me know if we have any other company," I radioed to the bomber pilot.

"Oh, I will," the pilot replied. "Tell Jerry we don't want to play today, won't you?"

I had been looking at the pilot through his windows earlier. With his goggles and his oxygen, I couldn't tell he was white, although I figured he was. He probably couldn't tell I was a Race man and might not have believed it if he knew. To anyone else looking at us, the stuff clamped on our faces wouldn't even make us look human.

I heard machine-gun fire as I came out from underneath the bombers. Hardcore had a Messerschmitt trying to get on his tail. This was my first up-close look at an ME-109. It was silver and green, with big black crosses on the fuselage and wings. The sun was glinting off the side glass of his cockpit and I couldn't see the pilot at all, couldn't even see the small shape of a head in the cockpit. He apparently was concentrating on Hardcore and he didn't see me or didn't act like he did. I'd like to say that we engaged in a running battle over miles and miles of green enemy territory, with him trying every trick in the book to shoot me down and me doing the same, but the reality is that he didn't expect anyone to come from underneath the bombers and he probably never saw me.

I killed a man by twitching a muscle in my thumb, which activated the machine guns so carefully placed in the wings of my aircraft. They cut his airplane nearly in two, and for some reason, he was unable to get out of the cockpit and pop his parachute. I flew down after him as his broken plane pinwheeled toward the trees below, and saw it explode. Hardcore whooped his thanks into my ears and I could hear the bomber pilots shouting their congratulations, but I felt no joy at all, or really anything at all. A man was dead below me, a man I had never seen and never would. We were tiny chess pieces arranged on a board by our two great countries and we spent a few seconds near each other in the skies over his home-land, and now I was alive, and he was charred and broken somewhere on the ground below. So now he knew more about life and death than I do.

TWENTY

The Letter

THE MAIL CAME ON A THURSDAY. It was usually a stampede around the base, like a new waterhole had opened up and all the lions needed a drink. I was used to ignoring it. But on this day, for the first time since I had gone to war, I got a letter. It was written in a clear hand, every letter legible, no lines blurred or out of place. It was addressed to Lieutenant Colonel Jonathan Nicholas, everything spelled out. I think it was more properly written than even my Army acceptance notice. I wasn't sure what it was until I saw the return address: Tuskegee, Alabama. And the name: Miss Virginia Scott.

I almost blacked out when I saw her name. Some of the guys were teasing me because I never got any mail, and they always offered to let me read their letters, then pulled them back when I jokingly reached out. This time, I saw the proffered hands again but ignored them. I knew some taunts were going around but could not make out what was said because my blood was suddenly a jackhammer in my head. My hand shook where the blood coursed through it. I thought I might have a heart attack.

"Is it written in Braille?" one joker finally said, the first voice to cut through my haze. "You trying to read it through your hand? You got some vision problems we need to know about, Nicholas?"

I realized I was standing there stroking the letter like it was a pet dog. Embarrassed, I put it in my pocket and walked outside. I heard laughter behind me but didn't know if they were laughing at me and didn't care.

I walked around the barracks to an empty spot. The sun was still up, hanging low in the sky, making the white paper look gold. I opened the letter, trying hard not to shake, and read it.

Dear Johnny,

I am sorry I have not written before now. I have been trying to decide how I feel about you, to be honest.

Oh, she was brutally honest. I wasn't sure if that was good or bad.

I thought about it for a long while. I wanted to buck up your spirits because of the fighting you are doing but I did not want you to get any false hopes if I did not have any real hopes to offer you. Also, I have imagined you surrounded by all those French or British girls and know I could not compete with them.

I looked around. The only person I could see was one of the crew guys smoking a cigarette and scratching his hairy belly. There were no girls of any sort, and I chuckled as I tried to imagine how Virginia imagined the war.

As I thought, I realized that you had become part of my daily life. I think about you nearly all the time. I know we have not known each other long, but it now feels that you have become a part of me in that short time. I know that I am taking a risk here. You may not feel this way about me, you may be with those other girls, you may not be thinking of me at all or even remember me. But I remember you, Johnny. You are in my heart now. I would like it very much if you would come back to me.

—Love, Virginia.

The crew guy looked over at me with alarm when I put my head in my hands and started to bawl. Big, choking sobs racked out of me and I couldn't hold them in and didn't particularly want to.

"You all right, man?" he asked, as he couldn't quite make out who I was.

"Fine, fine," I croaked, waving him away.

I needed to write back to her right away. I would write her the very next day, after our mission, if I survived it, and tell her how I felt. I would tell her that I was going to come back to her if I had any say at all about it, and that nothing would keep us apart after that except death itself. I think I sat there and wrote the letter in my mind. I took her letter and folded it again, then tucked it underneath my shirt. I wanted her words next to my bare skin. It was as close as I was going to get for a long time, I knew.

I did not know—could not imagine—how long it would be.

TWENTY-ONE

I Finally Get to Visit France

I DID NOT KNOW if I wanted to become an ace. I had one confirmed kill but to be an ace I would need four more, and now I was not sure that I wanted that tally against my soul, even if they were Nazis. My shoot-down of the German pilot did not gnaw on me. I did not lose sleep over it, I did not think about it that much. But, somehow, the dead pilot became a presence that would not go away. Sometimes while walking across the base, I would see a man move out of the corner of my eye, but when I whipped my head around, no one was there. Sometimes, I thought I heard a man trying to whisper an urgent message to me in German, but no one was there. So, it did not bother me, but it was also something I could not forget. One German ghost was bad enough. Four more might be a little bit much.

I wrote to Virginia, and she wrote to me. My letters were on cramped postcards supplied by the U.S. Army. They didn't let me say much, but I couldn't say much anyway. We didn't want to give anything away. Virginia's letters to me weren't much longer and were equally mundane. She was not a prolific letter writer, as it turned out, but I treasured each one she sent. We exchanged vows of love fairly early on in our correspondence, but after that we stuck to day-to-day topics, like what we had for lunch or whether we were sick or not. I didn't want her to know the reality of war; I kept my postcards as relentlessly cheery as a propaganda newsreel.

Our action stayed fairly heavy as the winter of 1944 lifted and spring began to spread across Europe. Men and women were dead everywhere, cities were ruined, great civilizations poked and stabbed blindly at each other, but Mother Nature did not notice or care. Blossoms poked around the ruined metal sculptures of destroyed tanks, vines curled around corpses, moving them aside, coming through.

We were steadily flying bomber escorts now, keeping the monsters safe as they pounded the guts out of Germany. We had a good reputation for a bunch of Race flyers. We had not lost a single bomber, and Colonel Davis intended to make sure we never did. "You stay with your bombers," he said, over and over. "Do everything by the book." So, we did, and the book was pretty good, because we never did lose a bomber to an enemy as far as I know.

We lost other things, though. We lost ourselves, sometimes. Hardcore, who had become my best friend while we were overseas, was shot down by an ME-109. It got on his tail and he could not shake it and his wingman could not get to him in time to save him. So, he died. And, like so many others, he knows more about life and death than I do. His real name was Walter Darby and he was from some nothing town in Texas, but for some reason he was eager to get back to it. I did not think there were any Race men in Texas, just like I didn't think there were any in Ohio, but he said there were, and he was one of them, and he intended to live there until the good lord called him home. The good lord called him earlier than expected.

Hardcore was the most restless man I have ever seen. He could not stand to be cooped up unless he was asleep or in the cockpit, so he wandered all over the base. He reminded me of something I read about sharks, that they have to keep moving all the time or they will die. Hardcore was the only one I told about the ghost of the German who tried to haunt me. I thought for some reason he would understand, and he did. Hardcore had shot down two planes. He figured the ghosts would be after him, too, but he never stood still long enough for them to catch up.

I lost myself on a sunny summer day in 1944.

We were supposed to escort some B-17s and B-24s to bomb the Herman Goering tank works in Germany. We had flattened pretty much everything else Germany had but they were still good at making things, including tanks, and the Allies really didn't want them to have tanks anymore. One thing they still had were guns and ME-109s, so we were going as heavy escort there and back. We didn't see a lot of action for a long part of the trip and I was getting kind of bored. We were observing radio silence and the bombers were responsible for all the navigation, so all I had to do was fly along with them, keep my eyes open and be quiet. I think I nearly fell asleep at one point. It was a bright, clear day, and the sun hung lazily in the sky, filling my cockpit with light and my head with thoughts of a nice long nap.

The buzz saw started up as we got closer. A flock of ME-109s rose from the ground like mosquitoes and headed for the bombers, flying in pairs just like we always did. Hawks and eagles might fly and hunt alone but that was deadly for fighter aircraft. We had to hunt in packs. We needed not only to protect the bombers but to protect ourselves.

Heavy shells from below started exploding around us, making a poom-poom sound like fireworks but releasing balls of fire and thick clouds of smoke. I heard the whine of the ME-109s and the ack-ack-ack of the big guns on the Flying Fortresses. The quiet of the day was gone. No more need for radio silence, everyone now knew we were there. I was the wingman to Bobby Masterson, a quiet man who turned up from Tuskegee just a few weeks before. I didn't know him well. He was from New York City but the vices of the big town had not rubbed off on him. He never drank, never cussed, seemed to smoke only grudgingly and absolutely refused to gamble. That meant he had more money than anybody else on the base, mainly because he never spent it on anything. He might as well have grown up in some small town in Iowa. He had a girlfriend who had already written him a sheaf of letters even though he had barely arrived in Europe. That didn't bother me now; I had my few letters, and to me they outweighed all of his.

"You got one coming on you, Bobby," I said. "I'll take care of him."

"Preciate it," he responded, as coolly as if I had just offered to buy him a soda.

A cool head in a firefight. That's what you want to be around.

The ME-109 saw me coming and the pilot realized he wasn't going to be able to out-turn me, so he dropped down and broke off the engagement. More fighters were coming up ahead at 11 o'clock, so this freed Bobby and I to get after them and chase them away. The mission continued on for a while then, with the MEs circling warily and us swiveling our heads around constantly, trying to spot them while also trying to keep from getting hit from below. I know that in the movies the airplanes are dogfighting constantly, but in real life you are acutely aware that your one and only life is sitting in a very expensive airplane, and you are careful. But you can't be too careful. We were nearing the objective and the flak was getting heavier. We never lost a bomber to an enemy fighter, but we certainly lost some to ground fire. I looked out the right side of my cockpit and saw a shell from below hit one of the B-17s right in the middle. The wounded Flying Fortress slowly fell out of formation, its crew leaping out of every window and door like ants. Jumping out of a plane was nearly as dangerous as being in one. The rear gunner pulled his chute too soon and went limp in the harness just after he cleared the plane, probably dead, which was just as well because his body hit the wing of the bomber behind him. It was strange that here I was in my little tin can and I felt much safer than those poor guys in an airplane bigger than several buses lined up.

"Johnny, you've got a girlfriend trying to sneak up on your tail," Bobby said, with no more drama than if he was telling me my shirt was untucked. "I'll see if I can make her leave you alone."

"'Preciate it," I said, borrowing his phrase. It seemed like a good, economical thing to say in such a situation.

He passed over me and I turned to see the ME-109 go into a steep dive. Bobby went after it, the right thing to do because he had his speed up and could catch this guy. But the German plane was apparently going faster than both Bobby and I thought because Bobby wasn't able to catch him as soon as he hoped. And, as it turned out, as soon as I needed him to.

I had hardly turned my head back around before I saw two more blotches on the horizon. I thought they were puffs of smoke from ground fire, at first, but soon enough I saw the wings and the tails of approaching ME-109s. They were headed for a B-24 that had pulled up to replace the B-17 that was now smeared all over the ground. I wasn't going to let them have it, Bobby or no Bobby.

"Forget that girl," I radioed him. "We have a couple of new dance partners."

"On the way. Don't dance with them both by yourself."

I didn't have a choice. They were headed straight for the bomber, probably figuring that a lone fighter was not going to put up much resistance with a lagging wingman. I have said before that we had never lost a bomber to enemy fighters, and I was damned if it was going to happen on my watch. I figured my best defense was a good offense, so I charged right between the fighters. They broke off, one to either side. I cut a hard left, slamming my body against the Mustang's metal frame. The Mustang could turn better than most airplanes and I thought I might be able to pick one of them off and even the odds a little. The Jerries weren't fooling around, though. The other plane went into a steep climb, a gutsy move because it exposed him to more fire from the B-24. But he probably figured—correctly—that the bomber wouldn't fire because the crew was afraid of hitting me.

I wish they hadn't worried so much, because he got on my tail and I couldn't shake him.

"My dance card's getting full pretty quick, here, Bobby," I said, trying to keep my voice as cool as his always was, but I was sure the shakiness was evident.

"I'm hurrying," he said. His voice sounded shaky too, and I knew then that I was in real trouble.

The ME-109 was right behind me, sending bullets whizzing past my canopy. I couldn't go into a tight turn to the right because that would send me flying right into the thick of the bomber fleet. I would almost certainly hit something, or, at the very least, I would defeat the entire purpose of my being there by escorting a German fighter right into the middle of a herd of U.S. bombers. I couldn't do a tight turn to the left because the other ME-109 was there, waiting for me to do just that. I couldn't go up because the Jerry was behind me and could probably out-climb me. And going down was stupid because I'd be closer to the ground and the flak.

Sometimes you have to do stupid things. I punched the stick and went down. I almost wished I was in a P-47 Thunderbolt right then. They were fat things, but they could dive like meteors, from what I had been told. The Mustang could dive, too, but no better than the ME-109. We went down together, me whipping back and forth, trying to avoid his bullets. He wasn't all that good a shot, but he was right behind me and didn't have to be. I could feel the vibrations as his 20mm slugs dug into the back of my fuselage, which caused jolts of pain as if they were puncturing my own body.

"Hang on!" Bobby shouted into my ear, his voice having lost all traces of its famous cool. "I'm coming!"

He wasn't coming fast enough. Smoke poured out of my right wing, which was bad because the wings held the fuel. I wanted to be flying a North American P-51 Mustang, not a crop duster. The plane was still responsive despite the damage, and I continued to whip it back and forth, missing most of my tormentor's shells. I hoped the smoke would blind him.

"Almost there!" Bobby shouted.

A dizzying explosion felt like it was going to knock my teeth out, and then my world started to spin. Vomit rose in my throat, and I had never thrown up while flying, or even gotten a little green around the gills.

I had indeed gotten too close to the ground, and a patient gunner had just given me a nice little present in the form of a shell that blasted through my left wingtip and set my plane spinning like a top. I managed to stop the spinning without throwing up, but this just gave the ME-109 behind me time to perfect his aim. My plane shook with what felt like one hundred little explosions and now smoke came from the engine, too, blinding me.

I dropped even lower. I was not going to let this Jerry shoot me down, and if I got low enough, it would be hard for the ground gunners to get me, as they were used to shooting at much higher targets. I was flying not far above the trees now, which limited my mobility. I didn't want to be waggling my wings too much because there was a danger I could actually hit a tree, and that could do as much damage as any German shell.

The smoke from my beloved P-51 was getting thicker, which was good in a way because it did blind the ME-109. He had to fly off to the side to see where I was and then fly back into the smoke to try to shoot me, which gave me plenty of warning. All I had to do was jog off to the side a little bit and let him shoot the air.

The strangest thing happened then. After a while he got tired of sucking smoke and just settled off to the right behind me, out of the smoke but off to where he couldn't get me. We cruised above the forests of Germany together, not all that fast anymore. I looked back and saw his head in the cockpit and gave him a little wave. He gave a little wave back. Nothing personal. I guess he just wanted to get a confirmed kill and make sure he actually shot me down, but he wanted to be gracious about it.

Another odd thing was that my Mustang was actually performing pretty well, considering it probably had more bullet holes than fuselage and was on fire. I carefully tested the controls, without making any moves that might startle the ME. Everything responded fine, more or less. I probably couldn't do any barrel rolls, but I could land if I had to. As it was, I didn't need to do anything for a while. We trundled on across the landscape for what seemed like hours, my plane spewing ugly gray smoke across a nice blue sky. The flak and armadas of aircraft that I had left behind seemed like part of a different world. It occurred to me that my war was about to be over. There was no way in hell I could get back to Ramitelli; I was nearly out of fuel. I couldn't go back because the ME was right on my tail, ready to end my world in addition to ending my war. There was really nothing for me to do but relax and enjoy the ride. Maybe I would get lucky and the ME would hit a tree and crash and I could claim it as a kill of my own.

I was almost starting to get bored again when the ME began to pull away. He was probably running out of fuel, too, and couldn't wait any longer to claim his prize. He gave a little waggle of his wings and fired off a couple of shots into nothing and banked into a slow turn. I didn't try to follow him—I wasn't that stupid—so I continued on until I couldn't see him anymore. My fuel gauge was banging on empty. The fire on the wing hadn't helped with that situation, at all. I tested the controls again and everything seemed to be working okay. I was pretty sure I was on enemy territory, and I didn't want to deliver a partially functional Mustang to the Jerries. I needed to get up higher and bail out.

I started a slow climb. I got to about 12,000 feet when I saw a dot on the horizon. The bastard was back! The ME-109 had tricked me! He was coming on fast, determined to get his kill after all. I didn't have enough gas to dive again and try to pull it out again. I barely had enough fuel to try to turn and evade him that way, and the truth of it was that I was scared the plane would fall apart under any sort of rough maneuvers. I basically sat there and let his guns chew into the plane. He got off a long volley and shot past me, probably figuring one encounter would be all it would take. He was right. I waited until his plane flashed by and bailed out. I had heard stories about German fighters shooting U.S. troops who were parachuting, which was against the rules. I didn't want to give him the chance. I figured that by the time he came around again I'd be too low for him to bother.

He didn't bother, anyway. He saw my chute and saw my North American P-51 Mustang plummet to the ground, so he had his kill. A little American flag would go underneath his cockpit, and I hated that it would be mine. I watched my plane corkscrew into the green hillside and explode. I had just cost the U.S. taxpayers tens of thousands of dollars. As I drifted down, I saw a small crowd assembling below, apparently coming out of the trees. I got closer and saw a road and some slow-moving cars, as well as cattle in the field and tiny moving human shapes here and there. I was outside some small town somewhere, but I didn't know where, or even which country. I started to pay close attention because the ground was coming up faster now and I didn't want to kill myself by slamming into a tree.

I managed to avoid a couple of trees and found a nice open field, coming to a textbook-perfect running stop. I dumped the chute as fast as I could and turned to face three rough-hewn women with knives in their hands. They were advancing toward me steadily, with looks of grim determination on their faces. I knew the Germans were tough, but I didn't expect to square off with three hausfrau the very second I hit the ground. I was tired and didn't want to deal with this, and I wasn't sure what I was going to do. The knives were a good size and the flight suit made it cumbersome to try to fight, but at least it might protect me from the blades and give me a chance to knock some good old American sense into them.

I was thinking that I should charge one of them, take the element of surprise, when suddenly they dropped to their knees and began sawing away at the cords of my chute, which was splayed out along the ground like a big dead jellyfish. They weren't after me, at all, with the knives. They wanted the silk from my chute. Things had been rationed so much that they needed the silk for clothes. One of them said she hadn't had a suitable dress to wear almost since the war began. I stood and stared at them, still in my fighting stance. Another, who was sawing away with some gusto, said she needed to make dresses for her daughters.

It took another few beats of my heart before I realized that I understood their conversation. I didn't speak German. They weren't speaking German. They were speaking French. I had flown over the border, somewhere back there beyond the trees. I had always wanted to come to France, and now my dream had come true. I thought of Dominique. She would have had a good laugh at this.

TWENTY-TWO

I Go Local

Looking back, what I did in France was stupid. I should have waited until a German patrol found me, surrendered, and been shipped off to a POW camp to wait for the end of the war. Even if it was the most vicious prison camp maintained by Hitler's minions, it would have been superior to what came next. But that was a little way off yet.

I was standing in this field, or what turned out to be the edge of a field, watching these women hack away at my parachute. They were going at it with the grim efficiency of stockyard workers in Chicago, and before long the fabric was chopped into manageable pieces and the cords had been cut up and buried. I stood watching them and they kept an eye on me but otherwise didn't bother me.

Finally, I pulled off my headgear and said, in French, "You are very efficient workers."

They quickly stood and looked at me, shocked.

"You speak French?" one asked. "Are you American?"

"Yes. And yes."

"Good for you," another said. "We have to go now. They will come for you soon."

"We could use him," said the third. "He speaks French. And he's Black. The Germans will never think he was the one flying that plane."

I found out later this was wrong, and the Germans knew all about the Tuskegee Airmen, but standing there in that field, somewhere on the edge of France, what they said made sense.

"Say something else," the first woman told me. "Talk for longer. I want to hear you."

I told them about where I had lived in Chicago and how I had moved to Alabama to learn how to fly airplanes.

"That's enough," she said finally, glancing over her shoulder as if expecting the Werhmacht to come marching along the field any second now. "You can pass. If you want to come with us, come with us. If you want to go to a prisoner camp, wait here."

"What do you mean, come with you? Who are you?"

"We are not going to tell you *that*," she said. "Especially not if you're going to go with the Germans."

I had the idea they were with the fabled French resistance, of course, but for all I knew they were going to force me to sew new dresses out of my old parachute. But I had heard rumors of German mistreatment of American prisoners of war and if I could pass for a French citizen I might as well give it a try. Hopefully, I could get out of the country and back in the game. So, in a hasty decision I would very much come to regret, I followed them down a little path that led out of the field and into the woods.

———

"Marianne," said the one who had been most skeptical of my involvement.

"Such a pretty name," I said, and she let something that resembled a smile get close to her lips.

She was Marianne. Her friends were Annamaria and Julie. They lived in Duborg, a small village on the other side of the woods. Duborg had once been pretty, they said, but it had been a hotbed of resistance and the Nazis had come through three or four times and just stomped it flat. The village was laid out in a square around a church, which still bore bullet holes and bloodstains against its rugged white walls.

They once had families, all of them. Now all their husbands were dead, and they lived together in Marianne's house because it was the only one of theirs that had not been destroyed. Like the town itself, it was a square house with four rooms that led to a small central kitchen. It seemed to have once been part of a barn; it had the feel like animals had once taken shelter in it. Whatever animals were around had long since been eaten, and Marianne, Annamaria and Julie were thin and rugged, their hands calloused and their faces as lined and craggy as hillsides.

There was not a lot they could do with the resistance. They had plans for blowing up German bases and killing scores of Germans with explosives placed in the woods, but they did not have guns, much less explosives. They mainly sheltered resistance fighters who were making their way through the village on their way to places where there was more action. When they weren't doing that, they sat at Marianne's table and plotted their revenge fantasies. I think it was easier for them to do that than to grieve for their husbands.

After they led me away from the duly disposed remains of my parachute, Marianne put me to sleep on her bed. I crashed just as surely as my North American P-51 had; all the stress of the mission and its disastrous conclusion melted away and I disappeared for a while in a dreamless black fog. When I awoke, I heard French being spoken by a woman, and for more than a few seconds I thought I was back in Dominique's bed. Then I remembered where I was, and the years came rushing back to claim me.

They fed me some rough peasant food—bread, cheese, a tiny bit of leathery meat—but it tasted better than anything I had eaten in a long time, especially nearly everything the Army had fed me. They gave me some vinegary wine, too, but I didn't care for it much and sipped it as slowly as I could.

While I slept, they had dreamed up big plans for me. The idea of having a man at their disposal, and a physically fit and militarily trained one, at that, was very agreeable. They were disappointed to learn that I did not know any more about explosives than they did, not to mention that I didn't have access to any, but they knew I had to be useful to them in some way or God would not have dropped me right in their laps the way He did.

The plans didn't take effect right away. There wasn't much going on in the town and we didn't have any equipment, so it was difficult to come up with anything workable. So, I settled into my life in France. The three ladies took my flight suit and cut it up into outfits for Annamaria's kids, who turned out to be two adorable little girls who bubbled over with energy and optimism despite having lost their father. They were five and seven years old, the eldest Marianne, the youngest Julie; Annamaria had named them after her friends, which was a nice enough gesture at the time but now reflected the fact that they were the only things she had left.

The girls seemed to like having me around. Marianne barely remembered their father and Julie did not remember him at all, so having a male pay attention to them was a novelty. They usually played by themselves, in the woods or in the town, as their mother became increasingly involved with the convoluted and pointless planning she conducted with her friends. I told the girls all about my life, about Alabama, which did not look all that different from this little town, and about Chicago, which was so large they could scarcely imagine it. Duborg was small enough that they knew everyone in it, and had a hard time believing I didn't know everyone in Chicago.

But these tales were our little secret. Annamaria warned her daughters they should never tell anyone I was an American, and especially that I had crashed my plane in the field beyond the woods. But my presence did have to be explained, because I was the only black face in town, as far as I could tell. There was one mysterious old woman who had apparently come from Mexico decades before. She was as wizened and dark as a rotting apple and about as talkative, and no one seemed to know much about her or remember why she now lived in a small town in France. Aside from her, the residents of Duborg were all as pasty as I had figured French people would be, so there was some explaining to do.

Marianne hit upon the idea that I was the Haitian husband of her cousin, who had gone missing in the war. I ordinarily lived in Paris but was looking for my wife who had said she might visit her cousin. The fact that I supposedly lived in Paris could let people think I had a certain amount of money and could thus afford to be waltzing around France during a ruinous war, looking for a wife who was doing the same, but it was a thin story, at best. Marianne liked it a lot because it would require me to mostly steer clear of town. Some of the residents of Duborg had actually been to Paris or had relatives there and might ask me about it, and my knowledge of it was all from books and mostly limited to its geography and to the locations of the places Josephine Baker had performed. Even with that, I knew more about Paris than Marianne, Annamaria and Julie did, so they couldn't even prep me properly. But because I couldn't spend much time wandering around town, I would have plenty of time to wander in the woods and help plan an attack on any Germans who might come through. The women, all three of them, were obsessed with the idea they needed to each kill a German soldier before the war ended or they died themselves.

And so, the war went on without me. I spent part of my time walking in the woods, talking with the weird sisters—which was how I thought of them as a group, borrowing a bit from "Macbeth"—about how we could hang chains from certain trees to sweep up Nazis by their necks, or even use them to prop up trees that we had cut, and then, when the time was right, drop the trees on the Germans. Nazi soldiers did come through not long after I crashed, looking for me. Or, rather, looking for a renegade pilot. The few people in town who knew of my existence either were not questioned or did not make the connection to me. The Germans, having little apparent interest in Duborg and no apparent desire to hang around, left. I should have gone with them.

The weird sisters were part of the underground, I will give them that. A few weeks after I was marooned, which was how I had begun to think about it, a man named Jean appeared at the door late at night. They had a password and he knew it, so they let him in. Over bread and bad wine, he said he was delivering the names of some infiltrators to Paris and he hoped the spies would be killed. It was vital that he get his message through, he said.

My presence surprised him a little. Jean was initially reluctant to talk around me until the women assured him I was not a threat. He looked at me from time to time while he ate and talked. He was deathly pale, had no extra flesh on him whatsoever and smelled bad, so I did not sit too close. He said he had never seen a black man before, but he didn't seem to attach much significance to my blackness. Once we established in conversation that I had never been to Africa and didn't know much about it, he started to lose interest in me. He was not interested in talking about airplanes. He had seen too many airplanes during this war and did not care if he ever saw another one. He was a farmer and liked to be near the ground, and if he was going to fight with someone, he would rather it be face-to-face, not have death rain down on him from some metal shell so high up he could hardly see it.

I did not sleep well with Jean in the house. I had gotten used to the household rhythm we had set up, or that the women had set up and I had joined. He slept on the floor in the room with me. Even after he had a bath, he still smelled pretty fierce and he fell asleep almost immediately and snored like a train. I dozed off here and there but, in the morning, I heard the patter of stealthy feet and the snoring abruptly stopped. I cracked my eyes open to see Annamaria tugging on Jean's shoulder. He followed her like a zombie to the next room, and later I heard squeaking sounds and a short, sharp cry of relief from her. I wondered if the poor man might get passed around from room to room and I would never get any sleep again, but he left after breakfast the next day.

The weird sisters were excited for a few days after he left because they felt they had accomplished something. The younger versions of Annamaria and Julie told me they were always this way after "company" came through, because they felt it was a blow against Germany, and it was. But the excitement faded as the dull day-to-day routine of life in a small, unimportant French town reasserted itself, and soon enough they were beginning to plot oddball schemes, most of which involved me putting together fantastic machines out of parts I could supposedly find around town. Flash Gordon had nothing on these ladies in the futuristic imagination department.

One night, I was trying to doze off when I heard something rustling through the room.

"Shhh, shhh," said a voice, which I recognized as Annamaria's. I had never been alone with any of the weird sisters, not due to any awkwardness or fear on their part, but just because they were all usually around. I had certainly never been alone with any of them in the limited privacy of my own room, which was how I thought of it now although it was obviously not really mine. Annamaria climbed slowly across the small bed, which shifted under her weight. I knew why she had come. I would have known even without seeing her take Jean away.

I heard the rasp in her breath as her face drew close to mine. There was a small window high in the wall that was useless for looking out, but it illuminated her face as it moved across the bed like an approaching moon. She planted her dry, coarse lips to mine. Her breath stunk of garlic and the bad wine that we all drank, but I knew mine did, too. Our tongues danced in each other's mouth and I could feel that she had a loose tooth on the left side of her jaw. I hoped it would not get any looser.

She broke off the kissing abruptly, as if that was enough to prove the point and cover the social niceties. She shoved a hand through the fly of my trousers and grabbed me, sending a jolt shooting down my spine. I had not been with a woman in a very long time. This was not how I pictured my return to sex, at all. It was to be with Virginia, and on our wedding night, and then we were going to travel together to some far-off place like Las Vegas or Hawaii. But now it was going to be in a bug-infested bed in a bug-infested house in a bug-infested town in the middle of nowhere, France.

She whipped out my penis and I gasped as it felt the cool night air. She stroked me like some farm animal, roughly, so that it was both painful and exhilarating. I grew in her palm. She tugged her nightdress up and sat on top of me. She was ready and I slipped in almost before I realized it. She did not give me a chance to move, not so much as sit up. She rode me like a donkey, rocking her hips, pushing down hard. I fired off my load very quickly, but she didn't seem to care, just kept rocking away, clawing at my stomach with her hard hands. I was about to slip out of her, spent, when she gave a little gasp like the one I heard last night and stopped moving. She looked down at me and the small trace of moonlight from the window caught her eyes. They were lost, two black holes in her thin skull that radiated animal need. She looked down at me and she saw a ghost. She saw a white French man, her long-lost husband. Without a word, she pulled away and vanished from the room, more silently than she had entered.

I thought about her a long time after she left. I felt nothing for her but pity. I suppose I was glad to be of service, literally, but it would not bother me if she never visited me again. I doubted that would be the case. She had found something, something she remembered she needed, and it was only in the other room, there for the taking. I thought it curious that the only one of the three weird sisters to have a physical reminder of past love—her sweet, innocent daughters—was the one who still needed love the most. The flame still burned within her chest and she could not bear to let it go out. She would do anything to keep it alive, even sleep with a Race man.

She did not act any different toward me the next morning, and I was glad. She barely looked at me, but then again, that's usually how she behaved. I spent part of the day whittling spikes that Marianne dreamed of hiding in the woods in a pit that Nazi soldiers would fall into. There was no useful ground cover for such a pit, and I was not eager to actually dig one, so I got by with sharpening sticks. That night I lay sleeplessly, waiting for Annamaria to return. I hoped to ruin the element of surprise and maybe make the process a little more enjoyable for myself. She did not come that night and eventually I drifted off to sleep.

I still remember my dreams from that night. They were troubled and uncertain and writhed together like snakes. I saw all the women I had ever loved and wanted to love. Sometimes they were walking down a hallway toward me, but when they were just about to reach out and touch me, they disappeared. The last in the line was Virginia, and it broke my heart when her fingers faded before my eyes.

Annamaria never appeared in the dream. She was nothing to me just as I was nothing to her. She came back the next night, after I was asleep. I think she waited to listen and make sure I was asleep. She didn't want me waiting for her and getting ready, didn't want me making anything out of it. I was just the pipeline to a dream for her and she didn't want me to do anything to mess up that dream. Again, she crawled across the bed like a thing possessed. The moonlight wasn't hitting her eyes this time, but I could see them anyway, burning like desperate embers. She used me for what she needed me for and then she crawled away, back into the darkness. I was sore, again, and relieved to hear her go. I don't know what she got out of our nighttime visits. They left me nearly despondent and not at all relieved; they were a drop of water to a man dying of thirst. Not nearly enough.

TWENTY-THREE

Into the Jaws of Death

JUST ABOUT A MONTH LATER, a group of Nazi soldiers stomped out of the woods, up to the little house we shared and shot Annamaria to death. She crumpled like a sack. I was in the kitchen helping Marie chop some half-dead herbs that she had found in the woods when we heard a commotion. There were shouts in German and Annamaria's answering shrieks in French, then the gunshot, a universal language. I walked to the door just in time to see the shot and see her fall. The life had gone out of her long before, the soldier just moved her body along. So now she knows more about life and death than I do.

Standing there, in that split second, and seeing her die, I realized that although I had sex with her, at this point, many times—it was never making love, never even close to love, barely on the same planet as love —I felt only the usual sorrow you would feel at seeing someone you know shot down like a dog. Her world had moved on years before and now she was racing to catch up with it.

The German soldier who shot her was younger than me. He was impressively clean except for his boots, which was how I knew they had come through the woods. He stood looking at me, and then looked at little Marianne and Julie as they ran out of the house, heedless of the danger, and hovered over their mother's body. Adult Marianne and Julie stood back by the door, their hands knotted together.

The poor little girls had seen a lot, but they had never seen this. They did not bend down to touch their mother. They just stood silently, looking down at her, holding each other's hands, their arms entwined. It felt like they had seen this coming someday, knew they would be on their own in this miserable world, and somehow, they were ready for it. Through all of this, the Germans just stood there. A couple of them in the back looked at the girls and showed traces of actual human emotion —sorrow, maybe?—but the ones closer to me might as well have eyeballs made of lead for all they saw and cared.

The man who shot Annamaria was the leader, I gathered. He kept the Luger in his hand but lowered his arm to his side. He had made his point. He had blue eyes the color of sea ice surrounded by whites the color of snow; there was little color to him and no emotion, at all.

"You," he said in English. "Come with us."

"I need to get some things," I said slowly.

If I was going to a POW camp, I wanted my identification. My dog tags and other papers were hidden under my bed.

"No. Come with us now."

"I have military identification. I need to get it," I said, even more slowly.

"You are military?" he asked, with a sneer. "What military?"

"The U.S. Army Air Corps."

"I suppose you are one of the Tuskegee Airmen," he said, the sneer still well in place.

"Yes." I could hear the pride in my own voice when I said it, pride that I had not heard there in quite a while. "Yes."

"Well, why do not we let you go back to your room for an hour or so? Get your gun, oil it up, get ready for us? I do not think so. We know who you are. You are a Haitian who has been transmitting messages to Paris. We have this on good authority. You are coming with us."

"I am telling you—"

The Luger reappeared, its black hole aimed between my eyes. I went with them. They surrounded me, like I would try to do something, and when I turned my head to say goodbye to the women and the girls, one of them hit me across the back of the head so hard I nearly blacked out. So, just like that, I was gone and never saw Marianne or Julie, or their tiny namesakes, again.

I see travel shows on TV now about small villages in France, so happy and bucolic and beautiful, and I wonder what happened to the women who cut up my parachute and talked me into a stupid mistake. I can't imagine any of them happy. Their grief and anger were as hard and shiny as diamonds.

We hiked through the woods. I thought of all the booby traps the weird sisters had begged me to build and suddenly wished I had. I imagined the soldiers before me falling into a pit full of sharpened sticks and screaming, but it did not happen. We walked in silence and the birds chirped in the trees, happily unconcerned with whatever the humans were doing below. The Nazis had a truck parked in the field at the edge of the woods. I don't know why they didn't drive right up to the house. Maybe Jean painted a picture of a much more dangerous resistance cell than we turned out to be.

The soldiers threw me in the back of the truck. Two of them got in with me and the others climbed in the front. There was some kind of wooden crate turned upside down. That was my seat. We bounced along for a while and then slowed down and slowed some more. The soldiers with me exchanged glances so I knew this was not part of the plan. They stayed with me, but the truck shifted as the others got out, and I heard the sound of the hood lifting and guttural German babbling. The Germans prided themselves on their mechanical aptitude, but our truck had broken down. The babbling continued. It was getting hot in the back with no air moving, and the soldiers gave each other nervous glances and exchanged thoughts on what might be happening, or so I figured, since I couldn't understand them.

"I can help," I said after a while. It might not have been in my best interest for us to get wherever we were going, but I was tired of sitting on the crate.

"What?" one of the soldiers said in a semblance of English—it sounded more like "vat?"—but that seemed to be about the extent of his fluency. He talked to the other one some more and then went to get the leader. The leader's flat, emotionless face appeared around the back of the truck.

"You have something to share?" he asked me, his voice full of irritation, at me, at the truck, at both.

"I can help. I know how to work on engines."

Aircraft engines weren't that different from automobile engines. They tended to be used for cruising more than stop-and-go driving, but the general technology was the same. I was better at working on airplane engines but had picked up a few automotive engine skills, as well, at the Coffey school, which seemed a lifetime ago.

"You know how to work on our German engine?" he asked, as if the engine in this miserable truck was somehow better than anything I could have seen in America. Then I remembered that he didn't think I was from America.

"Assuming it is an internal combustion engine, yes, I do."

I could probably have stripped it blindfolded if I had the right tools, but I decided not to push my luck.

"Get out, then," he said, before barking something to his men in German.

So, I got out, and they kept a gun on me at all times, although we were broken down on the side of a road that was surrounded by flat fields. If I had tried to run anywhere, they could have used me for target practice. I looked over the engine. It hadn't overheated. All the cables were hooked up properly. I started to ask them to describe how it had been behaving, but I thought it would be better if I figured it out without any help from them. For some reason, I wanted to impress them.

It would have been helpful to know how the truck had been maintained but given that it was a military truck run by a military that was losing a war, I guessed it had been done badly or not at all. A bolt of inspiration struck me. It seemed heaven-sent at the time, but given what it led to, I now have to think it may have come from the other place. I thought about where the truck had been just in the relatively short time

I had been on it; through a field and across dusty roads. I pulled the cover off the carburetor and could tell it was gunked up.

"This needs to be cleaned," I told the head Nazi. "I'll need some gasoline."

He gave me a long look, searching my eyes and face for traces of an escape plan. Maybe he thought I was going to somehow ignite them all with the gas and escape in their truck.

"Gasoline," he said. "But no matches."

"I don't want a match. It's for cleaning."

I took the carburetor out and apart, cleaned its parts in the gas and dried them on a piece of tarp the Germans laid out for me. No one offered to help me in any way. They seemed amused by the whole thing, as if I was the only one who was stuck. Finally, I got everything dried and back together. Nobody climbed in the truck but the driver. They didn't think it would work. He smiled when he cranked it up and the engine coughed to life, ready to go. The leader gave me a cool, appraising look and slowly nodded.

"I didn't think they had engines like this in Haiti," he said. "Very nice work. Now get back in the truck."

We trundled on for hours more, stopping only long enough for the soldiers to relieve themselves. They let me, too, although three of them stood behind me with guns at the ready, as if I would suddenly take off with my johnson hanging out. I did not know if we were still in France or in Germany, but if we were still in France, we'd entered a more heavily occupied section. German trucks were clogging the roads now, and in the distance, I heard the grumble-grumble-grumble of what I thought had to be a tank. It sounded like some kind of snorting dinosaur, but I never saw it.

At last, I was packed out of the truck and delivered to a large camp. A concentration camp. We had heard the Germans used them for undesirables who weren't actually soldiers. Human skeletons walked around the far edges of a large wall, wearing what looked like striped pajamas. And you didn't just smell the place; the smell attacked you, slithered up your nose like a snake. I sneezed three times rapidly just from the initial blast of odor. I really, really didn't want to be there. I had heard the scuttlebutt about POW camps, but I instantly had the sense that I would be much better off in one of those than in one of these. But with all my proof of identity back with the weird sisters, there was no way I was going to end up in one.

I was hustled inside the camp. I didn't get to say goodbye to the men who brought me in. Not that I wanted to, but somehow I thought I would feel better surrounded with soldiers, even soldiers from the other side who would kill me if they got the chance, than among the ragged crew I glimpsed out of the corners of my eyes. I was pushed into a huge concrete room with other inmates. I was the largest man in the room. I still had muscles and stood up straight where they were hunched skeletons. We were stripped and hosed off, then roughly shaved. My hair was not long, but it was gone when I got out. There was some muttering, very quiet muttering, as all this went on. I talked to a French inmate and learned that my new home was Bergen-Belsen.

"We will die here," the Frenchman said.

"You might," I told him. "But I won't."

I became less sure of that as the days crawled on. We were given hardly anything to eat. When people died, their skinny corpses were stripped and left on the ground. Ravens, vultures and other birds came to pick at them. When we had the energy, those of us among the living would try to kick the birds away but they always came back.

I was only there a week before I was pulled aside by one of the guards and taken to the camp director's office. I had not been fed this entire time and a headache had crept its way up my neck and into my skull.

There were four Germans in the room, two of them with rifles. Again, like I was going to try anything.

"I understand you are good with engines," a guy sitting at the desk said in halting French. He was the only one sitting, so I figured he was the director or some other muckety-muck. All of the Germans looked like muckety-mucks all the time; sometimes it was hard to tell who was in charge.

"How do you know this?" I asked.

Quicker than I could see, one of the Germans with a rifle clocked me across the back of the head with it, knocking me to my knees. My body exploded with pain to accompany the pain in my head. It felt like electric shocks were flying up from my knees. That pain met the waves of sickening pain flowing down from the back of my neck. I vomited on the floor, but it was nothing but watery foam. It's hard to throw up when you haven't eaten.

The German who hit me also kicked me, rolling me over on the floor. He only did it so I wouldn't mess up the carpet anymore.

"You do not ask the questions around here," the seated guy said. "You do not speak until spoken to. You do not speak even if spoken to. Do you know how to work on engines?"

"Yes," I said, as loud as I could. Fuck him and his impossible demands. I would speak. But until I got something to eat and a gun in my hand, I would speak only when spoken to.

"Good. We have something for you to do in the motor pool. Some of our trucks have been breaking down. We would appreciate your help. If we do not get your help, we will kill you. If you sabotage any of the engines, we will kill you. If they do not run in tip-top shape, we will kill you. Do you understand?"

"Yes."

"Then get to work. We will escort you there now."

I stumbled along in front of two guards, out the main gate and down an unpaved road to a cinderblock building full of trucks and cars. Just like the Nazis for you: starve you, beat you, but still expect you to work, and work right away. There must have been a dozen more men dressed in striped outfits like mine. They had obviously been here a while; some of the uniforms were little more than rags over bones.

There were other guards in place, so my guards gave me a shove toward the pool kapo. Kapo—rat—same thing. Kapos were prisoners who got benefits and extra food—or, in this case, food, at all—for cooperating with the Nazis and helping keep other prisoners down. It was just another example of the evil of the Nazi mind. It was not enough for it to be them vs. you; it was you vs. you. You starve a man for a while and he will do what he can to survive, including turning on his own. I was nowhere near that point yet, and I despised this kapo the instant I set eyes on him and was forced to breathe the same air as him. But you couldn't say anything to a kapo you wouldn't say to a guard. They would beat you harder than the Nazis, if they got a chance.

"Schwarzer!" he shouted at me in German. "Get this engine running!"

He carried a pipe wrapped in rubber tape and cuffed me across the side of my head with it. I almost fell to my knees again, but did not think I could take the pain, so I grabbed the front of the truck and held on. I nearly passed out. The kapo hit me again, twice, in the back, moving the pain to my spine. I could take him, I knew. These skeletons around me couldn't, but I had only been a week without food and I still had muscles. I had been eating better than this kapo for the past few years. But I knew that raising my hand to him would be the last thing I would do, and that was not how I wanted to leave this world.

Something else grabbed his attention and he walked away. I held on to the truck like a drowning man holds on to a raft. I looked at the engine. It was coated in grime and the rubber around the spark plug wires was rotted. The carburetor was probably plugged up, as well, and who knew what else. It was a mess. It was hard to know where to start.

"I need a wrench," I told the kapo when he came back around to check on my progress, of which there was none because I had no tools. "And some pliers. And some electrical tape."

I figured he would hit me with his stick again and steeled myself for it, but he didn't. At some level, he wanted me to work and get this done, and beating me senseless was not going to accomplish that. He had shown who was boss.

The work was slow once it finally got under way. I was not trusted with tools of any kind. Everything I did was done under the close and watchful eye of an armed guard. If they gave me a wrench unsupervised, they probably thought I would brain the kapo, and I would, no doubt, use the electrical tape to stitch up my shoes and patch the holes in my clothes, which were already starting to rot after only a week. It would not be good for me to get too comfortable.

I slowly got the engine in gear. I was not in a big hurry. I knew they would just use it to bring more victims to this hell, but that was out of my control. I wanted to minimize my beatings. I did a good job, as good as I could, but it was slow going. The truck really needed to be up on a lift, but the German mechanics had those in another shop and would take over that work once I was done. My job was just to raise the engine from the dead.

I ended up talking to the kapo a lot. His name was Seymour. He was a German Jew but had lived in France for a while and loved it. He liked to reminisce about it, although he had to be careful and do it only in small bits here and there. Otherwise, the Nazi guards would think he was being too soft, strip him of his kapo status, and throw him back among the regular camp inmates. This would mean his near-instant death. I despised him, too. I would have killed him if I had the chance, just because of what he represented. But his newfound friendliness was beneficial to me.

"Seymour. This engine work is hot and difficult. I could do it better if I got some food."

He hit me, but lightly, so the guards could see. He was getting very good at pulling his strikes. To a starving man they still stung, but they could have been worse.

"I'll see what I can do."

What he did was bring a very small ration of bread—if you fed it to birds you would feel stingy—and a sliver of hard sausage. My food for the entire day. I hid my face underneath the hood and ate it in three gulps. Most any other prisoner would kill me just for those scraps. The corpses were piling up outside in the courtyard like firewood and none of them had a spare ounce of flesh.

Seymour brought me the food every day. It was pathetic. In Chicago, I would have starved to death on it, but here I was eating like a king. I did not ask him where he got it and he never told me. It probably came out of the mouth of some other prisoner in the camp, but I would not let that stop me. I needed to eat. That is what the Nazi death machine had done to me in just one week. Some of the prisoners had been in the system for years. If it hadn't killed them—and most of them it had—it turned them into human rats or cockroaches; able to survive in almost any condition. Their eyes were flat and feral, their every move dedicated to gaining just one more minute.

I was not like them. I still had muscles, like I said, and although my head hurt nearly all the time as my body started to eat into itself, I was in better shape than anybody in the camp except the guards. I wanted to keep it that way, so I took my first step to becoming a human rat or cockroach by getting that food ration from Seymour. I had to. It was how things were done.

The bodies kept piling up in the courtyard. There was no place to put them. They rotted like trash and spread disease; typhoid and whatever you could think of. You could almost see it rising off of them, clouds of death rolling toward you across the filthy, muddy ground. Sometimes I wished I could join them, just sprawl there, a skeleton held together by skin, and barely that. But then the cockroach in me reared up and said, *No, you will go on.* So, I went on.

My work was good, despite the constant headache and the ringing in my ears that started to accompany it. The guard sometimes even wandered off while I was wielding large equipment. Not that he necessarily trusted me, he was just coming to the conclusion that I no longer had the strength to get up to much trouble, and he was right. Time was marching on and it was taking me with it, cell by cell. My hair, what was not shaved, was falling out. My teeth were falling out. My muscles were becoming ropes, and not strong ropes. Just connections to hold me together. Barely.

My good work got noticed. The trucks were running well. This meant they were better able to bring more miserable people into the camps. I was helping exterminate my fellow inmates. But that was just the cockroach in me. The better the trucks ran, the more food I got— though it was barely enough to keep a dog alive. I wouldn't even feed it to a dog. But again, my work got noticed.

A new batch of prisoners arrived. They saw the skeletons in the camp but said they were relieved.

"We thought we were going somewhere worse," one Frenchman told me.

"What on Earth could be worse than this?" I asked.

"Dora."

"Who is that?"

"It's a camp. I don't know where it is. It's called Dora. I have heard terrible things about it. No one comes out of there alive. They build machines for Satan there."

"What?"

"That's just what I hear."

He had been in camps for three years and was just a meat-wrapped skeleton. He fit in well with everybody else. It felt like I had lost half my body weight, but I was still the biggest guy in the camp next to the guards, and most of my pale, skinny fellow inmates avoided me if they could summon the energy. Some of them barely saw me, could not have cared less if I was coal black and eight feet tall. Others maybe feared me because I was stronger, or darker, or just different. This Frenchman did not seem to care one way or the other. He was weirdly relieved to be here. I started hearing some muttering; he wasn't the only one who feared Dora. There was talk of trains being rerouted there, full of doomed souls. There was also talk that anyone with a useful skill—bricklaying, welding, electrical work—was heading inevitably to Dora like water going down a drain. Dora was coming for us at Bergen-Belsen, they said.

TWENTY-FOUR

Dora

———

MY SKILL with the truck engines was something I should have kept hidden. A week after the Frenchman first told me of Dora, I found myself lined up in the square with my fellow damned, waiting to be loaded into a train and taken somewhere else. The camp officials did not bother to tell us where we were going, any more than you tell a dog where you're taking it. It didn't matter, we were going to go. There was muttering once we were crammed onto the train: We were lost; we were bound for Dora.

The ride almost made me miss the camp. We were crammed into the cars more tightly than firewood. There was no food and no hope of food, although the guards felt free to stuff their faces in full view of us when the train made stops. There was no water or hope of water. There were no bathroom breaks; but then, hardly anyone needed to pee or shit. There was no need. No raw material moved through our bodies. Our bodies were closed systems, feeding on themselves.

We traveled forever. There were numerous stops so the guards could rest and stretch their legs and eat. We sat motionless, not even shifting around to make our positions more comfortable. There was no point, we were never going to be comfortable again. Finally, one day the train stopped. We expected nothing unusual, but the doors were flung open and sunlight tore through our eyeballs.

"Schnell! Schnell!"

Although we had been immobile for days, with no food, we were expected to jump out of the car like children. Some of us hobbled down slowly. Others never moved again. They had died during the trip. They slumped over as we got out. In some cases, that was the only way we could tell they were dead. I looked back into the car as I got out. The dead lay there, a thin gray layer of paste across the floor of the car. The only difference between them and the dead back at the camp was that these had clothes, which gave them the thinnest scrap of dignity. I envied them. They were done.

They know more about life and death than I do, all of them. They earned that knowledge the hard way.

We were marched down a dusty road and past guarded fences. We were assembled like chess pieces in a large square. Kapos swarmed out of nowhere and smacked us into formation with sticks and sawed-off metal pipes. They wanted us to stand in orderly rows. They killed a few of us with vicious blows. It wouldn't take much to dispatch most of us to the next world. A good shove, a strong wind... A blow from a pipe was overkill.

Behind us was a gate that seemed to lead under the mountains that stretched off into the distance like a rumpled blanket. I didn't get a chance to look carefully. I turned so that I wouldn't catch a blow from a kapo. I didn't think one hit would kill me, but I didn't want to test my theory.

A row of Nazi scum stood lined up before us, well fed and well dressed. The dead from the train had been brought alongside us and were stacked to our right, like the bodies in Bergen-Belsen. The Nazis lined us up for a roll call. They wanted to know that we were all accounted for, the living and the dead. As long as the numbers matched their records, they really didn't care which category described us.

We stood out there for hours. The wind came roaring off the mountains and it was getting cold. The cold took a few more people out. They fell face down and didn't move and were carted off and catalogued with the others. Finally, the Nazis were done with the names and numbers. I didn't know what they wanted us to do next. Die, maybe. A line of zombies shuffled up behind us. They had been working somewhere under the mountains, it seemed.

"All right, move it!" a kapo shouted. "To work!"

"Day shift," one of my fellow prisoners muttered. "We're going to die now."

We marched into the gaping entrance of what was a tunnel cut into the mountain. We looked up in amazement until the kapos nearly cracked a couple of skulls. There were lights stuck high into the rough ceiling. The bulbs did their best to illuminate a series of tunnels that were crammed with rail lines and equipment that looked familiar to me. They looked like engine parts.

"What is this place?" I whispered to the ghost trudging along next to me.

"Hell."

We were led to a sizable flat area where several desks were stuck together. Men in white coats sat behind them with stacks of paper. Their coats were spotless even though the place seemed to ooze dust and grime from every direction.

"We are looking for skills," one of them said in several languages, German and French and Russian, repeating the simple message slowly each time. "We need welders. We need electricians. We need mechanics. We need construction workers."

What were they building here? They didn't give us much time to wonder. With each occupation, someone in our bunch raised his hand. One guy who volunteered to be an electrician had come from a village with no electricity. I knew because he told me when we were both at Bergen-Belsen. He wouldn't know which end of a wire to work with. He would probably end up being electrocuted. I didn't want to weld anything, and I didn't want to work as an electrician if I was going to be with people who didn't know what they were doing.

"Mechanic," I said in French.

"What sort of equipment?" one of the men asked. I could only see the top of his bald head. He was looking down at his ledger and did not look up. He just needed to fill a requirement. He didn't care who filled it.

"Engines."

"Truck engines?"

"Truck engines. Car engines. Airplane engines."

He looked up. I heard a quick intake of breath as he looked into the eyes of a man who was much darker than he expected.

"You are in the mechanical commando," he said, looking back down. "Get to work."

I stood back until we were all assigned, which took a while. The kapos hovered on the edge of the crowd like mosquitos ready to strike, but they didn't hit anybody because work was being assigned. This was nothing like Bergen-Belsen. There, our only job was to starve to death. My skill with engines had put me on the truck crew there, but that was unusual. In Dora, the first thing we did was sign up for work, and complicated work, at that. What were they doing here in this enormous cave?

Once we were all accounted for, the kapos marched us down the tunnels. The construction workers got pulled off right away but the rest of us kept walking. The electricians got pulled off later on, but my mechanical group kept walking. This place was huge, larger than anything I could have imagined. It was as if the entire mountain had been hollowed out, and maybe it had. The dust from this excavation still hung in the air, ever present, and I heard a constant coughing coming from somewhere and everywhere. Humans were not meant to be here. But here we were.

Finally, we reached our location. I sucked in air when I saw where we were, and nearly coughed myself. Towering above us were nightmares that I had not seen since I was a kid reading Buck Rogers comic strips. They were huge, tall as whales standing on their tails. They were rocket ships. The Tiger Men from Mars never had such weapons. We stood and gaped at them until the kapo hit a man on the back, nearly knocking him over, which would have knocked all of us over.

We were herded to a group of guards who stood on the other side of the rail line that must have brought these monsters here. They lined us up and showed us what we would be working on. We were going to help assemble the engines for these rockets. There were carloads full of parts that looked like metal guts pulled from some great beast. This beast had been brought here and disemboweled next to the tracks, and it was our job to take its guts and shove them into one of these sleek cylinders.

"What are these things?" a man next to me mumbled. "What are they going to do with them?"

"They will kill everyone on the planet," another said. "They will destroy all of Europe and America with these godless things."

The kapo hit him on the shoulder and he was quiet, but everyone glanced up at the rocket ships and believed him. These things could only be used to bring about the end of the world. They would kill us all, or we would die trying to make them.

More men in white coats accompanied the guards. It was their job to make these things happen, it seemed, and they were very serious about it. They instructed us, slowly, on what we were to do. The one who spoke to me talked even slower than the others. He seemed to think that I would not understand what he wanted me to do. He wanted me to connect a coolant hose to a valve. It was simple, the kind of thing I could do in my sleep. But if they wanted to think this was complicated work, I'd let them. If this was the worst that happened to me here, then maybe I could survive Dora.

Six hours later, we had one half-hour break, which we used to try to go to the toilets. Huge kapos guarded the door and they were reluctant to let anyone in, particularly a Black man.

"You wait, schwarzer," one of them said, his accent nearly impenetrable. "Wait until all the white men are done with their business."

There was another man with me, a scrawny skeleton who had to be near death. The back of his gray pants were streaked with brown and he smelled like a sewer.

"Let me in, please," he begged in French. "I have the shits."

"I can smell that," one of the kapos said.

The kapo took two steps and cracked the skeleton across the head with a length of pipe. The man crumpled to the side of the hallway and didn't move.

"Fucking shitters," the kapo muttered, and the other agreed. "Did him a favor."

I looked at the dead man, who knows more about life and death than I do, and felt nothing for him. The Nazis were starving the humanity out of me. I had been working for six hours straight, at this point, with no food, and this after a days-long train ride with no food. I just did not care about this man and his life and his death. I just wanted to dribble out what little hot pee there might be inside me and get back to work.

The simple valve attachment turned out to be much more difficult than I expected. I was tired, my head hurt, as it always did, and the German official was demanding in what he wanted. The tolerances for attaching the pipe to the valve were very exacting, he said in halting French. The engine for the rocket was a precision instrument.

If it was so precise, I wondered, why were they forcing half-dead men to do the work?

We worked for six more hours and were finished for the day. I was not doing anything very taxing, but I was permanently exhausted, and they did not feed us the first day. My stomach was busy eating my midsection. It was hard to focus and the kapo hit me in the spine at one point because I was too slow. My hands were shaking, and it was hard to do any kind of precision work. They did not care. When I died there would be other hands to take the load.

We staggered out of the cave and back into the sunlight. They did not give us time to let our eyes adjust, just marched us out into the sun. It was an overcast day and the light was weak, but the sunlight still blasted through my eyes and made my head, already constantly hurting, explode with pain. Still, I trudged out with the others and we stood for what seemed like forever for roll call. There were more bodies lined up nearby, workers who had worked their last. They were lined up in neat rows, one with his arm flung up away from his body, as if raising his hand to be counted.

Finally, they were satisfied that the living and the dead had been tallied and they let us go. The kapos herded us like sheep to the barracks, a squat building to the right of the roll call square. As we walked there, we passed another, smaller building, with a few women hanging out of the windows, blowing smoke from long cigarettes into the sky. They looked at us with disinterested eyes, as if we were dogs walking by.

"Who is that?" I whispered to a fellow inmate, quietly so a kapo would not hear and strike. He was a man who had been here a while.

"Whores," he muttered. "For the officers. Not for us."

He did not need to tell me that. There was nothing for us here but work and death, one probably leading to the other. We would help our enemy build machines to destroy us and die in the effort. It was the most vile situation I could imagine but I was in it and there was nothing I could do about it. All my years of working to fly, all my training in the Army, had led me to this. I was in the same place as some illiterate peasant from Russia who had never seen electricity. In the eyes of the Nazis, we were equal: useful tools, for a while. It did not seem fair.

TWENTY-FIVE

The Good Life

WE PILED into the barracks to sleep until the next twelve hours of work. There was no point in building enough barracks to house everybody. The Nazis just needed to build enough to hold one shift of workers, so that's what they did. We were collapsing onto the warm straw that the next shift had just vacated, as well as their lice and crabs and anything else they left behind. I found a place that seemed tolerable. No doubt, the person I would share it with would not want to share his bug-ridden straw with a Race man, but that was too bad for him. In all likelihood, he would be too exhausted to care.

"Put your shoes under your mattress," the man below me said. "Or someone will steal them. And you won't get any more, and your feet will rot and you will die."

"Thank you," I said.

There was not a lot of altruism in the camps, I had noticed. You tried to stay alive and that occupied most of your time. If you could help someone, you would, but most of the time everyone was just too tired, too ready to slip over into the next world.

"The guy that is usually there in your bed is dead," the man said. "I never liked him."

"Okay."

"You got it lucky," he said.

This was an unusual enough statement that I rolled over and looked down at him to see how crazy he might appear. He seemed to be no crazier than anyone else around here. He was thin, of course, just a skin-draped skeleton. He was, in fact, thinner than most. His wasted muscles were like strings under the skin, moving his puppet parts around. His eyes were like marbles, but he didn't seem off his rocker.

"How do you figure that I am lucky?"

"Oh, this is the easy life," he said and coughed out a laugh. "You should have been here last year. All those fancy tunnels there weren't built. We built them. We lived and breathed all the dust and dirt and shit from that mountain. We slept in the tunnels, not in first-class accommodations like this. You could never sleep, there was noise constantly. We had to shit in buckets. They just cut them in half and put a piece of wood across them and that was our shitter. Very fancy. Everybody got sick and everybody died."

"You don't seem to be dead."

"Oh, I'm dead. I'm dead, I just don't know it yet. We're all dead. You're dead. We're just two dead men lying here talking."

I fell asleep like I was dead. I seemed to remember having a scrap of a dream, and I was trying to hang onto it when the barracks commando woke us. It was time to go back to work. First, we stood in the square for roll call and then we trundled back into the mine.

I was very tired, and my head continued to hurt, but I couldn't do anything about it. The idea of asking a kapo or one of the guards for an aspirin was laughable and would only get me a clubbing that would make me feel worse. We had to move quickly, too, no matter how tired we were, or a clubbing would result. I saw at least seven men die from clubbings from the kapo as we walked down that hall day after day. Clubbings for nothing. Our kapo was named Georg. He was short but powerful, with arms sculpted from muscle and veins. He looked like a caveman so it was suitable for him to live in a cave. He even carried a pipe with so much rubber tape on the end that it looked like a club. Sometimes kapos fell out of favor with the Nazis and got thrown back into the regular camp population. I had never seen this myself, but I had heard about it. They were usually torn to pieces almost immediately; they almost never survived the night. I wished this would happen to Georg. He would be tough in a fight. It would take a lot of us to put him down, but it would be worth it.

"Your work is too good," a Frenchman named Zeller whispered to me once we had gotten in our places and gotten started for the shift. "You are too precise."

He was almost as short as Georg, but, of course, nowhere near as strong.

"I don't know how else to do it."

This was easier work than before; we were fitting inlet pipes together and soldering them. Our crew was smaller than it had been when we started. One of the Polish prisoners claimed to be a master solderer but he had never seen a soldering iron before. He ended up burning a hole in his arm and filling it with metal. He screamed until one of the SS men came along and beat him to death.

"If you do it too well, these things will work," he said, nodding his head down the hall toward where the monstrous rockets loomed. "You don't want them to work, do you?"

I didn't even know what they were supposed to do if they worked, but no, whatever it was, I did not want them to work.

"You can cheat," he said. "Make your work look good. But don't make it good."

He showed me the soldering he was doing. He made the solder as thin as he could so when the engine came under stress, the pipes would give way. It was tricky work.

"What if they catch you?"

"They'll kill me. They'll hang me. You'll see. But if I don't do it, they'll kill people with these things. My people, maybe. Your people, maybe. I'd rather they kill me."

I would rather they kill me, too. But I had a hard time embarking on my life of sabotage. I had spent my life learning how to do things well, particularly how to make mechanical things hum. It was easier to do that for me than to purposely do shoddy work, especially shoddy work that had to look like it was perfect. It took me a long time to even figure out how to go about it. I started by mimicking Zeller and using as little solder as I could get away with, but the Nazis kept shifting us around to do different kinds of work. Just when I would learn how to be falsely proficient in one area, they'd have me doing something else. It was hard to find the time to learn how to do things badly. But I was motivated. Those horrible shapes were coming along, and I did not want them to work. I did not want them to work, at all.

I started trying to get some tips by asking people how they conducted sabotage, but the man in the lower bunk told me to shut up.

"Nobody wants a schwarzer coming around asking about something that will get them killed. Sabotage doesn't happen here. Never. Our work is only of the best quality. And if you don't think you're the first person in the camp that everyone would like to see hung if they got the chance, you're not paying attention in this world, my friend. You look around this place. There are packs of Russians and Poles and French and Gypsies and whatever but there's no pack of Haitians. You are Haitian, is that right?"

"Actually, I'm American. I am a fighter aircraft pilot. I was shot down."

He gave a rustling sound I took for a laugh.

"Americans don't let schwarzers fly airplanes. If you were a pilot, you'd be in a POW camp, which would be even more luxurious than this place."

That thought had occurred to me many times as I stood in the square for roll call, and as I staggered, starving and exhausted, into the cave every day to help put those hellish machines together. But I figured that if I was in a POW camp, I would just be waiting out the war. Here, I could teach myself sabotage and do my part to throw a monkey wrench into the Nazi war machine. If it didn't kill me first.

TWENTY-SIX

Virginia and Life and Death

I THOUGHT about Virginia all the time. Even when I was trying to figure out how to sabotage something. She became a vast waking dream for me, a dream where she had been integrated in my life all along. When I moved from Alabama to Chicago, she moved with me. When we laughed in the kitchenette while Mother cooked dinner, tired after work, Virginia leaned on the counter and laughed along with us. When I went to school in Chicago, she studied with me. When I went into the air to learn to fly, she was there on my wing.

Most of us were like that. We were dead and we knew it, but hope was a brushfire in our hearts that the Nazis could not extinguish and we could not put out ourselves, however much we would like to, so that we could go peacefully to the grave. The men in the barracks moaned the names of their loved ones in their sleep, which sometimes meant calling for their mothers. I probably moaned Virginia's name; nobody told me if I did. I thought of her while I stood shivering during roll call, watching men die out of the corners of my eyes, falling over to be counted one last time. I thought of her while I ate my watery soup and tiny piece of bread, hunching over them to keep my ravenous fellow inmates from stealing whatever they could. I thought about her when I stood before the shop table and worked on these unimaginable machines of death.

I started trying to carve her name in the hellish cave that now seemed like home. I had a tiny bit of sharpened metal that came off a rocket fin and I carried it with me everywhere. It was small and I could hide it in my palm. I don't know what I intended to do with it—it was far too small to hurt anybody, and anyway, I no longer had the strength to try—but it made me feel better. And I could use it to carve Virginia's name. That would make this place more tolerable, give me something to remind me that there was a world outside. I wished I still had her letters to me, but those were long gone, eaten up by the Nazi machine like so many other things.

I started to carve her name into the wooden frame of my bunk. The wood was soft and half rotten and I could probably have done it with my fingernail, but I thought I would use my "weapon." That was until the man below me urged me to stop.

"It will take nothing for some of these fellows to turn you in to the kapo," he said softly when he saw what I was doing. "The kapo might do nothing or he might kill you. Only you know if this is worth it to you, but my advice would be to carve her name on your heart and leave it off your bed."

I decided to follow his advice on the bed, but I was determined to carve it in the underground factory. I kept my little piece of metal with me and got to work. Doing anything except trying to stay alive during roll call was foolish, and I rarely had time to try to carve anything on the walk down the tunnels. The kapo and the SS would have beaten me senseless for dawdling. So, I carved it when I ate, in tiny letters, on the wall where I leaned and on the small wooden bench where I sometimes sat. While I shoved the miserable food in with one hand I carved "Virginia" with the other. I never had a chance to look at my handwriting. I did not think that carving a name would count as sabotage, but you never knew with the Nazis. They considered everything to be their property, including the rocks inside this wretched mountain.

One day, I tried carving her name under the lab table where we worked. The civilian engineer in charge of our work, a bald, stubby man named Klaus, was busy supervising some of the other prisoners. I was connecting switches again, which required me to move my hands around a lot into various parts bins. I thought this would also give me the chance to do some carving. But I wasn't paying enough attention to my surroundings. I was working on the "G" under the table when a blinding pain shot through the back of my head. The next view I had was of an SS man leaning over me.

"What were you doing with this?" he shouted, holding my little bit of metal. "Are you trying to destroy our rockets? Are you a saboteur?"

He was not really asking in a way that would let me answer. His mind was made up. I was going to hang. He hauled me to my feet and waved my little metal piece in front of my eyes. It just did not look very threatening no matter what he did with it.

"What were you going to do with this?" he shouted. "Stab someone? Put it in a rocket engine so that it would explode?"

There was no way I could get that piece of metal in a rocket engine so that it would explode, but, of course, he did not know that. He was clearly not a rocket scientist. He was a dumb sadist and the creation of the Nazi state had given him the perfect world in which to thrive.

I had seen a couple of hangings by this time. They were carried out on the roll call square, and the people hung were announced to be conducting sabotage against the mighty V-2 rockets with which Adolf Hitler would win the war. That's what they called them, the V-2, the Vengeance weapon of the Third Reich. The only ones feeling the vengeance were us. The first ones I saw hung were a group of Poles. One man struggled and cried and had to be dragged to the noose; the other two waited patiently for him and went to their deaths without batting an eye. The second group were Russians, who obviously had once been huge burly men. One of them was rumored to have killed a kapo with his bare hands and everyone, from the SS men on down, and even the whores in the windows, looked on him with respect. They were dispatched with even less drama than the two laconic Poles. They were ready to leave, ready to let the Germans have their nasty little planet if they wanted it that badly.

So, now life was going to end for me. I wondered how I would go;

like that one terrified Pole, or like the others, who were already dead before they ascended to the gallows. The SS man continued to glare at me as if he was personally offended by my transgression. He was taking his job seriously, which I could have admired if he had a more admirable job.

My fellow inmates looked on without much curiosity or concern. There was nothing to do. There was no point in speaking up for me and they were all too tired to care. I figured they would hang me in the square the following morning. I would not be fed tonight and would work another twelve-hour shift. I was already a dead man, there was no point in feeding me or letting me rest.

"I do not think he was committing sabotage," a voice said.

We all looked around, surprised. It was Klaus. His voice was without inflection or fear; he was just stating what he saw as a flat fact.

"And why not?" the SS man asked.

Klaus adjusted his wire glasses on his owlish face.

"There is no place he could put such a piece of metal that would go undetected. We have been having trouble with parts coming from bad dies. There are lots of excess pieces of metal. I have asked him to remove the bits and give them to me. He has been doing this. He was going to give this piece to me, but I told him to keep it for a few minutes because I needed to go down the hall to look at the tracks. We have been having trouble with them and some cars of parts have derailed."

"So...you take responsibility for this?" the SS man asked. He did not seem to want to let it go. This incident would have to be reported somewhere and he wanted to make sure it wasn't his Nazi ass on the line in case I turned out to be a saboteur supreme.

"I take responsibility," Klaus said. "There will be no sabotage here."

The SS man gave me a long look, full of portent. *I'll be watching you*, it said. *I'll get you when this egghead is not around to protect you.* I could only hope that he would become fixated on one of the countless other prisoners around and forget about me. But since I was the only Race man in the entire camp, I had to figure that he wouldn't.

He released me and walked away. Klaus gave me a cold look and held out his hand. I picked up my little piece of metal where the SS goon had dropped it and put it in his hand. He folded his thin fingers around it and dropped it in the pocket of his coat.

"You weren't really going to sabotage my rocket, were you?" he asked.

"No."

"Good. I didn't think so. And no need to thank me. You're the best worker I have. You're the most technically sophisticated worker here, probably. Keep up the good work and you will keep up your usefulness. Let it flag and the next time our SS friend takes an interest in you, I won't say anything."

I didn't feel the need to thank Klaus. He may have saved my life, but he did it for the reasons he just said. He wasn't any more interested in me than he was the bit of metal in his pocket. As long as I was a good widget in the Nazi machine, I would be all right. The minute I gave him any real trouble, I would be hanging from a rope in the square, just another lynched Race man. Of course, if I had a chance, and the energy, I'd kill him and the SS man, too.

I abandoned my quest to carve Virginia's name under the table and renewed my efforts to find a way to sabotage these rockets for real. If I was going to swing, I wanted to swing for something I actually did. It was not until weeks later that I had my chance. We were building fins for the rockets, fins that would guide them to wherever they were going to go. I pretended that they were going to destroy my beautiful city of Chicago, or my adopted town of Tuskegee. I did not want these rockets to kill my parents or the love of my life, so I worked harder than ever before to make sure they didn't work.

Some of the equipment and materials we were getting in were not very good. Having a workforce made up of slaves will do that. I was trying to weld some sheet metal to the fin and noticed a hole in it, not quite big enough for me to stick my fist through, but big enough. A hole like that wouldn't bother an airplane much but I figured these things had to be much faster than airplanes, so it might cause a rocket some trouble if it should suddenly open up in flight. I should weld some metal over it, but I didn't want to. I wanted to do shoddy work.

I remembered all those afternoons spent watching my father work on his signs. I remembered that one, in particular, where he took wood and made it look like old metal. I had never done it myself, but I wondered if I could. If I could fill this hole and make it look like metal, then maybe when this rocket took off it would go out of control and crash down on Hitler himself. The trick was matching the metal. The rockets went elsewhere in the factory to be painted, and I didn't have access to that. Whatever I did would have to take the paint without falling through. I needed to make the hole look like metal without any paint.

The man who worked next to me was named Jean. At least, he said his name was Jean. About half of the Frenchmen in the camp used the name, seizing whatever anonymity they could to try to stay alive. My name was Jean, too, because that was how they pronounced John. I thought it was ironic, but not amusing, that I now bore the name of the very man who betrayed me so that I ended up here. Being Jean did not make me any more anonymous, as nothing would do that, but my "colleagues" would not believe that my real name was John and I was an American fighter pilot. I told a few of my fellow inmates, but they just laughed. Who would ever think of such a thing?

This particular Jean was already adept at making his solder as thin as possible. It was silvery and I thought it might work. I began studying how he used it, without being too obvious. He had little water to spare and needed to drink what he got, but he was able to dilute the solder by using a tiny bit of his soup, which was thin enough to be a close cousin to water. Then he could apply the weakened solder. He was starving himself to commit sabotage. I admired that.

I was loath to give up even a drop of my soup, as my fat and muscles were dropping off me at an alarming rate, but I didn't have anything else to work with. They barely gave us water and it could be dry and choking in the tunnels, so I needed every molecule of water. I needed every molecule of soup, too, but if Jean could do it, I could do it.

It took me a long time to get comfortable with my plan. That first fin was taken away and replaced before I could do anything with it. It was not like I could practice anywhere. The SS man watched me, the kapos watched me, Klaus watched me, and even the other prisoners watched me. They would turn me over to the SS in exchange for the tiny drops of soup I wasted. I could not walk around with solder on my fingers, either, so I squirreled away a tiny drop inside my shirt and then wiped my fingers off. Solder might not be so obvious on Jean's hand, but it would be on mine, and even though I could explain it away, I didn't want to take the chance.

Sometimes the stuff rubbed off or flaked off either during work or during roll call. Sometimes it managed to stick around, so I would have a tiny ball of it to practice on in the bunker, for the few minutes I could keep my eyes open after work. I carried my bowl with my tiny drop of soup and spread out a paste on the sideboard of my bed, in a small gap between the wood and the wall where the other man who slept here couldn't see it.

After a while I got pretty good. The work began to occupy my thoughts constantly, aside from occasional flashes of Virginia and the ever-present quest to stay alive.

It took a long time for another fin to come through that had a similar hole. The quality was going up. No doubt, the Nazis somewhere were killing people to make sure it did. But you can't build complicated, futuristic things with tortured people, so I was patient and another hole appeared before me. I was almost surprised to see it. It seemed like I had been preparing so long that what I was preparing for wasn't going to happen, but there it was. I ran my finger around the hole, testing the edges. They were a little rough and would grip the solder/paint well, I thought. I had some mixed up. I always had some ready now. I had gotten skilled at mixing it up on the sly and keeping it moist. My constant headache probably could have been soothed a little bit if I had put some of that watery soup down my throat, but I wanted to do whatever I could to fuck up these perfect Nazi murder weapons.

And here was my chance. Klaus was occupied on the other end of the table, and the SS man was down the hall, bothering someone else. Neither of them had seen the fin. It had arrived in a stack of equipment and Jean had handed it to me without comment. I think he knew what I was up to, but I had never asked, and he had never said anything. It was always best not to know.

As it happened, I had a good supply of my gunk on hand this day. I thought this was a sign that God approved of what I was doing. Maybe Virginia's father was praying for me and his prayers were paying off. I wasn't praying for myself, but it was nice to think that someone was. I got the fin halfway attached so that it hung down where I could get at the spot without being seen right away. Before I could put my goop on there, I had to fill the hole with something, because I couldn't "paint" on air. I had a small bit of wood that had fallen off one of the crates that were always rumbling by on the railroad tracks before descending even farther into this hell. A nice slice of metal would have been better, but after my last incident with a piece of scrap metal, I didn't want to try it. It wasn't worth the swinging it could get me.

I stuffed the piece of wood under the hole from the other side, using a tiny bit of solder to hold it in place. It wouldn't take a rocket launch to dislodge the wood. A well-placed finger could poke right through it. But the patch would certainly fail and that was the point. Now I just had to make the wood look like part of the fin. I thought of my father. I would not wish for him to be in this hellhole, but I could certainly use his skills. I thought of him in the window, smiling faintly as he turned wood into metal, or aged it 200 years, or made it do anything he wanted it to do. I hoped that the memory of those days had burned into my fingers and they would remember what to do.

I began by gently smearing the surface of the wood with my sad little paint. I moved it gently because the wood was barely hanging on there as it was, and the merest spike of pressure would send it clattering to the floor. If the SS man or Klaus heard, that sound could send me chattering to the noose. The solder seemed to be drying okay. The fin now looked whole, although it had a bright shiny spot that looked like a patch. Klaus would spot it instantly. He would probably blame the poor quality control, until he put his finger through my work and discovered what I had done.

Now I had the real task in front of me. This is where I hoped my father's spirit would come through the most. I needed to make the fake metal look like real metal, and fast. I had practiced this in my bunk, using grease as my second type of paint. There was no shortage of grease in the tunnels. I had squirreled some away just in case the Nazis got on a sudden cleaning jag. It was a small ball that I had stuck to one of my table legs. I reached down; it was a little dry, but it was still there. I got some of it on my finger and smeared it around. I wished it was wetter, but it would have to do. I could try to spit in it but that could bring unwanted attention, and I probably didn't have enough liquid in my entire body to make a good spit.

I smeared the grease across the solder, gently, gently. One false push and this would all be over. My hands shook most of the time as my body continued to eat itself from lack of food, but at this critical point, they were as straight and solid as a surgeon's. When I was done, and after a couple of small finishing touches, the open gap looked like just another part of the metal, which was a little lumpy to begin with. It wouldn't fool anyone on a really close inspection, but the light was variable in the tunnels and I was hoping it would, at least, get far enough along that they wouldn't be able to tell who had done it even if they found it. I bolted the bottom part together and it looked like a normal fin.

It seemed to work. I didn't hear anything else about it. But the next morning, in the square, as the wind threatened to suck the breath out of our lungs, it was announced that there had been sabotage and that the perpetrator would be shown to us as an example.

A cold bolt of fear shot up my spine. If I had any waste in my body, I would have shit myself right there. But as it was, my body just trembled. I waited for them to come and toss a noose around my neck, but I was just another gray column in the line and nobody was paying any attention to me.

Movement was visible on the far edge of the field and a shambling form was dragged up to the gallows. It seemed like a small, familiar form, accompanied on either side by larger prisoners. I felt my heart tighten in my chest. It was Jean, my tablemate, who knew I had been up to something as much as he had. The commandant made a piercing, sharp speech about how sabotage would not be tolerated. Jean was placed in the middle. The other two were probably just being hung to fill out the number of nooses. The Nazis were efficient that way. No point in wasting two perfectly good nooses just to get rid of one little sabotaging Frenchman. The other two men were obviously terrified, but Jean had no expression, at all. In some ways, he was a good, efficient engineer, as cold and calculating as the Nazi bastards that ran this hell. He had taken a risk and expected this outcome. Now that it had happened, he was ready.

I was far back but I imagined his eyes swept the crowd and found me and gave me some kind of signal. I don't think he actually did, or that he could have even seen me if he did. I was the only Race man, but color was fading from all of us now, we were the same ashen gray. From his view on the scaffold, we probably just looked like rows of dead, bent trees.

He knew I was up to something and he could have ratted on me, although I don't know that it would have gained him anything—maybe a few more hours of life, at most, maybe one more piece of moldy bread before he died. But men have given up much more for much less, and under these miserable circumstances I would not have blamed him if he fingered me just to gain another half hour, but he didn't, or I would have been up there with him. They would have loved to hang me, a Race man and a saboteur, and, they thought, a low Haitian. But Jean didn't and he went to his unmarked grave with a shrug. He swung in the noose and his legs kicked but that was an automatic reaction; his eyes showed that he was dead before the hangman kicked the stool out from under him.

TWENTY-SEVEN

White Coats

ONE DAY we had special visitors. We never had special visitors. I should say that the camp, the factory, had the visitors, because nobody seemed to see us lowly laborers. The clerical workers who high-heeled their way into the offices underground seemed not to notice the rag-clad skeletons that staggered around them, sometimes fell dead right in front of them. Just another day at the office. There were civilian scientists in charge of some of the operations, including my own "boss," Klaus. They knew intimately what was going on in the factory, but they had their own jobs to do, so it did not seem to bother them too much. They were probably irritated when one of us died and was unable to work.

On this day, we were called into one of the main halls. A line of white-coated civilian engineers, more than I had seen in one place, lined the walls. I didn't know if they were the regular ones who worked in other parts of the factory or a new bunch coming in for an inspection. The camp commandant was talking to another man who I also had not seen, obviously talking up to him. Being in the military makes it easier to sniff out bigwigs, people to whom attention must be paid, and this visitor was obviously a bigwig. He was tall and dressed in the black of an SS man. His black hair capped off the Nazi SS look. He seemed larger than life, full of more energy than all of us camp skeletons combined.

The commandant was explaining something to him about the workings of the plant, I figured. The man nodded and looked around, craning his neck to see the distant ceiling. He had a huge, jutting chin, which added to the impression of his size. He was an important man who looked important.

He didn't look angry, but apparently things weren't going well. Our miserable work was making itself felt on the production line because it seemed the V-2s weren't working as advertised. We still did not know exactly what they planned to do with them. Rumor was that they were trying to destroy London, but it wasn't going exactly as planned, and nothing makes a German madder than failure.

On this day, a show had been planned for the engineers and everybody. They intended an unmistakable demonstration of what happened to anyone who tried to throw monkey wrenches into the proud Nazi war machine. The enormous crane used to lift the rockets upright was going to be used to launch a dozen human beings into the next world. There apparently had been an underground resistance—literally underground—headed mainly by the French prisoners. I was nominally one of them; at least, I was considered one of them due to my fictitious Haitian ancestry, but I knew nothing of the movement. I wish I had known, I would have helped if they'd let me. But then I would have been with them and I didn't want to be with them on this day.

They were led to the gallows and small blocks of wood were placed roughly in their mouths. This was a new and unusual place to hang and the prisoners were scared even beyond the fact that they were going to die in full view of almost everyone in the camp. Work had been called to a halt and everyone, except maybe the secretaries, who probably had delicate constitutions, were made to watch. The crane that was capable of lifting so much metal did not struggle at all with the bodies of a dozen human beings who weighed next to nothing. The men were pulled into the air, twitching and snorting, their hands tied behind their backs. Even if they had tried to die with dignity it would not have been possible. Their bodies fought for life. Their legs flailed, trying to find support. They kicked and whirled but there was nothing there but fetid air. When they died, what remained in their bowels and bladders was released, a pitiful little storm of yellow and brown rain.

The engineers stood across the opening from me, but I could see them well. They looked very uncomfortable. They were probably family men in some other world, who studied at a university so they could work on advanced technology. But then their world was taken over by a monster and they found themselves in a cave watching the tools of their labor used to kill men in an ancient and barbaric way. Maybe they did not care. Maybe, like I suspected Klaus did, they just believed this was the price of doing their work. Maybe they believed in the monster and had helped it come to power. Maybe they were cowards and cried themselves to sleep at night. I didn't know, but I doubted that last one was true. I looked for the big man in the black coat, but he was gone. Probably some high-level official who didn't want his eyes sullied with the strange fruits of his labor.

We went back to work after the hanging. The crane was lowered, and it was someone's job to take the bodies off and carry them to the incinerator, which was attached to the infirmary, which should tell you how effective the infirmary was. Disposing of bodies was not something that would be done by the civilians or the kapos, and certainly not by the SS. The prisoners would remove their own. We were a perfect self-cleaning machine.

I finished my shift that day and was now thinking about my fellow prisoners like the SS wanted us to: We were all parts in a vast machine and if any part failed the other parts needed to get rid of it. I did not think the Frenchmen heroic for their sabotage, if they had actually committed any. I was able to completely separate their actions and mine. Mine did not seem heroic, either, just necessary. Their actions probably seemed necessary, as well, but they fucked up and got caught and now I would have to work a longer shift because time spent watching the men hang would not be deducted from my schedule.

I did think about Jean from time to time. His place was not vacant. A blank-faced Polish man worked there now who had obviously never seen much of the equipment on which he was supposed to be an expert. He was getting more behind by the minute and Klaus was beginning to glare at him. I hoped that when I died, I could go with as much dignity as Jean. Before I landed in this place, I had hoped to die in an airplane. I wanted to go at the end of some glorious dogfight. I hardly thought about planes now. They seemed to be part of someone else's life. I worked in the shadow of a weapon infinitely more deadly and now just dreamed of departing life with the same dignity as Jean, a French peasant to whom I had barely said two dozen words.

I did not know quite what to make of Klaus. I eyed him like a diver eyes a shark. He might not want to attack me, might not really be interested in me, but if he did want to bite, he could be fatal. Klaus was suspicious of me. He was actually suspicious of everyone. I did not think he had turned Jean in, though, because he seemed to be lenient with people he thought were good workers. But he was eyeing the Polish worker with obvious and increasing anger. I don't know why the guy volunteered to work with us. He should have worked in the infirmary, or guarded the shithouse, or something he could do. But more and more of the good jobs were in the skilled areas and maybe he was so ignorant of what that meant that he thought he could pass. Now he was in trouble and he knew it. Klaus had already yelled at him three times and the shift was barely under way. Klaus scrutinized everything the man did and the SS goon, maybe smelling blood, was starting to circle.

I think Klaus had a conscience of sorts. He was probably just a scientist who did not want to be here, but there was a limit to his patience. He let the Polish guy work most of the shift, making mistake after mistake. The man tried to ask questions of the other workers, but Klaus discouraged this, and all such talking stopped when the SS man came around. He was the hawk and we were the mice and we got quiet and tried our best to hide when he came by. The reason I say Klaus had a conscience of sorts was that it took him most of the shift before he told the SS man that the Polish worker was unsuitable for the task. The Pole was already pale but got paler when the SS goon hit him on the back of the head and hauled him away. It is possible that he was beaten and then reassigned to something more suitable. They didn't hang him because I would have seen that. I don't know what happened to him, but I never saw him again. I think it is safe to assume that he now knows more about life and death than I do.

I didn't think any more about the events of that day, not for a long time. I would never see those men again. I had no knowledge of their lives or their beliefs. Klaus was not having much more fun down here than we were, although he left to go home to his family every night while we slept in the sweat and stink of the men who worked the other shift. While we trembled and shivered during roll call, he ate breakfast with his family, probably tousled his children's hair. While we watched fellow inmates twitch and die on the square before us, or on the crane underground, he probably looked out a window at birds chirping in the trees. If this place even had trees. I pictured this whole area as gray and dead, just like our underground coffin, but the town outside was probably green and pretty.

Klaus had to leave all that and come down here every day with us and make sure we didn't mess anything up or he would have to have us killed, or maybe he would get killed himself. He had to hug his kids and kiss his wife and come down here with us. I am sure his wife and children smelled a lot better than any of us did, including the SS thugs. Klaus pinched the top of his nose hard between his thumb and forefinger every day when he left work. He probably got home with a splitting headache and had to numb himself to sleep with alcohol or pills just to make it back the next day.

I wonder if he thought his job was worth it.

TWENTY-EIGHT

The Awful Effects of Hope

Something terrible started to happen a few weeks after that. Hope crept into the camp, on clomping, staggering feet. New workers began to appear, trainloads of them, who were far more incompetent than the worst worker in Dora. The whispers explained: The camps east of us were being liberated. Germany was losing the war. If we could just survive, there might be hope.

Survival was a false oasis, a mirage. Production of the V-2 was not slowing; it was picking up. Apparently, Germany was losing the war on the ground but taking the fight to the air. So, hope was rising, however faintly, but it was hard to hope when the work never let up. With the new workers, everyone became edgy. There were plenty of replacements for those who made mistakes, and our little courtyard ritual of hangings continued without a break. But the Nazis looked a little nervous. This only made them more dangerous, like cornered animals. The kapos were really nervous. They could tell that everyone was eyeing them, studying them. If the iron hand of the SS ever lifted, the kapos would die in a horrible way. We would set on them like rabid dogs and they knew it. They had made their bargain and did not want to suffer the consequences.

So, hope arrived, but like the stink of the plant and the stink of our sweat, it just became another thing in the air. The work never stopped, never slowed. Complaints about the quality of the rockets had filtered down to my worktable. The parts that were coming in were better than they had been, so it was hard for me to do the painting trick that I had perfected. I could not punch holes where there were none, so I often found myself doing good work and sending it on. The welds were better, too, after everyone had seen Jean swinging on a rope. The man next to me now was Russian, an economy-sized Russian, only slightly larger than Klaus. If anything, he used too much solder, bulking up the seams like he was building a brick wall. Klaus bugged him about this but didn't yell at him, because he was at least building strong fins. Even if the V-2s blew up at launch, those fins would survive.

Given the rumors wafting around the camp, I watched Klaus's face for signs of worry, but if anything, he looked happier. He was sending through good material and whatever shit was rolling downhill wasn't quite reaching his head. I didn't look at the SS man. He was a deranged, wounded bear and he would be even more likely to kill me now if he had the chance. He was breaking heads wherever he went and was not worried about whether he knocked off a worker with experience or one of the bumbling newcomers.

I began to hear more talk of some kind of insurrection. This seemed unlikely, as no muscles had been imported into the camp. Even the new arrivals were scrawny and miserable because they came from other camps. The insurrection gossip soon splintered into a series of nationalistic fantasies. The Russians had a plan, which involved them leading the charge. The French burned to get revenge, to show that the defeat of their country was a fluke. The Poles had a plan that had them in charge, as did the few gypsies, but they never told anyone else what they had in mind and no one believed them. No one told me their plans directly, either, not even the Frenchmen. No one wanted me in on their plot because they were convinced I would either ruin it or draw too much attention to it. No one ever told me that, either, it was just my own conclusion.

I looked at the Russian next to me, ladling on the solder where Jean had used it so sparingly it cost him his life. He occasionally looked back at me, but his dead blue eyes betrayed no sign of a secret. If there was a Russian plot afoot, he was not part of it, or he was a good actor. When he looked at Klaus, there was also no spark of hatred or disgust there. Even when he beheld the SS monster that kept us in line, his eyes were placid, the sleepy orbs of a man watching the ocean on a dull day. He was either mildly retarded or cool as a snake.

Weeks went by and there was no revolt by anyone, least of all the gypsies. The monstrous V-2s were assembled on schedule, and they were getting better and better, helped along by Ivan's superior welding and by my inability to find enough weaknesses to exploit. Excitement in the camp perked up again, though, when we could actually hear explosions in the distance. According to the latest arrivals to the camp, Germany was getting its ass kicked everywhere, especially by the Russians, which made the ones in the camp stand taller. The Germans paid no attention. Roll call went on as usual, with the usual corpses left over afterward. We could hardly keep from smiling. Even the whores seemed restless now, maybe wishing they were plying their trade somewhere else. They twittered to one another like birds until an SS man would yell at them to shut up. Our time of liberation had to be at hand. Even the usual gray sky looked more inviting when we stood under it at roll call.

And yet no liberation came. More weeks went by. I think they were weeks; I had lost all track of time. I had been here so much longer than I ever expected, and I had been too busy with my various projects— carving Virginia's name, learning my subtle sabotage—to come up with a good system of keeping track of the days. At any rate, our liberation was taking longer than any of us wanted. Men fell dead waiting, happy enough just to know that the goddamned Germans were going to get theirs anytime now. We watched the gates at roll call, waiting for U.S. Army tanks to burst through, or Russian army tanks, or anybody.

And then, one day after the explosions had gotten closer and closer, making our hearts skip from the concussions, the bastards began to move us. The plant was closing. Klaus was gone. The engineers had vanished. The whores were gone, too. The nightmare factory was shutting down but most of us couldn't enjoy it because they were shipping the prisoners to other camps before this one could be liberated. The skeletons were being piled back on the death trains to other camps where they could continue their living death or maybe meet their real one.

I say most of us couldn't enjoy it: I didn't get on a train to another camp because I got sick. This wasn't a reprieve. I got the shits, finally, like so many had, and they didn't expect me to live. You have to understand how terribly sick I was. The Nazis were more than happy to move half-dead men onto trains where those men would probably die. The only way they would not move you is if you were so far gone, they thought you would be dead before the guards got their first smoking break.

I don't know why I got sick. I had been feeling the same before that: Tired, with a constant headache and little energy, the way I had been feeling for months, years, decades, centuries on end. I think maybe the sudden infusion of hope is what nearly did me in. It was like water flowing into cracks in concrete and then freezing, tearing the concrete apart. The hope flowed into my mind and cracked me open. All my secret hopes and fears came back to life. My body thought the war was over. All the tension faded away and I collapsed. The stress was the structure that had been holding me up.

I got the shits. I don't know exactly what they were, but they were nasty. I was barely eating anything, but what little I ate was going right through me and coming out as a brown goop on the other end. My dirty, stained, holey pants were ruined. They stunk of this vile shit and there was nothing I could do about it because I wasn't going to get any new pants. I would like to say that I hadn't sunk low enough to steal pants off a corpse, but I didn't do it only because the pants on the corpses were as nasty as mine.

It was odd seeing everyone packing up. The Nazis pushed us out of the tunnels. I think they blew up some of them. Our work in Satan's factory was done. My "colleagues" were packed on a bus. The SS pushed me and my newly sick colleagues into the infirmary where we were to die. There were no medicines left—there had hardly been any at all— and they didn't expect us to be alive to greet anyone who might liberate us. Because I felt like I had been hollowed out with a metal pipe, I figured they were probably right.

The thought of liberation was now nothing I could celebrate. I didn't know anyone who had gotten this intestinal bug and survived. The prisoners with the shits were despised and kept away from the toilets in a pitiful attempt to keep the disease from spreading. That's ironic, I guess. The ones who needed the toilets most were the ones denied.

I crawled into a pile with the other corpses and waited to die. Virginia, the Army Air Corps, Mother and Father in Chicago; they were all gone for me now. My life, my dreams, my plans, were all gone. For the first time, I realized for sure that I was going to die. I was not going to survive the great and terrible adventure that was this war. I would be one in a nameless pile of corpses that would be forgotten before the war was hardly over. This pile of pre-corpses I was in was only a start. There must be piles like this a thousand times higher, all over the world. And here I had been thinking I was special.

An overpowering light seemed to envelop me. I heard distant voices. They must be angels, and the light must be heaven. I felt a sense of relief that I had made it to heaven after all, because eventually, Virginia would join me. I think my face reflected my joy.

"This nigger's smiling," one of the angels said.

TWENTY-NINE

Be Yourself

"WHAT IS a nigger doing here in the first place?" another asked.

Surely angels did not talk this way in heaven. I opened my eyes to see two U.S. Army grunts standing over me, their faces drawn, eyes tired and dead. They had just gotten here and had already seen too much.

"Looks like he's alive," one said.

"He's alive and smiling? Does he know where he is?"

I tried to talk, to explain who I was, describe how glad I was to see some fellow Army grunts, even dumb rednecks who called me a nigger, but the words wouldn't escape. I don't know how long I had been lying there. I thought maybe it was hours, but it could have been days. I couldn't recognize the sounds coming out of my mouth.

"What language is that?"

"Polish, maybe."

"What niggers are from Poland?"

One of them turned and walked off. The other looked at me for a few seconds and then looked around at the sick and the dead. He was younger than me. I was too young to have seen the things I had seen. He was far too young. I could almost see the images burning themselves into his brain, past his unwilling eyes. He had signed on to fight an enemy, not shovel the horrible refuse an enemy left behind. I wanted him to look away, but it was too late.

The other soldier came back with some medics.

"This one looks a little more active than the other ones," he said. "We think he's Polish."

"Polish?" one of the medics asked, but they moved me onto a canvas stretcher without considering my origin further.

"Smells a bit ripe," one medic commented.

"Those others smell worse. They're dead," another said.

I couldn't tell if that was a joke. They moved me off and the shaking as they walked reminded me that my head was hurting, which I sometimes forgot. My head hurting was my natural condition. Earlier pain in my alimentary canal had taken my mind off of it; I wondered if it was a good sign that the pain between my ears had come back.

I woke up again under some kind of tent. My ratty, stinky clothes were gone. I lay under some kind of sheet. I couldn't tell if I wore anything else. There were lots of people around, moving quickly, talking quickly. There were other shrouded forms like me, barely moving, not talking, at all.

I could hear the chatter. They had heard about the amazing things underground. This is where they came from, they said. Apparently, our V-2s had been pouring down on London. Now, they saw where they came from, and the awful cost of building them, and were appalled by it all. They wanted to bring the dead sticks back to life, if they could, and then let them go to make their way back to their homelands.

Now and then, a doctor bent over me and stuck his face close to mine, checking for something. I wanted to tell them who I was, that I was an Army man, and that I needed to get back to the States as soon as possible, not to Poland. I tried to talk, but a tube in my arm filled me full of something that mangled the words before they left my brain. The doctors looked at me and nodded as I mumbled, as if they understood me. Then they moved on.

I lay in that bed for a long time. They fed me, by a tube at first, then paste, then actual food—bread and sausage and cheese. I didn't have to hunch over my food, I could eat it out in the open. There wasn't an unlimited supply, but there was much more than I'd had before, and it was better, too. I ate everything they gave me. When some of the other recuperating inmates didn't eat all their food, I ate that, as well.

In the bed across from me lay one of the other prisoners. I had never seen him before. He actually was Polish. Maybe they had put us together thinking we could talk. He was one of the serious skeletons. Even his skin was being eaten away, like he was disappearing into another dimension. He was on the tube, like me, but I moved off of it eventually. He didn't. He just looked at the doctors with his huge brown eyes, eyes that barely held a spark of life despite their size. His eyes were dying oceans.

After a while, I ate little sandwiches made of my bread and sausage and cheese, sat on the edge of my bed and looked at him. He looked back at me. He had a weird dignity about him, although he was naked under a sheet, with a big tube in his arm. As I looked at him, I could almost picture him as he must have been. I could see a brown knit cap on his head, one that didn't quite match his brown jacket. I could picture his gray trousers. Maybe he had three pairs, all identical. He probably used a bicycle for transportation, or maybe a horse and a rough wooden cart. I could picture him riding that cart back from town to his small farm, a loaf of bread under his arm for dinner. That was the life his father lived, and his father before that, and his father before that, way back to whatever wars or migration founded his country. He probably thought life would go on like that, only the world chewed up his life and spat him out, and now here he was, naked under a sheet on a cot from a country he could not imagine, his only companion a Race man who could not speak to him.

The stronger I got, the weaker he got. It almost felt like I was drawing energy and life from him, like some kind of vampire. The thought was stupid and yet it was a measure of how tired and depressed I was that it actually made sense, and finally I started to stay away from the man to see if he might improve. He didn't improve. He was on a one-way ticket out. The V-2 missile had claimed another one, right in front of my eyes.

I could talk now, and I wanted to go home. I talked to the Army medics and any other Army official I could find.

"You speak excellent English, Mr. Nicholas," one of them, a records clerk, told me. He was young, of course—they were all young, we were all young—and he was adept at pushing paper and swimming through the Army bureaucracy, but he had never seen something like the mess left behind at the V-2 plant and it showed.

"A lot of people from Chicago do."

"Well—I don't have any records on you. From what I was told, you're from Haiti and you lived in Paris."

I didn't want to argue with him. I wanted to show that I was a reasonable person, just a victim of mistaken identity.

"Sir, I am from Chicago. I serve in the same Army as you. I am a Lieutenant Colonel and a fighter pilot."

He was trying not to look as skeptical as he no doubt felt. He did not have much of a poker face.

"You were in the—what was that group of colored fighter pilots I heard about?"

"We're the 332nd Combat Squadron."

"I understood you were all in Alabama."

"We trained in Alabama. We're fighting here. I got shot down over a small village in France and then got sent here."

He leaned back in his canvas chair. I could tell he was going to unleash some logic on me.

"But if you were a fighter pilot and shot down, why aren't you in a POW camp? Why are you in this awful place?"

I thought it was interesting he considered a POW camp to be superior to Dora. He was right.

"I lost my uniform and my identification after I crashed. Some of the people in the town took them from me. I never got them back."

"And then you got captured and sent here."

"Not directly, but yes. I have some engineering experience and they seemed to think I would be useful building their rockets. Of course, I sabotaged them whenever I could."

"That's what they were building down there? Rockets? I heard something about it but I couldn't make out what they were doing. Wow. These were the ones they shot at London?"

"That's what I heard. They were very big. Taller than that tree over there."

I pointed to a fat, towering oak, and he whistled.

"Wow. What were those like to build?"

I thought of Jean, swinging on a rope, and the poor, incompetent Pole who disappeared.

"Awful. The worst time of my life."

He was embarrassed and looked down at his papers.

"Of course. Terrible, yes. I can't believe what I'm seeing around here. I don't know how one human being can do that to another."

"It seemed to be pretty easy," I said, and my words did not comfort him.

"Mr. Nicholas, I don't know quite what to do with you. If you will wait until we get some other people processed, we will get you back to France."

I guess he thought I was insane.

"I don't want to go to France. I'm not French. Do I sound French to you?"

"No, you don't."

I wasn't going to tell him that I spoke French fluently, and that I had always wanted to see Paris. No point in muddying his bureaucratic mind.

"Do I sound like I'm from Chicago?"

"I don't know. I've never been to Chicago. I'm from Florida."

"But do I sound American to you?"

"Mr. Nicholas, I have to say that you do. But there are some pretty skillful mimics here in this DP camp, and they all want to go to America, too. I don't have papers on them so I'm not going to send them there. You come here and tell me you're in the Army and that you crashed your plane, but I don't have any papers on you, either. You should be in a POW camp if you crashed your plane."

"I told you about that already," I said, my voice rising until I reined it in. Anger would not get me back to my own country. "The Army has records. You know that better than anybody. Check and see if a Lieutenant Colonel Johnny Nicholas crashed a P-51 Mustang over France on July 14, 1944. You'll see that he did. If you ask them for a picture of me, they'll send it. And you'll see it's me."

He drummed his fingers on the desk. He wanted me out of his hair, he had work to do.

"Mr. Nicholas, I will do that."

"So, I should come back later?"

"You should come back later."

And so, I did. The answer was always the same: "You should come back later."

I thought about writing to Virginia, renewing our correspondence, and asking for help, but I was pretty sure they thought I was nuts and wouldn't send anything I put to paper.

"Where are you trying to go?" an old man asked me after one of my fruitless visits to the American desk, which was not much more than a table.

"America."

"Ah, America. Me, too. Everyone is."

"I'm from there."

"You are? I wouldn't have guessed. I have said I am from there, too, but they don't believe me. I don't want to go back to France. There's nothing there, it's all destroyed. I want to go somewhere new. The world has been burned down and there's no point in trying to go back to where we were."

He was an odd old man. He looked something like the Polish man I had watched die, with one key difference—his eyes were bright. He was skinny and gray, like most of the people left behind at the camp, but his eyes were a blue so intense it was almost disturbing. They gave a spark to his face and, when he turned them your way, you almost felt heat from them. He also seemed—and there's really no other word for it—

happy. The first time I heard him laugh, while talking to some other DPs waiting to go home, I saw heads turn in search of this unexpected sound. We had laughed in the camp, but it was the grim laughter of the soon to be dead. His laughter was the laughter of the living.

His name was Pierre. He told me this one day while we were waiting in line to talk to the Army people again. He had been active in the French resistance, in a very low-level way, he said. He had been a banker and saw a chance to help by laundering money, but it wasn't his forte and he got caught. He was used to keeping track of money and didn't have a talent for crime. After being arrested, he lost contact with his wife and their three children, none of whom were far into their teen years.

He ended up in the camps, finally falling all the way to the bottom, to Dora. He had worked under a kapo who helped the Nazis keep records. They were meticulous record keepers, and he said he saw the numbers of the dead and dying every day. He knew he could die at any time, and yet now he could laugh again, before any of us.

I told him of my hatred for the Germans, how they used people like widgets and forced us to build the very weapons that would be wielded against us. He nodded but didn't say anything. He only became animated when he talked about the future, about his plans to go see the world now that the Nazis had taken everything he had and made him free. He did not like to talk about the camp and he did not like to talk about the past.

Now that I was healthier and out of the camp, my anger about being in that Hell continued to heat up. It felt good to let it out, to twist my rage and resentment into ever more elaborate shapes. I kept at it. I told Pierre any fantasy I could think of about the revenge I would get on the Nazis. He listened politely, a serene smile on his face.

"I don't hate them," he told me one day after enduring another of my rants.

That stopped me cold. I looked at him like he had just set his head on fire. He just looked back at me with that beatific smile.

"You don't hate them? After all they did? They ruined your life. They almost ruined the world!"

He extended his hands in a shrug.

"It is not for me to judge them. They did a great evil, yes. Does that make them evil? I don't know. That is not for me to say. I oppose what they did. I wish they had not done it. But they did it because they hated. If I were to hate, too, I could become like them. I don't want to be like them."

"But don't you want to kill them? If your kapo was right here right now, wouldn't you want to squash him like a bug?"

His eyes darkened ever so slightly. Everyone hated the kapos, even him. But he pushed the feeling away with an almost visible effort. "I would want to, I admit. But I wouldn't do it. I would look at him with sadness. Sadness because of what he was willing to do to survive. He was willing to become less than human, just to keep sucking in air."

"But look what they did!" I gestured around us, at the sad collection of humans, or former humans, who staggered around us. "Look what they did to all of us!"

He looked around, too. He knew what he would see, he saw it every day. But somehow, he saw it differently than I did.

"What did they do? They did it to themselves," he said. "We died without dignity, and they did that to us. They lived without dignity, and they did that to themselves. And that's worse."

I didn't agree with him. But he was firm. I couldn't change his mind. And I tried. We talked about it every day. There wasn't much else to do after I completed my daily fruitless plea to be returned to my own country. I was getting angrier by the day. I had volunteered to serve my country even though it really didn't want me to, and then I had nearly given my life. I had gone through hell, literally, and I just wanted to go home. But I couldn't, because of the same reason my country didn't want me to serve it. I had dark skin. If I had been a white soldier, speaking English as perfectly as I did, I would be on the next boat home. But because I wasn't, I wasn't. The knowledge made me furious.

While I fumed, Pierre pondered his options. He could go anywhere. He was untethered from his past. He said he missed his family and cried because they were gone, but I never saw him do it and never saw those bright eyes dimmed by sadness. He was always the same with me, hopeful and forgiving. We spoke French, but I was careful to do it out of earshot of any of the Army guys, so their suspicion that I came from Haiti wouldn't be confirmed in their minds.

"We are all trapped in ourselves," Pierre said. "No matter what you do, you are always with yourself. I would rather be with myself than be one of those Nazis and try to live with myself." He leveled those eyes at me. "Just be yourself, Johnny. Live with yourself."

I laughed, and he smiled back. I thought it would be easy.

THIRTY

Home

___

I HAD GOTTEN USED to rejection, but I was getting nervous because the camp looked like it was winding down. People were going back to countries they came from, or to where they wanted to go, and here I was.

"Mr. Nicholas," the Army man said one day. "I have done some checking. What you told me seems to be accurate. I had a photograph of you sent to me."

He held up a wrinkled photo of my smiling face from better days.

"I believe this is you. You've lost some weight."

I looked at his face to see if he was joking. A slight smile tugged at the corners of his mouth. He was.

"I'm sorry that it took me so long to check, Lieutenant Colonel Nicholas."

To my amazement, he stood and saluted me. I couldn't remember a white man saluting me, not since Tuskegee days, and then only rarely and grudgingly.

I saluted him back. He stuck out his hand for a shake, and I shook.

"You're going home."

He wasn't joking. I was angry at him for not checking sooner, but when I heard those words the anger stepped back into the shadows. I was going home.

They put me on a Curtiss C-46 with other returning soldiers and flew us to London, then put me on a commercial Pan American plane to New York. I wore civilian clothes and nobody paid any attention to me, except for the white woman who (very discreetly) asked the stewardess if she could move to another seat.

I didn't care. I wanted to be left alone. I just wanted to get home. I could have called home and told my mother I was still alive, but for some reason, I didn't want to. I wanted to feel my feet on the ground and then tell her. And then there was the matter of Virginia. I wanted to see her, to travel to her door and knock on it without warning...and hope that she answered it and not her husband or boyfriend. Despite her letters—long lost but written on my heart—as far as she knew, I was dead. I had stopped writing back. My reasons for stopping were unbelievable so I couldn't expect her to believe them. Better to hope and just show up.

I don't remember exactly when my feet touched the ground in America. I had been asleep on the plane and the next thing I knew I was stumbling across the pavement to the terminal. Day had almost faded into night. I'm surprised I didn't fall asleep in the terminal, but once I got inside, I started to wake up. The payphones were jammed with soldiers calling home, but I managed to find an empty one way down at the end of a hallway crammed with conversations. The noise was almost deafening; everybody was shouting into the phone, and these were people who had been taught how to shout.

I got through to my mother. I could barely hear her, so I was shouting, too. At first, she didn't seem to know who I was, then she started crying and laughing and praying into the phone, giving thanks right there to God for bringing me back. I couldn't tell, exactly, but it sounded like she had been given the official message that I had died more than a year ago. She wanted me to come home right away, but there was one problem with that. I wanted to see Virginia first. I couldn't tell Mother about Virginia because I didn't know what Virginia's reaction to me would be. I had mentioned Virginia to her in a couple of letters home, but I'm sure she had forgotten and, at any rate, she wouldn't have cared; she wanted me home. And I wanted to be home. But I felt now that home was where Virginia was, and I needed to find that location.

I told my mother I had to stay in New York for a few days for processing. I didn't, of course. I intended to get on a train to Alabama as soon as I could find one. But then Mother said something that caught me up short.

"I'm so glad you're back. You have just enough time to come see your Father. He's dying, Johnny."

Suddenly, I couldn't hear the shouted conversations of my fellow soldiers, couldn't hear the roar of the propellers outside, couldn't even hear my own breathing. I could hear my mother's words as clear as a sheet of ice and twice as cold. I thought of my father and what I had learned from him, and how it had probably saved lives somewhere. I didn't know what was wrong with him to take him from this life at such a young age, but I needed to tell him my story before he passed on.

Instead of getting on the next train to Alabama, I caught the next one to Chicago. There were a lot more of those. The train clattered miserably along but it didn't keep me from sleeping. When I wasn't sleeping, I was eating. I went to the bar car whenever I woke up, which was not all that often, and ate as much as I could stand.

Mother met me at Union Station. It was not cold, but she wore a tattered coat and pulled it close to her, hugging herself. Then she hugged me and nearly cracked my ribs. She was stronger than I was, at that point, I could feel it. I felt like a child again.

"You're so thin! It's so good to see you!"

I could hardly breathe, but I didn't care.

"What did they do to you? Why are you so thin? Don't they feed you in the Army?"

I couldn't begin to explain it to her. I wouldn't even believe it, and I had been there.

"It was hard, Mother, but I'm here now."

"Yes, you are."

She hugged me again, even harder this time. I thought she might break me in two. I didn't think I would mind.

"Let's go home," she said, still hugging me, and I felt the words vibrate through my scrawny chest. I did want to go home, even if it wasn't the home with Virginia in it.

I asked about my father on the ride home. We took a cab. My mother looked out the window at the passing lights.

"He's not been well for a long time, son. He's—he's not been living with me."

"What?"

"He has not been the same since he got out of prison. He took to drinking, a lot. He got to be as useless as those bums down the street. He hangs out with them now, sometimes. I don't know where all he goes. Your uncle Abe is worse. I haven't seen him in more than a year. The last time I saw him, his eyes were as yellow as a cat's. Evvy left him and moved out West somewhere. Your family is gone, son. There's just me. Me and your sister, but who knows where she is."

My father was in the hospital. I was exhausted. Mother wanted me to wait until the next day to see him, but he sounded in such bad shape that I was afraid to wait that long. We went straight away. It was morning and they were letting visitors in. Mother knew the nurses now; they greeted her like a friend.

"He's down here," mother said, her face tight with concern.

She led me to a room and pushed open the door. I saw what she must have seen: Myself. On the bed lay an older me, just as thin as I was. This was how I must have looked on that Army cot back in Germany. I shuddered at the sight of him. He was what I saw when I looked in the mirror, and I didn't like what I saw. I could stand looking like that. I did not want my father to look like that. I stood at his bedside. Mother looked at us both and then mumbled something and left the room. She was looking at two skeletons, two skeletons she loved, and she couldn't stand it.

I looked down at my father. He was sleeping. His skin was stretched over his skull in a look I knew so well. His color was off. He looked gray, like an unfinished clay model of a human being. His eyes moved under his lids, but he did not wake up. I felt my own lids growing heavy; soon I would look still more like him. We would both be lying in our beds, eyes closed, half dead. I knew he was likely to go before me, but I didn't think it would be this soon. He wasn't an old man. He was twice as old as me. We looked the same, for vastly different reasons. I wasn't ready for him to go, although I could understand the pain he was in and why he might want to.

We left shortly after that and went back to the kitchenette. We walked down the hallway, which looked even dingier than I remembered. Mr. Roswell was not in the hallway to greet us. There was just the bare bulb and nothing else, not even an old newspaper. I started to ask what happened to him, but I didn't really want to know. I assumed something bad.

The kitchenette was smaller than I remembered, cramped, and Mother no longer made much of a pretense of cleaning it up. Nobody came over anymore, she said.

Mother fixed me a sandwich.

"You're so thin," she said, and I knew she wanted to add, "just like your father."

We were both physically and emotionally tired and didn't talk much, but it was the best meal I ever ate. It was a toasted cheese sandwich with some peanuts on the side and a glass of ice-cold milk. She was embarrassed that was all she could give me, I knew, but it tasted better to me than the finest steak. Mother wanted to know about my experiences but I couldn't tell her, not while we were eating lunch. Really, I couldn't tell her, at all. I told her about being shot down, but it looked like that was going to upset her, so I was very vague about the rest. I didn't tell her I was in a prison camp. I didn't even say I was in a POW camp, as she wouldn't really know the difference. I said I spent the end of the war in a "facility," and left it at that.

We ate on a card table that I had never seen before. Probably it came from someone else in the building, but Mother didn't say, and I didn't ask. Our original dining table was gone. I had a flash of memory of Uncle Abe and Aunt Eveline sitting there, Uncle Abe splitting the air with his big laugh while my father looked upon him with a shy smile and Mother and Aunt Eveline just rolled their eyes. He would never sit there again. The table was gone, and he was gone, and now it was just me and my mother, sharing cheese sandwiches and peanuts on a folding card table.

It was the best meal I ever ate but afterward I had a bad taste in my mouth because sitting there thinking about my family and the stupid dining table, a piece of furniture I had never really thought about before, made me realize how quickly a family can die. You grow up surrounded by these people and learn their rituals until they are in your bones, but it takes much less than you realize for it all to disappear. Maybe you hate going to Grandmother's for Christmas dinner but one year you won't have to go and then you'll never go again, and you'll miss it. It can just take one bad day to kill a family. Mine was done in by World War II, but a car crash will do as well, or a bad rainstorm, or even a headache. Much less than you think.

My father died sometime that day. After eating the sandwiches, Mother and I both settled down for a nap. Our beds were five feet apart. Mine was my father's, I knew, without her having to tell me. Even before he drifted away, they had been sleeping apart, just like people in the old TV shows. I had slept on the train but was still exhausted and fell into a dark hole immediately. I woke up disoriented, expecting to feel straw under my back, not some stiff mattress, but then I remembered where I was. I was safe and I went back to sleep.

We went back to see my father in the morning, but his spirit had left. Maybe his thin, tired body just didn't have room for it anymore. Mother clutched my arm tightly when we got the news and I prepared to catch her if she fell, but she stood upright. She didn't cry. They had moved him to a room in the basement and I went to identify him. It was my father, of course. The nurse looked from him to me and I could tell she was thinking that there wasn't much difference between the man on the table and the man nodding his head and saying sadly, "Yes, that's him."

Only my father was dead, and I was angry. He knows more about life and death than I do, but it wasn't that. I had come through a war that I was sure would kill me and returned just in time to see him die. I worked in an underground hellhole building nightmare weapons while he was safe in Chicago the whole time. I would have given anything to be safe in Chicago. But here I was alive and there he was dead, for nothing. My enemy was the Nazis. His enemy was himself. He had the worst end of the deal. It took me a long time to understand that, even though Pierre tried to tell me that very thing.

Mother wanted to have the funeral the next day but was in no shape to make any arrangements, and neither was I. The neighborhood had changed. Aside from the buildings, it was as if I had never lived there. The people were different, and the people were what made the neighborhood. The war had come and sucked all the men away, men both white and black. The white men to fight, the black men to fight (sometimes) but otherwise to help, or, at the very least, to take some of the jobs there were no white men left to perform. The old men shuffled around on the edges of their lives and history, and the IV-Fs—the draft washouts, those deemed physically, mentally or morally unfit even to be cannon fodder—hung around, playing pool and letting the war go on somewhere else. I knew some of them, or the old me knew some of them, but I didn't feel like talking to them.

I walked to the funeral home down the street. It had been a store and then a church, like my uncle's old church, and now it was a small but tidy funeral home. Business had never been better. It even made more money as a funeral home than it did as a church, or, at least, that's how it looked. I explained the situation to the owner, who didn't know my father or me, because he had only moved into town the year before. Everybody was a stranger to me now, including myself. I didn't mind dealing with strangers. We agreed that the funeral should be the next day, two days after he died.

"If you want," he said, "I can arrange to have some mourners there. If you would like a larger crowd, I can do that."

I had told him the circumstances of my father's death, as I was not ashamed of it. We're all going to die and should all die however we choose, if we get the chance. He assumed this meant my father had no friends, but I remember seeing him light up the neighborhood with his smile. Once word got around, his friends would appear like animals walking out of a forest after a rainstorm.

Mother was in the kitchenette, alone, looking at nothing.

"There's one more thing you have to do," she said, focusing her eyes on me when I came in the room. "You have to find Katherine."

I had not seen my sister in years. We didn't talk about her anymore. I wasn't even sure she was alive, and I wasn't sure that Mother knew, either.

"Where is she?"

Mother nodded toward the window.

"Out there. Out there somewhere. You can find her."

I could only imagine the shape that Katherine would be in. I wasn't sure I wanted to find her.

"Mother—"

"No arguments. She needs to come to her father's funeral. I don't care if you have to tie her up and drag her. You get her there."

I thought it would be easier to find her if I dressed up as a soldier. I didn't have a uniform, though. Mine was long gone, and the Army had thought I was dead and hadn't given me a new one. I did have an Army hat that someone had loaned me on the long trip home, so I put that on and wore a green shirt that I pressed so that the creases were knife sharp. I was going to have to look for my sister in places that no little brother should ever have to look for his sister. I thought it would be easier if I were dressed as a soldier, or as close as I could get to one, because no one would think it odd that a soldier was in town and looking for a girl.

Before I got started, I needed something else a soldier would have. I bought a pistol at the first place where I started asking around. The Army had given me a little money and I spent most of it on a cheap .45, identical to those everyone in the military was issued. This one had probably been swiped by some fellow soldier and resold.

I started my search at some of the pool halls where I thought women were available. I was afraid I might see someone I knew, but I didn't. I didn't know for sure that Katherine would be among them, but there weren't many options for girls who dropped out of school and needed money for their vices. She had once had so much promise, but now she only had one thing to sell.

Once I got in the area and found out for sure that women were available, I started getting specific. The only problem was that I no longer knew what my sister looked like, or what name she used. I still saw her in my mind as a young girl on the verge of ladyhood; I was pretty sure that was not who I would find. The only thing going for me was that Katherine was tall, and not many of the available girls were tall. I got very specific on that point.

"What, you get tired of fucking short Japanese girls?" one pimp asked me.

"I was in the Atlantic theater."

"I don't care if you was in the movie theater, I ain't got a girl tall enough for you."

I kept moving on, looking for someone who did.

"Since when they let niggers fight in the Army?" another pimp asked me. "And why don't they give you a full uniform? They ashamed of a Black man? And where your medals?"

I could have bored him with my whole story, but he wouldn't have believed it and, anyway, I didn't have time. I needed to find my sister, and fast. My journey took me from poolhall to pimp car to juke joint to alleyway. I did come across some Japanese girls for sale and wondered where they came from. There were German girls, too, and French girls, of course, which made Dominique flash across my mind. Pretty much, all of the world was for sale, and pretty cheap, in the back alleys of Chicago. Even my sister. She was for sale here somewhere, and I needed to find her.

Finally, I found a pimp who said he had tall girls. He worked out of a pool hall and had gotten word of me.

"I heard there's a nigger soldier looking for a tall piece," he said when I came in and was directed to him. "I guess fighting for the white man makes a Race man horny."

"Just show me what you got."

He had the girls in a dark back room, so the clients couldn't get a very good look at them. The building got rattier and darker the farther back you went, until it felt like you were in a cave. The girls slouched against a big, tattered couch, uninterested in me. They didn't even look at me and I didn't blame them. I scanned them quickly. He stood behind me, glaring. If he had heard about me, he had also heard that I hadn't bought anything, but had spent the entire day wasting the time of hard-working entrepreneurs like himself.

One of the girls caught my eye. She was tall and stoop-shouldered and looked like there was no hope in her, at all, but there was something about the shape of her cheekbones that caught my attention. This girl had cheekbones like Mother. I had just a couple of seconds, so I took a chance.

"Katherine Mary."

I used her middle name the way Mother always did when she was mad. The girl's face snapped up and she looked at me in surprise.

"Oh, my God," she said, and I knew it was her. Her voice was deeper and scratchier, but the whore on the couch was my sister.

"I don't know what you're up to, but I don't like it," the pimp said.

I had hoped that I could pretend to buy her and then run off with her, but now I doubted the pimp would let us alone. Time for the backup plan. I took my pistol out of my belt and pointed it at his head. I didn't even know if it would fire, and I hadn't bought any bullets, but I was counting on not having to actually use it. Before the war, I wouldn't have needed it. I could have wiped the floor with the pimp and his thugs, but not now. I needed a little help.

"I'm taking her with me."

"Man, you are making a mistake. A big mistake," the pimp said, slowly measuring each word so I knew he was serious.

"Johnny, you get out of here," Katherine said. "You gonna get me in trouble."

She even talked like them now. Mother would have been appalled to hear that grammar.

"You already in trouble," the pimp said.

"Come with me, Katherine."

She did as she was told. I guess she was used to that by now.

The other girls looked at me now. They were all smiles. This was probably some fantasy they shared, getting rescued by a strong Race man. I felt a flash of sadness because it wasn't going to happen for them.

We backed out of the club, me pointing the gun at the skull of anyone who looked like they might try anything. Once outside, I hailed a cab and practically threw Katherine into it.

"God damn you, Johnny, what did you have to do that for?" she snarled at me. She pushed up against the window, getting as far away from me as she could. "I was fine. What did you have to go and do that for?"

She didn't even ask about my appearance. I guess she was used to gaunt men; maybe that's how she thought we all looked. Probably the only men she saw were the ones who bought her.

"Father is dead," I said, not really wanting to talk to her, much less argue with her. "Mother wants you at the funeral. It's tomorrow."

"Tomorrow? He—"

"He's dead."

"What he die of?"

"Drank himself to death."

She looked out the window at the passing buildings with no more than concern—or maybe even less concern—than if I had told her it was going to rain.

"Aren't you going to say anything?"

"You want me to say I'm sorry that he's dead? What he ever do for me? Brought me out of my home and up here, watched as I went out on my own. I left and I thought y'all might bring me back. None of y'all even looked for me." She faced me and her eyes were glistening. "None of y'all even looked for me."

"I was a *kid*, Katherine."

Her facade melted, just a tiny bit. She raised a hand and I flinched, but she only used it to briefly caress my jaw.

"I know you were. But Mother and Father didn't look for me, either. Uncle Abe and Aunt Eveline didn't look for me."

"Everybody looked for you, Katherine, all of them. You know they did."

This was true, but it didn't fit into the private mythology she had built in her head. The mythology that told her it was all jake that she had let go of life. It wasn't her fault she was drowning.

"No," she said quietly. "None of y'all even looked for me."

She stared out into the gloom for a while, and then got started on more practical matters. "You got me out of there, and now what am I going to do for money? Are you going to keep me? You and Mother? You look like you don't have two nickels to rub together."

"You can get a job."

"I had a job."

"You can get a real job."

"What, cleaning floors? Taking care of some white man's kids? I'd rather just get paid for sucking a white man's dick."

I hit her on the side of her head, knocking her forehead into the window with a loud crack. The cabbie jerked his mirror so I could see his angry eyes.

"Don't you go breaking my glass. You'll have to pay for it."

Katherine sulked in silence for the rest of the drive to the kitchenette. I gave the cabbie a little bit extra for his trouble. Katherine walked down the hallway like she had never been in the building before. She stepped into the room and saw Mother, who had cleaned up a little and found a cot for me. I was giving my bed to Katherine. We wanted to make her as comfortable as possible, for just a little while. Not to be nice, but to keep her from running off immediately.

Mother was putting a pillowcase on a pillow for me when Katherine walked in. Mother stopped, stock still, like a rabbit spied by a hunter.

"Katherine," she said, her voice weak but not trembling.

"Mother," Katherine said, shaky. All her bravura from the car gone, but wary.

Mother put down the pillow and walked toward Katherine, very slowly, as if fearing she might, at any moment, be attacked. I stood in front of the door because I feared the opposite, that Katherine would bolt for the comfort of the night that she knew so well. She did neither. She just stood there, thin and tired and frail, waiting for my mother to approach. Mother wrapped her arms around her daughter slowly, as slowly as a cloud enveloping a mountain. Katherine moved more quickly once embraced; she hugged her mother tightly and rested her face in the hollow of her shoulder. I expected to hear sobbing but neither woman cried. They were both all cried out, probably long ago. They just stood there and swayed, hanging on to each other although they knew the years were gone and would never come back.

"Thank you for coming," Mother whispered to Katherine. "It's good to see you again."

Katherine didn't tell Mother that she really didn't have much of a choice.

"It's good to see you, too. I miss him."

"I miss him, too, honey. Oh, I miss him, too."

They just stayed there and swayed for another minute. I started to go and hug them both, but it didn't seem the right thing to do. It wasn't as though the years had dropped away—there were far too many years gone for that—but, just for a little bit, the lost years didn't matter quite so much.

Katherine stayed in the kitchenette that night, in the little bed that mother made for her, and it felt almost like we were a family again. Almost. We barely talked, and the ghosts hung heavy in the air. But we were together, almost all of us, united by the loss of one of us, and that was the best we were going to get.

The funeral was small, as shrunken and wizened as my father had been at the end. The owner of the funeral home looked at me, and when he thought I wasn't looking, he shook his head. He had offered to find me mourners to put on a better show, but I declined. I wished then that I had not, and he knew it. I don't know what had happened to my father's friends. Maybe they were all dead like him, or near death, or maybe the war had arrived like a hurricane and blown them all away somewhere, but they were not there. There was just me, my mother, Katherine, and a few people from the neighborhood. They sat patiently through the service, muttered a few words of condolences and left.

We were the only ones at the gravesite. Mother and Father bought their plots years before, back when times were good, or at least better. The city had continued to grow around them; it took an hour to get there. We were the only ones standing by when his body was lowered into the ground. Father had died, had left this life and all he knew in it. His passage was not unmourned but it was almost unnoticed.

Then the funeral and gravesite visit were over, and he was gone, never to come back, never to be reached again. I think this is the worst part of being human. People die and you can't talk to them and they can't talk to you. You might think about something they said to you once and, years later, you finally understand it, but they're gone, and you can't tell them. I've had people tell me that the beloved dead are all around us and they know our dreams and our thoughts, and they sense what we wish we could say to them. I don't believe it. They're just gone. Some ghost of them rattles around in your memory but they're gone, and they don't hear, and they don't care.

I had wanted to tell my father how those times spent watching him paint signs had paid off, had probably saved lives, but I couldn't while he was asleep and then he was asleep forever.

We went back to the kitchenette and had dinner. Mother fixed some chicken and we sat around the small table and ate it, each lost in our thoughts. I have heard about Irish wakes where family and friends get together and laugh and get drunk and toast the life of the one who's gone on. My father had been buried in silence and after he was gone, we sat in silence and ate, and then Mother went to sleep. She laid down on her meager bed and went to sleep so fast it was alarming, almost as if she had died, too. I walked down the hall and brushed my teeth and used the bathroom, and when I returned, Katherine was gone, along with the gun and what little money I had. I never saw her again, never looked for her again.

Once in a while, I imagine her as a grandmother somewhere, in a small house with a nice yard full of grandchildren and a smile on her face because she has finally conquered her demons and become at peace with herself. But I'm sure she's long dead. She knows more about life and death than I do.

When I came back into the room and saw she was gone and Mother was asleep, I decided to do what I had wanted to do earlier. I caught the L and went back to the graveyard. It was locked but the brick wall that contained it—to keep the dead in their place, I guess—had crumbled in places and I was able to get in easily. I walked back to my father's grave and squatted in the grass. I know I said I don't believe the dead can hear, but I talked anyway. I told him everything, my whole story since I left Chicago. It all led up to that moment when I remembered what he had taught me, when I felt him live through me, and I wanted him to know that.

I talked for a long time, low and calm. We did not have the money for a proper headstone, so he just had a small stone cross, but I didn't talk to that. I looked down at the ground where he lay and talked to the dirt over him. Occasionally, I heard people walking around. I wasn't the only one able to get through the fence. But if they saw me or heard me, they left me alone. Maybe they knew that nobody in here had any money, or anything at all, and so everyone deserved some peace and quiet.

THIRTY-ONE

Virginia

—————————

I WANTED DESPERATELY to talk to Virginia, to see Virginia, to hold her. I had exactly no money. What little I had possessed was spent on the gun or gone with Katherine and she probably didn't even have it anymore. I couldn't call because Virginia's family didn't have a phone. Writing a letter would be too slow. So, I told Mother about her and she gave me some money for a telegram. I had fought my way into the white man's Army, helped beat the Nazis, spent time in the worst hell they could create, and I had to borrow money from my mother to send a note to my girlfriend. I felt like I was twelve years old again. But I did it.

Virginia. stop. Am alive and back. stop. Would like to see you. stop. If you want to. stop. Write me back. stop. If you want to. stop.

I sent it off and went for a walk. For the first time in years, I had no direction in life. I had absolutely nothing to do. There was nothing to do in the kitchenette and nothing to do in the apartment building that wouldn't get me into trouble. I was out of the military. I had no job. So, I walked. I walked the old paths of Washington Park, where I hadn't been in years, and tossed rocks into the lagoon.

I looked up at the trees I used to climb. They had seemed huge and towering back then. Now, I saw they were just average as trees go. I was tempted to try to climb one, but given my current health, I probably couldn't do it. I'd fall out of it and break my neck, and I wasn't ready to depart this veil of tears just yet. I wanted to hear from Virginia first. If she told me she wouldn't see me, or if her husband wrote back, or if I never heard anything from her again, then I'd think about climbing.

I walked back to the telegraph office at the end of the day. No message. I went back the next day after lunch. No message. I could imagine any number of reasons why not. Maybe she was married now. Maybe she was on vacation. Maybe she had just given me up for dead and didn't want to see me. All good reasons. I kept going back, day after day, and finally the man would see me coming and shake his head, and I wouldn't even have to go in the door.

This kept up for a couple of weeks. I ate breakfast and lunch with Mother and helped her around the kitchenette, then I went for my walk while she went to work. I could feel the strength flowing back into my body. At night, my legs would hurt, and I would massage them and smile when I felt the muscles coming back. I enjoyed my walks, at least the time when I wasn't brooding on why my Virginia was silent. But it was time for me to look for work. Mother was working every day and feeding me, and that didn't seem right anymore. I was a grown man, I should be supporting her.

I could have gone back into the airplane business, once I got my health all the way. Maybe. The Postal Service was looking for pilots, but I was competing with all the pilots coming back from the war, healthy heroic pilots, and I doubted a Race man had much of a chance without putting more energy into it than I could muster. I could go back to the Coffey School. I could teach there, for sure. But something kept me away. The same force that kept me aimlessly wandering the city also kept me away from Coffey. I didn't want them to see me, not yet, not the way I still was. And I didn't feel like telling war stories. They would want to hear the good news, the news that the *Defender* liked to print. That wasn't the kind of story I could provide.

I actually went down to the Coffey School one day, took the L and then walked, not even bothering to stick out my thumb to try to catch a ride. It was a nice day and I watched a small plane buzz its way into the air and disappear into the distance. It faded from view, but I could still hear it, buzzing like a tiny mosquito. I leaned on a fence post at the edge of one of the fields adjacent to the runways, close enough to look, not close enough to be seen. I'm not sure that anyone I knew there would even recognize me, and I didn't want them to even if they could. Really, the only person I wanted to see was Willa. Seeing Coffey would be nice, but if I wandered down there, I would want to see Willa. Just to soak up some of that spirit. I could use some of that spirit. I could use some of that spirit today, as a matter of fact, right this very instant, but I could have definitely used it then.

The mosquito buzzing grew louder, and the plane reappeared. It looked like a Piper Cub. It circled the airport once and then made a pretty good landing. Two people got out, but I couldn't see who they were from this distance. The distant shapes merged briefly; probably one patting the other on the back. Another successful training flight. Another person getting their wings, probably a Race man, too. I realized something in a flash then, although it took me a very long time to admit this, even to myself—I just wasn't interested in flying anymore. I wasn't afraid. I had just lost the sense of joy that airplanes once provided. I had flown too near the sun and gotten burned.

A little Piper Cub was all right, probably, but the airplanes I was most used to were weapons of war, and I didn't have any use for weapons of war anymore. I had not seen what they could do, not first-hand, but I saw what it took to make them, and I wanted no part of them. I mean the V-2, of course. Once I got home, I saw some newsreel footage of London picking itself up after the rockets—rockets that I helped make, however unwillingly—rained down on the city like a lead rain from Hell. The first time I saw them on a newsreel the images of the rockets were small and fuzzy and distant. I think if I had seen close-up footage I would have gotten up and walked out. As it was, just seeing the damn thing move was enough to make tears flow down my cheeks. I was sitting in the balcony, of course, and there were strangers on either side of me. They didn't know me at all but I'm sure they saw me crying. Maybe they thought I had family in London, or I was just so damned happy that the war was over. I don't know. They didn't ask, I didn't explain.

I kept checking the telegraph office. There was nothing there. I checked the home mail, too, but it was all bills. No one sent Mother anything after Father died. Not a card, not a letter, nothing. Nobody sent me anything, either, but nobody knew I was there, I guess. Hardly anybody even knew I was on the planet anymore, and I sort of liked it that way. There was one person who I did want to know that I was on the planet, but I didn't know if she was still on it.

So, I kept checking the telegraph office, and. my walks started getting shorter and shorter. I was going shorter distances, seeing less and less, walking in circles. Circling the drain.

One day, about ten o'clock in the morning, the buzzer sounded in the kitchenette. Mother was getting ready for work and I was getting ready to go for a walk before returning and trying to figure out what I wanted to do with the rest of my life. I walked down the dark hallway, past the empty chair, and looked out the window on the side of the front door. And there was an angel, a ghost, a vision. There was Virginia.

I almost yanked the door off the hinges. I grabbed her up in a bear hug like the one Mother had given me when she picked me up. I literally picked Virginia up. I would have swung her around but there was no room. There were so many things that I wanted to say, years' worth of things that I wanted to say, but they fought with each other to get out of my mouth, so I ended up sputtering in her ear.

"I know," she whispered. "I know. It's good to see you, too."

We stayed like that for a long time until I noticed some of the young men in the neighborhood wandering by, their attention drawn to Virginia like wolves attracted to some wounded beast. She would not be their prey. I ushered her inside, down the dim hallway—hoping she wouldn't notice how shabby it was—and into the kitchenette.

"Well," Mother said when we came in. "Company."

"Mother, this is Virginia. Virginia, this is my mother."

Mother's expression softened. I don't know who she thought I was bringing in. Some floozy off the street, I guess. I had told her about Virginia but hadn't mentioned that she was coming for a visit, because I didn't know myself.

"I've heard so much about you," Mother said to her with a gracious smile.

"And you," Virginia said.

They shook hands in a friendly way. I was grinning from ear to ear.

"Dear, would you like something to eat?" Mother asked, since I was just standing there being useless.

"Oh, no ma'am, I'm fine. I had something on the train."

"Johnny didn't tell me you were coming."

"He didn't know."

Virginia gave me a sly look. There seemed to be a sense of confidence behind her eyes now, a sense of playfulness, that I didn't remember seeing before. We had all gotten older, we had all changed. I had changed for the worse. I was glad to see that Virginia had changed for the better, if that was even possible.

"I have to go to work," Mother said. "Hopefully, my son will recover some manners and entertain you properly. Will you be staying with us?"

My heart leaped at the thought. There were only two beds. But Mother would be in the room. Maybe she would—

"No, ma'am. I have a hotel down the way," Virginia said, destroying my little fantasy before it could take wing. "I've dropped my bags there."

"But I will see you later. You two have a lot of catching up to do."

Virginia gave me that playful look.

"Yes, ma'am."

When Mother was gone, we just stood and looked at each other for a long while. She looked even better than I had remembered. Her hair was shorter and tighter, and a little more bronze. Her figure was the same, but there was something about her that was different. She carried herself a little taller, seemed more taut. I had gotten softer and weaker and she had gotten stronger and harder, and the changes looked better on her than they did on me.

"You look good," she said at last.

I waved my hand, shrugging away the compliment.

"But you're so thin. Didn't they feed you in the Army?"

"They did. But not enough."

She just looked at me for a little while, didn't move to touch me. I stood there like a statue.

"Johnny, I didn't hear anything from you for more than a year. They told me you were dead. Where were you? In a POW camp?"

That would be the better story. I couldn't tell her the truth, at least not yet. I felt such joy bursting in my heart upon seeing her and touching her again that I didn't think I could stand to go back into those tunnels. Those nightmares happened to another person, not to me. They couldn't happen in a universe that could create something as good and pure as Virginia.

I nodded my head.

"Oh, baby."

She held me then, opened her arms and I was drawn back to her. I held her tightly, as if she might fall away, and she rested her cheek on my chest and cried.

"I was so sad. We were writing and then you stopped writing. I didn't know what had happened. I thought maybe you had found some girl over there. I kept asking at the base and they didn't know, and they didn't know, then they said you just flew off one day and never came back. They thought you were dead. They told me you were dead. I thought you were dead until I got your telegram."

I thought I was dead, too. Maybe I really was dead, and this was now heaven. But surely heaven would be a little fancier than the kitchenette.

"I got shot down. And imprisoned. I don't know why they didn't know what happened to me."

"I'm so sorry. Did they mistreat you?"

Her words cut me to the heart. How could I tell her about the plant, about the hangings, about the endless murder? I couldn't. I decided then and there I never would.

"No. They didn't feed me as much as I wanted. But, no."

"Still, that's awful."

Her arms moved up and down my back. They were strong arms.

"You know what I kept thinking, Johnny? When I was wondering what had happened to you, and I was asking and asking and asking, it occurred to me that if I were your wife, they would tell me something."

I think I stopped breathing. I think I may have even passed out standing up, because everything went black for a bit before I heard her asking, "Johnny? Johnny?"

I knew what I had to do then. I had to grab life. I had seen, over and over and over, how quickly it could slip away. Life is a flash of lightning. Without a word, I released my hold on her and dropped to my knee.

"Miss Virginia Scott. Will you marry me?"

Now it was her turn to stand speechless, but not for long. She recovered faster than I had. She pulled me to my feet with those strong arms and looked me in the eye.

"Mr. Johnny Nicholas, yes, I will. Yes. I was going to ask you if you didn't ask me."

She kissed me then, soft and gentle at first, the kind of kiss you get at a wedding, and then harder and more insistently, the kind of kiss you get on the wedding night. We kissed for a long time, and after a while it was barely kissing anymore, it was a desperate embrace. The kitchenette was empty, my bed was empty, we were both ready. But I knew it wouldn't happen then and didn't want it to. I wasn't sure how I would be. I still felt weak, a shadow of the man she fell in love with. I was afraid she might crack me in two. And this wasn't how I wanted it to be. Not with her. I was not going to go to bed with Virginia Scott until she was no longer Virginia Scott; not until she was Mrs. Johnny Nicholas.

We broke off and she brushed at strands of hair she imagined had fallen in front of her face. It was a delaying tactic until she decided what she wanted to say.

"I'm so glad you're home."

"Me too, baby. Me too."

"Would you like to come to dinner with Daddy and me tonight? I'm sure he'd like to hear the news. Maybe your mother could come, too."

"Daddy?"

"Yes, I came up here with Daddy. You didn't think he'd let me search for a strange man in a big city all by myself, did you?"

I did not think the Rev. Scott would allow that, come to think of it.

"My mother gets off work late."

"We'll wait. Maybe we'll have a snack to tide us over. There are places that stay open late in Chicago, aren't there? I hear that's one of the advantages of the big city."

"Oh, yes. Yes, there are. There are even a few worth taking a lady to."

She went back to her hotel then, because I wanted to get dressed up, or as dressed up as I could get, before having dinner with her father. I wasn't having second thoughts, I didn't think Virginia was, and I didn't want Rev. Scott to, either.

Mother came home hours later and I surprised her with the news. She looked happy for me. Tired from her day, and from her life, but happy for me in that moment. This really wasn't how I pictured the day I would tell her I was getting married. I had thought about it once or twice over the years. I pictured everyone gathered around, laughing, swapping stories, maybe getting a little drunk. In some of the versions, depending on how old I was, Katherine was even back for the occasion. It never occurred to me that it would be just Mother and I, in the same old kitchenette. And we'd be dining with a preacher so we wouldn't even be getting drunk.

I didn't have much in the way of dress clothes. I would have worn my Army uniform. I had always worn that well and I knew Virginia liked how I looked in it. But I no longer had one and had not tried to get another, and, anyway, I doubted they would give me one. They were done with me. I had a brown suit jacket that had been handed down from my father. Before the war, it wouldn't have fit me, especially not in the arms. Now it fit fine. I had a decent pair of pants. I had one nice white dress shirt with a stiff collar. I had exactly one good tie, nice wide striped one with several different colors in it, red and gold and blue and brown. I had a pair of nice brown shoes that could use a shine but looked all right. This was what I wore to the dinner where my mother met my father-in-law-to-be. It was exactly the same outfit I had worn to my father's funeral.

Mother and the Rev. Scott got on fairly well. They had Alabama roots in common, although they didn't know any of the same people.

"We were too poor to know anybody," Mother said, earning a laugh from the Reverend.

She was very gracious toward Virginia. I think she thought—

correctly, maybe—that Virginia was above me, although she would never admit anything like that. Or maybe she saw a bit of her lost daughter in my lovely's face; I don't know. But she treated her well. They laughed a little and occasionally leaned their heads together like old friends conspiring when they talked about me.

Mother only made me nervous once during the dinner. The table talk had wandered from Alabama to Chicago to the war and finally, lightly, landed on religion. The Rev. Scott told us about his church and how it had grown.

"I have to ask you, Reverend, are you truly a man of God?" Mother asked, and I almost dropped my fork onto my steak.

"Mrs. Nicholas, I like to think I am. I try."

"There are some who say they are of God, and they can talk the talk, but they have larceny in their hearts," Mother said. "I have known men like that. I am ashamed to say that my own brother was one. He hurt a lot of people with what he did."

"I am sorry to hear that," Rev. Scott said. He looked as though he was going to reach for her hand to reassure her, but he did not. "I do try my best. I want you to know that."

"I think you do," Mother said. "You look like you do."

The reverend poked around at what had happened to my father. Mother made some veiled references to Uncle Abe's brief criminal career but did not seem interested in telling the tale, so she didn't. I needed to talk to Virginia about it, I knew, but I was like Mother. This was a nice dinner, a happy dinner, and I didn't want to spoil it.

On the L ride home, Mother folded her arm in mine like she was a girl on a date herself. "She's a nice girl, Johnny. You take good care of her."

It made my heart grow warm to hear her say that. I could tell by the way she held my arm and smiled up at me that she meant it.

"I will, Mother. I will."

And I did try, I really did.

The reverend had a meeting with other reverends the next day, and since I continued to be unemployed, I was free to show Virginia the city. I showed her as much as I could, the Field Museum and Wrigley Field and the Hancock Building. I didn't take her anywhere I might actually know anyone. My old life was over, and I didn't want to see anyone from it. In a brief flush of panic, I wondered what would happen if we bumped into Dominique. I pushed that thought away. I had never bumped into her when I was actually looking for her, and she probably wouldn't recognize me now. I was still a boy in her mind, if she was still alive or thought of me at all. I hoped that she would be happy for me, but I had to quit worrying that she might see us.

I did take her to Washington Park: To the lagoon, where I had imagined German submarines to be lurking. I had thrown rocks to scare them away and it worked because they never did surface. The trees where Nelson Ray and I imagined ourselves as fighter pilots. I never imagined myself falling out of that tree, falling to the Earth, falling beneath the Earth. That never occurred to me, back when playing at war was a fun way to pass a hot day. I told Virginia about these imagined perils. Better that than tell her about the real thing.

As the day went on, Virginia wanted to plan. We were going to get married, that much was decided. The question was when, and where. I admit that I was not much help because, having arrived at this point, I just didn't care about the specifics. We could get married at the finest church in Chicago, in a mud hut in the Congo, or in her father's church in Alabama; it did not matter to me in the least. As far as I was concerned, we were already married. She had my heart and I did not want it back.

Mother would not want to leave Chicago, I knew, particularly to go back to Alabama. But Virginia gradually became more and more insistent on getting married in her father's church, and with him doing the honors. And it made sense. I didn't particularly want to go back to Alabama myself, but my mother didn't have a church and her father did, so it made sense. I didn't know any ministers, not anymore, and wouldn't have trusted the ones I had known. Alabama it was. I was going back to Tuskegee whether I wanted to or not.

THIRTY-TWO

Hitched

I RODE down on the train with Mother while Virginia made all the arrangements. There really weren't many arrangements to make. From my side, there was only Mother and myself. Mother looked around the train with some interest and watched the porters carefully. The trains and the porters were the ones who had spread the *Defender* to the South and prompted Race people to head to the North in droves, including her. But this did not really seem to interest her much, and she didn't say a whole lot to the porters. She just looked out the window at the scenery, which was flat and not very interesting. We didn't really talk that much. Our bond wasn't fraying but there just wasn't a whole lot to say.

The wedding was on a Saturday. It was April, so it was not too hot. Storm clouds massed on the horizon the day before but had the courtesy to go away before the actual wedding. On the day we got married, April 16, the sky was clear and crisp and blue and limitless. Mother did not buy a new dress for the occasion—she didn't have enough money, and I didn't have enough either—but she had sewed some new lace on an older one and it looked as good as anything.

Virginia didn't buy a new dress either, as it turned out. She wore the same dress her mother had worn at her wedding. It had been carefully stored in a closet in the Scott household for all these years, waiting for this day. Virginia could have worn a cement sack and looked lovely, but she looked especially beautiful in this dress. Her mother cried to see her in it, and I think Mother almost did, too. I know it's the ordinary thing to say, but it's true: Virginia looked like an angel.

The wedding wasn't like a lot of them that I read about today. It wasn't fancy and it wasn't big. Like I said, my side was just Mother and I, but Virginia's side wasn't much bigger. She had her parents, of course, and two sets of aunts and uncles, and an old childhood friend of hers that I met for the first time. She was Virginia's age but had been married years before, when she was really too young. She had two kids now. Her name was Cindy. She was beautiful but had lost her figure. She looked like a beautiful woman who had been pulled and stretched until she was much larger. I wondered, briefly, if this might be what would happen to Virginia someday, but she was so magnificent that I couldn't picture it.

Even with a small crowd we did not feel lost. The sanctuary of the church would hold many more, as the God business was booming, but somehow the soaring ceiling and the high, thin curved windows made the number of people within seem inconsequential. As for me, I only had eyes for my wife to be.

There was no organ. Cindy led us in a couple of hymns and then the ceremony began. Our vows were simple, picked out by the reverend. They used the quote from the Bible about how life would be only a tinkling cymbal without love, or something like that. I wasn't really listening. I was focused on Virginia's beautiful face, and how it was only inches from mine, obscured by a white veil that signified she would soon be my wife.

And then she was, and her father told us we could kiss, and we did. There was no purpose to us walking down the aisle because there weren't enough people there, so we just turned to face them, and they stood and clapped. I caught my mother's eye and saw her smile. It wasn't as big a smile as I had always thought it would be. It wasn't a beaming smile. I think, at this point, that Mother was beyond joy.

There was one other guest at the wedding that I hadn't seen earlier, but I saw now when we faced the audience: Willie Mason, my old friend from Tuskegee. Mother wasn't beaming but Willie was and clapping his hands loud enough to cause an echo. He looked like the same old Willie, and when it was over and done, he came up and wrapped his big arms around my shoulders.

"Man, it's been too long," he said.

"Yes, it has. How'd the war treat you, Willie?"

"Made a lot of money off my fellow soldiers, man. How about you?"

"Oh, it was kind of interesting. Glad it's over, though."

He gave me a laugh and a clap on the shoulder and then we both ended up talking to other people for a while. We met up again later, outside the church, standing on the lawn, looking up at the clear blue sky.

"I'm really glad you came, Willie."

"Me too. Virginia tracked me down, and I'm glad she did. I wouldn't have missed it. Never thought you'd actually get this girl."

"Me either. Me either."

"I'm glad you did. It's good to see you, Johnny. I hope you don't mind me saying, you are looking a little rough. What happened to you? We thought you were dead."

"I know. I got shot down. It took me a while to get back." I didn't really want to talk about this now, today of all days. "It just took a while. So, what happened with you, Willie? They managed to keep you busy?"

He gave me that trademark smile. "Man, yeah. They got me started working on engines and doing training for that. They had me teaching classes at Tuskegee and then going up to Michigan to work on engines and teach there. I didn't get any exciting war action like you flyboys, but I got my hands dirty."

"You kept us going. It wouldn't have happened without you."

"Ah, me or somebody else. One good thing about it is I really learned a lot about engines. I mean, everything. I thought I knew a lot, but now I could probably build you an engine out of this grass here."

"Wish you would. I could use a car."

"You can borrow mine."

"No, that's all right, I'm just kidding around. We've got that Mercury over there for the honeymoon."

It was the reverend's car. We were only going down to Montgomery for one night; I didn't want Mother to go back on the train alone, but I didn't tell Willie that. It wouldn't sound very romantic.

"So, what are you going to do after that? When are you going to come back here so I can win some more money off you?"

Willie had his smiley face on, but I knew he was serious, at least in terms of wondering what I was going to do. I wished I had an answer for him.

"I'm not sure yet. I've been kind of sick. Just getting my strength back."

"Sick? You mean those Nazi bastards worked you over, don't you?"

"Something like that."

"That's kind of a sickness, I guess."

"What are you going to do, Willie? Stay in the Army?"

"Nah, I'm done with the Army. I want to sleep late again before I'm too old to enjoy it. I'm not really sure yet, either. I thought maybe you had some good ideas."

"I'm sure something will come to me. I've got a woman to support, now."

"Yeah, and you don't need to be worrying about this on your wedding night, do you?"

"I sure don't."

"You think you might do something with airplanes? Maybe fly the mail or something?"

"I don't think so."

Willie looked a little surprised by that. I don't know but that it made him a little sad. He had washed out years ago and hadn't flown, but maybe it made him happy to think that I could.

"You got all the flying you want on Uncle Sam's nickel, I guess."

"That's probably it."

"Flying the mail would be boring after flying a Mustang. Hey, Johnny, something you said reminded me of something. You know what? While you were gone, some of those Nazis were brought over here as prisoners. They rode them around on the train and put them up at some of the military bases. And you know what? They treated them better than they did Black men. They didn't have to ride on the backs of the trains. They didn't have to eat by themselves. They were treated better than Black soldiers."

I must have had quite a look on my face because he added, "Those Nazi bastards."

I wasn't really reacting to that, though. He had mentioned moving them around on a train, and for just a second, I was back on that train in Poland, moving along with the other living dead, surrounded by the stench of vomit and piss and shit and death. I felt beads of sweat push their way through my skin.

"Johnny?"

I snapped back. Willie was looking at me with concern.

"Listen brother, I didn't mean to make you mad. Don't listen to me. This is your wedding day and you need some happy thoughts. You go with your bride now. You treat that lady right. She's too good for you, you know."

I must have gotten back to normal because his slow smile had returned.

"I do know that."

I turned and she was moving toward me across the lawn, her brilliant white dress floating over the bright green grass. Her eyes were fixed on me, full of love. She did look like an angel, there's no other way to describe her. She was an angel.

"Mr. Nicholas, have you abandoned me already for your old Army buddies?"

I wrapped my arm around her waist and pulled her close for a kiss. Willie looked away, mostly, although I caught him stealing a look out of the corner of his eye.

"No buddies here, just Willie. And I think he won't mind if I take you and skedaddle on our honeymoon."

So, we gave a final wave goodbye and got in the car, a big white Mercury that ran like a ground-based version of the P-51 Mustang; it was flat fast. I had to keep pulling my foot back to keep from getting a ticket.

"Why are you in such a hurry, Mr. Nicholas?" Virginia asked with a sly smile.

"You'll see in a little bit, Mrs. Nicholas."

We made it to Montgomery in record time and checked into the hotel, The Fairton, the nicest place that would allow Race men and women to stay there. It was on the north side of town and overlooked a scrubby patch of woods. It could have overlooked the Alps, or the Taj Mahal, and I wouldn't have cared. I peeled my bride out of her dress, helped her carefully fold it and place it in the closet, and then fell upon her on the bed. We made love furiously, Virginia clutching me with strength I did not know she possessed. I had always pictured her as being maybe a little too pure, beyond such an animal thing as sex; I was wrong about that. She needed me and she needed it and she could finally have both.

I awoke sometime in the night. We had shoved our bodies together as much as we could stand and then fell asleep without even going out for dinner. A bright moon shone its white rays into the room, illuminating a sleeping Virginia. She slept with her lips together, breathing almost silently through her nose. Very well composed, even in unconsciousness. I thought she was composed all the time. Now I knew different. I thought of her pushing her hips hard against mine, wanting all of me inside her, and smiled. I put my head back down and fell asleep against my wife.

At some point in the night, she needed more. She moved off the bed and then I felt her climbing back on it, from the foot, crawling almost silently toward her goal. The moon outlined her silhouette as she loomed over me and grabbed me with a rough hand, urging the blood to go where she wanted it to go, getting me hard and ready. Her actions were much faster now, faster and coarser. She just wanted it and she wanted it now. She finally got the desired effect and climbed astride me, arching her back so far that the moon glanced across her face. She was not my Virginia. She was Annamaria riding me with her cold, dead eyes. I shouted at her to get off and kicked at her. I would not have her taking me in my own honeymoon bed, with my wife lying right beside us!

"Johnny!" she shouted, but I would not listen. I kept kicking at her, trying to push her out the window.

"Johnny! What are you doing?"

Her shout was louder this time. I realized it was not in French. It was not Annamaria's voice. I sat up in bed and saw Virginia lying on the floor, a shocked look on her face.

"Virginia! Virginia! I'm so sorry!"

She didn't say a word, just got up and went to the bathroom. She came back a few minutes later to find me shaking and sweating on the bed. She looked at me silently for a long time and then cupped my jaw in her hands.

"What was that, Johnny? Was that the war?"

I nodded and, as I moved my head, the tears started. She slowly drew my head to her shoulder and let me sob.

"What did they do to you over there, Johnny?"

I shook my head as I continued to sob. I didn't want to tell her. I had decided that I should never tell her, and I certainly didn't want to bring it up on our wedding night. She continued to hold me but didn't ask again. My tears subsided, replaced by a headache, that old familiar headache. I hadn't had one in a while, had almost forgotten what they were like.

"Did I hurt you?"

She showed me her leg, that silky leg I had been kissing just a few hours before. "I think it might have a bruise tomorrow, but nothing bad. You think you can go back to sleep? Without knocking me out of bed?" She smiled faintly to show me that this was joke, that everything was okay between us.

"I think so. I hope so."

"Let's go back to sleep. But first, since we're still awake..."

She took me in her hand, a much softer hand than the one Annamaria wielded in my nightmare. Virginia stiffened me up and then pulled me on top of her. She still wanted me, was still wet for me. I pushed into her slowly to show that I loved her.

THIRTY-THREE

Idle Hands

I LOVED BEING MARRIED. Loved everything about it. I was used to being alone, stuck inside my own head, so it was wonderful to have Virginia around all the time. And we were together a lot because neither one of us had a job. The downside to marriage was that because we had no income and no money, we were living with the Rev. Scott and Mrs. Scott. We had a small room upstairs, directly over theirs, so we grew very quiet in our lovemaking.

I needed to work, so the reverend found me odd jobs to do around the church and for parishioners. I cut lawns, fixed broken cars, repaired windows, even painted signs, which sort of gave me the willies. I wasn't as good at sign painting as my father, and I didn't want to get good at it.

Virginia did some work related to the church, as well, including picking up some of the little old ladies in the Rev. Scott's Mercury. We went to church every time the doors opened, which meant we were there all-day Sunday, half the day Wednesday and for days on end during special "revivals," which seemed to occur every few weeks. I had no idea that Christianity was so tenuous in Alabama that it required constant reviving.

Reverend Scott occasionally tried to engage me in conversation about religion, but I didn't want anything to do with it. I would go to church because he was helping me out and because I was married to his daughter, but those were the only reasons. I did not recognize the personal god that the reverend preached about. I did not believe in a god that cared not a single whit for what happened to his creations. I had been to Hell. It did not make me believe in Heaven.

I also did not care much for being back in Alabama. I didn't particularly want to be in Chicago, either, which had skyscrapers full of bad memories for me. I had returned Mother to Chicago and she resumed her place in the kitchenette, returned to a life she was no longer living with any enthusiasm. Part of her wanted me to stay, I think, but part of her wanted me to go. I was the last thing reminding her of her old life, and I think she had grown happy—if happy is the word—in her new, small, quiet, gray one. She let me go back.

But living in Alabama was making me mad. I was used to Chicago, where white people had the upper hand but there was still some room for a Race man to get ahead. In Alabama, the wind was in your face all the time. Willie was right. German prisoners of war, the worst of the worst, were treated better than patriotic Race soldiers. And I was starting to hear stories about how Race soldiers coming back from the war were being mistreated, beaten, even killed in the South. It was a background muttering among the Rev. Scott's flock, and the *Chicago Defender* spoke out against it in almost every issue. The *Defender* was still distributed throughout the South, put out hand to hand by the train porters, but I didn't read it much. It reminded me of too many things, and it reported on another world that was no longer mine.

One day that other world came very close. A soldier from Tuskegee, an airman in training, in fact, wandered into town and got too close to a white woman. According to the mob who beat him half to death, he had whistled at her and chased after her, which I doubt. Maybe he looked at her. Maybe she walked into his field of vision and he turned his head to see what was causing this movement, and that was enough to earn him a lifetime of disability, according to the redneck thugs who beat him up.

The man had not served in the war—he was too young—but I heard from Willie that he was a promising pilot and would have made the country proud. Hearing about the beating, and reading the local newspaper's account of it, infuriated me. The newspaper reported the incident as if the man had it coming. Of course, no one had seen who had done the actual beating. No one would be charged; nothing would happen to them. Reading the story made my blood boil, even worse than hearing about it by word of mouth. I got so angry that my vision dimmed for a while and my pulse pounded in my neck. I thought I might have a heart attack, but I didn't.

I don't care if the man was the worst Race soldier on the planet, he was better than a hundred of these ignorant white men. He was serving his country, even if his country wouldn't serve him.

"The Army is complaining to the sheriff," Willie told me about a week after the beating.

We had started playing cards regularly, but we just bet bottle caps because I didn't have any money.

"Complaining how?"

"Hauling his dumb redneck ass in and yelling at him. Telling him that soldier was U.S. government property and shouldn't be damaged by his local dumbasses."

"We're always someone's property." I threw my cards down in disgust. I had a pretty good hand, but my heart wasn't in the game anymore.

I badgered Rev. Scott about the incident. "Why isn't the church taking a stand against this?"

He had mentioned it in sermons but that was it, just words. I don't know what I expected him to do, but I wanted him to do something.

"I'm meeting with some ministers from around here. We're talking about what we can do to protect our men and women."

"Talking."

"Talking is what I can do right now, Johnny. I'm not a soldier like you. I can't fight anyone. And the Lord told us to turn the other cheek."

"I think we've done that. Enough."

I think I was made even more angry because I didn't know what to do about it, either. Should I try to beat down every white man I saw? I was nearly back to my old strength but that would never be enough. I would get my own ass beaten down at some point and then everyone would say I deserved it, and I would set my own cause back. It was frustrating and it made my pulse pound. Because there was nothing I could do about it.

Six long months after we moved in with Virginia's parents, I got wind of a good job, where I could use my skills without working on things that would give me nightmares. I heard about it from Willie, who always kept his ear to the ground where money was concerned. He probably just wanted to stop playing for bottle caps.

"I heard from my cousin that a guy up in Huntsville is going to start a car company," Willie said.

"A car company? Hasn't he heard of Ford and Mercury and Chrysler and Studebaker?"

"I guess he has. He wants to make something more affordable. Something for the common man. I'm just telling you about it, I'm not saying it will work. If you don't want a job, don't ask me about it."

I didn't know anything about Huntsville, hadn't even heard of it. Willie said it was up near the Tennessee state line. That had some immediate appeal. It was farther North, and I wanted to go farther North. And, more importantly, it was hundreds of miles from the reverend and Mrs. Scott. They were fine people, don't get me wrong, but I was ready to live with my wife, and I'm sure they would be happy to get us out of the house. I knew that Rev. Scott wanted me to get a full-time job. He was probably getting tired of saying, "Idle hands are the devil's workshop" and then finding me something to do around the church.

I expected a fight from Virginia. After all, we'd be miles north and getting around in those days wasn't as easy as it is now. I could have flown, I guess, but I was done with flying. I was going to crawl along the ground like everyone else from now on. Virginia seemed a little disappointed at the location, but she said, "Johnny, if you want it, take it, and I'll go with you." I think the strain of living in the house with her parents as man and wife was getting to her, too.

And so, I told Willie yes. I should have checked out the job, found out more about this man and his car, but the truth was that I didn't have the money to go up there and find out. A job had been offered to me, and I was going to take it, sight unseen. If I could work on an airplane engine, I could work on a car engine.

I took the train up to Huntsville to sign on and get started. I would rent a room for a while and then find us a place to live, and Virginia would join me. I would have been bored with the place, but Willie came with me, as he took a job there, too. We swapped bottle caps back and forth the whole way up to Huntsville. I was not impressed by my first sight of the place. It was just another sleepy little town, dusty and slow, cars and people trundling by as if they didn't have to be anywhere at any particular time.

"Where are all the Black folk?" Willie asked, and I looked around. Sure enough, there weren't a lot of Race folk, at least not within sight of the train station. That could not be good.

We spent part of the tiny amount of money we had on a taxi out to the Huntsville Arsenal, where Willie said the car company was setting up.

"Why are they in an arsenal?"

"Lots of space, I guess," Willie said. "With the war over, not much use for arsenals."

I wished that were true, but I doubted it.

The area did not seem industrial. We saw lots of cotton and corn and cows, even after we passed a sign telling us we were on Huntsville Arsenal grounds. We got out to face a guard lounging near an unpaved road with a long gate that stood open. He did not seem excited to see us or interested in us. The end of the war had not ended the training in Tuskegee; but it had ended whatever had been done here.

"We're supposed to go to Building 481," Willie said. "We have jobs at the car company. Dixie Motors."

"I heard you was coming. Go on through, it's down the road and on the right. You'll see the sign. Only, I think it's Keller Motors now. I don't remember if they changed the sign. It'll say one or the other."

We headed off down the road so he could return to staring into space.

"Dixie Motors," I said. "I don't like the sound of that. I like Keller Motors better."

"I'll like whoever signs my paycheck," Willie said.

We found a building with an open front and not much else. There were wooden shapes here and there, which I guess were meant to hold a car chassis. There was a row of lights along the ceiling and, aside from the wood, not much else. It was considerably less advanced than what the Nazis had built, even under a mountain, but at least no one had died here.

"Hello?" Willie asked to the empty space. "Hello?"

A door was cracked open on the far side of the room, and after about half a minute a head poked out. It was a white man with a crew cut.

"Help you fellas?" he shouted, not bothering to show any more of himself.

"We're here to work for the Dix—I mean, Keller Motors."

He looked at us for another few seconds and then disappeared. We looked at each other. He had seen us, two Race men. We probably weren't going to get the jobs now. We hadn't specified that we were Race men in our letters, but we hadn't run from it, either. Anybody paying attention to where we were and what we did would have figured it out, but a lot of people didn't bother to take the time. I had heard about situations like this, and the thought that I was in one now made the blood start to pound in my ears. Then the white man reappeared, walking out the door and over to us with a big smile.

"Hey, fellas," he said, his accent thicker than any I had heard even farther south. "Sorry about that, wasn't told to expect anyone today. My name's Jim. Jim Dupuy, director of production."

He shook our hands and smiled at us like we were old friends, and it was genuine. The pounding in my ears subsided.

"Come on back, you should talk to Mr. Mitchell. We're glad you're here, we're ready to get started. Don't look like much now, I know."

We walked across the floor, our steps echoing in the cavernous interior. This place was huge.

"Got a good deal on this," Jim said, as if reading my thoughts. "They used to make gas masks here during the war. This arsenal made a lot of chemical weapons in the war. They probably needed the gas masks just to do their jobs."

He gave a big barking laugh, and I smiled but felt my throat tighten up a little. Jim walked us through to a smallish office that was crammed with mechanical manuals, motor and aircraft magazines, odd little plastic pieces and other random junk. It looked like a little boy's room, except messier. Seated behind a scarred metal desk was a rotund man in an ill-fitting suit. When we entered, he popped up to meet us so fast he almost made me jump.

"Fellas, this is Mr. Mitchell. Mr. Mitchell, this is Mr. Nicholas and Mr. Mason."

He called us mister and used our last names. I was beginning to like this place.

"Please, call me Hubert. Sit down, sit down, I'm glad you're here. I checked up on you a little and I understand you are both excellent mechanics."

"We like to think so, sir," Willie said.

Willie was more deferent than I expected. Either he liked Hubert Mitchell, or he really wanted the job.

"I know my stuff, too. I built my own airplane when I was a kid, and it actually flew, and I'm still alive. So, I know what to look for, and you fellows have it. This should be easy for you. You're used to working on very complex engines. The one we've got for our cars is simple. It's just an inline four, less than sixty horsepower. A one-barrel carburetor. You could probably put one of these together in your sleep."

He was right about that.

"What I'd like for you to do, if you want the jobs, is to verify the construction of our engines. We'll put our cars together on our assembly line, but I want to make sure they're tested and they're good. You'll examine every engine we build and then work with Jim here to make any changes that need to be made."

I detected a note of nervousness in his tone now, and Jim's eyes were beginning to dart around the office as if he were afraid to look at anything too long. Now the situation was pretty clear. The Keller Motor Company wanted to hire good quality technical workers without paying the going rate for white ones. As Race men, Hubert knew that we would work for less. As former military men, he knew we'd do a good job. But the rest of his workers would probably be white, and it wouldn't do to have a Race man giving orders to a white worker. So, we would do the quality checks, but Jim would be the go-between. He would put the muscle behind our ideas and suggestions. He would probably get paid more than us, too, for a job that didn't even need to exist if white people had any sense. I looked at Willie, and he gave a slight nod. He understood what was going on. I could also tell that he was willing to take the job, and I was, too. It could be worse. We'd be doing work that would call on our skills, but that wouldn't force me to mess around with airplanes. And Hubert Mitchell, although trapped in his white insanity, didn't seem to be a bad sort, and Jim Dupuy didn't, either. It was almost certainly the best we could do. An image of Rev. Scott came to mind. The idea of continuing to do busy work at the church had lost its appeal. I was going into the car business.

THIRTY-FOUR

The Keller Super Chief

The work at Keller Motors was less than exciting. I moved Virginia up to Huntsville and we got a small apartment near the edge of the arsenal, where I could walk to work every day. Willie lived closer to town and usually thumbed a ride in, so his schedule was very flexible. You could never tell when he would turn up.

The thing is that it did not matter. The assembly line did not grow more complex; it was still just a series of boards, like the frame of an abandoned house. There were no workers for us to instruct, even through Jim, who was not around much. He and Hubert Mitchell and other officials of the Keller company were out barnstorming the country, raising money to build a small, cheap woodie wagon. We essentially got paid for showing up and keeping the place clean, although when the brass stopped by with the car, we had to tune it up and get it ready for its next stop. When the car was gone, Willie and I studied the blueprints for the thing and tried to figure out the best way to build a bunch of them. Willie had never worked on an assembly line. I had, but it was the one in Germany under the mountain and I wanted to forget about that.

We began to have our suspicions about the car after we became familiar with it, at least on paper. The thing was stone simple. Too simple. The whole back half of the body was made out of wood, which posed no technical problems at all. We could probably get in a truck and drive around the backroads near the base and round up two dozen men who could build a station wagon body out of wood. Willie objected to it on practical grounds.

"You get one of those things out in a wet Alabama winter, and in about six months it will rot right off."

"They'll have to keep it in a garage," I said.

"A garage? This is supposed to be a working man's car. Now we say he's got to be a working man owning a house with a garage to buy this inexpensive car? Man, nobody's made a car out of wood since the horse and buggy days. There's a reason they quit doing it, too."

He was right, of course. Whenever the Keller was around it was treated like a prize racehorse and kept warm and dry. That was about as far as you could take a racehorse comparison with this car. It was as slow as a snail in the snow. On one stopover, when the car needed a little more work than usual, Willie and I managed to take it out for a drive. It took forever to hit 50 miles per hour, the little engine churning away under the rounded hood. We tried to keep it on good roads but hit a couple of bad ones, too, and the thing nearly shook our teeth out. Its interior was as spartan as an old buggy. It was only slightly more comfortable than the Nazi truck that had knocked me around.

"This thing is a piece of junk," Willie said when we got back, although he was careful to say it so that only I could hear.

It was, too. We rolled it back into the shop and propped open the hood to do some work. The car had round headlights on either side of a grill that curved upward on the ends just a little. I used to think the car was smiling at us; after driving it a while, I knew that it was laughing at us. But the company kept growing. Hubert Mitchell and George Keller, the man the company and the car were named after, were on the road a lot. They had signed up dealers all over the country. Of course, they only had one car so far.

Willie and I put our plans for construction together, and even started working on some modifications that would make the thing run better. A new engine would be nice, but we had to work with what was at hand. We managed, at least on paper, to eke out another 12 horsepower. Our modified Keller Super Chief—maybe it should be the Keller Super Super Chief—wouldn't win any drag races, but it would be slightly less of a slug than the one we had. We were ready to go, but the brass kept winging in and out on their endless sales visits. No other construction workers were hired, not even anyone to hammer wooden bodies together. Mitchell kept saying good things were about to happen, but I had developed a very bad feeling about the whole thing. There were lots of new cars hitting the road, some not more expensive than what he wanted to sell the Keller for, and they were much, much better.

But if they wanted to pay me for doing nothing, that was fine with me, for the time being. When I got home, I wasn't tired from having a long day. Virginia and I lived cheap so we had decent money, so we went out as much as we could. We couldn't eat in most of the restaurants but there were a few good Race ones and we got to know the people there well. Willie was similarly relaxed, and even found a girl. Her name was Eileen. She was awfully young, about five years younger than us, but she was both smart and knowledgeable and she fit in so well that we all soon forgot there was an age difference. Willie and Eileen often joined us on our outings. You might think that meant that I looked at Willie virtually all day every day, but the Keller job was so slow that half the time Willie got bored, wandered off, and started a card game somewhere.

Looking back, that was the best time of my life. I was bored but relaxed. I had energy to explore Virginia's body and she mine, and we did that a lot. Not every day, but often. She was a preacher's daughter, but she was learning new tricks, and she was learning them with me. It wasn't long before she started becoming ill in the morning. We both knew what that meant. I actually had sensed it on the horizon long before it happened. I knew that we were going to bring new life into the world, and I believed, based on nothing, that it would be a boy.

While Virginia continued to grow, Willie and I whiled away the days for the Keller Motor Company and Willie endured good-natured teasing from Eileen about when she could expect to become a wife and mother. Willie and I started going out fishing, something I had never done. The Tennessee River wound its way near the arsenal like a lazy snake and gave us plenty of opportunity. I didn't like fishing as much as I thought I might, but it was something to do. While the company chiefs tried to drum up interest in the Keller, we learned how to dredge up catfish. I decided that, some day, I would take my son fishing and teach him everything I knew about it, which wasn't much.

Just when it finally seemed we were going to be ready to start building cars, George Keller up and died. He died in a motel room in New York City. Word didn't reach us right away. It ricocheted around the dealers and the salespeople, but didn't get to us technical folks for a couple of days. Hubert Mitchell ended up telling us himself during one of his swings by the "office."

"Now, you don't worry about that," he said. "Everything is going to be fine. We'll just find a new man to head the company and we'll press ahead."

His face was paler than usual, which put the lie to his words. He looked like a man who worked for a dead company. So, Willie and I put down the fishing poles and started looking for work. I had a new mouth on the way, and I needed to make sure it got fed. And Willie, of all things, wanted to get married. We needed some cash and we would be lucky if we got our last couple of paychecks from the Keller Motor Company.

Virginia was getting larger by the day. She was starting to feel it, too, and most mornings I woke up to the sound of her retching into the toilet. Our fairy tale had come to an end and the real world was intruding again. I looked around the apartment. We didn't have much. We had bought a ratty couch that we had recovered, and some nice tables that were turned so visitors couldn't see the chips in the wood. We had a radio, an old one from before the war. Televisions were out but we couldn't begin to afford one. I knew I needed more money. I needed a more stable job. I wanted my son to have things I never had.

"I hear there's going to be hiring at the arsenal," Willie told me one day. "Lots of people starting to move in."

"What, are they going to start making gas masks again?"

"I wish. That would be even easier than designing a car no one is going to build. No, it's something about rockets."

"Rockets?"

We were on the concrete balcony that encircled the second floor of my apartment building, feet up on the metal railing, beers in hand, watching the sun go down somewhere over the arsenal. It was a beautiful day and I was relaxed until I heard that word.

"Yeah, something about rockets. Missiles. Like those things the Germans rained down on London in the war. You heard about those, right?"

I almost dropped my bottle.

"Right?"

"Uh, yeah."

"You okay? You look kind of funny."

"I'm fine. Just the heat, I guess."

"Heat? It's not hot. You're getting soft, man. You need to find you some hard work. Anyway, they're bringing these German guys over here. They're the experts with the missiles, I guess, 'cause they built them."

They were the experts, all right. I tried to keep calm and keep drinking my beer like nothing happened. For a couple of seconds there I felt like I was back in that hellhole, that literal hell, building the devil's weapons and trying to escape the noose, or worse. A cold sweat push its way to my skin, as if fleeing the very thought of the place.

"Are you sick, Johnny? It's not hot, and you're sweating." Willie brought me back to Earth.

"I'm fine."

"You really are getting soft if you think this is hot. The Keller Motor Company has not been working you hard enough, obviously."

"You know that is true."

"Those Germans will, though, I hear. They'll work you to death. Very efficient."

I spit out a mouthful of beer and was coughing.

"You sure you're okay?"

"Fine," I croaked. "It went down the wrong pipe."

"You just need to relax. I can't believe they are bringing those guys here to work, though. Didn't we just beat them in a war? I wonder if they'll keep them under guard or something."

"I hope so."

I wondered where they would keep the Germans. They would probably need to build some kind of prison on the arsenal. Or were they still prisoners?

"Anyway, I'm going to see what kind of jobs they have. I hope they know a couple Race men can work on their rockets. I don't have any rocket experience, though. I'm a piston man. I've seen a couple of the new jet fighters, but I haven't worked on them. I think that's a whole different thing, though."

I let Willie prattle on while the sun moseyed out of sight. It was taking its time going away, a big kid not wanting to go to bed.

"You ever worked on a jet or a rocket?" Willie asked.

I was back on an even keel by this time. His question didn't even faze me. "No. I'm a piston man, like you."

"So, you want me to see what kind of jobs they are going to have?"

Working with Willie was always fun, but working with Germans again did not appeal, even if they were on my ground now.

"No, I don't think so. I'll find something else."

THIRTY-FIVE

It Gets Better and It Gets Worse

THERE WAS NOTHING ELSE. At least, nothing else that could use my technical skills. But I needed money, so I took to mowing lawns, shoving the blades across the yards of white folks. After all this time, I was like my mother, doing things for white people that they didn't want to do for themselves.

Willie went to work for the arsenal, working on engine valves for some motors they were developing for mysterious purposes. And then, sure enough, the Germans came. They weren't coming as captured enemies, either. The local white paper had it all over the front page, treating them like they were heroes. I couldn't believe it. I read the story about ten times, and it always said the same thing. The Germans were going to revitalize this town and build the country's missiles against the looming Soviet menace. I felt my face burn and my pulse pound in my head, and the white paper darkened before me. These were the very same Germans who built the V-2s that blasted London back to the Bronze Age. The paper said so. But it didn't say anything about how they were built. They were just miracles that assembled themselves. And these Germans were being treated better than I was.

Virginia didn't understand why I didn't get a job with Willie. I never answered her and eventually she stopped asking, but she would look at me when I came home bathed in sweat and I knew she was trying to figure it out. She knew it had something to do with the war, but I wouldn't discuss it. She didn't need to know there was such evil in this world, especially not while carrying our son. I didn't want those thoughts to leak down to him and affect his mind.

And so it went. The Germans arrived in Huntsville and became absorbed into the fabric of the city, eating at fancy parties, being fed at the best restaurants. I knew this because the white newspapers reported on their every move, who they talked to, where they went for fun. They never reported on what the Germans did during the war. Never that. From reading the papers, I learned that many of the Germans had settled on the slopes of Monte Sano Mountain because it reminded them of the green hills of Germany. So, I knew where they were. Sometimes I walked outside the house and looked toward where I thought the mountain was; it was smallish as mountains go, and dark. I looked up there and just wondered what they were thinking. They were probably blissfully asleep.

I was mainly angry because I knew that before long, I was going to have to work for them again. I would get paid this time, and would not be worked to death, most likely, but I would have to work with them. The shadows were lengthening, our baby was getting more due by the minute and there was no way I could make enough money cutting grass to support even myself, much less a wife and child. I had mentioned moving back to Montgomery a time or two, but Virginia always changed the subject. She loved her parents but, as it turned out, was quite happy living several hours away from them.

I held out as long as I could. I want the record to reflect that.

Our son was born on October 1. It was a beautiful fall day. The humidity had taken a vacation and gone further south, but the leaves were still hanging on, showing their colors. The sky was a deep blue. The sun, which had been roasting us all summer long, turned down its intensity a little to let us enjoy the day. And James Scott Nicholas chose this fantastic day to arrive, at 10 a.m., a courteous time for a courteous boy. It gave us all time to get to the hospital to greet him: Me, the Reverend Scott, Mrs. Scott, Willie and Eileen. My mother sent her regards but couldn't make it; she didn't have time enough. She requested a photograph of her only grandchild.

He arrived loud and crying. He was tall, twenty-two inches, and heavy, nearly seven pounds. He yelled his head off, as if we had disturbed his sleep, which I guess we had. We all looked at him and laughed with joy as the nurse cleaned him up. Eyes were gleaming all around, even Virginia's, although she was exhausted from hours of labor. I had never felt such love flowing around me before, love that transcended each of us as individuals and brought us all together. I think even the nurse felt it; her eyes were shining. I want to keep the memory of that feeling for as long as I live, and maybe beyond. It was that strong. I believe that most people never get to feel it at all. I am lucky that I did.

Like I said, I held off working at the arsenal as long as I could. I had managed to scare up some roofing work in addition to the grass mowing, which brought in more money and was picking up just as the mowing season was winding down. But after we brought little James home, I knew those days were numbered. Virginia made the apartment as fit for a child as she could, but suddenly what was big enough for two wasn't big enough for three. Babies are tiny but they seem to come with a lot of attachments and extras. James was squeezing us out of our place. Virginia began giving me those long glances that carried a lot of meaning.

So, finally, I had to ask Willie if he knew if something was available.

"Man, do you not read the papers? We can't get enough people in there. Just tell me what you want."

Of course, what he meant was, just tell me what you want, and I'll see what's there out of jobs they might give to Race men. Our jobs at the Keller Motor Company, such as they were, were the exception, especially for Alabama. The dumbest white man in North Alabama would get a better job at the arsenal than I would. We had proven ourselves in war, but that would never be enough. Ironically, I would probably never have a job as technically demanding as what the Nazis had given me.

"I don't want to work on missiles."

"What? Are you kidding? That's like saying you want to go to

Chicago in December, but you don't want it to be cold. That's like saying you want—"

"All right, I get it. I just don't want to work on them."

He found me something in the motor pool. The Army was pouring into Huntsville and they needed jeeps and trucks and transports for the assorted bigwigs coming through, not to mention the missile parts. They also needed someone with mechanical experience to keep those engines and transmissions running, and I had experience in that. My time working in the motor pool at Buchenwald was no less hellish than my work on the missiles underground, but for some reason it didn't affect me the same way. I didn't swear off using cars or trucks or working on engines. I'm not sure exactly why this was the case. I think maybe I was used to trucks and cars and engines. I understand them; everyone understands them. But working on a missile, something you've only ever seen in the comics pages, was a whole different thing. It was something out of a nightmare, one from which I never woke.

The end of the war had alerted the United States and everybody else that things were going to be different now, and worse. Hitler showed that death could rain from the sky from far away and hit you before you knew it was coming. We showed we could create a weapon that would turn entire cities to glass. And not only did we have it, we would use it.

I was vague to Virginia about what I was doing. I knew I could do better, and she would, too. But little James was occupying her time and my income went up dramatically, so she didn't push too hard. We needed to get out of the apartment, so we saved up over the next couple of years and bought a little house a little further north of the arsenal. We bought a car when James arrived, in case he suddenly needed to be whisked off somewhere. Virginia, being the worried mother, pictured him needing to rush to the hospital in the wee hours of the night, and we'd have to go out of our way to get to the Race hospital. I figured he would be a fighter and would be healthy, but I bought the car anyway.

It sure as hell wasn't a Keller Super Chief! Not that what we bought was much better. It was a 1938 Ford Fordor Deluxe. The Deluxe—or "dux," as James started to call it when he could talk—had been a nice dark green at one point but now it was various shades of green, brown, tan and black, like it was trying to camouflage itself. Its V-8 engine ran on six cylinders most of the time and it liked to mark its passage through the world with a modest cloud of black smoke. Virginia had the car most of the time, but I brought it into work with me now and then to try to improve it when I had a little spare time in the shop. There was something deeply wrong with the car. I replaced all the parts that I could without taking it completely apart, but it steadfastly refused to perform up to specs. I got a couple of the dead cylinders going again but it then dropped a pair of the other ones. Six cylinders was enough for it, thanks.

Life settled down this way for a long time. They weren't the best years, but they certainly weren't the worst. We made more friends and started attending the Bethel Baptist Church. It was just a little way down the road from our house but we drove there more often than not just to show that we could. I have never known Baptists who didn't like a little financial competition. Our car was nothing fancy, but it was not the worst in the parking lot, and after I painted it one spring it looked pretty presentable. I was surprised how fast those years went, though. Even though nothing was happening—we were just growing older together—it seemed that the planet had picked up speed and was whirling around the sun at a dizzying speed.

James sprouted from a tiny grasping infant to a rangy boy who could nearly outrun me. I started slowing down and spreading out, and my clothes reflected it. My pants didn't get any taller, but they did get wider. My time in the war had been much more exciting, too exciting sometimes, but it seemed to crawl compared to the way things move now. I wondered if that was why old people walk with canes. The planet must be spinning so damned fast by then they can hardly stand upright.

THIRTY-SIX

Memories

———————

OCCASIONALLY, I saw the Germans. They would suddenly appear in the corners of my eyes, walking together, speaking German. I think my ears would pick up their language before my brain was even aware and I would begin to tense. When it got colder, they wore long black leather coats, just as they had back then, and walked around like vultures. I would walk the other way when I saw them. I didn't have access to most of their buildings anyway and didn't want it.

One day I was elbow-deep in an eight-cylinder Ford truck when I heard that unmistakable sound, the one that made the hairs on my arms stand up: German. Someone was speaking German and they were close by. I extricated myself from under the coffin-length hood and found a thin man standing before me. He wore round black glasses but, aside from that, nearly everything about him was khaki colored. He wore khaki pants, khaki shoes and an off-white shirt that was almost khaki. Even his face and hair were close to khaki. He looked like he had been modeled out of clay.

He stood there looking at me as if expecting me to do something, and so I just stood there and looked back at him. After a few seconds of this, his khaki face started to darken.

"Oh, my goodness," he said. "I spoke to you in German, didn't I?"

"Yes." I should have said, "Yes, sir," but I didn't feel like it.

"I must apologize. I talk to my colleagues in German all day and sometimes I forget."

His English was good but heavy with accent, so I had to concentrate to be able to understand him.

"I know this is unusual, but I was wondering if you had a few moments and could look at my car."

"What's wrong with your car?"

"I don't know. I study rocket fuel. I'm not really good with mechanical things. That's why I wondered if you could take a look at it."

"I'm not really supposed to work on people's personal cars."

"I know. Please. It's causing me a lot of trouble."

He looked so upset that he might cry, and I didn't want to see that. I told him to drive the car into the shop and be quick about it. He pulled in behind the wheel of a wheezing Studebaker. I expected something German, so I could excuse myself by saying I didn't have the parts for it. But I could probably fix a Studebaker.

"Keep it running," I told him.

He got out and I popped the hood. He hovered over me like I was a doctor operating on his child. His child was a mess. The valves were clacking, the timing was off, there was an oil leak somewhere down below and the excess was burning off in sharp puffs of smoke, and the remnants of a bird's nest poked out from behind the engine block. I was surprised he was even able to drive it into the garage.

"Where did you get this?"

"I bought it in Texas."

"When were you in Texas?"

"They brought us from Germany to Texas. Fort Bliss. Then they brought us here. I bought this from an Army guy."

My guess is he bought it from an Army guy who was still mad about the war and who didn't like Germans. Nobody would sell a heap like this to anyone they liked.

"Well, this thing is a mess. You need to take it in to a shop. It's going to take a lot of work."

"Is there—is there any way you can do it? I could pay you—over time."

He looked very nervous now. I was really starting to get irritated.

"This is the arsenal motor pool. I'm not supposed to be working on employees' cars. Just take it in to a shop."

"The problem is—the problem is I don't have much money. I send a lot of my money home. Most of my family is still there. I bought this car because I thought it would be reliable, but it's terrible."

"I thought the government brought your families over here."

"Most of them. But not all. Not mine. I have a big family. I'm one of the younger scientists. Not so special." He stood before me, rubbing his hands in worry like a cartoon character.

I almost felt sorry for him. Almost. I leaned against the Studebaker's dented fender and looked back at him. "Where did you work over there?"

"In Germany? In Peenemunde. A little town on the coast."

"What were you developing?"

"Some of it is secret."

"Some of it is secret, and I'm not supposed to work on employees' cars."

He got my drift.

"We were working on rockets and aircraft. Then the Allies bombed us and most of the work was moved somewhere else."

"Underground?"

His handwringing wrung even more. He was worried about talking too much, but he also wanted his car fixed.

"Yes, underground."

"Did you work at the underground plant?"

"No. Some of us stayed at Peenemunde, even after the bombing. I was one of them."

"Did you ever go to the underground rocket plant?"

"No. I heard about it. I heard it was not a fun place to work."

"Did you have any slave laborers in Peena—penna—"

"Peenemunde. Slave laborers? I don't know what you mean by that.

We had some prisoners of war who worked there, but I didn't work with them. Why do you ask? How do you know so much about this?"

I wasn't going to answer that. "When you're with the other Germans in there, do they ever talk about the rocket plant? That underground plant?"

"At work? No. I have never heard it spoken of. We just talk about technical problems. The rate of flow needed for the fuel, the best mix of fuel, that kind of thing."

I didn't think they would be riddled with guilt.

"I'll fix your car. Just this once. I probably won't get everything fixed but I'll make it run smoother. But I want you to do something for me."

"Anything," he said. "Anything legal."

WHAT I DID WAS, I WROTE DOWN NAMES. ALL THE NAMES I COULD remember.

I started simply. I wanted to write the names of the people from Dora. In neat, precise, easily readable handwriting, I put down the name: JEAN. Poor Jean, hung up before me in the camp, swinging for an act I was also committing. Now he was gone wherever the dead go, to Heaven or Hell or Valhalla, and I was alive and free, with a family, working on a German bastard's car.

I then wrote ZELLER. Zeller, who steered me on the path to sabotage, to what good end, I do not know.

I realized there were so many more people there, so many more members of the gray walking dead that had surrounded me, and I did not know their names, or if I had heard them, I did not remember. So, I wrote down the names of anyone I could think of.

KLAUS (ENGINEER). That should get their attention. Klaus might even be here, for all I knew, but I had never seen him or heard anyone mention the name.

GEORG. SEYMOUR. (KAPOS). They would know that term, too, and I pictured them nervously looking at each other as they read it.

I even wrote MARIANNE. ANNAMARIA. JULIE. Those names

would make no sense to them, but I realized the list was really not for them. It was for me. I was going to remember one more time and then I was going to let them go.

And then I wrote: DORA.

I gave the note to the German with the broken Studebaker. His name was Franz.

"Is there some place where you and the other engineers gather?"

"There are lots of places like that."

"Take this paper and leave it in one. Leave it in one of the more popular places. Don't let anyone see you. But make sure you leave it somewhere it will be found."

"I don't see—"

"Just do it. And if you connect it to me, I will guarantee you that your car will never run right again. It will fail you just when you need it most."

He looked at his battered transportation nervously, as if there was some magic spell I could cast on it.

"I will do it."

He took my paper, and I felt a sense of lightness in my chest. My war was finally over.

THIRTY-SEVEN

The Coming Storm

VIRGINIA'S MOTHER died when James was ten years old. So now she knows more about life and death than I do.

Virginia was sad but not inconsolable, because she had a child to look after and did not have time to be inconsolable. That must be one reason why the human race has survived and thrived. We have kids and they keep us busy, too busy to see how terrible life can be.

Lillian, the wife of Rev. Scott, mother of Virginia, visited us often while James was growing up. She liked our house. It was smaller but no smaller than the one she and Rev. Scott had lived in for forty-five years. She absolutely adored James, and he was adorable in the years she saw him. The Scotts kept a small bench just inside their front door, where they would sit to take off their shoes and put on house shoes. One morning, she went out for a long walk, came back, told her husband she was tired, sat down on the bench and died. Her heart gave out one massive final pulse and then stopped. The Rev. Scott was in the kitchen, working on a sermon about the impermanence of material things. He could not see the bench from the kitchen table, but he heard a loud thump and went to investigate. He laughed when he first saw his wife lying there, because she moved a little and he thought she had just fallen off the bench. Then she did not move again, and he realized something was wrong. He felt terrible about laughing afterward. He told the story over and over through the years, but he never left out the part where he laughed. I think he left it in to punish himself.

Virginia asked her father to move in with us after her mother was dead and gone for a month, but he refused. He said something was going on in his part of the state and he wanted to stay close to it. Race men and women, choking under the indignities they had to face every day, were talking about how they could gain their rights under the Constitution. They did not have them in Alabama. They would have to either take them or persuade the white majority to grant them. I did not think either outcome was possible, but my father-in-law did, and the work began to consume him more and more.

He had never come to visit us as much as his wife had done, but now he was around the house almost every other week. He was working to end segregation and discrimination and had volunteered to be a liaison between the southern Alabama churches and those in the northern part of the state and in Tennessee. James never quite warmed up to his grandfather as much as he had to his grandmother, but he did like having him around, and not only because the Rev. Scott rarely showed up at the door without bringing several small bags of boiled peanuts.

Rev. Scott invited me to some of his meetings, but for reasons that I don't understand, even now, I didn't want to go. It wasn't like the issue of being free didn't apply to me. I just couldn't stand the thought of getting in a room with a lot of angry Race men and whining about what we could do. I didn't think we could do anything, and I had had enough of feeling powerless during the war.

My son was growing taller and stronger. He was nearly the size that I was when I first started walking down to Harlem Airport. I was stronger and healthier now but had not regained my full size and strength, and never did. The war diminished me in a lot of ways, including physically. I was happy to leave the futility to someone else and just enjoy watching James grow up.

We used to sit around the dinner table and talk when Rev. Scott was in town. He told us what was said in the meetings, how some Race men from churches all over the country were starting legal challenges to segregation laws in the South that were clearly unconstitutional.

"Think of it," he said. "We could eat where we want, in the best restaurants. We could live where we want, in the best neighborhoods. We could swim in the best city pools. We could be doctors, lawyers, congressmen, not just for Race people, but for white people and Jewish people, too."

"Oh, Daddy," Virginia said. "You like your house, and you don't ever go out to eat."

She was teasing him, and he knew it, and laughed. James joined in.

"Or swim."

"That's all true enough," he said, pushing back from the table and patting his stomach, which had actually grown larger after his wife's death.

He and those other preachers would get together and eat and talk and eat and talk. I sometimes wished I ran a food service so I could get rich off their appetites.

"Johnny, I wish you would come with me. We could benefit from your experience during the war. You're a hero! You remember how those war experiences helped integrate the military. We could still use those stories."

President Truman had finally gotten disgusted with the treatment of Race men in this country after the war, when Race soldiers came back home and were beaten or lynched by white mobs for the usual tiny infractions of whatever rules the rednecks had laid down. It was obvious to all that Race men had fought for their country and its freedoms only to come home and be denied them once again. Most of the white people didn't care, but Race people resisted, and some said they would never again fight for a country that wouldn't fight for them. President Truman desegregated the military.

So that was done, and I didn't see how it would help to tell my stories to the Rev. Scott and his little band. I wouldn't tell them the biggest story of all, the one I have told here, because all it would illuminate is that there is evil in the world and in the hearts of men, and they already knew that very well.

I asked Willie if he wanted to go, and he was even more reluctant than me.

"I can't stand to be in a room with that many preachers."

Finally, though, Virginia wanted to go to a meeting and asked me to come with her. It was during one of her father's more frenetic visits, so she saw it as a chance to spend more time with him, I guess, or maybe she was just worried about him and didn't want him to get too excited. I got Willie and Eileen to look after James and off we went. Willie and Eileen had gotten married and had tried to have kids, but it never took, so they adored James and spoiled him and roughhoused with him as if he was their own.

The meeting was larger than I expected. Rev. Scott had been telling me that crowds were growing, but I hadn't paid much attention, and in my mind, it had been just a few guys sitting around on folding metal chairs. Instead, we drove to Bethel Baptist, one of the larger Race churches in the area. There were a lot of cars in the lot and I had to park far away so that we trudged through the dust to get to the church.

"Beginning to worry about you, Reverend," said a man at the door.

He was tall and lean and dressed in a crisp black suit. He had to stoop over to shake my father-in-law's hand, and when he did so, he clasped my father-in-law's arm with his other hand. I had not dealt with too many lawyers, but it struck me that he was one, or should be, if he wasn't.

"Toussaint," Rev. Scott said, "this is my daughter, Virginia, and my son-in-law, Johnny Nicholas."

"Pleased to meet you," the man said, turning all his considerable charm and attention to us, and kissing Virginia on the back of her hand. "Toussaint Guthrie."

"Toussaint Guthrie," I repeated, unable to help myself.

His smile nearly broke his face half in two. His teeth were as white as our picket fence.

"I know. My parents were fans of Toussaint L'Ouverture, but our last name was Guthrie. So that's what I got. You can call me Tony, if you like."

"Toussaint is fine."

"Great. And I've heard a lot about you, Johnny. I'm very proud of what you've accomplished."

"Thanks."

"Come on inside, then, let's get started."

Toussaint led the meeting with my father-in-law acting as a second-in-command of sorts. The pews were filled with men in suits, men in work shirts, men in something in between and ladies in nice dresses. A few of the ladies wore hats as if they were attending a regular church service, standing out like mushrooms studding a field. Toussaint outlined activities that were going on around the state and in the rest of the South. There were plans for sit-ins and strikes, but those plans seemed a little vague. And I'm not sure, but I think this is the first time I heard the name of Dr. Martin Luther King. I didn't know who he was, even though he was from Alabama. Toussaint didn't dwell on him, just mentioned him in passing, but it was the second person I had heard of that evening who was named after a historical figure and the name stuck in my mind.

After a while, the meeting devolved into an argument between Toussaint and my father-in-law. Mr. Guthrie thought that some amount of violent resistance might be good and necessary. Rev. Scott did not think so.

"They will take any chance they can to beat us down," Rev. Scott said, to quite a few _amens_ from the crowd. "We should not give them a chance. We need to show the white folks that we're better than them."

"We've been showing them that for thousands of years," Toussaint said. "We need to show that we're tough, too. We're not just victims."

He got a few _amens_, but not as many as Rev. Scott. Probably, everyone in that crowd had experienced some kind of run-in with hateful white folks: police, a bunch of drunks on a street corner, anything. Whatever it was, it was enough to make them wary of sticking their necks out. I don't remember all the rest of the meeting. I never had a very good attention span for meetings. Probably it involved setting up plans for another meeting for some kind of civil disobedience.

What I do remember are those two names: Dr. Martin Luther King Jr. and Toussaint Guthrie. I remembered them at the time because I thought they were unusual. Later, I would remember them because I would have to choose which one to follow.

THIRTY-EIGHT

The Fire Next Time

Things were heating up. You've probably seen all the old black-and-white news clips of police dogs and fire hoses and marches and Dr. Martin Luther King Jr.'s "I Have a Dream" speech. But there was so much more to it than that. That was just the big wave, but there was a lot of water under that wave. There were hundreds of people like my father-in-law, and like Toussaint Guthrie, who made it happen. Some of them rode the crest of the wave to get to the shore and some did not reach the promised land.

I started going to more meetings. Virginia was happy because she thought I was bonding with her father, making the family stronger. I was really going because of Toussaint. The second time I went to a meeting, leaving Virginia at home, this time, to keep an eye on James, he pulled me aside after the meeting was over.

"Hey, military man. I want to talk to you."

We went straight from the church to a bar. I'm sure that's not the first time that has happened, but it was the first time I had done it. It was a dingy bar that, of course, catered only to Race folk. If the big bad wolf came up outside and sneezed, the whole place would probably fall down. Toussaint, without asking, ordered himself a Coke and me a

Miller beer. We sat at the far-right corner of the bar, out of earshot of the other inhabitants, who were playing snooker at the lone table.

"What do you think about these meetings?" he asked after he took a long sip of his Coke and let out a little sigh.

"I'm getting more interested."

"But it's a slow thing, isn't it? It's slow. Everybody has to take time to get their minds around the fact that Black folk are being kept down and there's something we can do about it."

His manner of speaking was unusual. I had never heard anything like it before, and it took years before I heard anything like it again. That moment came when I was watching late-night TV and came across a rerun of Bela Lugosi in "Dracula." Toussaint talked like Bela Lugosi in that movie, sort of. When he wanted to emphasize a word, he paused and drew it out. "It's sloooooooow." "Everybody has to take tiiiiiiiiime." It was effective, though. It made me listen, just to hear when he would let that Alabama drawl go even slower.

"So, how would you like to speed it up?" I asked.

"You're from the north, right?"

"Well, I was born in Alabama, but yeah, I grew up in Chicago."

"See, the brothers down here are beat down. Some of them. A lot of them. They've been raised to expect nothing and so they expect nothing. If you offer them a little something, just a liiiiiiiitle something, they're happy with that. Let them vote, maybe, if they own property, but don't let them run for office and don't let them move into a nice part of town. Don't let them in the schools. Do you understand what I am saying here?"

"Of course."

"They're cowed. They live with these white folks and they have come to believe things should be the way they are, with maybe a little more freedom for them. Just a little. But up north, they think differently. You got the *Defender*, man! The porters bring that down here and people pass it around like it's the Bible. In the north, a Black man can live where he wants, get the job he wants—"

"You ever been up north, Toussaint? To Chicago or New York?"

He shook his head sadly and peered into his Coke. "Nah. When I had the time, I didn't have the money, and when I had the money, I didn't have the time."

"I'm just asking because it's not the way you think. A Race man can't live where he wants. He can't get any job he wants. He can do the jobs that white folks don't want to do, or he can do jobs that serve only the Race community, but that's about it."

"Race man," Toussaint said with a chuckle. "I like that. Anyway, I guess you're right, but you have to admit that things are better for Black folks up north than they are here."

"Absolutely."

"Glad I'm not completely wrong. But here's the thing. Some of the Black folks up there think that maybe a stronger approach is needed."

"Stronger?"

"Stronger. Maybe showing white folks that we're not weak. They've been scared of us this whole time, you know. Scared of what we might do. Scared that we might pull something like my namesake did in Haiti. I think we should show them that they do have something to be scared of."

"You mean armed resistance."

"Yes."

"Toussaint, they could cut us down like dogs. And they would give us nothing after that. That would set us back a hundred years."

Toussaint finished his Coke with a gulp and clapped the glass back on the bar, hard enough to make the barkeep glare at him and the snooker players to look up to see if a fight was going to break out.

"I expected more out of you, man. You fought Hitler. When we appeased Hitler, did it work? No, it did not work. What worked was showing Hitler that we would kill him if he did not back down. And we did."

"That's not the same situation, at all."

"It's exaaaaaaactly the same situation. Someone is doing something you don't like, you call it to their attention that you're not going to stand for it. And if they don't believe it, you show them that you mean it."

Toussaint was energetic and on fire, but he wasn't suicidal. He planned to take his violent revolution slow. He knew that to try any sort of frontal attack, or even a good frontal defense, at this stage, would mean death, and an undignified one, at that. He'd swing from a tree or get beaten to death in a jail cell.

"You know that guy, Marsten? On the county council?"

"I've heard of him."

"He's the one pushing to keep things segregated. Well, one of the ones. He's not alone, you know that. But he's the ringleader. I've had some people looking at him for a while. He used to be in the Klan."

The Ku Klux Klan wasn't what it used to be, but that was like saying a knife wasn't as sharp as it used to be. It could still kill you.

"So, what are you going to do to him? Shoot him?"

"Shoot him? Are you crazy? They would actually investigate something like that. No, I've got a better idea."

And so, one dark June night, we followed James Marsten as he went about his evening. There was a council meeting that day and it went late. I don't know what they talked about because we didn't go in, but nobody seemed excited about anything when they came out. After the meeting, James Marsten drove to a trailer park just outside of town and was greeted at the door by a woman who was not his wife. This fact, and her address, were duly noted. I was wishing that I had a camera with a fat lens like the one Jimmy Stewart used in "Rear Window," but a setup like that cost money. So, we just used our eyes. After about an hour, Marsten reappeared and drove home, stopping first at a Shell station for some gas.

Toussaint drove a Buick and we used his car for our quiet pursuit. It was a few years old and more bulbous than the newer cars, which were getting lower and longer, but there were still a lot of cars like it on the road, so nobody paid it much attention. It had big doorsills that were easy to duck behind, which was good because two Race men hanging out in a car for hours would attract attention, and we didn't want that. We parked a couple of blocks away from his house, in a particularly dark patch of street. Marsten lived in a neighborhood that would definitely object to having two Race men in it for any length of time, but it was late, and everybody was inside.

"It is just a gift that he stopped to get gas," Toussaint said. "That is a sign that this is supposed to happen."

We got out of the car and crept up behind Marsten's car. He didn't have a garage. Toussaint quietly poured some gasoline from a metal can under the back of the car, then went quietly back to his own. Crouching out of sight of the house, I lit a small piece of paper on fire and then tossed it under the car. Toussaint pulled the Buick up behind me just as the gasoline under Marsten's car caught fire with a whump. Toussaint had crawled down the road with the passenger door open, and I ran around and got inside. He didn't peel out, didn't want to attract attention, just quietly motored off and out of the neighborhood. We were three houses away when Marsten's car exploded, sending his hood hurling into the sky like a piece of trash caught in the wind.

Blowing up his car made us happy but didn't really have the desired effect. The police theorized that Marsten had done a sloppy job of filling up his car. A neighbor had been burning trash earlier in the day, so they figured that the two incidents came together in that explosive moment. This was what was reported in the white newspaper. The good news for us was that meant the police were not looking for us, because they did not feel that a crime had been committed. The bad news was that it could not possibly strike fear into racist white hearts because it was thought to be an accident.

Toussaint and I gathered later over beers and Cokes to theorize about how we could change this. We needed to strike fear in white hearts without getting caught. I have to say, at this point, that I was not completely on board with Toussaint's approach. I was mainly talking to him because I was bored and he had interesting things to say. My job was going fine but there was little hope of advancement. Race life in the South was just a long stretch of lingering resentment, and the stirring movement to change things did not interest me too much because I did not think things would change. Virginia was as beautiful as ever, although her thin body was getting diluted in the excess flesh that comes with age—as was mine, I might add. I never regained the size I was before the war, but now my burgeoning size was of a different, softer, kind. James was growing and growing and needing less from me, although my desire to give him more led to the greatest mistake of my life. But that's getting a little ahead and I don't want to tell it now.

Toussaint and I couldn't agree on a good strategy or target so, for a while, we just talked and plotted. We met at the same little bar, Smokey's, and our conversations were weirdly disjointed. When the bartender or anybody else came within earshot we talked about family life or sports or places we had visited, and when they moved away, we talked about arson and strikes and assorted violence.

Then one day Willie told me that a cousin of his had been beaten up when white policemen had broken up a planned sit-in at a Birmingham lunch counter. It was a dumpy little lunch counter, according to Willie, and white people barely bothered to eat there, but let a Race man try to get a sandwich and suddenly it was holy ground. The police—and somebody in the white crowd that gathered, most likely—beat Willie's cousin George until he was nearly in a coma. He lost the sight in his right eye and had trouble talking forever after. He had ordered a grilled-cheese sandwich.

I didn't know the details until Willie told me. The white Huntsville paper did carry something on it, but it was a tiny news brief that was written as if the police had broken up some criminal activity. It didn't even mention that a Race man had been involved. It was just some random police action, nothing to see here, folks. As it turned out, the sister of one of the policemen who did the beating lived in Huntsville. Willie knew this because his cousin George had once given the policeman a ride to Huntsville when his car had broken down. George saw the stranded motorist by the side of 65 and gave him a lift to his sister's place. The white cop had not minded being in proximity to a Race man then, apparently. I wondered if he had recognized George when he was beating him. Probably not; probably thought we all look alike.

We found her house. It was in east Huntsville and was nothing special: A single story with wood siding and a slab driveway without a cover. Similar houses were all around it, each separated by low white fences that needed painting. A couple of half-dead live oaks stood watch and occasionally dropped limbs onto the fences with a crash. We knew this because we watched the house for a long time. We saw the policeman's sister come and go, but she didn't do much. She had two kids and chased after them and, aside from that, she took care of the kids and waited for her husband to come home.

There was hardly any cover, aside from the fences, and even they didn't provide much. The trees were also of little use. Cover was important because it seemed to be a neighborhood where everybody knew everybody else's business and kept an eye on each other. The people there were probably good folks, but their goodness had a definite limit as far as we were concerned because they would almost certainly not take kindly to two Race men driving through their neighborhood on a regular basis. So, we mostly stuck to the relatively busy road behind the house and kept on moving. This is one reason our surveillance took so long.

Another reason it took so long was because we couldn't figure out what we should do to the house, or to the sister. Toussaint favored burning a cross in the front yard and tossing a note indicating it wasn't done by the Klan, but by a new organization of strong Race men and women. The Clan, maybe. We couldn't decide on a name. This idea was problematic for a lot of reasons. We didn't have a big cross, we probably wouldn't have time to get it upright in the yard properly, and we'd probably end up setting ourselves on fire. We could set the car on fire again, but that would be too close to what we did to Marsten's car, and that would set the police on our tail not only for this torching but for that one.

We needed something bigger. Or, as it turned out, something smaller.

THIRTY-NINE

Our Secret Weapon

Virginia had started complaining to me that I was gone too much and was not seeing enough of James. We had tried and tried to have another child, to give James a brother or a sister, but it didn't happen, and Virginia turned her full attention to our only child. She fussed over him and burrowed into his life as much as she could, even well after the point when it embarrassed him.

Toussaint and I needed to do something to this policeman's wife to keep our plan of revenge afloat. I needed to spend more time with James. To my everlasting regret, I solved both problems at once.

Toussaint and I thought and thought and decided the worst thing we could do to this nice, upstanding white lady would be to inspire fear. Fear not only of Race men, but of Race men being able to penetrate into her house at will. We decided we would leave a note on her kitchen table. It would say only, "We are watching you and your brother. For George." We would include a picture of George that had been taken after his beating and circulated in the Race press. The *Defender* never picked up the story, but the *Chattanooga Call* did, so we cut that one out. It was an elegant solution, one that could be equally deadly for us as blowing up a car, if we got caught, but also one that carried a little less immediate risk to life and limb.

The problem was getting into the house. Her two boys were tearing around the house at all hours, and when they weren't wandering in and out, the neighbors were. This is where the lack of adequate sneaking around cover was critical. And this is where it occurred to me: use James. I wish I could say that Toussaint put me up to it and I just went along out of weakness, but the truth is that it was my idea. I could never tell Virginia, of course. I approached James directly.

He was sitting on his bed reading one evening while Virginia was at the store buying groceries. He was reading a comic book, *The Flash*, about the fastest man alive. It was his favorite, as its tattered cover would attest. I came in and wandered up so casually that he instantly knew that I wanted something. Without going into a lot of detail, I explained what I wanted him to do. I even explained a little bit of the why, so he would understand why it had to be done. He smiled when I finished talking. James looked at *The Flash* as if he would be joining the ranks of superheroes soon, once he had done this thing.

"It will be great!" he said.

He was too big and cool to hug me anymore, but he gave me a light punch on the shoulder. Not a hug, but almost as good. I can still feel a tingling in that shoulder when I think of that moment now.

"When do we start?"

It took a while for all the pieces to come together. The policeman's sister and her family had company for a few days, company that came with more kids, so that made it impossible. Then it rained hard for several days and I didn't want to have James mucking around in that. But still we watched and waited. James got more and more eager, drawing little lines of attack in pencil on the back of his notebook. When Virginia saw them one day and asked him what they were, he said they were football plays. Sometimes he drew the Flash running through the lady's backyard.

Finally, all the elements came together. The family packed some suitcases in their car, which meant it was their turn to go visit someone and inflict their children on them. They weren't big bags, which meant they weren't going to stay long, but that would give us a couple of free days, at least. They also took the dog, which was a very good thing. He wasn't much to look at, but he was noisy.

James had plotted his route as best he could without going into the yard. There was a gap in the back fence that appeared to be just big enough for him to climb through, and assuming there were no unforeseen pitfalls in the yard, he should be able to get to the house without being spotted. Getting into the house was another thing. Most people didn't lock their doors. We had to hope that this family didn't, even when they were away on vacation. If that wouldn't work, I trained James on how to pick locks. Or, rather, we figured it out together, as I didn't know how to do it, either. We practiced on our back door so the neighbors wouldn't see us and wonder what we were up to. I never quite got the hang of it, but James was fast and good. I was proud of him for that. I still don't understand why.

The evening after the couple left, Toussaint and I parked the car a few blocks away from the house, where the neighborhood petered out and the woods began. Nobody would see us here or look for us here. There was a small creek running through the woods, so if anyone did happen to spot us, we could get out of the car and say we were going fishing. Fishing at night in that little creek was a fishy excuse, but the white folks would probably expect Race men to be doing something like that.

The position was good for us but of little use to James because he would be on his own. He had the picture and the note in a sack, but he would have to make his way to the house in the dark without being seen. We had driven him around a few times to visualize where everything was, and he had plotted out several options, but now it was up to him. I got out of the car, bent down and gave him a hug.

"Be my little superhero," I whispered, and he chuckled and then he was gone.

"He's a good boy," Toussaint said. "Smart, too."

"Yes, he is. Just like his daddy."

He laughed. "Which one? Good or smart?"

"Both. Of course."

James took longer than I hoped, but finally I saw his small form darting from behind a tree across the road. Then he was in the back seat, telling us his story so fast I could hardly make out a word. He had nearly gotten to the fence when he heard the sniffing of a neighbor's dog from behind a fence, then he had to sit quietly for several minutes until it went away. He made it to the back of the house all right, but the door was locked. James poked around and found an unlocked window and entered the house by crawling down the back of a couch. He made his way to the table and left the note and the photograph.

"They had a cookie jar," he said at the end. "I brought us each back a cookie."

We laughed and we ate the cookies. They were chocolate chip and a little stale, but the moment was good. That was my little activist, coming back from a mission with cookies.

***

"This is ridiculous," the Rev. Scott said.

He was reading the *Chattanooga Call*, which he had subscribed to and which he had sent to our house. It wasn't as good as the *Defender*, but it was easier to get. Rev. Scott slid the paper across the table to me. "School Integration Causes Riot in Mississippi," the headline screamed. "National Guard Called in to Keep Order."

"They are rioting to keep little Black children out of their schools," he huffed. "It's just absurd. I don't understand these people. What do they think will happen? That our black will rub off? What are they so afraid of?"

"Losing power," Virginia said. "We were going to have a nice quiet dinner and now you bring that up. I told you not to bring the newspaper to the table."

"Well, I shouldn't have, I'm sorry. I don't mean to get my dander up. It just seems that we climb and climb and then fall back, fall back. We can't get ahead. Like that Greek fellow who was always pushing that rock uphill. Sen—sen—"

"Sisyphus," I said. I had a good education and liked to show it off now and then.

"Right. Sisyphus. I need to write that down. That would make a good sermon."

He scribbled in the margins of the newspaper.

"Maybe Toussaint and some of those Nation of Islam people are right," Virginia said. "Maybe nonviolence isn't the way to go."

We all stared at her, the Rev. Scott, James, and me. She had never said anything like that before.

"I know they're not, I know they're not," she said quickly. "I'm just tired of hearing news like that. It's so frustrating."

"I know it's frustrating," her father said. "But Toussaint and his kind are not right. You don't get ahead by being worse than the people who are keeping you down."

"Maybe that's the only way to do it," James chimed in.

His grandfather and mother looked at him now, but I kept my eyes on my plate. I would have kicked him under the table if I could have reached him.

"What are you saying, son?" Rev. Scott asked.

"Maybe violence is the only thing they understand. That's what they use on us, and it has worked for a long time. Maybe there's no other way for them to see."

Rev. Scott looked at James with sadness in his eyes, and it hurt me to see it. I was the one who had brought James into Toussaint's orbit, but I wanted to keep that part of his life away from his mother and his grandfather. The less anyone knew about what we were doing, the better.

"Son. That isn't what the Bible tells us to do. We should turn the other cheek."

"But the Israelites were always fighting people and wiping them out!" James protested. "They would move in some place and kill everybody there!"

Rev. Scott shook his head.

"They did, too!" James said, his voice louder than it needed to be.

"Yes, they did," his grandfather said. "But that was the Old Testament, James. Those days are gone. Now we are to turn the other cheek."

James put his napkin on the table and stood up, his chair squealing against the floor.

"We've been doing that for a very long time. We don't have any cheeks left to turn."

He stomped out of the room and up the stairs. Virginia, so furious that her face was a deep maroon, began to stand to go after him. I grabbed her hand and pulled her back into her chair.

"Let him go," I said. "He's a teenager."

"Barely," she said.

"Still, he is. Let him cool down."

"He's right, dear," Rev. Scott said. "He's a good boy. This news would turn anyone's head."

"He probably won't even remember it tomorrow," I said, with a forced laugh. "He'll be thinking of some girl at school."

"Oh, I hope not, not yet," Virginia said, calming down, giving me a smile.

I knew what I said wasn't true. Toussaint had lit a fire within James, and I had spent a lot of time fanning the flames. That fire wouldn't go out easily.

FORTY

Burning Down the House

"WHY DON'T you and Eileen come by the house?" I asked Willie one day when I ran into him at the hardware store. "Been a while."

"Yeah, we'll do that," he said, his eyes resting on me for a second and then glancing off.

I hadn't seen Willie in a while. Since I wasn't working with him directly, we had to make an effort to get together, and we hadn't made that effort in a long time. He paid for his bag of nails and gave me another nod and headed out. He was almost to his car when I caught up with him.

"Willie, seriously. Come by the house. Maybe tomorrow night? I feel like I haven't seen you in forever."

Willie had a big white Lincoln with dark green leather seats. He was doing well for himself, had moved up to chief of his section at Redstone. I was sure there were things he was working on that he couldn't tell me about.

"I'll have to see," he said as he sank onto the Lincoln's bench seat. Willie had picked up some weight to go with his gravitas. "But tomorrow night's probably not good. I'm putting in a lot of hours."

I don't know why I pushed it so. In that moment, I felt Willie slipping away, and he was a bond to my past that I suddenly realized I didn't want to break.

"Willie. Please."

Willie pulled himself back up off the seat by leveraging the door frame, which made the whole car creak. He leveled his eyes on me, his fat lids at half-staff, which I knew meant that he was serious.

"Johnny, to be honest, I don't like the company you're keeping."

"What do you mean?"

"You know what I mean. The last couple of times we were at your house you spent most of the night complaining about the white man and what he's doing to us. I see that every day, I don't need to hear about it when I'm visiting my friends."

"But—" I didn't know what to say. "I'm just talking about the news, what's going on around us every day."

"I know what's going on around us every day, Johnny. You're not the only Black man to be affected. And it's not anything new. What's new is that you're angry about it. You and that Toussaint Guthrie."

"So, you don't think I should be friends with Toussaint?"

Willie descended back onto the seat. I felt a trickle of cold sweat run down my spine. I was losing him.

"You can be friends with whoever you want, Johnny. But what has Toussaint done up against what you've done? What does he know up against what you know? Nothing. He's all mouth, Johnny. And you're all ears, for some reason. But just because you're listening to him doesn't mean I have to."

"Willie—"

He shut the door and rolled down the window a little.

"Call me when you wise up, Johnny, and we'll be glad to come over again."

He started the Lincoln's massive engine and drove away.

"I'm not going to call you!" I shouted at the vehicle's departing backside. "You just stay in your place, Willie! You seem to know where it is!"

I didn't really feel that way about Willie, and I don't know why I shouted that. There are a lot of things that I did in that time, and in the years to come, that I don't understand. It was almost like I had actually died in the war but wasn't buried, and someone else took over my body and lived the rest of my life. When I think about those times and feel bad, that's what I like to think. It wasn't me. I was dead and gone and peaceful in the ground, and someone else made my mistakes.

Virginia was losing patience with me, too. As time went on, James' enthusiasm for the struggle—and for making the struggle an actual struggle—became impossible to ignore. She was no dummy, she knew where it was coming from, too, as surely as Willie did.

"Look at what's going on all around us," she said when the Freedom Riders started moving into the South and signing up Race men and women to vote. "This is the way to do it, not with violence. I don't want you filling our son's head with this, Johnny."

"It's what they're afraid of, Virginia. It's what they've always been afraid of. White people understand violence. They can dish it out, believe me. But they can't take it. Especially from us."

"Getting down to their level doesn't make us better. It doesn't even make us equal. It makes us worse. I am telling you, do not fill James's head with this."

"Or what, Virginia?"

It was a question I should never have asked. She gave me a long, hard, level look. I had seen fire in her eyes before, but it had never been aimed at me as a weapon.

"I will do whatever I can to protect him from that, Johnny. Whatever I think I need to do."

That could cover a lot of ground. I backed down. I didn't really want to know how far she was willing to go.

So, I began lying to her. The truth was I was proud of what James was becoming. He was becoming a warrior. I was done with that life, was exhausted by it, but he was just beginning, and he would be a much better warrior than I ever could be. I protected our country from outside forces. But I came home and despite my sacrifice, I was just a Race man in white America. Nothing had changed. James was going to be part of a new generation of warriors, one that would extend freedom to our own people. How could you not be proud of that?

I thought that fighting back was the hard way. Working through nonviolence, like Dr. King advocated, like Gandhi had advocated before him, was the easy way. Was it not easy to do nothing in the face of continuous and eternal oppression? Was it not harder to risk jail or even death to help others? That is what I thought then, as I talked with Toussaint and watched James begin to swim in the waters we warmed for him. That is what I thought for a long time.

I could not convince Virginia otherwise, or her father. I became an underground supporter to my little warrior, underground even in my own house, in my own life.

"Son," I told him one night while we were sitting in our car, looking at the house of someone who had attacked Freedom Riders, wondering what we could do to them—"son, there are people who don't understand what we're doing, and some who do understand it but don't approve of it. Do you follow me?"

"I follow you, Father," he said.

I had taught him to call me Father and to call Virginia Mother, instead of Mom and Dad. It was how I was raised, and it seemed right to me.

"So, we need to be quiet about it. You know we've talked about not saying anything at school. You haven't said anything at school, have you?"

"No, sir."

I thought he answered a little too quickly, but he looked sincere, so I didn't press it.

"That's good. I'm just saying we also need to be quiet when we're around anyone else. Anyone but you and me."

"What you mean, Father, is don't tell Mother. And Grandfather."

"Yes, James. I know that sounds difficult, but that is what I'm asking."

"Would they count as people who don't understand what we're doing? Or people who understand but don't approve?"

"That last one, I think. But I'm not so sure that anyone who really understood it would oppose it. You've read your history, right?"

"I have. Are you going to ask me again if I know where Toussaint got his name?"

I looked over at him and he was looking away, but grinning.

"Oh, I've asked you that before, have I?"

"Yes, sir." Still with the grin.

I reached over and gave him a playful box on the back of the head.

"I knew that. Just seeing if you were paying attention, is all."

"Uh huh. Sir."

I matched his grin with my own. And so, I continued training and molding my weapon in secret.

———

THINGS REALLY WENT SOUTH WHEN HE GOT BUSTED. THIS WAS WHEN I learned several things about my son. One was that he had started going out on his own with his friends, doing what he called "operations." Toussaint and I were too old and slow for him, and too soft. He and his friends had developed a taste for the harder stuff. Blowing up a car, breaking into a house to deliver a cryptic note, hanging pro-Race signs off the front doors of known racists, that was all nothing. It would not right the wrongs, not the way a beating could.

James and his friends, as they got older and stronger, liked to deliver their message wrapped in pain. They never attacked a white man openly —that would be suicide, even they could see that—but they were as watchful as sharks and became skilled at following a white man on a narrow road as he tried to make his way home after having too much to drink. A sudden acceleration from behind, a flash of the headlights, maybe even a gentle tap with the front bumper, and that man was very likely to careen off into the trees to break an arm or leg, or worse. If the man was very, very drunk, and they knew no one waited for him at home, he might get a beating from a group of masked toughs as he stepped out of his car and fumbled with his keys at the door. He would never be able to say who hit him.

James and his gang scattered their attacks all over North Alabama. Decatur one week, as far as Scottsboro the next, maybe a quick hit in Florence. They delivered no actual message with their message, just quick and blinding pain. They never touched women, or course, or even tried to be noticed by women, especially white women. That was the real kiss of death, of literal death, far more dangerous than even taking on a white man in the daytimes. James and his friends were angry and increasingly violent, but they were not stupid, and they were not suicidal.

But they did make mistakes. They got too active too close to home. One day a policeman showed up at our door, looking for James. A white policeman. I was at work. Virginia let him in and asked what it was all about. He showed her a baseball cap that had been left at the house of a man who had been beaten by several people. No one had seen anything, but the hat was there and, written neatly inside, was the name James Nicholas. It was a little smeared with sweat but it was still legible. Virginia had written it there, had inscribed his name on most of his clothing, for some reason. James probably forgot all about it.

Virginia called him at the church, and he came home. He was working there, doing the same sort of odd jobs that I used to do at the Rev. Scott's church in Tuskegee. The policeman asked James if he had been at the house where the beating occurred, and he said no. He had been at his friend Jeff's house, several miles away. Jeff could vouch for him and so could Jeff's mother. The policeman showed James the hat and asked him if it was his, which of course it was. James said he had lost the hat and didn't know what had happened to it. He thanked the policeman for bringing it back. The policeman asked him if he was sure he hadn't lost it at the scene of a beating, and James said he was sure.

And that was it. The policeman, in talking to Virginia, had already given up that he had no witnesses. He was either expecting James to fold up and confess, or he didn't really care about solving the case and threw away his only lead. Maybe he didn't much like the guy who had been beaten up and didn't care who did it. Whatever the reason, he left, but he took the cap with him.

I heard about all of this an hour or so later when I came home, tired and dirty from a long day and expecting dinner. Instead, I stepped into a battle. Virginia was hot, and James wasn't much cooler.

"You," my wife said, pointing her finger at the center of my head like she was holding a gun. "You filled his head with this nonsense. You and that Toussaint. And now he's a criminal."

"I am *not* a criminal," James said, shouting at her loud enough to make her flinch. "I didn't do anything."

"You know you did," Virginia said. "You know you did."

"Don't you raise your voice to your mother," I said.

We were all talking at once, giving each other orders instead of listening. It set the tone for how things were going to be from then on. I had thought I was coming home to just a normal evening after a normal day at work, but instead I walked into the beginning of the end. These things sneak up on you sometimes.

That particular evening, James ended up sulking in his room and I ended up sleeping on the couch after making myself dinner out of whatever I could find in the fridge. Virginia stayed in our bedroom and I could hear her crying on the phone to her father. I couldn't sleep. I watched TV until all the stations signed off and then I lay there, rigid and angry, my body finding new lumps in the couch that made me squirm. Looking back, I think that was probably the worst night of my life. Worse even than all the horrible nights in the camp. There, I had lost hope but felt it was not my fault, it was the fault of forces much bigger than me. Here, I knew it was my fault.

I went back to work the next day. Virginia was in the bathroom, so I snuck into the bedroom, got my clothes and left. James went to school, I guess. Things went on as if things were normal, for a while. Virginia was distinctly frosty to me for a long time, and James was becoming an inscrutable teenager, so I threw myself into work. The vehicles in the motor pool had never run so smoothly. After a while, I got promoted, and became the assistant to the commander for the entire motor pool: trucks, airplane engines, generator, whatever there was that had pistons. I could have run the whole thing myself, but that still wasn't a fitting job for a Race man in Alabama.

"You should build the engines for our rockets," one of the German engineers joked when he climbed down from a plane flight one day. "We could get to the moon faster."

I gave him a little chuckle but no actual smile. He was right, though.

Redstone Arsenal's motor pool had the least downtime of any Army base, or any NASA facility.

But anyway, I'm a little ahead of myself. I worked hard, and James got good grades despite his growing hooliganism, and Virginia actually began to remember that I was her husband and that she loved me. And then James got arrested for real.

FORTY-ONE

The Wild Blue Yonder

I HAVE BEEN a little too focused on my own family situation and have failed to give the bigger picture. In 1961, President John F. Kennedy said the United States should go to the moon "not because it is easy, but because it is hard." This came in the wake of the excitement of Sputnik, when it was feared that Russian children were ahead of our own and they would soon be raining down death from the sky. It was white people against white people, and I did not pay much attention. But with the moon race, I paid attention.

NASA went on high alert for years. Planes went back and forth to various centers, which had been Army centers not too long before but then became civilian. And our center was leading the way. Our Germans were leading the way. These people we had fought so hard to conquer—these people who had tried so hard to kill me—were leading the way. They flew all over the place, carried to and fro by the engines that I made sure were safe and functional. On the ground, they moved about in jeeps and trucks that were in better shape than anything else on the road. I was doing my part for the moon race by keeping our Germans safe and healthy. Just for the record, I never thought they'd do it. I knew we had enough trouble getting oxygen at high altitude in the cockpits of fighter planes, and I couldn't imagine willingly going to a place where there was no oxygen, at all. I liked to look at the moon in the sky and was happy to leave it at that.

What also happened was that Huntsville was growing all around us. People were moving in all the time, from all over the place. Just walking around the arsenal sometimes you could hear accents that you would never hear in Tuskegee or anywhere else in Alabama. It was not cosmopolitan, not exactly, but its claim to fame wasn't being the water-cress capital of the world anymore. A sign at the city limits still declared that proud fact, but the city itself was moving on.

And everywhere, there were Germans. Constantly in my mind or in my line of vision or in the white newspaper. There were lots of them and they were very busy. And one of them was on my television. Dr. Wernher von Braun told us what spaceflight meant, what it would be like to live among the stars. He told us this in his German accent with his swept-back hair. And I remembered where I had seen him before. I had seen him in the underground camp. That had been his doing, and now our race to beat the Russians to the moon was his doing. He was coming up in the world.

All of this was happening in Huntsville while the civil rights move-ment was blooming everywhere else. Race people were trying to get the right to vote and to be treated like normal human beings but the heads of the white people in Huntsville were in space. All the teachers were trying to instill a love for math and science into the heads of the kids, but James wasn't interested. He didn't believe a Race man could ever go to the moon.

"How many Negro astronauts are there?" he asked me one time when I complained about his math grade and told him he was selling himself short. I tried to get him to use the word Race instead of Negro, but he wouldn't do it, and he wouldn't apply himself, either.

"This is your fault," Virginia told me one night when we were still together. "Yours and Toussaint's. Filling his head with this garbage about how he can be more violent than white folks and make himself better."

"He's just a kid," I said, as if that answered anything, and we didn't say any more about it.

We had long since stopped talking about Toussaint and his beliefs because it just made us fight. She believed that when I was with her, I would be swayed by her, and that when I was with Toussaint, I would be swayed by Toussaint. She believed that, on this issue, the issue of the very future of Race men and women in America, that I was weak. And it was true.

I could think about my weakness more clearly when I was by myself. I understood this fact more clearly when I was by myself. I understood it more clearly when Virginia was asleep and I was alone and on the edge of sleep, because that was when I dreamt I was back in the camp. That was when, in my half-awake dream, I returned to the state of living where you obeyed, or you died. Where you did what you were told or you found yourself at the end of a rope, or worse. Where you did what you were told, or your head was bashed in with a pipe. More than at any other time, that was when I realized they had drilled the very core out of me, made me into this weathervane.

I still went back and forth between them. I told Virginia that I was no longer associating with Toussaint, but that was a lie. She did not know my work schedule and did not check it, but I still got with him now and then. He was not around as much as he used to be. Toussaint was not burdened with a steady job so he was free to go where the action was, and if you look at old photographs of sit-ins and Race protests of almost any sort from those days, particularly ones where fires and fighting were involved, you're likely to see him somewhere in the background.

I was not involving James with Toussaint anymore, not after his visit from the police, but it didn't matter. It was too late. I had no influence on him, just like the Nazis lost influence on their missiles as they roared their way to London. James was a self-guiding missile. One Saturday night, he and his friends beat a man halfway to death, and this time they got caught. James was going to jail. The saddest thing was that it wasn't a white man that they beat, it was another Race man. One of James's friends thought this man knew what they had been up to and were going to tell on them, so they beat him down to teach him a lesson. James told me that it was all his friend's idea, and I believed him because I wanted to believe him, and he wanted me to believe him.

He got arrested in the afternoon. He called me at the motor pool from the jail. I went to see him as soon as I could leave. We sat across from each other at a metal table, with a bored-looking cop watching us from nearby as he filled out some paperwork.

"James, what is going on here? Your mother is going to be devastated."

He looked at me with eyes that were flat. I had never seen him look that way before. He was just a kid, but his eyes looked as cold as a snake's.

"She won't be devastated when the white folks give us what's coming to us," he said, his voice flat.

I kept looking into his eyes and they weakened. Tears pushed their way past his lids and ran down his cheeks, and then he put his head down on the desk and sobbed.

"I'm sorry, Dad. I'm sorry. I let you down."

I went to put my arms around him, but the policeman got up and steered me to the door. He was a pasty, rumpled man and I expected him to say something rude to get me out the door. Instead, he walked me outside, stood close and looked me in the eye.

"Your son seems like a good boy who made a mistake," he said, his voice low as if James could hear. "I had that hunch and I let you in here so I could confirm it. I did. We'll keep him for a while and get to the bottom of this, but I don't think we'll have him for too long. When we hand him back over, though, you need to be sure to keep an eye on him."

I was so startled by his obvious concern that I could just nod my head in agreement and stammer.

They did have him for a while, though. They had him for the next eighteen months. The man he helped beat was not in a forgiving mood and did not see the same good character that this policeman did, and James did not have a good defense. We spent as much as we could for a lawyer, but no good lawyers wanted to spend time with a case like ours. The good Race lawyers were busy with the struggle and didn't want to defend a Race man accused of a crime that, to them, was just a white stereotype of what Race men were like. Most white lawyers didn't want to be bothered, at all. In the end, we got a public defender and paid him a little, but we got what we paid for—virtually nothing—and James was transferred to a juvenile facility outside Birmingham.

The chill in my house deepened into an ice age. Virginia believed that I had tried to move James away from violence, but she also blamed me for steering him in that direction in the first place, which was true. With James gone, I moved into his room, and my wife and I began sharing a house instead of continuing a marriage. We drove down to see James every weekend at first, then every other weekend as the chores and duties of everyday life crept back into the crevices on our calendar. James was always happy to see us and told us of how he had seen the light, how well he was doing in juvenile hall, and how he was studying hard so he would not fall too far behind. Although we always drove home in complete silence, his stories cheered us up. The only thing James was not telling us was the truth.

FORTY-TWO

The Nation

JAMES WAS hard when he got out. I started to say that he was a hard man, but he was still just a boy. He was a boy trying to be hard and tough. Virginia and I, and Rev. Scott, drove down to pick James up when he was released. He had on regular clothes, like he was just getting out of school. There was a difference about him, though, a lean and wary way of walking. An older boy was with him, a muscular boy who had some chunk on him, as well. His face was round, his head was almost conical, and his hair was shaved down to the nub. He looked like a human missile.

"This my friend Addis," were the first words out of James's mouth.

"This *is* my friend Addis," Virginia said, unable to help herself. "Hello, Addis."

"Ma'am," Addis said, and nodded to me and to the Rev. Scott.

"I have to go now," James said.

"You go then," Addis said, and patted him on the shoulder. "I'll be in touch."

He walked off, heading along the side of the busy road. There was no one to greet him.

"Addis, would you like a ride?" Virginia called, but he turned and shook his head.

"No, thank you, ma'am."

We each gave James a hug, which he endured stoically, his body tense. It was like hugging a fence post.

"Let's get you home," Virginia said.

The conversation on the way home was awkward. What do you say? How was prison?

"You tell me that they treated you all right, son," Rev. Scott said.

James nodded. "They treated me all right. I met some interesting people. We started looking out for each other."

"That boy Addis?" I asked.

"Addis, yes. Him and some others."

"And they made you study?" the reverend asked. "And let you go to church? I would think that would be the best thing in the situation."

"We studied. And they let us go to church. After a while I didn't go to church, though."

"Why not?"

"After a while, I went to mosque."

James tossed it out there lightly, but it landed like a hand grenade.

"A mosque?"

James's grandfather looked like he was going to be sick.

"It's something called the Nation of Islam," James said. "A Negro man's religion, not this white European stuff that's been handed down. Authentic. Addis told me about it."

Rev. Scott pushed himself back into the seat, exhaling with a grunt like someone had punched him. Virginia just stared at the back of James's head.

I knew about the Nation of Islam. They were headquartered in Chicago and I would see some of them around here and there handing out newspapers and asking people to come to the mosque. They said white people were blue-eyed devils, and it was often hard to argue with them about that. Uncle Abe used to argue with them sometimes, about how they weren't really Islamic and how they ought to try some Baptist preaching sometime. It was good-natured arguing, and they smiled and argued right back, accusing him of carrying the white man's water by preaching his religion. It was the kind of arguing men do with smiles on their faces.

Aside from that, I didn't know much about them, but I knew they were more hard-edged than some in the struggle. I just hadn't realized they were in Alabama, and that specifically they were in a cell with my son.

"Son, are you...are you a Moslem?" Rev. Scott asked.

He tensed as he awaited the answer but allowed himself to relax when James said, "No. Not yet."

"Why not?" Virginia asked, her anger evident in her voice. I glanced at her in the mirror and she was as tense as her father. "What's keeping you from it?"

James's face lost some of its hardness. He didn't look at them as he answered, just looked at the passing scenery, the flat green landscape that whirled by. "I don't know. I just wasn't ready yet."

"What is it about it that appeals to you, James?" I asked. After watching my Uncle Abe for so long, I wasn't under the illusion that someone's religion could tell you if they were a good person. I didn't have a dog in the fight, so I could just ask my son some honest questions.

"It's not handed down to us," he said, turning to me and talking to me like I was the only one in the car. "It's authentically Negro. Black people were the first people and everyone else came from us. The Bible always shows Adam and Eve as white, but it wasn't like that. Dr. Muhammad tells it like it is. His teachings show us what we were, and that shows us what we can be."

"Oh," Rev. Scott groaned from the back, but I kept talking over him. I wanted the conversation to be civil for as long as possible.

The heat was on James after that. His mother kept an eye on him to keep up his studies and stay out of trouble. She was not happy with his flirtation with the Nation of Islam but that was not her first concern. He needed to stay alive and out of jail first, and then she could worry about what church he went to later.

With her on his back about his studies, her father was left with nothing to focus on but his grandson's eternal soul. The Rev. Scott was not doing it to be annoying, although he was. He genuinely feared that James would roast forever in Hell if he didn't turn from the false path of Mohammed, and he wanted to make sure that didn't happen. He came to visit us even more but spent less time at civil rights events and more time reading the Bible with James. He pointed out that James was the name of the brother of Jesus, and it would be a shame to change it or add anything to it. When he wasn't around, he sent tracts and pamphlets for James to read, some of which espoused things that the reverend didn't even believe. He was willing to try anything.

James endured it all with good grace. He even seemed a little amused. He read the Bible with his grandfather, although I noticed he didn't touch it when he was by himself, and he studied enough and got enough good grades that he wasn't far behind in school, which made his mother happy. He started dressing better, too, wearing stiff cotton shirts and ironing them himself. His bearing was more upright, too. I didn't recognize it at first but then I remembered where I had seen such a bearing, and where I continued to see it every day. He looked like a military man.

I asked him about it one day, when he came home from school wearing a crisp white shirt and creased black pants. His answer warmed my heart.

"I'm trying to be like you."

"Like me?"

He fixed his very serious face on me and said, "Like you."

There is very little more a father needs to hear in this life than that.

"I thought about how you did things. You wanted to learn to fly so you learned to fly, even though Negro men weren't allowed to fly for the military. But you wanted to fly for the military, so you found a way to do it. And now Negro men can fly for whoever they want."

"I was just lucky," I said. "I was in the right place at the right time."

"No, you did what you wanted to do, and everyone gets to benefit from it. That's what I want to do. You came back from over there, but things are still bad here. It's my time to change it. I want to do it the way you did it. The right way."

I think I had tears in my eyes when I hugged him. He was still a tough nut, but his mother and his grandfather were getting through to him. I acted like I was, but I don't think I was really playing much of a part, except for being a role model years ago. I was proud of what he told me at first, but later I thought about it and felt ashamed. I had made a difference, it was true, but that had ended twenty years before, five years before James had been born. After I came back, or whatever version of me it was that came back, I wasn't a role model for anything but how to get a menial job and work at it until you died.

I had seen cartoons and movies where old soldiers, reminiscing about their young, dashing days, went and poked through their memorabilia, which was usually stored in a moldy trunk in the attic. I didn't have an attic or a trunk, and I didn't even have any memorabilia. I had come through the war with nothing. At the time, I was happy just to be home, but now I wished I had something to look at, to point to, to convince myself that my son was right. I had my letter of acceptance to the Tuskegee flight training, and my letter of acceptance to the Coffey School, but that was it. I didn't even know where they were. Virginia had wanted to frame them and put them up, but I said no, because, at the time, I didn't want to think about what they had led me to.

I went for a walk later that day, after dinner and after the sun had gone down. The evening was refreshingly chilled and quiet, just the occasional sound of cars swooshing by or dogs barking. Cicadas shouted from the trees, a gentle wave of sound that washed against the hills. It was peaceful and quiet and yet I knew it was a war zone. It was a war zone for me and every other Race man and every Race woman and every Race child, and it always had been since we had been brought over from Africa, and it always would be. It made my heart heavy to think about it.

I thought about what James had said. Sometimes it is good for fathers to listen to the wisdom of their sons. I wished—not for the first time—that he had been able to meet his grandfather. I think he would have liked my dad. I think they would have laughed and gotten along, and I wish Father could have been stronger and held out longer. He had not been an old man when he died. He didn't have to go when he did.

"I will be stronger," I said out loud, to no one but myself.

I decided that I would rejoin the fight. I would show James that he was right, that I could still do things the right way. I got my chance to show my worthiness almost right away. Rev. Scott was waiting at the kitchen table when I got back in the door.

"Did you hear what happened in Selma?"

FORTY-THREE

The Bridge

H UNDREDS of civil rights marchers had planned to walk from Selma to Montgomery to protest that Race men and women had been kept away from the polls in Selma, which was one of many ways the white man kept the Race man down. Stupid white troopers had killed one young man for nothing more than demonstrating for his constitutional right to vote. I had heard about the march but had not thought much about it. It seemed like a nice enough thing to do but not something that would compel me to drive down there and take part. The marchers were filing quietly down the road on the other side of the Edmund Pettus Bridge when the Alabama state troopers attacked them.

"It's on the TV," Rev. Scott said, his voice hoarse and hopeless.

We walked into the living room where James was doing his homework with one eye on a Western. Virginia was away at a church function or something similar, I can't remember that exactly. I do remember what happened next. I switched the channel and heard people talking about Nazi Germany. They were talking about war crimes. It was "Judgment at Nuremburg," and I wasn't expecting to hear those words, and it shook me for a second.

"There's nothing on," I said, but right then the face of the new anchor, Peter Jennings, appeared and said they had some terrible footage to show America. And they did. I didn't want James to see it, but it was too late. He slammed his book shut and we all watched. The cartoon violence of a Western was nothing, a joke, but the real thing reached out of the tube to grab us by the throats. What was this land we were living in? What happened to the land of the free? What freedoms had I fought and nearly died for, if stupid white men could keep law-abiding Race men from even walking to protest their lack of rights?

It was unbearable. I said some things I would not ordinarily say in front of James. I believe the Rev. Scott said some similar things. As the hours passed, everyone was angry about it. You could feel the anger and hatred in the air, it coated your teeth. The next day was Monday and I called in sick. I don't think any Race men went to work that day unless they had to. James and I accompanied Rev. Scott to a meeting at the church where we talked about the response. There was to be another march, led by Dr. Martin Luther King. It needed to be big. But the marchers wanted a court order to keep the troopers from attacking them again.

"Showing John Lewis's bloody head has brought us a lot of sympathy," Rev. Scott said, to a murmur of agreement from the crowd. "But I doubt he'd want to get his head split open again, and I don't want mine split open, either. That isn't how it should be done. We shouldn't cause violence, but we shouldn't have to suffer it just to get our point across."

There were murmurs of agreement to that, too. I scanned around the room and spotted a familiar face, one I hadn't seen in a while. Toussaint Guthrie. He was eyeballing the crowd, too, and we locked eyes from about thirty feet away. He gave me a slight smile and a dip of the head. Then he rolled his eyes quickly to the right. He wanted to talk to me.

"Haven't seen you in a while," he said. His mouth was smiling but his eyes weren't quite.

"I've been around. I haven't seen you."

"I've been traveling, it's true. Getting the lay of the land. I've been talking with some people and we have some ideas for the next march to Montgomery. I think a man like you could be helpful."

It was getting hot in the church, so we stepped outside. The cool wind hit me and before my body could acclimate, I shook with a sudden chill.

"Someone's walking across your grave," Toussaint said with a chuckle.

"At least maybe they're visiting it. So, what is your idea?"

"The Rev. Martin Luther King and the other fellas putting this next march together are saying that it will be safe. We'll have a court order to keep those crackers off us. But me and some people who think like me want to go on the march and be sure. The whole world will be watching this one. If any of those redneck cops try to beat any of us, we fight back. On national television. Race men fight back, and everyone will see that we don't just take beatings, we can give them, too."

I wondered if the state troopers would be that stupid again. They probably would. It did not pay to overestimate them.

"So, are you going to have people walking around with sticks?"

"No, man. Nothing obvious. Just Race men on the lookout, dressed nicely but ready to protect their brothers and sisters if they need to. If nobody messes with us, they'll never know we were there."

"What if somebody messes with us when the cameras aren't rolling?"

"We'll be ready for that, too."

After watching the footage on TV, the idea of busting heads sounded like a good one. I could still feel the anger coiled inside me like a spring, tense and ready to pop.

"I'll do it," I said. "Who are these people doing this with you?"

Toussaint motioned with his sharp chin toward the parking lot, where a stocky man was walking up. When he got closer, I saw he was just a boy. He looked familiar.

"Mr. Lee," Toussaint said, shaking hands with the newcomer. "You lost your watch? You were supposed to be here an hour ago."

"Ah," the boy said, shooing the complaint away like a fly. "Don't have much time for talking. I've been organizing."

After hearing his voice, I remembered where I had met him. We had met him in jail and had tried to give him a ride home.

"Addis Lee," he said when he shook my hand.

"Johnny Nicholas. Did you get home all right that day you got out?"

"Oh, that's you," he said, a smile faintly showing. "I thought you looked familiar. How is James?"

I had an idea then. It was a stupid idea, but it burst into my head fully formed and I mistook that for wisdom.

"He's inside," I said. "Hold on and let me get him. He'll want to hear about this."

"Wait—" Toussaint said, but I didn't.

I stuck my head back in the meeting and saw James looking at the ceiling, bored by the adult droning. I waited until his eyes found mine and then motioned for him to come outside. The Rev. Scott noticed the movement but was busy in the middle of the conversation and his eyes didn't linger on his grandson.

"Hey, Addis," James said when he came outside.

"Hey, James."

"You think he can handle this?" Toussaint asked.

I think it was the only time I knew him that he was the voice of reason. What hurts me is that it was also one of the few times I didn't listen to him.

"He can handle it."

James looked at us in confusion until we explained what we were talking about. Then he looked at me with undimmed admiration. There is nothing better for a father to receive, no better gift than that. His eyes were almost level with mine—he was going to be tall—and I can picture the way they looked right now and will never forget it.

I pictured us walking together, father and son, fighting the good fight that I had begun so many years ago. I had walked that lonely road for such a long time that I forgot I was on it, and he had reminded me, so I owed him that. That's the way I thought of it then. We would walk together with other Race men and women and children and would go the extra step to protect them. It would be best if there were no trouble at all during the march so we could be heroes only in our minds, but to be honest, I was hoping there would be at least a little trouble. It's hard to demonstrate you are a warrior when there is no war.

We planned how we would get together, which was difficult because none of us knew Selma very well, we weren't familiar with the planned route to Montgomery, and James and I had to keep our participation quiet. I would never hear the end of it if Virginia saw James and I walking around with Toussaint and that jailbird Addis Lee, who was a Moslem, to boot. We eventually settled on a plan that would get us together in a parking lot at a Walgreens outside of Selma, and Toussaint planned to scout out other meeting locations as we moved along.

I walked home that night with the Rev. Scott and James, sometimes resting my hand on James's shoulder. My father-in-law smiled to see it, but he did not really understand the secret bond we had forged, the bond of soldiers.

Two days later, we were in Selma, dressed in our best jackets and ties —the men, that is; Virginia and the other ladies had on their Sunday dresses.

Cars were everywhere, and they were big in those days and took up a lot of space. We had to park blocks away from our hotel and just leave the car next to the road. The hotel was nothing fancy and we were lucky to get one room for all four of us, even though it was small and cramped. Some people were sleeping in their cars, but Rev. Scott had friends in this town and managed to pull something together for us.

Selma was jumping like it had probably never jumped before. Airplanes full of celebrities were coming in from all over, including Hollywood. I heard about that on the radio; I didn't see any myself. They were way off in the front somewhere and were going to be in the middle of the pack, at best. There were news cameras everywhere, and reporters stopping people to question them and scribble in their notebooks.

I did bump into one person I didn't expect to see: Willie. Years ago, we might have done something like this together, driven down in the same car, windows rolled down, laughing all the way, even for serious business like the march. Now we came down separately and didn't have too much to say when we came together outside a diner where we had all waited in line for an hour to get lunch.

"Johnny," he said, and shook my hand.

He smiled but didn't crack a joke or make an inappropriate comment. It was like meeting only half of Willie.

"Willie. How is Eileen?"

"She's fine. Doing well."

"Is she here?"

"Nah, she couldn't make it. We have a little girl, Johnny, I guess you didn't hear. We had given up on it ever happening but then one day it did. She's a cutie, but she's a handful, so Eileen's still in Huntsville. She says she's too old to be a mother, but she loves it."

His smile grew like a flower in the sun as he talked about his daughter.

"Her name is Ellen. Eileen and Ellen. Like two little peas in a pod. They even have the same birthday, which is weird."

"That's great, man. Do you have a picture?"

"Do I have a picture? Do I have a picture?"

The Polaroid he showed me was Eileen holding a tiny replica of herself. Little Ellen resembled her father only in that she was stumpy and round. The picture was beautiful but seeing it made me sad. Ellen was at least a year old and we hadn't even known she had arrived on the planet. Willie and Eileen had been there for us when James was born, but we had drifted apart since then, to the point that I was only seeing his daughter in a tattered picture.

You think the things in your life are forever, but they're not. Not even close. People move in and out of your life like the tide. It's a hard thing to get used to and you can't always predict when it will happen, or to which person. Willie and I had been through a lot and I thought we would always be close but now we weren't and that was all there was to it. Nothing against him, nothing against me (I thought) but now we were distant, standing on icebergs that were floating away from each other.

We chatted a while longer and Willie asked about Virginia and James, and then we shook hands again and parted ways. I walked back into the diner and saw my family at a back table, studying the tattered menus. I had just gone to park the car and had instead seen a ghost from my former life, and it made me sad. I looked at them as I approached. Virginia, tired but alert, scanned the menu for something healthy, prob-ably in vain. Her father, already having decided on a hamburger, looked around at his fellow marchers. And James, squinting at the menu with the same intensity as his mother, but very likely to order a hamburger just like his grandfather. The light was shining in on them from behind and from certain angles they looked like people you would see in those Renaissance paintings: kissed by light, sacred, holy. My family. As permanent as things could get in this life.

FORTY-FOUR

Lost

———————

THE MARCH WAS, for the lack of a better term, fun. We walked during the day, stopping for water and snacks and even a picnic lunch here and there. In some of the towns we passed along the way, the residents, white and black, gave us food, and most of the restaurants were happy to serve anyone passing by. There was always some singing going on, and the songs would drift through the crowd the way the call of the cicada floats through the trees in the summer. At night, we slept in the fields that we passed, huddled in blankets or tents. The Rev. Scott had a small tent that one of his parishioners had pushed on him and begged him to use. He pulled it behind him on a wheeled trolley and wouldn't let anyone else carry it or pull it.

In the fields, the singing continued but it became softer and lower and reminded everyone of the slave spirituals that we had heard about and sometimes still sang in church. I looked out over the fields that first night, at the small candles twinkling in the night, illuminating the huddled forms, and felt an ancient connection stir inside me. I felt connected not only to our slave ancestors but to every man that had walked the Earth before, all the way back to Adam and Eve. It was a deep, heavy, satisfying feeling, like I was a wave in a mighty ocean. I have never felt that again, never felt such a sense of peace and belonging. Virginia sat with me after a while and we held hands and listened to the snatches of song, and eventually lay down and fell asleep.

The second day felt a little longer because sleeping in a field is not restful and the sun drove away that satisfying feeling. We walked, most of us a little more disheveled and without coffee and without having brushed our teeth. But as the day went on, we got some food and stopped at stores and gas stations along the way and managed to change clothes and make ourselves more presentable, so when evening rolled around, we were a little tired but good as new. I took a break from Virginia for a while and walked with James and Addis, but we didn't run into any trouble. The crowd was even bigger now, gaining in size as it moved along like a tidal wave of justice. Our little patrol made us feel better, like we were a big part of the reason why the march was going so well. It was a big crowd and we were protecting it, we were needed, we were necessary.

The evening went about like the evening before, except the Rev. Scott had been taken away to stay at a parishioner's cousin's house so Virginia and I inherited the tent. The time spent listening to the singing was lessened because we were so exhausted, we fell asleep quickly.

At some point in that night, or early the next day, James disappeared. I have searched my heart and mind so often for some evidence that I was aware of his absence during the night or that morning, but there was nothing. He just up and left our lives and never came back and there was less than a ripple in an ocean to mark his passing. I looked for him in the morning but did not find him or Addis. I did find Toussaint, who said he had not seen them since the day before. I figured that they had gone on ahead, powered by the energy that propels youth, and that we would reconnect later in the day.

We had identified some spots where we could meet up during the march if we got separated. These had initially been set up for us to conduct our patrols but now they became a way for me to find James. Virginia and I waited but he did not come. We scanned the faces as they passed, and some looked at us in return, but he was not among them. Eventually, we gave up and marched on ourselves, sure he would turn up with childish stories of his exploits, until we fell into an uneasy sleep.

We stumbled into Selma with a sense of foreboding hovering over us like a cloud, while all around were happy faces. The march had taken place, but we had lost something and were frantic. Virginia told her father and he put out the word through his network and Toussaint did the same.

While the happy crowd listened to speeches as the shadows lengthened in Montgomery, we filled out a police report with a white junior officer who was clearly not very concerned by the whole thing.

"He's probably just playing with his friends and lost track of time," the policeman said.

He started to say something more, maybe lecture us on how Race children did not have much of a sense of time, but then he thought better of it and didn't say anything else. He asked us about James, and he asked us about Addis and wanted to know if they had ever been in trouble. I said no at first, but Virginia placed her hand firmly in the middle of my arm and said we should tell everything we knew so the police could help.

"They've been in juvenile detention?" he asked, and what little interest had flickered in his eyes went out. "Maybe they've done something, and we've got them in custody. We'll let you know."

"Can you check and see if there have been any reports of trouble?" Virginia asked.

"I can do that. I will let you know."

We called him dozens of times over the next few months and he never knew more than that. Or if he did, he never told.

As we went through the story that day, again and again, I gradually opened up about who James might have been with and what he might have been doing. Virginia increasingly fixed me with her stare, the stare I knew so well not so long before. The gulf between us cracked open again and grew wide in an instant, like a crevasse opened instantly by an earthquake. This one made no sound as it yawed before us. Or maybe it did make a sound, and that sound was my own voice, telling the story and adding damning detail after damning detail and no longer caring about what recriminations Virginia would throw in my face if I could only get my son back.

We stayed near Montgomery for two more days, staying in a cheap hotel room miles outside the city. We stayed in one room because money was tight, but we moved in separate worlds. I mostly sat out on the concrete balcony, reading a newspaper by the weak overhead light until Virginia went to sleep, then I crept in and slept on the couch.

Sitting under that light reading the paper, or looking at it more than reading it, reminded me of old Mr. Roswell back in the dark hallway of the kitchenette. I could picture him with his paper, propped up against the wall like I was now. He was surely dead by now, so he knows more about life and death than I do. I wondered what prompted him to sit there, what story led him to that single chair in that dim hallway. I never thought to ask him. Kids never think to ask, but I don't think any of the adults in the building thought to ask, either. Did he ever have a family? Had he made a mistake and lost them? I thought of my own vanished James and the fury that was my wife moving about in the room behind me. Sometimes it can take so little for your world to end and you find yourself sitting in a chair, alone under a single bulb, wondering what the hell happened.

We had a term for it when we flew: the point of no return. It was the point at which you no longer had enough fuel to get back to your base, so you would have to keep going and land somewhere else. The thing about the point of no return was that it wasn't always easy to figure out. The more you flew, the more fuel you burned and the less you weighed so the faster you could go. The point would just arrive without warning, without any kind of notice at all, but when you reached it your flight profile changed and there was nothing you could do. It's the same way in life. One day you just push too far, and you can't go home, and no amount of wishing will get you back.

As the days dragged on, it became clear that something had happened and James was lost to us. There were a few reports of scuffles and violence along the way of the march, but that was not surprising given that it was the equivalent of an entire small town getting up and changing its location. There were no reports of murders or of bodies found, but he just didn't come back. We had given him the phone number of Rev. Scott's church for emergency use while we were in south Alabama, but he never called, or if he did, he never called when anyone was there. Rev. Scott had a party-line phone in his house, but James never called that, either. We had our own line but now when it rang it was only to convey condolences.

I like to imagine that James didn't die and wasn't killed. He just decided to chuck it all and move away somewhere, and he felt he couldn't tell us because we would worry. So, he moved to Point Barrow or Moosejaw or somewhere like that, far away and cold, and became a beloved town eccentric, maybe working in the diner or training sled dogs, a friend to everybody. I think about him like that and it makes me smile, even now.

One month to the day after the march to Montgomery, Virginia asked me to leave. It was done very quietly. You could have stood outside our door on that fine spring day and not heard a thing, not realized anything was amiss. She stood before me, hands twined behind her back as if she was in prayer, and said she would like for me to go.

"It's not that I don't love you," she said in a calm voice. "But you made a mistake and I can't live with you here."

I was tired and hollowed out. I didn't raise my voice, either. I looked at her, my wife, and saw her anew. She was the same height but seemed taller, as if age had made her even more regal. Her face bore lines that had not been there before, and her body may have been a little more plush but she carried it the same way she had done when she was just a girl in her early twenties. She was a beautiful woman and the years had made her even more so, and I had disappointed her for the last time.

She went away while I gathered my clothes and my things. I didn't really have much, as it turned out. I had been living as if I knew I was going to be kicked out, so I had packed my closet lightly so as to be ready when the day finally arrived. I packed my favorite clothes and left behind things she had given me, even a couple of nice suits. She could give them to someone else now if she wanted to. I moved into an apartment near the arsenal. It reminded me of our first apartment in Huntsville, only it was worse. The floors were uneven and the wallpaper was stained. It came furnished with a bed, a dresser and a mirror, and someone had wedged a small cross made of cornstalks between the mirror and the wall. I started to take it down but feared that maybe it was some religious force keeping the devil at bay. I had enough trouble and didn't want more; I left the cornstalk cross just where it was.

At first, the novelty of being in a new place was interesting. I didn't have the car anymore, so I figured out a bus route to get me to work. My social circle had dwindled to nothing so I made friends with a man down the way and we leaned over the iron rail that looked out onto the parking lot and watched the sun go down a couple of times and drank a couple of beers and talked about nothing. The interesting part of my new life did not last long. Soon I begrudged the extra time it took me to take the bus to work and I started to hate my room, the cornstalk cross, the neighbor, everything. I went to sleep angry and I woke up angry.

It was not my fault that my son had disappeared. I was not the one who set up a society that refused to treat him as an equal and expected him to take it without complaint. I had tried to teach him, first by example and then by direct action, not to put up with that. It was not my fault that my society had made me fight to serve my country when it needed me most and then treated me, and every other Race man, as trash. It was not my fault that white people had devised ways to be evil that even Satan had not considered. None of this was my fault and yet here I was, alone in my ratty apartment, looking at a stupid rotting cross made of cornstalks. A Race man had once been hung on a cross like that but even he had been bleached of all his color and taken away from us.

At first, work was fine, too. It was a novelty not to have to go home right after work. I could hang around and talk to people or even go out to a bar, something I hadn't done in a while, since those plotting nights with Toussaint. The problem was that I didn't want to talk to anyone after work and I didn't want to go to bars. I certainly didn't want to talk to Toussaint and I didn't want to talk to anyone else, either. At work, I stewed in my anger, and at home, I stewed in my anger. I didn't even find peace when I slept. I heard the voice of the weird sisters in Germany calling me, begging me for help, especially Annamaria. Once I thought I saw her glowing eyes before me, but it was just a car turning around in the parking lot, shining its lights through my partially open window. I also heard news of James. I heard the phone ring and a policeman told me he had been found and was safe and sound. At this point, I would always wake up, only to feel my joy crash into confusion and despair when I realized where I really was.

I never saw James in a dream or even heard from him directly. Virginia was in my dreams, even Rev. Scott, even Dominique from back in Chicago, but never James. I thought about him constantly during my waking hours, but I never dreamed about him, not once. It was as if he had left me entirely, not just my life but my subconscious, as well.

I was not sleeping well. It made me very tired. I made mistakes at work. One day I forgot to have a plane prepared in time and a gaggle of engineers from the Manned Spacecraft Center in Houston were left cooling their expensive heels for two hours. It was entirely my fault, but I managed to cover that up and eventually it was forgotten, and, anyway, the people at Redstone did not care all that much for the people at the Manned Center, so it blew over.

But there were other mistakes, piled one atop the other like the stacked parts of a rocket, until that rocket got too tall to ignore. One day the assistant to the deputy center director said he wanted to talk to me. I walked up the stairs to his office, which was in another building. I would say it was a nicer building, but it wasn't much nicer. Everybody was really pushing on the moon mission and corrugated metal was the preferred construction material for most of the buildings there. We were building spaceships in glorified barns.

The assistant to the deputy center director was a small man named Tompkins who wore a dark suit and a fat tie, although those wouldn't come back into season for a few years yet. He had a whole list of my recent mistakes, and there were a lot of them. My supervisor had been keeping track, obviously.

"Mr. Nicholas, do you have any alcohol or drug problem that could be causing this lapse in your work habits?" Mr. Tompkins asked.

He smoked and a ring of white cloud hung over his head like a ghost.

"No, sir."

"You do acknowledge these performance deficiencies?"

"Yes, sir."

"Your supervisor speaks highly of you and you have moved up

through the ranks in a very orderly fashion, with no performance deviation until recently. There must be some explanation."

I had not told my supervisor about James. That was something for me alone, not him. He was white and would not understand the march and what it was about. I had taken the time off but had not said what for, and he didn't ask. He probably saw the march on TV and thought about it but never connected it to me, never thought it could affect anyone he might know. When I came back and there was no more James, I did not tell him because there was nothing he could do and because I did not share my personal life at work. My work was about engines and transmissions and tires and schedules and grease and not about missing children or separations or divorces.

"I can't think of one," I said. "I will do better."

He looked at me and the smoke lay over his head like a blanket. He didn't believe me but wasn't sure what to say about it. I knew that I could easily be replaced as a car or truck engine mechanic but the aircraft engines we worked on were more complicated. I could be replaced there too, but it would not be as easy. It would be easier to fix me. I knew this was what he was thinking, almost as if he spoke it out loud.

"See that you do, please. I'd rather not have this sort of meeting again."

"Neither would I."

We didn't shake hands, and I left. As I walked back to the motor pool office it occurred to me that I was in danger of losing my job and I did not care one bit about it. I began to wonder what I should have for dinner that night.

The situation did not improve. I could simply not concentrate on my work, and the work suffered. The things I did hands-on were botched; the schedules I made were wrong, the planning I did, flawed. There were several meetings with my supervisor and one more with Mr. Tompkins, who looked very unhappy to see me again. Even his smoke cloud looked unhappy to see me again. I would like to say here that there was a big blow-up one day, that I got tired of my supervisor's criticism and knocked him out with a single punch to the jaw and left my job with my head held high. That would make for a better story, but that is not what happened.

What happened was that my performance did not improve, and my supervisor increased the work of those around me until at least a couple of people were capable of doing my job, and then, after a string of warnings, he let me go. It was a long time coming; it took months. I didn't realize it at the time but, looking back, I see that my time there was like the mission that ended my flying career. I was flying over that endless French terrain in my wounded bird, enjoying the view even though I knew it was not going to end well, Jerry on my tail to force me along. This time it was me coasting along at work, knowing it was going to end. The difference was that I was not enjoying the view and the only one on my tail was me.

So, it came to be that I lost Virginia, lost James, and lost my work. I had come unglued from the world.

FORTY-FIVE

Years of Wine and Roses

A BODY in motion tends to remain in motion. I had learned that years ago in school and now I set about proving it with my own life. I had started going down and I kept going down. Paying the rent for my apartment was too difficult without a job and the thought of getting another job was unpleasant. I had spent so many years—most of my life—being in places where other people wanted me to be at the times they wanted me to be there, I simply lost interest in continuing that practice. So, I did not get another job and before long I could not pay for my apartment, and not long after that my landlord threw all my stuff into the parking lot.

I stuffed a few changes of clothing in a bag and left the rest of it there. My neighbor gave me a beer and said goodbye and waited until I was out of sight to start rooting around in my leftovers. I had come out of the war with nothing and I could live in peacetime with nothing. I drank the beer as I walked down the street with my bag and decided that I should have another beer. Later, I found a place to relieve my bowels and later still, a place to sleep. For the next several years, this was the cycle that defined my life. I boiled it down to the essence, and it was beautiful in its simplicity. All I needed was alcohol, a place to shit and a place to sleep.

Some days, I walked down by the river, taking care to avoid any of the nice neighborhoods that had sprung up there. Some days, I walked up the mountain, wondering if I might bump into one of the Germans who lived there. Some days, I wandered into the swamp that bordered Redstone Arsenal. The mosquitoes didn't bite me. I was rejected by all life forms, including them.

One day I saw an alligator. I didn't know there were any alligators this far north, but there it was, its colossal scaly back poking above the gummy water. Its kind had floated in the water like this back when the dinosaurs were fresh, and here it was now. I was wading in the water and I guess it could have attacked me, but I had no fear of it. The mosquitoes wouldn't even bother to suck my blood, surely this lumbering beast would not bother with me. And it didn't. It submerged as I approach and was gone, with barely a ripple marking where its bulk had been.

I came out of the woods one morning to find a car on fire on the side of the road. It was a fat old American car and there was no one around to watch it burn. Flames licked the sky, but it was a show that only I witnessed. The entire world was deathly still except for the crackling of the flames, and I was the only human being in that world. I watched the car endure its personal hell for a little while until even I got bored with it and moved on, and in all that time not another soul appeared anywhere on the horizon.

Sometimes I came across parcels of food, little sandwiches and apples and bottles of water, things like that, just abandoned by someone and left like manna. I felt like a child eating his lunch at school, but I ate them anyway.

There are things that you see and notice when you are by yourself, and I mean truly by yourself, that you do not see any other time. I have listed some of mine, but they were mild compared to what I heard about. Some of the other unglued men that lived in the area used to congregate now and then under the bridge that spanned the Tennessee River on the far eastern side of town. There were seven or eight of us and we huddled under our stinking blankets and talked. There was nothing much around here, just a gravel road that ran alongside the river. The Tennessee is pretty enough in places, but it was tired and brown here, as if its trip through town had worn it out. We would gather and tell our stories because no one else would believe us, and really, we didn't even believe each other half the time.

One of the men, who called himself Ezekiel, said he had seen dozens of "little people." We asked him if he meant midgets, and he said no.

"They are just about two feet tall," he said, his eyes glowing at the memory. "I saw them in the Paint Rock Valley. They come out by the creek at night, when the moon is bright. And they dance. They have on tiny little clothes, little suits and dresses, and everything is leafy and green."

I figured he had been staring at the side of a soup can too long one night, but he said he had seen them over and over. The rest of us just laughed, and he laughed too, but he was serious. He was as serious as I was when I told about the alligator, but I got the same response. They asked what I had been drinking because it must have been good stuff and proposed that we organize a hunting party. But I could tell, underneath the laughs, that some of them believed me, and some of them believed Ezekiel. To tell the truth, I believed Ezekiel.

One day I came across a broken mirror on the ground. I looked into it and saw my father. I saw my father as he looked right before he died. The man staring back at me from this shard of glass was gaunt, gray, dirty, tired. It was me, and I had become him. I had become him at his worst. The sight staggered me and I stepped back. When I did, the sun glanced off the mirror and caught me full in the eyes, blinding me. I sat down hard on the ground, having seen a ghost and been blinded by the vision. The mirror was outside an abandoned store and I leaned my back against the rusting metal wall and rubbed my eyes until I could see again.

I was not drinking as much as he did, I don't think, but I drank whenever I could. I would say it helped the time pass, but the time passed with no help. The mornings faded into the afternoons faded into the evenings faded into the nights. It got hot, then cool, then cold, then warm, then hot again. The leaves appeared, turned green, turned yellow and red, turned brown and let go and crunched underfoot.

I stole to get by. I watched houses from the woods until I knew that their owners were gone and then I broke in and stole food and, when they had it, beer and liquor. It reminded me of when James, Toussaint and I staged our pointless little raids. Those flashes of memory were more painful than the shot of light from the mirror, more painful than stepping on a nail, more painful than anything else I experienced in those years. One night I was beaten and robbed of what little I had by some dirty young men; but the memories of James made that pain fade to nothingness.

The worst part of it all was the loneliness. I could tell my "friends" under the bridge about the odd things I had seen, but there were countless sights and thoughts that visited me, and I had no one to share them with. One evening in the Paint Rock Valley I watched a huge orange sun settle below the horizon, lighting the sky with orange and red loveliness that made my breath catch in my throat. I can understand why Ezekiel saw the little green people. Sometimes the world is far too beautiful to look upon by yourself. But I was done with the world, and the world was done with me.

FORTY-SIX

The Point of No Return

Something tugged at my foot. A rat? I kicked it away. It kept tugging. I crawled out of my unconsciousness and pulled the tattered blanket away from my face. I was hallucinating, early in the morning. I saw Virginia, standing over me with a look of pure disgust on her face.

"Get up. Your mother is sick. We're going to Chicago."

I must not have moved because, in short order, she kicked me.

"Get up."

I got up. A couple of young men I did not know took me back to my old house and marched me into the bathroom. While they ran a hot tub of water, one of them motioned for me to get undressed. I handed him my clothing piece by piece, and there was quite a lot of it as it was September and getting cold. Because I didn't have a closet in which to store things, I tended to wear whatever I had. He handed each piece out the door to Virginia. I never saw any of those clothes again.

When the tub was full and I was naked, the young men left. I stepped into the tub and almost cried out. I hadn't felt water that hot in a long time. I stretched out and a wave of relaxation coursed through me, so strong it almost knocked me out right there. I had taken baths here and there, when I could, but this was the best bath in years.

I lay in the tub for what seemed like hours, until the water started to cool and turn a faint brown from the grime on my body. Then I washed and scrubbed and washed again. When I stood up, I felt human again. A razor and shaving cream were placed below the mirror atop the sink: very subtle. But I used them, and when I was done, I looked better. I looked like my old self again. My old self, but the thinner version; I looked like a much healthier version of the man who labored in the underground rocket plant.

I put on the robe and slippers that had been left beside the door and walked out. The young men were sitting at the table, and it was then I recognized them. They were from the church. They had been little the last time I saw them. They stood up and walked into the kitchen and returned with a plate full of ham and grits and green beans. I sat down at the table and ate hungrily, just above the level of an animal. They watched me with no expressions on their faces; no fear, no hatred, no disgust, nothing. When I was done, one of them brought me a slice of pumpkin pie and I gobbled it down in three bites. They took my plates away when I was finished.

"There are some pajamas over there," one said, pointing to the couch. "That's where you'll sleep."

The couch. My old couch. On closer examination, it wasn't my old couch, it had been replaced with a newer one, but it was the same color and in the same place. I was back to sleeping on the couch, while Virginia was away in bed. I did not feel like I had made much progress, but I put on the pajamas and crawled onto the couch, covering up with the fresh blanket Virginia had placed there. I could see the young men in the kitchen, sitting in the darkness, watching. They were going to watch me all night. I thought that would bother me, but I closed my eyes and I was asleep.

I had a dream. In it, I walked across an endless field that was broken here and there by lovely little streams. The grass was fresh and bright green, free of brambles and bugs. The sky was a shining blue, as was the water. The streams were so narrow I could step over them easily. Golden fish swam in the water and showed no fear when I walked over them. Red birds flew in the sky, shining cardinals that called to each other in long, musical songs. And that was all that happened. I walked and stepped over the water and the birds flew and sang and the fish swam. The scenery was slightly different as I moved but it never really changed, it stayed green and lush and water-fed. There was no one else around, no one to appreciate this beauty. A tall hill rose before me in the distance, capped with a white peak. No matter how long I walked it always stayed the same distance.

At first, I was disturbed by the lack of people and the unmoving mountain, but as my journey continued, I came to enjoy the rhythm of the trip and felt a kinship with the grass and the sky and the fish and the birds. I felt I was a part of everything, and my job was just to walk and see it all and if I never made it to the mountain that would be all right. Despite all that walking, I awoke refreshed.

The young men were asleep in their chairs, the sunlight pushing their shadows against the kitchen wall. I went to the bathroom to pee and heard their chairs scraping on the floor after I shut the door; they probably heard the noise, woke up abruptly and wondered where I had wandered off to. They looked relieved when I came back. They made bacon and eggs for me while I got dressed, then watched me while I ate. I felt like a prisoner, but the food was good.

Virginia did not appear until Rev. Scott showed up at the front door. She nodded to me and let her father in. The reverend had aged considerably. He still moved fairly rapidly, but was stoop shouldered, as if always on the verge of bending down to pick up a penny. I stood when he came in and stuck out my hand. He shook it with his own dry hand, then pulled me closer in a gentle hug.

"It's been a long time, son," he said softly.

Virginia walked out of the room.

"Yes, it has," I said.

Virginia returned.

"It's time to go. We have a long trip ahead."

We drove to the train station, Virginia and her father up front with one of the young men, the other two of us in the back seat with lots of room. Virginia did not want to sit with me and probably didn't want her father to, either, although he kept tossing sad glances my way. The young men left us at the station. Apparently, I had passed some kind of test and been declared trustworthy, so I no longer needed guards.

We took our seats on the train. We had sleeping cars from Chattanooga to Chicago, but the trip from Huntsville to Chattanooga was not long so we just had regular seats.

"I brought you a magazine," Virginia said, handing me an old issue of *Popular Mechanics*.

It had an article about the space program and how the Mercury and Apollo flights were progressing. I had no interest in reading it, but Virginia obviously did not want to talk so I ran my eyes over it to be polite. I had picked up newspapers and magazines and old books from time to time in recent years but had gradually fallen out of the habit of reading. I preferred to just sit still and listen to the world around me. I could hear the wheels clicking on the track and the wind pushing against the cars and occasional nearby traffic and Rev. Scott's uneven breathing and Virginia's silent disdain. I didn't analyze or dwell on any of it, just let it wash over me.

You will notice that I have not mentioned having a drink, because they certainly did not give me one, and by the time we got to Chattanooga, my head was hurting and I was shaking, although I hid it as best I could by putting the magazine down and pretending to sleep, making sure to keep my hands folded tightly under my arms. When we changed trains, I had a sleeper car to myself, and once in it I doubled over and rocked and moaned to myself. I wondered if I could get to the bar car, but I didn't have any money and Virginia wasn't going to give me any. Maybe the porter would take pity on me and bring me something. After a while, I heard the door to my car swish open and I started to ask the porter for help, but I saw it wasn't the porter. It was Rev. Scott.

"Son, you look bad," he said, and sat down across from me.

"I feel bad."

He fumbled in his pocket and then I felt something metallic and warm against my hand. He was handing me a small flask.

"Don't tell Virginia about this," he said. "I don't want to argue with her. But I know a few more things about the world than she does, and I know how alcohol works. You need to get through this and, unfortunately, that means you need to drink."

"Reverend," I said, my voice a sly admonition.

"Son, if you're a minister and you don't know a few sinners, you're not doing your job."

We shared a belly laugh at that and I tossed back some of the liquor. It took a little while to hit but then, I have to admit, I felt better. I had liked to think I was not a drunk like my father but here was the proof. Ninety proof, at that, and once it coursed through my veins and got its hooks into me, goddamn it, I felt better.

"I don't know what you're used to drinking. This is vodka. It doesn't smell as much as some of the others. I'll give you some mints, too, so Virginia won't notice."

"She's not going to get close enough to notice."

"No, son, I don't think she is."

We rode on in silence for a bit and I drank a little more and felt a little better.

"It's good to see you, Johnny," Rev. Scott said after a while. "I'm glad you're still around, but I don't like what you're doing to yourself."

"Sometimes it's not my favorite thing, either."

"Why are you doing this, Johnny? Is it the war?"

"Isn't that enough?"

"But—we won, Johnny! And you showed them what a Black man can do!"

I started to tell him. I really did. We had the time. It was a long ride. I could have told him about a hell he could only imagine, a hell that was right here on Earth. But I didn't. And he wanted to know.

I took another sip, felt the burn, and even though I've never particularly liked gin, I felt better still. I looked him hard in the eye. His eyes were watery with age and had collected various spots and veins, but you could tell a spry mind still lived there.

"You don't win wars, Reverend. You survive them."

"I'll have to take your word for that, Johnny. I don't doubt it. You're living proof, to me."

I finished off the flask and handed it back. "At least I'm good for something. Any chance of a refill before too long?"

He didn't laugh but tucked the flask away. I wonder what he did with it when he wasn't loaning it to drunks.

"Maybe one more on the train. And I think there may be liquor in Chicago. But you can't have too much. Just enough to get you through this."

"Fair enough."

"You should get help, Johnny. What's happened between you and my daughter is none of my business, but I still feel like your father-in-law and I want you to pull yourself together. For my sake. For your own sake."

"I know."

"There's that Alcoholics Anonymous. I've talked to people who work with them and it helps, it really does."

"I've heard of them."

He stopped talking and just looked at me sadly. I examined my shoes. There was no argument that could be made; he was right, of course. He was right and what remained was only the will I had to pull myself out of this dive, if it wasn't too late already.

"Get some rest, Johnny. I'll come check on you in a little while."

"Yes, sir."

"It is good to see you again."

"You, too."

I didn't blink, afraid that a tear would run down my cheek, and I didn't want him to see that. I didn't blink until after he had left my car and closed the door. I should say that I spent the night thinking about my situation and resolving to do better, but actually I just fell asleep.

I didn't see Virginia again until we arrived in Chicago, and I mostly saw the back of her head at first, even then. Rev. Scott hailed a cab and he and I got in the back seat. Rev. Scott put a cautioning hand on my shoulder as we entered the hospital.

"Your mother has cancer, and it's made her demented. She may not know you."

I felt ashamed that he knew this and I didn't. I felt sad that it took me a few moments to recognize the woman on the bed. She was knotted in the sheets like a trapped insect. She was bone-thin and wore a scarf on her hairless head. I recognized her by her eyes. Her eyes were the same.

"We'll wait outside," Rev. Scott said.

I pulled up a chair and sat beside my mother. A nurse came in to verify that I was family.

"He's my husband," my mother said, her voice thin and weak as a wisp of smoke. "He's come to see me."

The nurse gave me a look of severe disapproval and left.

"Oh, Carleton, you've come home," she said. "I'm so happy."

As I learned when I looked in mirrors now, I looked just like my father, for both good and bad.

"Yes, I'm here. And I will stay."

"Yes, stay."

She closed her eyes and clutched my hand in her wiry fingers. The bed next to hers was empty but there was a small vase with wilting flowers next to it. I got my little folding knife out and cut one for her, a pink daisy that was still in good shape. I had found the knife in the woods months or years ago and cleaned it up. It was very small and not sharp because I used it to open cans, and it left a ragged gash on the stem of the daisy, but it finally cut through and I was able to slide the flower through her hair and rest it on her ear. She opened her eyes.

"I'm so glad we're back together. And how's Johnny? Do you see Johnny?"

"I see him. He's fine, he's happy, he sends his love to you."

"Oh, good."

"He's healthy and happy and married."

"To that lovely girl, Virginia?"

"The very one."

"And James? How's our grandson?"

"He's—he's fine. Big and strong and healthy. He plays football."

Her smile stretched wide across her face and seeing it was the only thing that enabled me to keep it together. We're always taught that lying is bad, but sometimes it's the best thing you can do. Sometimes it's the only thing you can do.

"It's so good to hear it. Everything is all right then, isn't it, dear?"

"Everything is fine. We're all together and we're happy."

"Then we've made it. We've made it."

She opened her eyes again and met mine. "We've made it, haven't we, honey?"

"Yes, dear. We've made it."

She closed her eyes again, savoring the moment, and then drifted off to sleep, her fingers gradually growing slack in mine.

She didn't recognize me at all the next morning and shouted for the nurse in fright when I came into the room. She died that afternoon. So, she knows more about life and death than I do.

I don't really remember much of that day. I didn't cry or make a scene, but I just drifted off. Mentally, I was back in the woods, alone. I remember being at the hotel and eating, waking up later still in my clothes, and Rev. Scott came to talk to me from time to time. I'm sure he brought me some alcohol, too, but I don't remember it. I believe Virginia stuck her head in the door once in a while to check on me, but she didn't talk to me except to hug me once and tell me how sorry she was. My memories of her on that day are mostly that of a shadow head framed in a doorway.

The funeral was two days later. Virginia and her father handled all the details, and thankfully, Mother and Father had worked out their burial arrangements long before, like proper adults. I didn't have to do a thing. I felt like a child, and I guess I was behaving like one. Virginia didn't know who to invite, and I didn't either, so the funeral was as small as my father's. A couple of her friends got wind of it and came to see me, and squeezed my arm afterwards. I don't know when they had actually seen her last. One of them looked me in the eye and called me by my father's name and said she hoped I'd be all right.

So now there was no one left, no one, at all. Katherine was in the wind and Mother and Father were in the ground. There was only me. This was a whole family, as happy and full of plans as any other, and now it was gone, worn down by war and time and bad luck and bad choices and weakness. It had crumbled like a statue and there was nothing left, nothing left but me, the feet of clay.

I listened to the preacher eulogize someone he had never met. He couldn't know of Mother's struggles, how she gained and eventually lost her husband, her brother, her daughter, her son, her grandson, her mind, her life. He couldn't know that, but he tried. He read from some script and it fit her life well enough. All the rest was up to me. Nobody would remember my Mother but me. I didn't go up to the casket and look at her that day. Rev. Scott assured me that she looked fine, she looked peaceful, but I knew she was gone from this earth and only lived now in my mind, a rickety place, at best.

At one point, the preacher looked at us and asked if anyone would like to say a few words. I thought I should but wondered if I was up for it; I wasn't in the habit of speaking in complete sentences anymore. Virginia just caught his eye and slowly shook her head no.

Some son I had turned out to be. Too destroyed to eulogize his own mother. While I stood there, clutching the back of the pew, feeling the shakes and the shame begin to come on, I decided that I would do my best to remember Mother. I would do my best to remember Father. I would do my best to remember Katherine, to remember James, to remember Uncle Abe, to remember Aunt Eveline, to remember Anna-maria, to remember Marianne, to remember Julie, to remember Jean, to remember Pierre, to remember them all. They lived now only in my mind, and I would make that as good a place to live as I could. I would remove the cobwebs and pack the anger and fear into the attic so they would have room.

And then I thought I needed a drink. I wanted to head out to a bar after the funeral, any bar, anywhere, but I didn't have any money. I would have begged on the street for a while to get some, but I think Rev. Scott could sense that temptation and kept himself close by. Virginia hovered, too, but she didn't touch me and didn't get too close, like a moth afraid of a flame. So, we headed back to Alabama. Rev. Scott appeared again in my berth and extended the flask. I drank it like a vampire on a neck and I felt better.

We got back to Alabama and Rev. Scott gave me a hug, dropping another flask in my pocket as he did so. Virginia stood before me then, as close as she had been in years. She looked me over and I guess I found some small amount of favor in her eyes.

"I'm so sorry, Johnny," she said softly.

She gave me a hug that lasted just a little longer than it needed to. It felt good when I noticed that, and I thought about that for weeks and years to come.

"And, hey," she said. "Did you hear? Men are on the moon. Right now, right up there."

"What?"

I had missed that completely.

"They announced it on the train last night. You must have been asleep."

I looked up into the sky, but it was daylight and there was no moon. "So, they did it."

All those rockets had finally worked. Those German bastards had put a man on the moon.

"Johnny—are you okay?"

"I'm fine. Just thinking."

"Do you—can we take you somewhere? Do you need some money?"

"I'm fine."

"All right. You take care of yourself. I know my father talked to you about pulling yourself together. You should."

"I will."

"Look me in the eye and say that."

I looked her in the eye and said it. It was easy to say. I hoped I meant it. She didn't look convinced.

"Take care, then, Johnny."

"Goodbye."

I waited until they were gone and then walked away from the train station, headed for town. I felt the weight of the flask in my pocket and it was comforting. I transferred some of the weight from the flask to my stomach and felt even more comforted. I repeated this a few times.

After a while, I noticed a lot of people were walking near me, and traffic was getting heavy. I looked around and people were flowing downtown. For a second, it reminded me of the march from Selma to

Montgomery, but in this case, most of the people walking were white. I wanted to ask someone what was going on, but everyone seemed focused, and I had become pleasantly unfocused, so I just let myself get pulled along by the crowd. I could hear a loudspeaker in the distance now, and cheering. I got down to Main Street and saw that a small stage had been set up across from the First National Bank. Finally, the words blaring at me made sense, and I realized they were talking about the moon race. We had won it.

He had won it. There he was, on the stage, beaming at the crowd, hair slightly askew: Dr. Wernher von Braun. He was fatter than when I had seen him in the underground rocket plant. He shouted something into the microphone, and I could hear all of Germany behind him. I heard that voice and thought of the plant, and for a second, I was back in the crowd in the square, half alive, looking at the stage, wondering who was going to be hung. My vision narrowed to a black cone, and in the center was his Cheshire Cat face. I knew what I had to do. I had to kill him.

FORTY-SEVEN

The Moon Above

I STARTED MOVING toward the stage, but it was slow going. A thick crowd had assembled and they were throwing up their hands and laughing and sticking sharp elbows in my face. Some politicians were speaking now, talking about von Braun, about Huntsville's contribution to putting men on the moon, but I ignored it and moved forward slowly but steadily, a shark on a mission. I had nothing to kill him with and, to be honest, he was not a small man and it could prove difficult, but my rage and alcohol had mixed and sparked something I didn't want to put out.

Then a miracle happened; he was in the crowd, moving toward me. They were carrying him, cheering and carrying him, and he was laughing and grasping their outstretched hands in joy. We had put people on the moon. Those horrible things I had helped build, and tried to sabotage, had been perfected by this man and they had put people on the moon. I wondered what all those people in the plant would think. I wondered what Jean would think, if he were here on the stage, swinging from the noose.

Now von Braun was nearly close enough to touch. I could maybe pull him down hard and hope he landed face down and cracked his skull. But there were too many people around, it wasn't a good bet. I could maybe clutch his neck and choke him, but he was too high, and the crowd was too thick and boisterous. I wouldn't stand a chance.

Then I remembered my knife. It had a thin blade that made it difficult to use for opening cans, or even cutting flowers, but it would be perfect for opening a man, for cutting a man. He might not even know what had happened until he had gone past and suddenly someone in the crowd cried out about the blood, and by then I could have gotten away. It was perfect. It was in my pocket.

And then he was next to me, laughing down through his graying hair that blew in the hot summer wind. I reached out to touch him, to exact my revenge. My knife was folded against the underside of my wrist, ready to strike. Then another miracle occurred. I touched him and felt my hatred blast away, vanish like a firecracker in a puff of smoke. It caught me by such surprise that I closed my eyes when I felt it, so that I didn't actually see Dr. Wernher von Braun at the time that I touched him. But I know what I did. I helped hold that son of a bitch up.

FORTY-EIGHT

Inhabiting Life

It's hard to describe, but I felt like a great spring inside me had let go. Years of tension vanished. Put simply, and for no reason at all, I forgave the man as he passed over me. I did not realize how much a part of me my hatred had become until it was no longer there. The loss left me staggered. I literally would have fallen down right there, spineless as a jellyfish, if the crowd had not been so thick that it held me up.

With what little strength I had, I slowly moved to the edge of the group and made my way out. They were still yelling and whooping and talking, but now I felt peace and wanted silence. I wandered a couple of streets away and sat down heavily on a park bench. I felt something hard in my pocket and found the flask. I opened it and poured out what remained and threw it away. I had lost my knife, too, but I didn't want it anymore.

I spent the rest of that day looking for an Alcoholics Anonymous program and found one. And, from that day to this, I have not had a drink. That isn't to say I haven't wanted one. I have wanted a drink nearly every minute of every day. I want one right now. But I won't take one, and I won't let one take me.

My sponsor helped me get another apartment. It wasn't even as good as the last one I had, but it was mine. I got another job, working on car engines for a man who restored old cars, from Model Ts to shiny 1950s Cadillacs to little British convertibles. He was a white man, but it didn't bother me to work for him, and he paid me well and said I was the best mechanic he had ever seen. I know this part is boring but that is only from the outside. It was how I got my life back. It was a huge struggle for me, and it makes me a little sad that I can't tell it better.

I attended my AA meetings faithfully, in the basement of the Tried Stone Church of Christ. I even saw Rev. Scott once in a while. He said he was coming to visit the preacher, but I think he was coming to keep an eye on me. Which I did not mind.

"You still got my flask?" he asked me one time.

"I threw it away."

"I give you a gift and you throw it away?"

He looked a little hurt. I started to apologize but then a big smile spread across his face and gave away the game.

"That's a gift I don't mind you tossing."

And so, for the second time in my life, I started building myself back up. I had done it after the war, but never quite got as healthy as I was before the war. And this time, I never got as healthy as I had been before I dropped out of the world. I was gradually going down, but I decided I would try to slow my decline. I started eating better, began lifting weights again, ran a little. Things were looking up.

One evening after our meeting, when I was heading upstairs to go home, the preacher at Tried Stone pulled me aside. His name was Brother Roberts and he had a grave look on his face.

"I believe you are close to Rev. Scott. He's a friend of mine, too. I hate to be the one to tell you, but he has passed away."

"He—how?"

"In a car accident. He fell asleep, apparently. It was a single-car accident, anyway, late last night. He had run off in a ditch and wasn't found until a few hours ago. There was nothing anybody could do."

Rev. Scott was getting up there and his death should not have been a surprise, but death often is even if you think you're expecting it. He was very spry and sharp, and I figured he'd have several more years left, but he was also old and tired, and it had caught up with him. I hadn't pictured him dying in a car accident, but it was all tied together. He had probably been in North Alabama or Tennessee for a meeting and got headed home late and got sleepy. He was working, right until the end. And now he was dead. He knows more about life and death than I do, but I think he always did.

I called Virginia when I got home. She answered the phone with little more than a whisper.

"I heard. I'm so sorry. Can I do anything?"

"Thank you. No. Well—yes."

I could almost hear the indecision in her head, crackling over the phone line. "Anything."

"Go with me to the funeral."

"Of course."

"It's in Tuskegee. We can take my car."

"That's fine. But we should take mine."

She knew I was doing better, but she didn't know how much better until I showed up the next day to pick her up.

"I can't believe it," she said, standing on her front porch and watching as I got out of a Jaguar XK-150 to pick her up. A polished, sleek, British Racing Green XK-150.

"Can I help you, sir?" she asked then, a smile breaking through her grief. "I don't believe I know you."

"I am your humble chauffer. A man named Johnny Nicholas hired me to transport you to Tuskegee."

"Well. I hope that fancy car of yours has some trunk space. Because I have a few bags."

I knew she would, which is why I finally had settled on the XK-150. It was fancy but had a little room for bags. What she didn't know was that I had access to all the cars we worked on. The Jaguar wasn't mine, but I had brought it back into terrific tune and I wanted to see how it would be on the road. We had a beautiful E-Type Jaguar, too, but it was too impractical for a road trip and the little convertible MGs were out of the question. I could barely fit in one of those by myself. We had American cars, too, but they seemed kind of dull and familiar. So, the

XK-150 it was. I actually drove an old Pontiac GTO that I had fixed up, not this sleek British beauty. But she didn't need to know that.

It was a beautiful day for such a depressing journey. Virginia was obviously tired and said she hadn't slept well the night before. I could see why. I didn't pry but let her talk when she felt like talking, which was not often. Occasionally, she would comment on some passing scenery, but that was about it.

The funeral was large. His congregation, though small, was out in full force, and people from the churches all around came, too. There were also officials from the civil rights movement—John Lewis, Jesse Jackson, Ralph Abernathy—and even the U.S. attorney, who gave a little speech; Virginia's father was even more connected than I knew. It was a long service, with lots of laughter and crying, and when it was over, I was exhausted. The reverend himself appeared very peaceful and dignified in his coffin, but there was a lot of ruckus involved in sending him off.

I couldn't help but compare it to the funerals of my parents, both of whom slipped into the ground almost without notice. I couldn't help but see that if you want a big funeral, if you want people to notice when you are gone, you have to be part of their world. You have to keep your connections. My parents had lost theirs and I had lost mine. My funeral, when it comes, will be small and quiet, if there is one at all.

We stayed overnight after the burial and left the next morning. Virginia seemed less tense on the way home. It was not as good a day weather-wise, as menacing clouds bunched on the horizon, but Virginia had slept well and seemed much more at ease, a weight having been lifted off her shoulders and sent to heaven.

"You know, we're the only two left," she said at one point, watching me to see my reaction.

"I know."

"My parents are both dead. Your parents are both dead. Your sister has disappeared. And James—"

"James is gone," I said, not wanting to hear her add him to that list. "Let's just say James is gone."

She wasn't angry with my interruption. "So, it's just us now, and we're not even an us. We're completely alone."

"Yes."

"But you look better now, Johnny. Do you feel better?"

"I feel much better."

"Someone is watching over you. You keep heading for that cliff, but you don't quite go over it, do you? You always get pulled back."

"What cliff? Where?" I tugged the steering wheel from side to side like a pirate at the wheel.

Virginia laughed and punched me lightly on the shoulder. "You know what I mean."

It felt good to hear her laugh. I couldn't remember the last time I had heard her laugh.

"Someone watching over me, that's funny. That reminds me of something." I told her the story of my days on the street, when I would stumble across little caches of food, and how I felt like they were manna.

"You don't get it, do you?" she asked.

I looked over to see a sly smile on her lips.

"What?"

"Who do you think left you that food?"

"God?"

"No. It was me. Well, me or my father, and sometimes one of the boys from the church. We knew you were hungry and left it out for you."

"But—how did you know where I was?"

The smile faded, replaced with a look even more meaningful. "Oh, Johnny. I always knew where you were."

I didn't know what to say. I blinked and felt a film of tears in my eyes. It was getting hard to see out the windshield, and I could not afford to crash this car.

"Did you like the food?"

"I loved it. I loved it."

"I'm glad you loved something. Everybody has always loved you, Johnny, even when you didn't love yourself."

My mood darkened almost instantly, like the sky in the summer storm that seemed to be headed our way. "Did you love me even when we lost James? Because it didn't seem like it."

She didn't rise to the bait, didn't fight back, just spoke as someone telling the truth because she was too tired and sad to tell anything else. "Even then. I was mad at you, Johnny, don't get me wrong. But even then. But I was never able to be as mad at you as you were with yourself. I just never understood your anger, where it came from. You didn't use to be like that."

I thought about telling her about the war. I had never told her about that. Had never told anyone, come to think of it. Maybe it would help.

"There was a time when I was lost, and you didn't know where I was. When no one was watching over me, even God."

"I don't know what you mean."

And so, as we drove back to North Alabama, on that skinny black road under the endless blue sky that was beginning to be eaten up by cancerous dark clouds, in that beautiful British car, I told her about the war and the rocket plant. I left out a few details, like my true relationship with the weird sisters, but I didn't spare her anything from the rocket plant.

"My God, Johnny. You've been keeping all this inside for all that time. No wonder. Like eating batteries, all that acid."

I also told her about my encounter with Wernher von Braun.

"I've let it go."

"You don't have much else to let go of now, Johnny."

We were almost back to Huntsville and the visit was going to end. She reached across the seat and held my hand over the gearshift.

"Are you going to let go of me, too?" she asked. Her voice was flat, but her eyes were bright. "If you want to, now's the time. We part ways and it's all done."

"And if I say I don't want to let go of you?"

"Then you stay the man you are right now. No more holding things inside, no more going off to play in the woods by yourself."

"I don't want to let you go. You're the only thing I have left."

"Don't you answer so quickly, Johnny. This is a big decision. Once you make it, you need to stick with it."

I pulled over to the side of the road because I was having a hard time looking at her and driving.

"When I make up my mind, I stick with it. That's how I got you in the first place. If you'll remember."

"I never forgot. Not for a day."

When I dropped her off at her house, I stayed too. We made love and then she cried in my arms until she fell asleep.

FORTY-NINE

The Thin Thread

AFTER A WHILE I went back to my place less and less and one day, I realized that all my belongings were back in the house, and I was, too. It wasn't anything we talked about, it just happened. We were past the point of thinking we could control the flow of our lives, so we were content to see what fate had in store for us.

One day she came and sat down next to me on the couch, where I was reading the paper. It was a Saturday, in the spring, and the smell of fresh-cut grass wafted through the open windows.

"I need to tell you something," she said, touching my arm so that I would put down the paper. "It's something I've only told you once before."

My heart started racing when I heard that. I knew what it meant, but I almost didn't believe it. It was a miracle, it was too good to be true, it was some cruel joke by God.

"It's not going to be just us anymore. I'm pregnant."

We had not been trying to get Virginia pregnant, not specifically. We had not talked about it as a goal, but occasionally the topic would rear its head and we had decided she was too old. She believed it and I believed it, but as it turns out, she wasn't. She had a child before so that made it more likely that she could conceive later in life.

And so, when I was nearly fifty-two years old, we began planning for a child. Virginia threw herself into decorating the guest bedroom, which would be turned over to the baby. James's room, which we rarely set foot in except to clean, was not considered for the new need. Walking in there to tend to a new child would be too much, and by silent agreement we left his room alone.

The months seemed to fly by, for me, at least. This pregnancy was rougher on Virginia than the first one. She was sick a lot and I stayed home as much as I could to care for her. The garage let me bring cars home to work on them, which was very nice, so I was close by most of the time. It was a nice time, although again I wasn't the one having the baby. I would work a while and then go in and chat with Virginia, or bring her food, or wipe her mouth when she was sick. It felt good to be needed and to be able to help.

We were six months into the pregnancy when the doctor called us both in to talk about the results of a checkup. I was a little nervous. This was the first checkup I had been to.

"The baby is fine. He's a very active little boy, as you probably know," Dr. Lumpkin said.

We hadn't known, and hadn't intended to find out, but now we did.

"But his activity is not the only reason for the extensive sickness you've been experiencing."

Dr. Lumpkin did not live up to his name. He was not lumpy at all, but bone thin and nearly as white, with a shock of white hair on the top of his head. He looked like a big Q-Tip and would have seemed comical except for the grave expression on his face. Virginia slid her hand into mine and we waited for his next words.

"I'm afraid you have Hodgkin's lymphoma. I would like for you to get another opinion, but I would also like for you to start treatment right away. This form of cancer can be quite aggressive."

As it had in the past when I was in a rage, my world narrowed to almost nothing. I focused on Dr. Lumpkin's shock of white hair and everything else went black. I could feel Virginia's hand gripping mine with almost painful force, but my hand seemed to belong to some other dimension somewhere.

"And the baby?" I heard her ask. "What about our son?"

"The treatment will be very difficult to carry out effectively if you are pregnant. I strongly recommend that you have an abortion, fight this cancer and then try to get pregnant again later."

He said it as if we were discussing throwing out bad fruit in a refrigerator before buying more. It was just another option, another check on the paper.

"We've lost one child," Virginia told him, her voice as flat as a snake. "We won't lose another. We might not get another chance."

"I wish you would talk about it. Talk about it tonight and think about it. But you need to move soon on treatment."

We didn't talk about it that night. There was nothing to talk about. Virginia would not hear of anything else. We sat on our couch, holding each other close, and cried until our tears mixed together and our arms and shirts and necks were wet.

"This is just a challenge," she said. "We've gotten this far, and now we're down to you and me. But God doesn't want it to end there. He wants us to be a family again."

We fell asleep on the couch and later I woke up with a pounding headache. I woke Virginia up and we staggered to bed with sore necks. I lay in bed and the headache did not go away but danced around my skull and sent sparks coursing through my eyeballs. I was probably dehydrated. I had cried out all my liquid. Lying there in pain, I prayed to a God I no longer believed in and asked for help to get through this one last thing. I wanted Virginia to live and I wanted my son to live. I wanted it all and I did not think that was too much to ask, not after all I had been through. I got no answer back, but I figured that meant God didn't say no.

Virginia started her treatments two days later. She couldn't do chemotherapy without risking the health of the baby, but she could do radiation treatment with shielding to protect the fetus, the doctor said. It would not be as effective a cure as doing radiation and chemotherapy together, but Virginia would not hear of any course of action that might harm our child. I dropped her off at the hospital in her car, a Buick, but picked her up in a car from the shop: A '56 bright pink Cadillac. I thought it might cheer her up, but she was so weak she could barely muster a smile, and the smile looked almost like a snarl. She fell asleep immediately on the way home, her head drooping limply on the door, her hair blowing lifelessly in the wind.

And so, she grew, and she shrank. She became thin and drawn except for her belly, which began to bulge with our son. She ate frantically for the baby's sake and threw up when the radiation attacked her.

"Darling, maybe the doctor was right," I said one day after she spent most of the day in the bathroom, sick. "This is going to kill you."

"No," she said, so faintly that I could barely hear her, even with the door open. "This is just my cross to bear. You've gotten through some tough times, Johnny, and so will I. You got sick and thin and you got through it."

"I wasn't carrying a baby, though. It was just me."

She turned her head away from the toilet and to me. She was thin and gray and sick but still beautiful, still my Virginia, and no soldier on any battlefield has ever displayed more courage.

"But you came through it and got me back. And I will get through this and we will have a son. God doesn't make us suffer for nothing."

"You will get through this and we will have a son," I repeated, and sat down next to her and held her hand. That was the only part of her statement that I believed.

After a couple of months, it seemed God was easing up. Virginia began to gain weight to catch up to her belly and her color and her energy returned. The therapy was helping, and the baby, as if responding, became more lively, kicking to get out. Life returned to normal, or as normal as it can get with a baby on the way. On one particularly nice day, Virginia and I drove downtown in a black '62 Thunderbird that I borrowed from the shop. It still needed a little work and coughed dramatically now and then, threatening to die, but it was the perfect car for a perfect day. We walked the same street where Wernher von Braun had been carried, and window shopped. I bought her some ice cream from the drug store soda fountain. A decade before they wouldn't have served me in there, but now I was just like anybody else, a man buying his pregnant wife a cool treat. We stopped at Dimont's jewelry store and

I bought her a little silver bracelet. It didn't have any rare stones and it wasn't expensive, but it looked nice against her skin and it made her smile.

"Thank you, Johnny," she said, and kissed me, something she rarely did in public.

There are some days that burn themselves into your memory, whether for bad or good; this one was for good. While it was happening, I thought, I want to remember this, and I worked hard to do that and I'm glad I did. I still remember the warmth of the sun pushing against my forehead and Virginia's lips pushing against mine.

It became harder and harder for Virginia to go out as the baby neared. She was still strong, but she was going through two traumatic experiences at once: saving her life and bringing forth new life. It was more than any woman should have to bear, but she did it with all her strength. Two days before the birth, Virginia had to be hospitalized. The drugs and the stress of a birth at her age had worn her down. She still was tough, and her color was good, but she needed more rest and attention than even I could give her.

There are days that burn themselves into your mind, for good or bad. Sometimes there are years between them, sometimes they follow as close as the moon and the sun. The day the baby arrived was not long after our walk downtown. It was not a day I had to prompt myself to remember. I couldn't forget it if I tried.

The labor was relatively short. I held Virginia's hand as the contractions started to get more numerous, and she made the usual jokes about how this was all my fault, the same jokes she had made when James was born. The doctors shooed me from the room for the actual birth, and I slouched in a chair, feeling guilty that I felt so tired when I wasn't the one trying to pass a bowling ball through my body. The baby's cries pierced the fog of sleep and pulled me to my feet. Virginia was there with our son, both of them swaddled and exhausted and clinging to each other like survivors of a shipwreck. I kissed her on the forehead and tried to kiss him on his little wizened apple forehead, but he was too curled up for me to reach it, so I made do with the back of his head.

"We're a family again," she said, and we were, dazed, confused, tired, but alive, happy, a family.

The doctors wanted Virginia to rest and to keep the baby for a while for observation, because of what his mother had been through to produce him. After receiving increasingly pointed hints, I kissed them both again and went home and fell into a deep, dark, bottomless, dreamless sleep.

Virginia died in the night. I did not feel a thing, received no premonition or ghostly message. No goodbye.

FIFTY

My Greeting and Farewell to You

IF MY SON had not been born, I would have returned right then to the woods, drank myself to death and waited to be picked apart by the raccoons and the alligators and the buzzards. But Virginia was not my last tether to the earth; my son was.

I could not raise him alone. I put him up for adoption, with the condition that I be allowed to live near him, to keep an eye on him, to watch him grow. I interviewed many candidates because my son was a bright, healthy boy, and I picked a young family that promised to raise him right. I have always lived near him, sometimes right across the street, but I have kept my distance and let this new family thrive. The new parents loved him as their own but agreed that when the time was right, he should know the story.

And so, I am telling you the story.

You are the boy I used to babysit every once in a while. Your mother gave me some books to read to you, but you weren't very interested. They were stories about love and war and things like that, with talking animals and knights in shining armor. You told me that your mother said I had better stories to tell, real stories about love and war, and you wanted to hear those. Particularly the ones about war. But those stories I wouldn't tell.

Until now. You're not ready to hear it yet, though, so I have written it down for you. When you are old enough, when you are ready, you can read it.

I don't know what you will learn from it, I just wanted you to know. You can push your way past all the cruelty and meanness and loneliness and take what you have learned from life and travel with it as far as you can and make something good. You can take the pain—the pain you have received and the pain you have learned to give—and stick a trembling finger out from this world and touch another world. You can build an aluminum can and put a man in it and land it right on another world. And it means everything. And it means nothing.

And you can love another person. One person out of billions, the same as any other, another person fated to live in pain and die. You can treat that person badly and you can treat that person well and you can love that person and keep them in your memory until you die. And it means nothing. And it means everything.

The Young Guardian

COMING SOON

During the family's desperate search for a place to rebuild, they learn that the Communist soldiers who control the country are intent upon killing any man who fought alongside the Americans. Nou's family must flee their homeland or live under constant threat of torture and imprisonment. But escape from Laos requires a guide able to smuggle large numbers of refugees through the jungle's high mountain paths and across the Mekong River into Thailand, routes watched by patrols instructed to shoot to kill. While the number of dead who litter their escape route increases, Nou draws upon the folklore heroes who inspire her, tales that strengthen her determination to bring her family to freedom.

www.scarsdalepublishing.com

www.ingramcontent.com/pod-product-compliance
Lightning Source LLC
Chambersburg PA
CBHW032100180726

48284CB00002B/378